ANTHONY RICHES

ARROWS OF FURY

EMPIRE: VOLUME TWO

Complete and Unabridged

CHARNWOOD
Leicester

First published in Great Britain in 2010 by
Hodder & Stoughton
London

First Charnwood Edition
published 2011
by arrangement with
Hodder & Stoughton
An Hachette UK Company
London

British Library CIP Data

Riches, Anthony.
Arrows of fury. - - (Empire; v. 2)
1. Great Britain- -History- -Roman period,
55 B.C.–449 A.D.- -Fiction. 2. Historical fiction.
3. Large type books.
I. Title II. Series
823.9′2–dc22

ISBN 978–1–44480–623–6

Published by
F. A. Thorpe (Publishing)
Anstey, Leicestershire

Set by Words & Graphics Ltd.
Anstey, Leicestershire
Printed and bound in Great Britain by
T. J. International Ltd., Padstow, Cornwall

This book is printed on acid-free paper

For Dorothy and Edwin, with all my love

Acknowledgements

Writing the second book in the *Empire* series was always going to be harder than the first, and not only because of the sudden and necessary imposition of a deadline as opposed to the leisurely approach that was possible with the first. Writing a debut novel was, for me, an activity fuelled by aspiration and ambition, whereas the delivery of the sequel featured the addition of a decent sized dash of nervousness to the mix. Everyone has one novel in them, or so the cliché goes, but from the moment I knew I'd sold three, the big question in my head was whether I could even deliver a second commercially acceptable story. Of course I knew the back-story that will see Marcus through the decades of the empire's difficult transition to rule by Septimius Serverus, and that controversial emperor's reign, but could I actually write a story about the months following the battle of Lost Eagle?

The answer, to my eventual relief (and a good deal of eye rolling by those close to me), was yes, I could. Successful delivery of *Arrows of Fury* can be credited primarily to the assistance of the usual key people in the writing side of my life. First and foremost, my partner Helen told me in no uncertain terms to stop worrying and get on with it, and chased me to write when internet car reviews held more attraction than the next 500 words. My agent Robin Wade told me much the same thing, albeit in his usual breezy and convivial style, and my editor Carolyn Caughey gently pointed out what was needed to make the first draft of the manuscript into a second draft that really worked, and didn't ever let me believe I could get away with nearly good enough. Carolyn's assistant Francine Toon was always on hand with prompt and effective assistance when needed.

I was provided with valuable factual assistance by several people who have expertise in the period. Adrian Wink, purveyor of authentic Roman military equipment at www.armamentaria.com, helped me with both kit to play with and insights as to its maintenance and carriage by the soldiers of the day, and equipped me for the charity walk I'll be plugging later. John Conyard of Comitatus (www.comitatus.net) was kind enough to take time out from knocking soldiers over with his cavalry horse at Maryport to give me a fresh perspective on Roman archery. Pete Noons and the Roman Military Research Society (www.romanarmy.net) were hospitable and helpful, and demonstrated their equipment with both zeal and demonstrable enthusiasm. Dr Jon Coulston gave me some valuable insights into the reality of the Syrian archer in 2nd century Britannia, and dispelled the myths of men in long flowing skirts once and for all, and Jon and Dr Mike Bishop's excellent and learned book *Roman Military Equipment* is recommended reading for anyone with an interest in the subject.

Lastly, the draft manuscript was beta tested by a few people, notably Paul Browne and David Mooney, and their critical input was of great value in picking out a few points that could be improved.

Robin Wade and I plan to walk Hadrian's Wall for charity when this book is published, and we've chosen:

Help for Heroes (www.helpforheroes.co.uk), an organisation which highlights both the worst and the best in Britain's attitudes to its armed forces. If you're interested in reading more about the walk, please go to my website (www.anthonyriches.com), where you can find further details.

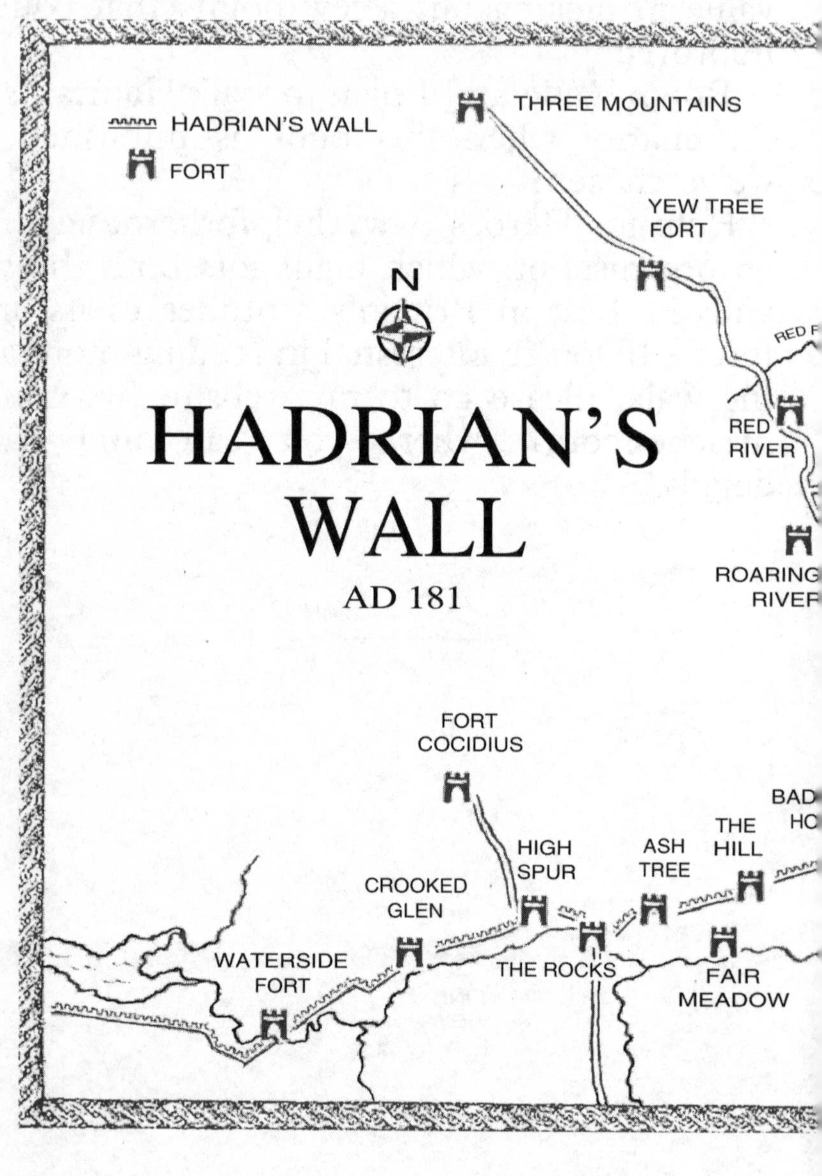
HADRIAN'S WALL
FORT
THREE MOUNTAINS
YEW TREE FORT
N
HADRIAN'S WALL
AD 181
RED RIVER
ROARING
FORT COCIDIUS
THE HILL
HIGH SPUR
ASH TREE
CROOKED GLEN
WATERSIDE FORT
THE ROCKS
FAIR MEADOW

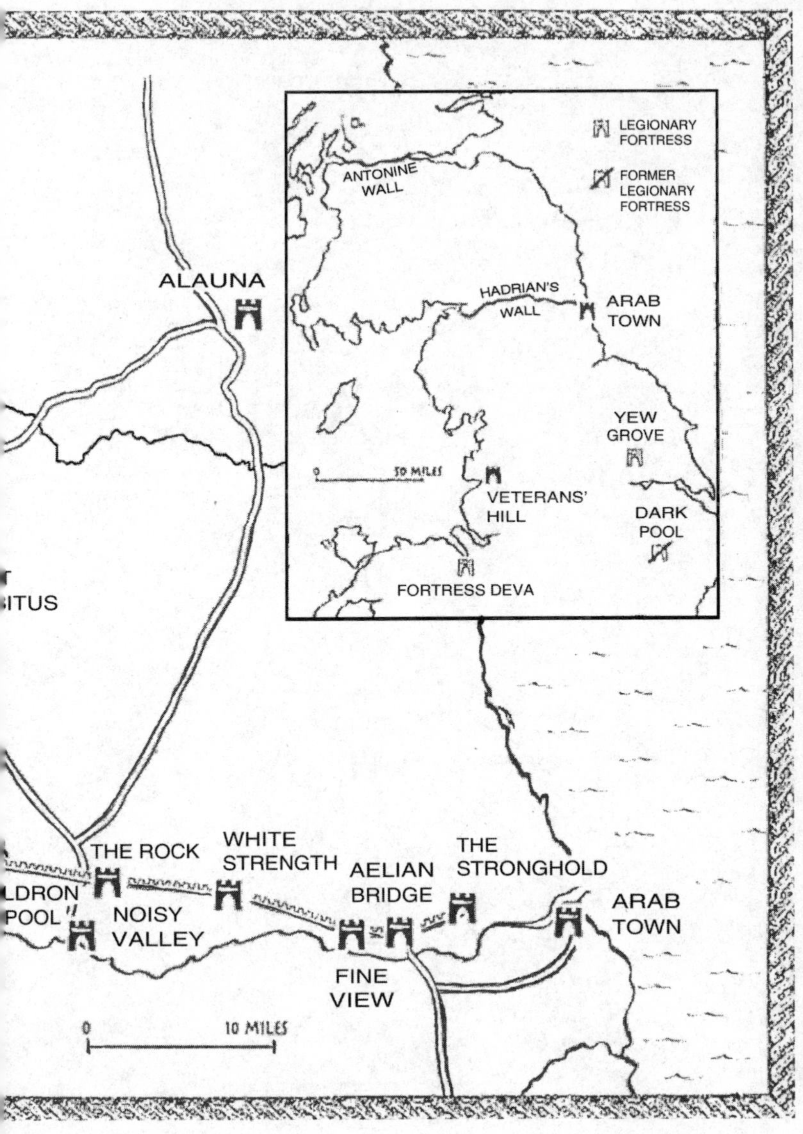
LEGIONARY FORTRESS
FORMER LEGIONARY FORTRESS
ANTONINE WALL
HADRIAN'S WALL
ARAB TOWN
YEW GROVE
0 50 MILES
VETERANS' HILL
DARK POOL
FORTRESS DEVA
ALAUNA
THE ROCK
WHITE STRENGTH
AELIAN BRIDGE
THE STRONGHOLD
ARAB TOWN
POOL
NOISY VALLEY
FINE VIEW
0 10 MILES

1

September, AD 182

The Tungrian centurions gathered round their leader in the warm afternoon sunshine, sharing a last moment of quiet before the fight to come. Marcus Tribulus Corvus winked at his friend and former chosen man Dubnus, now centurion of the 9th Century, which Marcus had previously commanded, then nudged the older man standing next to him, his attention fixed on the ranks of soldiers arrayed on the hillside behind them.

'Stop mooning after these legionaries, Rufius, you're a Tungrian now whether you like it or not.'

Rufius caught his sly smile and tip of the head to Julius, the detachment's senior centurion, and picked up the thread.

'I can't help it, Marcus. Just seeing all those *professional* soldiers standing waiting for battle takes me back to the days when I stood in front of them with a vine stick. And that's my old cohort too . . . '

Julius turned from his scrutiny of their objective and scowled at the two men with an exasperation that was only partly feigned. Rufius nudged Marcus back, shaking his head solemnly.

'Now, brother, let's be fair to our colleague and give him some peace. It's not his fault that it's taken all morning and half the afternoon to get two thousand men and a few bolt throwers into position. Even if my guts are growling like a shithouse dog and there's enough sweat running down my legs to make my boots squelch for a week.'

Dubnus leaned over and tapped the veteran centurion on the shoulder.

'I think you'll find we call that wet stuff 'piss' in this cohort, Grandfather.'

The older man smiled tolerantly.

'Very good, Dubnus. Just you concentrate on taking your lads into action as their centurion for the first time, and I'll worry about whether I'll be able to hold my bladder in a fight for the fiftieth time. Youth, eh, Julius?'

Julius, having turned back to his study of the defences looming before them, replied in a tired tone of voice that betrayed his growing frustration with their prolonged wait in front of the tribal hill fort they would shortly be attempting to storm.

'Might I suggest that you all shut the fuck up, given that it looks like we'll actually be attacking soon? Just as soon as those idiots have been cleared from the top of their wall that'll be us on the march, and ready for our starring role in Tribune Antonius's great victory over the Carvetii tribe. When I send you back to your centuries you get your men ready to advance, you repeat our orders to them all one last time, and remember to keep your bloody heads down once we're on the move.'

Julius cast a disparaging glance at the batteries

of bolt throwers ranged alongside his four centuries, their sweating crews toiling at the weapons' hand winches as they ratcheted the heavy bowstrings back ready to fire. He tugged at the strap of his helmet, the crosswise crest that marked him as a centurion ruffled by the breeze as he turned back to stare at the wooden walled fort to their front.

'I don't trust those lazy bastards not to underwind and drop the occasional bolt short. And when we do attack, let me remind you one last time that our objective is to break in and take the first rampart. Just that, and only that. Tribune Antonius has been crystal clear on the subject.'

Marcus managed to keep a straight face despite Rufius's knowing smile. It was an open secret among the officers of the 6th Legion's expedition against the rebellious Carvetii tribe that the legion's senatorial tribune, the legatus's second-in-command, was desperate to prove his readiness to command a legion of his own before his short tenure in the position ended to make way for another aspiring general.

'Once the way's clear to the second gate we let the legionaries through to take their turn, got it? So, clear any resistance behind the first wall and then hold your men in place. No battle rage, and no trying to win the fortification crown. Not that any of us would ever be so favoured with two cohorts of regulars all vying for the honour. Once we've done our bit I'll call the bloody road menders forward and they can do the rest.'

The officers clustered around him turned to

watch as the bolt-thrower battery to the right of their soldiers loosed a volley of three missiles at the hill fort's outer wooden palisade, barely two hundred paces from the ranks of their soldiers. At such close range the weapons crews were taking full advantage of their weapons' accuracy, and another of the barbarian warriors lining the fort's wooden walls was plucked away by the bolt's savage power, most likely dead before he hit the ground behind the palisade. After a moment the remaining defenders ducked into the cover of the fort's thick wooden beams, and the artillery crews grinned their satisfaction as their officer shouted at them to get back on their weapons' hand winches and prepare to shoot again. Julius nodded.

'That'll be it; their heads are down. Get back to your centuries.'

The four centurions saluted him and turned away, heading for their places in the two columns of auxiliary infantry waiting to either side of the heavy wooden ram that was key to their assigned task of breaking into the hill fort. Dubnus, the leader of the century that led the right-hand column, a tall and broad-shouldered young centurion with the frame of an athlete and a heavy black beard, spoke quickly to his chosen man, who in turn set the century's watch officers to one last check that every man was ready to fight. While they fussed over armour and weapons for the final time Dubnus shouted the century's orders across their ranks, repeating Julius's command to take the first rampart and then hold to allow the legions through with their assigned task complete. That done he drew his gladius and picked up a shield he'd left on the ground in front of his men, smiling wryly at Marcus, who stood at ease beside him in front of the century with his helmet hanging from one hand.

'When I got my vine stick last month I assumed I'd never have to carry a shield again in all my days . . .'

His friend's eyes were alive with the prospect of the impending action. He was as tall as Dubnus, and if his body was less massive in its build it was still impressively muscled from the months of incessant conditioning since he had joined the cohort in the spring. His hair was as black as a crow's wing, and his brown eyes were set in a darker-skinned face than was usual in the locally recruited auxiliary cohorts. A long cavalry sword was sheathed on his left hip, while the shorter infantry gladius, which usually hung on his right hip, was in his right hand. Its ornate eagle's-head pommel gleamed in the afternoon sunlight, the intricately worked silver and gold polished to a dazzling brilliance.

' . . . and yet here you are, hefting a painted piece of board again as if you were still in the ranks? Perhaps you'd rather go forward with just your vine stick for protection, eh, Dubnus?'

'No, I'll put up with the burden this once, thank you, Marcus. Those blue-nosed idiots aren't going to keep their heads down for long, and they'll throw everything but the water troughs at us once we're through the gate. If we get through the gate. Now, you're sure you don't want to lead the Ninth Century forward one last time?'

His friend shook his head, gesturing to the front rank of the century arrayed behind him.

'No, thank you. These are your men now. I'm only along for the ride. After you, *Centurion*.'

A sudden bray of trumpets stiffened their backs, calling the waiting centuries to readiness for the inevitable command. Marcus pulled on his helmet, his features suddenly rendered anonymous by the cheek guards' brutal lines, then took up his own shield.

'Infantry, advance!'

Julius turned back to face his men from the head of the left-hand column, drawing his sword and pointing it at the fort.

Tungrians . . . *advance*!'

At his command the detachment's two columns marched steadily forward down the gentle slope that ran down to the hill fort's perch high above the valley below. Three sides of the fort's position were utterly unassailable owing to the heavily forested and precipitously steep slopes that fell away from the pinnacle to the north, south and east. The only possible approach to the hill fort was from the west, where a flat and treeless ridge angled up to meet the hill on which two legion cohorts and their supporting artillery were gathered, ready to follow up on the advance of their Tungrian auxiliaries. Bordered on both sides by the wild forest of oak and birch that made the hill fort's steep approaches so difficult, the space beneath the trees thick with holly, alder and hazel that made it practically impassable, the ridge's wide path led arrow straight down to the fort's massive outer gates. Only here was there any realistic prospect of an attacker's advance meeting with anything but disastrous rebuff, but in anticipation of such an obvious approach, the fort's occupiers had long since constructed an elaborate series of defences across the fort's western face. Three successive palisades of thick wooden beams defended the innermost point of the fort, the hill's flat summit.

The Tungrians hunched behind their shields as the fort's wooden rampart loomed in front of them, casting nervous glances at the thirty massively built barbarians striding purposefully between them. An iron-tipped battering ram fashioned from a tree trunk hacked from the surrounding forest hung between the two ranks of prisoners, and swung to and fro as they marched down the ridge's slope. Each pair of men on either side of the ram was shackled together at the wrist, their chains wrapped around the tree trunk to remove any chance of flight, and every man was naked from the waist up, while a legion centurion and a dozen hard-faced soldiers marched alongside them in grim silence with drawn swords. The legion officer barked a command into the oppressive silence that greeted their advance.

'When we reach the gate you barbarian bastards will swing that ram as if your lives depend on it. Which they do!' He waited a moment to allow the men among them that spoke some Latin to translate his words for the others. 'When the gate's breached you will be released from your chains, and you will then go forward into the fort and take on the defenders with any weapon that you can get your hands on. Any man that runs will be put down by the soldiers alongside you or behind you without a second thought, so if you think that's a better choice than going through the gates you can think again. Those of you that survive the attack will be freed to return to your villages with your second brand.' Some of the men glanced down at the mark crudely burned into their right forearms, 'C' for '*captivus*'. 'Let me remind you that if you decide to run, and in the unlikely event that you actually get away with it, the lack of that second brand to cancel out the first one will get you crucified when you're recaptured. And that, my lads, is not a pleasant way to leave this life. Far better to die cleanly here in the sunlight than choking out your last miserable breaths in agony, and with your back opened up like a side of bad meat.'

Dubnus nudged his friend.

'Keep your eyes open for them once we're inside. I'm pretty sure that half of them fought us at Lost Eagle, I even recognise a couple of them, and they'll probably be only too happy to take one or two of us with them. Especially men wearing crests on their piss buckets like you and me.'

Marcus nodded grimly as the attacking force came to a halt in front of the massive wooden gates.

'Archers, ready . . . '

He glanced back, seeing the century of Syrian archers arrayed behind their small force taking up positions from which to shower the ramparts with arrows if the defenders were sufficiently unwise to show themselves. The legion centurion commanding the ram's conscripted bearers pointed at the gates, bellowing the command for them to start their assault. With a collective grunt of effort the ram-bearers swung the tree trunk backwards, then heaved it forward with a collective lunge, the iron head's arc ending against the gates' timbers with a rending crash, sending a shower of dust cascading down on to the leading Tungrian soldiers waiting alongside them. A tribesman popped up from behind the wall and lifted his arms to hurl a rock down on to the ram's bearers, but fell back with an arrow in his neck and a dozen more studding the palisade's wooden wall before the missile even left his hands. Twice more the ram swung back and hammered into the gate's creaking timbers, and with the fourth blow the left-hand gate sagged tiredly on to the ground, ready to fall. Julius barked an order back into the expectant silence.

'*Tungrians, wait for my command . . .*'

The ram's fifth collision with the fort's defences ripped away the left-hand door; its shattered remnants fell back into the gap between the fort's first and second palisades in a cloud of dust and splinters. Without the strength of its support, the right-hand gate surrendered after another two blows of the ram's massive iron head, leaving the gateway open and empty. The waiting legionary guards tossed keys to the barbarians' chains to the shackled men, waiting behind their shields with drawn swords as the prisoners freed themselves from the ram. Some of the barbarians gathered their chains to use as crude weapons, while others simply looked about them at the Roman troops gathered to all sides in a combination of hatred and simple terror. With the last of them freed, the centurion pointed his sword at the gateway.

'Go! Go and earn your freedom!'

For a moment longer the prisoners hesitated, until a shaggy-haired giant who had hefted the ram's heavy nose with straining muscles bellowed his defiance and loped forward into the fort, triggering a collective howl of anger and a sudden mad charge from the men behind him. As the last of the barbarians vanished through the gateway, Julius flashed his sword down.

'Advance!'

The four centuries trotted quickly towards the smashed gate's opening, flinching involuntarily as the bolt throwers on the hill behind them spat their heavy missiles over their heads in a salvo of shrieking iron. As Marcus rounded the gateway and stepped over the fallen gates' shattered timbers a falling man rebounded from the palisade in front of him and hit the ground with a wet crunch of shattered bones, a bolt buried deeply in his chest. He stepped forward and hacked reflexively at the dying man's head to make sure of the kill, then stared up and down the curved face of the inner wall. There seemed to be no other target for his sudden urgent need to take his blade to another enemy, only the half-naked barbarian prisoners milling about between the walls to either side of them and a few scattered corpses of the bolt throwers' earlier targets. He started as a scream sounded from the rampart to his rear, suddenly feeling horridly vulnerable to whatever was happening above and behind him. Instinctively raising his shield as he spun to face the outer wall, he felt a clanging thud as a spear intended for his back found only the iron boss in the shield's centre. The spearman howled his frustration at the miss, then staggered forward off the wall and turned a neat half-somersault to the ground with an arrow buried in his neck, the price of standing to make the throw.

A flicker of movement caught Marcus's eye, a mob of a hundred or more barbarians streaming round the fort's inner wall from his right, waving swords and axes in the air as they charged towards their attackers with berserk howls. They ripped through the barbarian prisoners without mercy, clearly aware of their former allies' need for redemption through victory and taking no chances with their loyalties. For whatever reason, and whether it made sense or not, the defenders had committed most of their strength to meeting the Tungrian attack head on. Any chance that the legion cohorts would be bearing the brunt of the battle once the auxiliaries had broken the fort's first line of defence was clearly no longer a reality. Dubnus had seen the barbarian charge, and stepped forward with a bellowed command that cut through the moment's confusion.

'Form a line!'

A good part of the 9th Century was through the gate already, and in seconds they had an unbroken wall of shields raised across the gap between the first and second palisades, the other centuries clustering to their rear in the thin space between the walls. The wave of attackers crashed into them, hammering at the shield wall with swords and axes, while the Tungrians held them at bay and stabbed back at them with practised skill, aiming killing blows at their throats, bellies and thighs. Stuck behind the line, Marcus craned his neck to see what was happening behind the fort's enraged defenders. As he watched, the massively built prisoner who had headed the first wave of attackers through the gateway got back to his feet a dozen paces behind the rearmost enemy warrior. A red smear across his forehead indicated that one of the defenders had clubbed him to the ground without taking the precaution of checking that the blow had been sufficient to put him out of the combat. He was pointing to something that was out of sight to Marcus around the inner wall's curve, bellowing words that were inaudible over the battle's cacophony of screams and curses. With a sudden flash of insight Marcus realised what he must be pointing at.

'The next gate . . . '

He turned to Dubnus, pointing urgently past the seething mob of barbarians on the other side of their shield wall.

'The second gate's open! Give me ten men, quickly!'

He sheathed his spatha and tossed the shield aside, climbing nimbly up the rough wooden ladder that led on to the wall's wooden fighting platform with a sudden burst of energy born of his realisation that the way to the heart of the fort had been left open behind the mass of warriors throwing themselves on to the Tungrians' shields. Climbing on to the narrow platform, he looked out for a moment across the ridge, back to the legion cohorts waiting in the afternoon's sunshine, their standards gleaming prettily in the sunlight. He waved down at the Syrian archers with the agreed crossed-fists gesture to indicate that the wall was taken, the signal to stop shooting at anything that moved along the wall's length. The archers' centurion waved back, barking to his men to stand down, and another man joined Marcus on the rampart, his face dimly remembered from his time commanding the 9th Century earlier that summer. Their eyes met, and as Marcus raised a hand to beckon him on down the wall in his wake a hot spray of the soldier's blood stung his eyes. A heavy bolt had opened his throat with the precision of a surgeon's scalpel, the man's blood fountaining across Marcus's mail armour as the soldier toppled choking back into space and fell on to the men fighting below them. Another bolt slammed into the timber an inch below the top of the wall, directly in line with Marcus's stomach, and the third screamed past his head with a hand-span to spare and no more, burying itself in the rough timber of the second palisade. Another man climbed on to the wall, and

Marcus recognised Scarface, a 9th Century soldier with little respect for the cohort's officers.

'Best keep you fuckin' head down, Centurion, or those legion tosspots'll put a dart clean through it.'

Marcus nodded, ducking below the rampart and beckoning the other man on.

'Follow me!'

He scuttled off down the line of the rampart bent almost double, slipping and almost falling on a patch of still-wet blood, and looked back to make sure that the men who had climbed up after him were following. Thirty paces around the outer palisade's curve from the point he had climbed up he dropped from the platform's eight-foot elevation to land beside the massively muscled prisoner, drawing both swords as the man spoke in rough Latin, his voice a bass rumble.

'Gate open. We close, they trap.'

Marcus nodded, beckoning his men to jump down.

'What's your name?'

The Briton spoke without taking his eyes from the open gate.

'Lugos.'

'Come with me, Lugos. I may need someone that speaks the language, and you'll be safer with us than staying here. If this works you'll be a free man by the end of this fight.'

The big barbarian nodded curtly, and Marcus led his small party along the curve of the inner palisade to the gate, still open despite the obvious risk to the fort's security. Marcus peeped round its timber frame, seeing a cluster of a dozen warriors standing next to the much smaller opening in the fort's third and last wall. He pulled his head back, speaking quickly to his men.

'There's only one more gate. It's still open, and they've only left a few men to guard it. We've already captured this one, and if we can stop them closing that one we've got the fort at our mercy. Are you with me?'

The three 9th Century men who had followed him nodded readily, Scarface glaring round at his comrades in a way they knew only too well, while the three others, from other centuries and therefore less used to his way of doing things, stared back with a mixture of uncertainty and apprehension. It would have to do. The barbarian had acquired a spear from somewhere, and stared down at him without any visible expression.

'Very well, gentlemen, let's go and win ourselves a fort.'

He threw himself round the gate's wooden frame and shouted a challenge at the warriors guarding the last gate, wanting them to see the small number of men charging along the wall at them with a single officer at their head. They dithered for a moment, caught between the need to deny the Romans the gate they were entrusted to guard and the opportunity to kill their enemy, and in that time his sprinting pace halved the distance between them. Glancing back, he saw that only the barbarian, his three former soldiers and one other man had joined him, but it was too late to do anything but face the enemy warriors, suddenly confident as they realised that they outnumbered their Roman attackers by two to one and came forward with their swords drawn.

Jinking to right and left, Marcus batted aside the leading warrior's sword-thrust with the long blade of his spatha and hit the man hard with his right shoulder, punching him back into the men behind him and gaining a moment's confusion in which his small group could gather their strength. Spinning away from the tangled knot of barbarians, he readied himself to take on another warrior, only to see Lugos leap at his intended victim with a blood-curdling howl, spitting him through the guts with a downward lunge of the spear he had found and leaving it buried deep in the man, taking the sword from his nerveless fingers. He raised the weapon over his head and hacked it down into another warrior's unprotected head, his eyes bulging wide with the bloodlust. Marcus dragged his gaze from the spectacle in time to parry a sword-blow from his left with the gladius' short blade, spinning to his right and chopping the spatha's heavy blade through his attacker's spine, severing the man's head in a shower of gore. The headless corpse toppled stiffly backwards to the turf. The other Tungrian soldiers were in the fight now, crowding in behind Scarface's lead, and the gate guards were abruptly on the defensive as they found their strength almost halved.

Marcus looked beyond them to the last gate, knowing that their unexpected run of luck could still end in stalemate if the men remaining inside managed to get it closed. The eight-foot timbers of the fort's innermost palisade were more than stout enough to hold off the attackers for long enough for the remaining occupants to have time to make their escape over the walls on the fort's far side, and down the steep slopes into the surrounding wild forest, whose secret paths only they knew.

'Scarface, hold them! You . . . '

He pointed at the panting Lugos, hooking a thumb at the last gate.

' . . . with me!'

The other man nodded, understanding the Roman officer's purpose if not his words, and the pair burst past the knot of fighting men and ran hard for the gate. A single man hurried through the gap just as they reached it, drawn by the sounds of battle, and died on the barbarian's sword without ever quite comprehending how badly the fort's defence was undone, the slippery rope of his guts falling through his torn stomach wall as Lugos pushed him back against the timber rampart and lunged at him again, shoving the sword's blade up into his chest to skewer his heart. Marcus burst through the gate and stopped, his swords held ready to fight as he took in the scene before him. A wide-open space crowned the hill's crest, perhaps fifty paces in diameter and surrounded on all sides by the final wooden palisade. A single timber-built hall stood against the enclosure's far wall, and the open space between gate and building was studded with smoking cooking pits and the scattered remnants of their last meal. A single warrior stood outside the hall, and as Marcus stood breathing heavily in the gateway he shouted something through the door behind him. A massively built warrior stalked through the doorway, a fighting axe held in one hand and a round shield in the other, the thick gold torc around his bull neck marking him as the tribe's king. He stood for a moment, taking in the sudden reality of his defeat before setting off towards Marcus at a lumbering trot with his bodyguard running alongside him.

The centurion looked back at the gateway behind him, seeing that the prisoner was still the only man to have reached as far into the enemy's defences. He stabbed his spatha's long blade into the grass at his feet, pointing to the gate and chopping at the air with a bladed hand.

'Destroy the gate!'

Even if he lost this last fight there would be troops following up soon enough, once the battle between the first and second walls was resolved, and the fort's last gate had to be kept open if that were to mean anything. The barbarian nodded, taking the sword's heavy blade to the uppermost of the gate's wooden hinges in a flurry of blows, and Marcus pulled his spatha from the turf and turned back to find the fort's chieftain and his companion less then ten paces distant. Pointing to the barbarian prisoner, the big man growled a command, locking his eyes on Marcus as his bodyguard trotted warily round the Roman officer and ran at the prisoner with his sword held high.

With a growl of anger the chieftain stepped in to attack the young centurion, hacking down at him with his axe, and the savage attack left Marcus with no option but to step back beyond the blade's humming arc. Out of the corner of his eye he caught a glimpse as the man's bodyguard and the barbarian prisoner fought in a whirl of blades, the two men almost perfectly matched in their skill and strength. The chieftain stepped forward and struck again, slashing the axe horizontally at Marcus's belly in a backhanded blow that knocked aside his sword and connected solidly with his mail armour, sending him staggering backwards, winded by the blow's force even though his mail had stopped the blade from penetrating. As he struggled for breath the big man whooped in triumph, raising his weapon for the killing blow that would split the Roman's helmet and cleave his head apart, only to stagger and fall as an impact of unimaginable force dumped him on his back.

The artillery bolt had missed Marcus by inches before punching through the big man's mail shirt and burying fully two-thirds of its length in his chest, a chance hit by a shot fired at random into the figures struggling in the gate's skylined opening by some frustrated artilleryman on the far slope. The chieftain struggled to get back on his feet, making it no farther than one knee. He stared stupidly down at the bolt protruding from his body, feeling the strength ebbing from him with the blood coursing down his chest, then gave Marcus a beseeching look as he dropped the axe and shield, holding out his arms in readiness for a mercy stroke. The Roman looked into his eyes for a moment before nodding, and then dropped his gladius and wielded the spatha two-handed to sever the grievously wounded tribal leader's head from his shoulders with an executioner's stroke. The dead man's bodyguard stopped fighting and stepped back from the exhausted prisoner, dropping his sword and prostrating himself on the ground. Gathering his strength, the barbarian lifted his sword, looking to Marcus for a decision. The centurion shook his head tiredly, pulling the big man out of the gate's deadly opening before any more bolts could be sent their way, and sat down heavily on the turf, his body suddenly trembling as the relentless urge to fight burned out of his blood to leave him shivering in the afternoon's warmth.

* * *

'Let me make sure that I've fully understood this. Once the fort's first gate was open you took half a dozen soldiers and charged off like a man with his arse on fire, ignoring your instructions to hold and let the legion cohorts come forward?'

First Spear Sextus Frontinius fixed Marcus with a fierce stare from behind his desk, raising an eyebrow in a silent invitation to comment.

'Yes, First Spear.'

'And as a consequence of disobeying your orders, you proceeded to secure both of the gates that the regulars were supposed to capture, once you'd made the initial break in and cleared the way for them?'

Marcus kept his face stony, only too well aware of the first spear's swift temper. He shifted his stare from the wall of The Hill's hospital, visible through the office's open window, to the heavy gold torc sitting on the first spear's desk. Frontinius caught the quick glance and his face hardened.

'Never mind the jewellery, Centurion, just answer the question.'

'Yes, First Spear.'

'And to round things off nicely, you also engaged the tribal leader of the Carvetii in single combat?'

'Yes, First Spear, although I should point out that I can't . . . '

' . . . take the credit for his death? Yes, I read the dispatch that Julius sent ahead of your return march so I've had a day to consider the implications of this latest feat of arms. He stopped a bolt in the middle of the fight. Has anyone got anything to add to this tale of disobeyed orders and glorious victory?'

Rufius spoke quickly, his tone light.

'Yes, First Spear. You should have seen Legion Tribune Antonius's face — he had a golden fortification crown all polished up and ready to hand over to whichever of his officers was first man over the fort's last wall and he ended up having to put it away again, or else hand it over to an auxiliary cohort centurion.'

Marcus shook his head ruefully at the

memory of the legion tribune's amazement on hearing that the Tungrians had taken the hill fort in less than ten minutes, and with only a handful of casualties. On the other side of the desk from the four centurions standing to attention in front of him, still in their mail armour from the march back to The Hill, the first spear raised his eyes in amazement to the low ceiling of his office in the cohort's headquarters before turning his glare on the subject of their discussion. Marcus kept his eyes fixed firmly on the view through the open window and his face expressionless.

'You may well shake your bloody head, Centurion. Once again you present me with the ultimate conundrum, young man. Once again I've allowed you out into the countryside only to have you come back with your reputation enhanced and your profile raised. You've drawn more attention to yourself than either you or this cohort can bear. It's a mystery to me that we've not all been nailed up months ago . . . ' He rubbed reflexively at his bald scalp, turning to Julius. 'I know Tribune Antonius isn't the sharpest officer you've ever served under, but surely even he could see that there's something not quite right about a man so obviously Roman serving in an auxiliary cohort?'

His deputy shrugged.

'In truth, First Spear, I think he was somewhat preoccupied with the fact that a pack of auxiliaries had whipped whatever glory there was to be had from stamping the remnants of the Carvetii flat out from under his nose.'

The first spear mused on the comment for a moment.

'Yes. With a bit of luck he'll have been too busy working out how he's ever going to distinguish himself enough to get command of his own legion, and not looking too closely at *you*, Centurion Corvus. Very well, I'd better go and report to the prefect. You four can go and get ready to march to the coast tomorrow. We've had word that our replacements have arrived from Germania, so you'd best get over to Arab Town and get them before someone less deserving finds out they've arrived and has them away. And *you*, Corvus, can reflect on whether there's any way that you could manage a simple march to the coast and back without taking on and defeating any more barbarian warbands. Dismissed.'

The four men saluted and trooped out of the office, heading for the officers' mess. The oldest of them, a stocky veteran with iron-grey hair, put an arm around Marcus's shoulders and ruffled his coal-black hair affectionately.

'Not to worry, young Marcus, I was watching the wet-nosed aristocrat like a hawk and I'll swear he never made the connection. Let's go and get a drink, eh? You and I have new centuries to collect tomorrow, eighty big strong Tungrian boys apiece and an end to marching around alongside our old centuries while other men undo all our good work.' He ducked away from Dubnus's playful slap. 'Current company excepted, of course.'

* * *

First Spear Frontinius made his way from the headquarters building to the prefect's residence with a reflective look on his face, the heavy torc carried in one hand. The new prefect had been posted to take command of the cohort less than two weeks previously, a post made vacant by the promotion of their previous commanding officer to lead the 6th Legion earlier the same summer. The two men had hardly begun the gradual process of getting to know one another, so essential if they were to lead their cohort successfully once the fight with the rebels north of the wall was rejoined, and yet there was already something about the man that made him feel uncomfortable. Unlike his previous prefect, now the legatus of the imperial 6th Legion and privy to the secrets behind Centurion Corvus's position with the cohort, Gaius Rutilius Scaurus had made no attempt to seek any sort of relationship with his first spear.

He nodded to the sentries standing guard on the residence and stepped into the building's cool shade, waiting while the prefect's taciturn German bodyguard went to fetch his master. After a moment's delay his superior appeared at the door of his office. A tall man in his early thirties with a thin, almost ascetic face, he was dressed in a simple white tunic with the thin purple stripe on his left shoulder denoting that he was a member of the equestrian class. Scaurus's eyes were a watery grey, their seemingly soft gaze set below black hair in a narrow face and with a chin that the first spear was unsure whether to characterise as aristocratic or simply weak, but his bearing was confident and his voice was cultured, almost urbane.

'First Spear. Won't you come and join me?'

Frontinius stepped into the prefect's office, accepting a beaker of water and taking a seat opposite the prefect. The room was lit by a single lamp, its shadows pressing in on the two men. Prefect Scaurus took his seat on the other side of his desk, his face half lit by the lamp's soft glow, and took a sip from his own beaker before speaking.

'The detachment has returned, I hear. I presume that the job of dealing with the locals went well enough, since we don't seem to be overrun with wounded?'

'Yes, sir. We played our part as requested, broke into the fort and dealt with the defenders easily enough. Three dead and half a dozen wounded, none of them seriously enough to need transferring to Noisy Valley. Flesh wounds for the most part. The officers also managed to retrieve this . . . ' He put the heavy gold neck ring on the prefect's desk, watching as the other man picked it up and inspected the finely worked bull's heads that knobbed both ends of the torc. ' . . . a nice donation to the burial club.'

The prefect put the torc back on the desk and nodded with satisfaction, but his next words instantly put the older man on his guard.

'And centurion Corvus?'

'Prefect?'

'I said, 'And Centurion Corvus?' By which,

First Spear, I meant to ask you how your youngest officer performed during the defeat of the Carvetii.'

Frontinius shifted uncomfortably.

'Centurion Corvus played a full part in the action . . . '

'Despite only having gone along for the experience, eh? My man Arminius tells me that the rumour around the fort is that Corvus did in five hundred heartbeats what the legion cohorts might have toiled to achieve in five thousand, and with a good deal more losses, if the natives had managed to get their palisade gates closed. And that a certain legion tribune has had his nose put out of joint in a quite spectacular way by his inability to reward one of his own centurions for finishing off the campaign. Which would probably be just another war story for both of us, except that I've been reading the cohort's war diary, First Spear Frontinius.' He lapsed into silence for a moment, fixing Frontinius with a level gaze, his grey eyes unblinking in their scrutiny of his subordinate. 'And in the record of his cohort's war to date your man Corvus seems to have played a full part in just about everything that's happened in the last six months. He must be quite the man with his colleagues, not to mention the troops.'

An uncomfortable silence played out for several seconds before the prefect spoke again. 'As I read the story of your cohort's actions early in the campaign I began to wonder two things, First Spear. I began to wonder just how one man could cause so much disruption to the enemy's plans . . . '

'He was commanding the scout century, Prefect, and so he was always going to . . . '

'And more importantly, First Spear, I found myself wondering just how on earth he managed to avoid the eye of the succession of senior officers who must have heard of his exploits and decided that they wanted to know more about this remarkable young centurion of yours. I'm sure you can understand my pondering on these questions about this cohort of mine, given that it's my responsibility to ensure its complete loyalty to the emperor.'

The first spear opened his mouth to reply, but found himself forestalled by the prefect's raised hand.

'Before you answer, First Spear Frontinius, I've got one more question that I'm pondering. And I would be very careful with your answer if you value your place here. Just why is it, I'm wondering, that I find myself commanding a cohort which has an officer who, as we speak, is still being hunted by the emperor's secret police as a traitor to the throne?'

Frontinius sat in stunned silence for a moment, the prefect's face darkening with his failure to reply.

'Come on man, just how stupid do you think I am? The man's obviously Roman. The name 'Marcus Tribulus Corvus' shouts alias, and he's blessed with skill and speed with arms that probably cost him ten years' training with the best teachers. As it happens, I hear that the son of Senator Appius Valerius Aquila, a man of high position and reputation who was tortured and executed for treason earlier this year, is known to have spent most of his young life having fighting skills drilled into him by his father's tame gladiators in preparation for service with the praetorians. He is known to have shipped out for Britannia on faked orders only weeks before his father's death at the hands of the emperor's investigators. And, First Spear, he is known to have vanished into thin air after two attempts to kill him, both of which ended with other men's blood spilt, but not, apparently, that of their intended victim. This man Valerius Aquila, who was more or less the age that your 'Tribulus Corvus' appears to be, is believed to have benefited from the assistance of local troops, and the finger of suspicion was pointing squarely at the Sixth Legion's former legatus until he was careless enough to leave both his legion's eagle and his own head on the battlefield last spring. Perhaps Legatus Sollemnis was fortunate that his death was both quick and honourable . . . '

He paused, raking the first spear with a long, hard stare.

'The man *behind* the throne, First Spear, remains convinced that the Aquila boy is sheltering with an army unit somewhere in northern Britannia. And if Praetorian Prefect Perennis ever lacked motivation to have him found and killed, the death of his own son in this province earlier this year, coupled with extraordinary rumours of the younger Perennis having been murdered while apparently executing an act of treason, will only have stiffened that resolve. The emperor's 'corn officers' will be out in force across the northern frontier, with orders to kill not only the fugitive but the leaders of any military unit found sheltering him, and to exercise their discretion in further punishing the men of that unit. I think we both know that the dirty-jobs boys have never been backward when it comes to handing out summary justice, and I'd imagine that you for one would end up choking out your last breath on a cross, with every centurion in the cohort likely already dead in front of you. Your men would be decimated at the very least, and as for your previous prefect, now Legatus Equitius, I believe, well, I wouldn't care to occupy his shoes either. So, First Spear, you'd better explain to me just why my cohort is sheltering an enemy of the empire, and why on earth I should tolerate the situation for a minute longer?

'*Start talking.*'

* * *

The Hill's officers' mess steward was contentedly dozing off in his quiet corner when the door opened and a centurion stepped into the mess's lamplight and looked about him, seeking out the steward. The newcomer was a grey-haired man with a stocky build, in late middle age to judge from his seamed face, and at first glance more likely to be a trader than a soldier, but the man behind the mess counter knew better.

'Steward! Wine, four cups and make it

something decent if you've any jars left fit for anything better than unstopping blocked arses. No doubt our brother officers have been throwing the stuff down their necks like Greek sailors while we've been away defending the cohort's reputation.'

More officers were crowding the doorway behind him.

'Shift your backside, Rufius, I've got a thirst that demands prompt service.'

Julius clapped a hand on Rufius's shoulder and manoeuvred past him into the mess, dropping his cloak on to a table and stretching with genuine weariness. He was a head taller than the older man, his build both muscular and athletic while his grey-streaked heavy black beard reinforced the slightly piratical look of his face. Dubnus came through the door behind him, his physique if anything more magnificent, even if he looked less comfortable than his colleagues, still not quite at ease with his exalted status. Centurions, the steward knew from experience, were uncertain for their first few weeks with a vine stick in their hands, but very quickly never to be proved wrong in all the days that followed.

'Come on, Dubnus, stop lurking, get in here and get your cloak off. You're an officer now, so there's no need to simper in the doorway like some bloody virgin invited to her first orgy.'

Dubnus favoured his brother officer with a dirty look and stepped inside, turning back to beckon Marcus in with a curiously deferential gesture as Rufius stepped up to the counter and slapped down a coin of a decent if not exceptional value.

'If your wine is worthy of the name we'll be drinking here all night and you, Steward, will earn this for keeping us well supplied. Come on, Marcus, let's have you at the bar with your right arm ready for action.'

The steward nodded deferentially. This was the kind of officer he could cope with. Over the older man's shoulder he watched the youngest man step into the lamplight. Gods, what a collection, he mused. Rufius, legion-trained and a seasoned blend of piss and vinegar; Julius, the supreme warrior in the prime of his fighting career, all muscles, scars and confidence; Dubnus, the former Chosen Man newly promoted into a dead man's boots and still adapting to their fit; and the Roman, leaner than the others, lacking their obvious muscle but known to every man in the cohort by the respectful title 'Two Knives'. The other three were all good enough centurions, respected and feared by their men in equal measure, but the Roman was the one officer in the fort that any man would follow into danger without ever needing an order.

Rufius passed a cup each to Julius and Dubnus, beckoning Marcus to join them.

'Get a grip of one of these cups.'

Marcus fiddled for a moment with the pin holding his cloak together, and Rufius gave the heavy piece of jewellery a knowing look.

'Still wearing that pin, eh? Don't say I didn't warn you if the bloody thing goes missing. Julius, let him through to the counter.'

Julius turned to look at the young centurion as he twisted the ornate badge to open its pin. He looked hard for a moment at the ornate replica of a round cavalry shield, decorated with an intricate engraving of Mars in full armour, sword raised to strike.

'So that's what the pair of you rode all that way to find. Very pretty . . . '

Rufius took the younger man's cloak and tossed it on to the piled table.

'It's just about all he's got to remind him of his father. There's a personal inscription on the shield's rear too, which makes it even more precious to him. That was all we could recover from the bundle we buried that morning Dubnus and I pulled his nuts out of the fire outside Yew Grove.'

The hulking young officer standing behind them laughed softly, his discomfort with the novelty of his status suddenly forgotten.

'Dubnus and *I*? I seem to recall that all you did was wave your sword about while I had to throw myself around like a fortress whore on payday.'

Rufius grinned, poking his friend in the belly.

'One well-favoured axe-throw from no more than spitting distance and the butchery of a defenceless horse and suddenly he's One-Eyed Horatius. Anyway, the point is that when we dug up the bundle we buried back then that was all there was worth keeping . . . that and the lad's last message from his father.'

Marcus shivered at the memory of opening the

watertight dispatch rider's message cylinder and reading a few lines from his father's message from the grave into the cold dawn air a few days before.

'*By the time you reach Britannia, I expect that Commodus and his supporters will have laid formal charges of treason at our family's door. I will have been tortured for information as to your whereabouts, then killed without ceremony or hearing . . . Whatever the ugly detail of their ending, our kindred will be taken and killed out of hand, our honour publicly denounced, and our line almost brought to an abrupt full stop. You are almost certainly all that remains of our blood . . .*'

He shook himself free of the momentary introspection, raising the cup of wine to his friends.

'And enough of that, there's wine waiting. Let's have a toast, gentlemen. Tungrian comrades, living and dead.'

'Living and dead.'

They raised their cups and drank.

'Here's a toast for you.'

Julius raised his cup and looked around the small group with a wry smile.

'I'll drink to that moment at Lost Eagle when Uncle Sextus started humping that chieftain's severed head in front of twenty thousand wild-eyed blue-noses. That was the moment I was sure I was going to die.'

They drank again. Rufius nudged Dubnus with his elbow.

'Your turn, *Centurion*.'

After a moment's silent thought the young officer raised his cup.

'To Lucky, wherever he is now.'

Julius drank and laughed sharply.

'Not so lucky after all. All those years with never a scratch only to get his hair parted by a blue-nose axe. His loss, your gain.'

The four men nodded silently, sharing a moment of memory. Marcus raised his cup to Rufius, a questioning look on his face.

'And your toast, Grandfather?'

'My toast . . . ? I'll raise my cup to those we loved who are no longer with us.'

The other men nodded, lifting their cups in silent salute, Rufius draining his and hammering it down on the long wooden bar with a smack of his lips.

'A refill, Steward! We'll be sitting over there by the stove. It might be late in the month of Junius, but it's bloody cold for all that.'

⋆ ⋆ ⋆

'It began, Prefect, back in the month of Februarius. One of my chosen men brought a young man in peasant clothing to the fort's main gate . . .'

Frontinius told Prefect Scaurus the story of Marcus's fight to gain a place with the cohort in swift and economical sentences, taking care not to exaggerate his recollection in any way. When his story was complete Scaurus sat in silence for a moment before speaking.

'First Spear, you present me with a dilemma

greater than any puzzle requiring a solution during my years of learning.'

A long silence hung in the air between them. Frontinius judged it best to keep his mouth shut as he waited for the prefect to resume what he expected to be a one-sided conversation.

'It occurs to me that while I know what you have done, I do not yet understand why. So, First Spear Frontinius, help me understand your decision with regard to this fugitive from imperial justice. In your own time . . . '

The prefect rose from his chair and paced across the room, turning to look straight into his senior centurion's eyes. Now his face was in shadow, unreadable, while the lamp behind him would show him any emotions crossing the first spear's face. The first spear pondered his response for a moment before abandoning any thought of attempting to put any particular shine on the story.

'You want to know why I agreed to allow a man wanted for treason to take sanctuary with the cohort. There is no one reason, but I'll try to make why I did what I did clear for you. I suppose we can ignore the fact that both the man and his father were innocent of any of the charges laid against their family, although I'm convinced that was the case . . . '

Scaurus shrugged without interest.

'It's immaterial, First Spear. He could be as pure as a novice priestess and that would change nothing. My question wasn't about his widely accepted guilt, I want to know why he's *here*.'

Frontinius nodded.

'Very well. In the first place it was my prefect, Septimius Equitius, who made the request of me, and he is a man whose judgement I had learned to trust during his time in command here. He owed a debt of honour to Sollemnis, the former legatus of Sixth Victorious. The legatus was the boy's real father, and this was the way in which he was being asked to discharge that debt. And don't mistake this for an attempt to shift the blame to Legatus Equitius. If there's a hammer and nails in my future then I'll do my own dying. However protracted the agony might be I can only cross the river once. All I'm trying to say is that there was a man's honour involved in the decision.'

He paused for a moment, picking his next line of attack.

'There was benefit to the cohort too. I exacted a price for Corvus's acceptance from Legatus Sollemnis in addition to the large sum of money that he contributed to the burial fund. Corvus was accompanied here by a legion centurion not long retired, a legion cohort's first spear, in fact, and I made his service here for a year part of the bargain.' He chuckled darkly, unable to resist the humour in his memory of Tiberius Rufius's smug smile once he had a vine stick back in his hand. 'Turns out the man would have killed with his bare hands for the chance to bellow his lungs out at a century one more time . . .

'There was one more reason for my decision, the most important of all. I would have given Prefect Equitius the hard word if I hadn't seen something in the boy, and neither his honour, nor the gold, and not even the bonus centurion that sweetened the deal would have swayed me. I'm not stupid enough to go risking my life, and those of the officers I serve with, not without a good reason.

Scaurus shifted, staring hard into his eyes.

'What reason?'

Frontinius stared back at him, his eyes flint hard in the half-light.

'He's a born soldier, Prefect, simply that, a born soldier. I've spent most of my adult life chasing recruits round these hills, teaching them how to take their iron to the barbarians that threaten their people. I've seen thousands of them, good, bad and indifferent, and I'll tell you now, without hesitation, that he's the most able warrior I've ever met, and the best leader to boot. He knows what to do, he does it without hesitation, and he's faster and more skilled with a blade than any man I've met. The men of his former century would cover his arse with their shields even if it put them at risk of catching a spear themselves. Given a different roll of the dice he would have risen to command a legion without breaking sweat . . . '

He stopped, unable to read the prefect's expression in the shadows.

'You weren't at the battle of Lost Eagle, Prefect, but if you had been you wouldn't be asking me to explain my decision. When you get the chance to see him fight, then you'll know what I mean when I tell you that you'll never see a man throw his iron around with so much grace, or so much purpose.'

The prefect laughed quietly.

'Very poetic'

Frontinius shook his head dismissively.

'Fuck poetry, that was simple fact. And now, Prefect, you've toyed with me for long enough. You've made your decision, now have the decency to tell me what it is. If you want me on a cross then that's how I'll depart this life. But I warn you, if you plan to nail him up then you'd better have something good up your sleeve because there's at least one century of Tungrians that will paint the floor black with their own blood and that of anyone that gets in their way before they'll stand still and watch that happen.'

* * *

Far to the north of the Roman wall whose stones he had so recently trodden as conqueror, in a forest clearing not unlike the one in which the war had been set in train a few short months before, Calgus, lord of the northern tribes, was arguing his corner against growing opposition. While only one of the tribal leaders dared to speak out against him, half a dozen other implacable faces were arrayed behind the old man, mirroring his grim obduracy. Calgus shook his head and scowled at the old man, raising his hands and eyes to the skies as if to seek guidance from their gods.

'No, Brennus. We have *not* lost this war. In fact this war has barely begun, and yet already we have two mighty prizes to parade in front of our people.'

The king of the Votadini tribe leaned back tiredly in his chair, glaring back at Calgus from beneath the hood of a heavy cloak.

'As you keep saying. My people are expected to be happy with the head of a dead Roman officer and a meaningless metal bird on a stick when what they really need is their dead menfolk back. That, and an end to the killing. Can you magic forth either of those things from your bird on a stick, Calgus? At least we had peace with the Romans before this war, unlike your troublesome Selgovae. There were no forts on *our* territory before this revolt, whereas your lands were already studded with their outposts. You argued for us to abandon our ties with the Romans when you had already long since soured your relationship with them, like a fox without a tail convincing its brothers to go without theirs.'

The old man looked around to his fellows, holding his hands out in apparent exasperation.

'Now they will litter *our* territory with their soldiers in the way that they already control your tribe's land. We will live under their control, no longer trusted to run our own affairs but instead jealously watched, and herded like the cattle we will become.'

The old king was pushing harder than Calgus had expected, encouraged by the knowledge that he had more than enough supporters around the grove to give Calgus's bodyguards a decent fight, and made bold by the combination of his anger and apparent security. Calgus took a deep breath and started again.

'They *used* to control our land, but not any

more, King Brennus. You *may* recall that we burned out every fort on Selgovae ground in the first two days of our war with these usurpers. The Selgovae are newly freed from their oppressive presence on our land, and we will not lightly fall back under their domination. The prizes that we took in battle with the Romans will draw the northern tribes back to us. They are the symbols of an empire grown newly vulnerable. They tell us that the legions can be defeated, that we can be free again, they tell us that . . . '

The Votadini king laughed at him in shockingly open defiance, stiffening Calgus's posture with astonished anger.

'They tell us that we got *lucky*, Calgus. They tell us that you turned a Roman against his own, to lead a legion on to ground that made them helpless against our attack. We cannot expect such fortune again, if indeed I should call it fortune. We may have defeated a legion, but before the end of that day we were running like frightened children with two more legions on our heels, and their bloody cavalry. I lost a son to their spears, a son I will never see again thanks to this adventure of *yours*. A son whose head will have been taken by their soldiers to decorate some barrack or other . . . '

His nephew Martos, a scar-faced warrior with a fearsome reputation in battle, stared at Calgus from behind his uncle's chair with a look of thinly veiled anger, a half-dozen of his men at his back. Brennus sat back in the chair, his eyes locked on Calgus's, and with a flash of insight the Selgovae king knew that the challenge was coming. He strolled easily across the ground between them, looming over the old man and bending to speak quietly into his face. Martos and his men stiffened, ready to air their blades if Calgus as much as touched their leader.

'Got a new champion, have you, old man? Could it be your sister's boy that's stood behind you, perhaps? Or will you do this the old-fashioned way and turn your men loose on mine, see who prevails, eh?'

Brennus looked him straight in the face, no sign of fear in his eyes.

'There will be no challenge if you agree to make peace with the Romans. They have two full legions on our soil even now, they dominate the land around their destroyed forts on the north road as they start to rebuild them, and yet you claim to have broken their grip on us for ever. If we seek to offer them resistance those legions will roll over us and grind us into the ground we stand on.' He shook his head at Calgus, then turned to the men behind him. 'This rebellion is *over*! We're back in the iron fist, but this time there'll be no Roman tribute payment to soften the indignity of our lost sovereignty. The best we can hope for is to trade those cursed spoils of battle, and humble promises of peace and good behaviour, for some measure of normality. Until we do their legions will trample our land and people under foot, forever seeking revenge for their wounded pride.'

Calgus turned away, affecting to consider the suggestion. It was more than a suggestion, of course, more like an order from the leaders of the other tribes arrayed behind the old man, and an assured death sentence for him. If the tribes negotiated with Rome he knew that nothing less than his own head, alongside that of the Roman legatus currently sat in a jar of cedar oil in his tent, would satisfy their lust for revenge. Not unless they could take him alive, of course, for a lengthy humiliation and eventual ritual execution. He turned back to face the implacable faces with a slow secret smile.

'So, it's to be peace at the price of my head. If that's how you all want it, I suppose I have little choice. And I'll have the satisfaction of knowing that my sacrifice won't be the only one you have to make.'

He stood and waited, watching a glimmer of understanding dawn on the old man's face while the others around him frowned their incomprehension.

'You have hostages?'

Calgus shook his head sadly.

'Brennus, Brennus, what do you take me for? Of *course* I've taken hostages. Since you're all culpable for our defeat, you can all pay the price for our surrender. If you betray me, you betray your closest family members.' He pointed at each man in turn. 'Your sons will never reach manhood. Your wife will never warm your bed again. Your daughters will never run to their father's arms again. And, to be quite clear, they will all leave this life in slow, hard ways. I've sent the right men to make sure of that.' He spread his arms wide, encompassing the gathering with a feral grin. 'So, if you want to take my head for your would-be Roman *friends*, go ahead.'

He waited ten long seconds for anyone to move. 'I thought not.' He stepped close to the seated elder, a grim scowl replacing the smile. 'In that case, let's get back to business as usual, shall we? And in case any of you are tempted to put a sword in my back, I'll warn you that if the men holding your family members don't receive messages from me as expected, then you'll be killing your loved ones just as if you'd put the knife to them yourselves.'

Brennus stared up at him with a look of horrified distaste.

'Do you expect to rule us in this way for ever, Calgus?'

'*For ever*, Brennus? Of course not! But I *will* keep you under control for long enough that we can finish the job we started. The Romans may have twenty thousand angry troops in the field, but they're on unfamiliar ground in a land filled with hostile tribes, and the legions from the south and west can't stay up here for ever. The first sniff of trouble in their own areas and the governor will have them away down the road to their fortresses, leaving the Sixth Legion and the auxiliaries to hold the line. I'll have them bottled up behind their wall by the end of the summer, and then we'll see if your people still want peace on Roman terms. I'll chop our invaders up piece by piece, I'll make them rue their desire to expand into our lands, and I *will* send them away with their tails between their legs. And you, Brennus, all of you fools, you should worry less about *for ever* and more about the next few days.'

⋆ ⋆ ⋆

Marcus was still discussing the next day's march to Arab Town with his friends when the prefect's orderly delivered a polite request for the centurion to join Prefect Scaurus and the first spear in his residence. He went back to his quarter, changed into a clean tunic and hurried up the hill just as the evening's quiet gloom was finally surrendering to night, and the torches were being lit along the fort's streets. Inside the building he was conducted to the prefect's private rooms, where he was surprised to find Scaurus sitting opposite Frontinius, a sword unsheathed in his lap. At the room's far end stood a foot-high statue, surrounded by a ring of small candles. It was a representation of a man in the act of stabbing a bull to death, his left hand pulling back the animal's head while the other wielded the knife buried in its throat. The first spear nodded to the chair set facing the two men.

'Take a seat, Centurion.'

He sat down with a questioning glance to both of the men, already pretty much sure of the reason for the summons. The prefect nodded a greeting, tapping the sword's blade.

'Forgive the impolite nature of this meeting, Marcus Valerius Aquila, but given the circumstances I decided that not to take the precaution would be foolhardy.'

Marcus nodded his understanding, keeping his eyes fixed on the prefect's.

'You'll know why I've asked you to join us . . . ?'

He nodded again.

'You've uncovered my secret, Prefect, and you want to talk to me before you decide what to do with me.'

The senior officer raised an eyebrow.

'You're assuming that I haven't already made that decision.'

'Yes, sir, I am. If you'd already decided to have me arrested I would have found myself at the point of a sword without warning, my hands bound, and then thrown into the punishment cells for safe keeping. And if you'd already decided to ignore my situation I probably wouldn't even be here, you'd be agreeing with the first spear the best way to keep me out of trouble. As it is you have a sword ready to use, which implies either mistrust of my potential actions or a lack of confidence in your own abilities. Or both.'

Scaurus laughed, flashing a glance at Frontinius.

'Confident even in the face of execution, Valerius Aquila?'

'I've lived with the prospect of an unjust death, like the one visited on my father, my mother, my brother, my sisters, my uncle and my cousins, for several months now. It's hard to stay scared for that long, Prefect.'

He closed his mouth and waited for the prefect to speak. Scaurus looked into his eyes for a moment, then shrugged slightly and continued.

'Like you, I was born and raised in Rome. Unlike you, although I am the son of an old and respected line, I was not born to a wealthy family. Our clan fell on hard times during the Year of the Four Emperors. My ancestor was unlucky enough to back the wrong man a hundred years ago, and the Emperor Vespasian made him pay for it with enough severity that for a while it was touch and go as to whether the family name would survive at all. We've managed to rub along well enough since then, but we've never been sufficiently well connected to amount to very much beyond the usual imperial service, a rather shabby existence for a family that can trace its line almost seven hundred years, back to the overthrow of the last king of the city. My mother died in childbirth, and my father was killed serving on the German frontier when I was young, and so I found myself living with my uncle's family, essentially a burden to them and, if not resented, hardly welcomed with open arms. It was inevitable that I would seek a means of escape from their charity, and I found it in the patronage of a man of great power.'

He paused, a half-smile playing on his lips as he surveyed the listening men.

'And now you're wondering in just what way I prostituted myself to make that connection. Exactly what was it I had to offer an older man that would make him take me into his house and treat me like a son? What did I give him in return for the status and favour that he bestowed on me?' He laughed harshly. 'I've lived with the sideways glances and innuendos for half of my life now, but in point of fact my benefactor simply took a chance on me. He plucked me from a life destined to disappoint everyone involved, not least me, and he raised my face to see the heights to which I might climb. He did this because he saw something in my wildness that he believed was worth his time and effort to bring to fruition. He looked into the eyes of a disaffected youth and saw a warrior waiting to be released.'

He stood, raising the sword to point at the complex statue standing amid its ring of tiny bright flames.

'He made one small change to my life, almost insignificant compared to what you've been through, Valerius Aquila, but just as deep in its impact as the traumas you've endured. He brought me to the worship of the god Mithras, the Unconquered Sun, the soldier's true god, and in doing so he gave me the purpose I was lacking. I won't bore you with the changes that my service to Mithras has wrought on my life, but I will tell you this — his decision to take the chance that I could be rehabilitated led me to the path I still follow, a life of service to Mithras and the warrior code followed by my sponsor and his brothers. Men who became, through my service to the god, my brothers too.'

He stared at the statue for a long moment before continuing.

'Don't underestimate Mithras, either of you. I have been in more than one tight situation, with weaker men around me reduced to little better than panic, including some that were appointed to lead their fellow men into battle, and my faith in him has kept my sword hand steady, and ready to exploit the opportunities that he always provides.'

He turned, pointing the sword's long blade directly at Marcus.

'I can see in you the same restless purpose that I felt fifteen years ago, and which my sponsor chose to harness in the service of our god. You can do great things, Valerius Aquila, or you can continue with your current path and eventually be discovered and put to death alongside those you have come to regard as your brothers. Every day that you remain here is another toss of the coin, another chance for the emperor's head to land face down and destroy everything you hold dear. I have a choice for you to make, between service to a noble god in the pursuit of the soldier's ideal and hanging on here until the day that your hiding place is discovered.'

He paused for a moment, raising an eyebrow at the younger man.

'You offer to . . . *protect* me, Prefect?'

The prefect smiled, his teeth a white flash in the gloom.

'I offer you rather more than that, Valerius Aquila. I offer you friendship, a kind of kinship if you like. I can never replace your family, but I can give you something to which you can belong without forever endangering it simply by your presence.'

'And as the price for this bargain you will take me from this place and these people?'

'When the time is right, you will leave here.'

Marcus frowned slightly.

'There is a lady . . . '

Scaurus nodded.

'I know. First Spear Frontinius enlightened me on that subject. And when the time is right she can accompany you to wherever you travel, if she will. Mithras wants your service, for you to live the life of a warrior, not for you to cut yourself off from the world. There is room in your life for both your god and your woman.'

Marcus nodded slowly, his face creased in thought.

'It is a generous offer, Prefect Scaurus, although I still wonder exactly how you can protect me from the empire's hunters.'

Scaurus smiled tightly.

'So do I, given your apparent talent for drawing attention to yourself. In time you will come to better understand both the forces hunting you and those arraigned behind me, but for the time being it will be enough for you simply to trust me. So, your decision?'

Marcus thought for a long moment, staring into the room's shadows.

'I will do as you bid, Prefect. I will follow you as you command, and I will serve your god to the best of my ability.'

Scaurus nodded decisively.

'Good. Perhaps in this way we'll be able to keep you from the throne's hunting dogs, and avoid the danger of your friends and comrades being taken down alongside you. Quite how we are to keep you out of public scrutiny in the meantime is a different question altogether.'

2

The first arrow missed its target by less than a foot, hissing unheard past the heads of the rearmost rank's soldiers. Of the other four arrows, fired a second later, one flew cleanly past the astonished faces of four soldiers near the back of the century's column, another fell short owing to a weak bowstring, and the last two found targets among the marching soldiers. The first flicked off the metal boss of a shield slung over its owner's shoulder in the marching position, ricocheting into the throat of one of the soldiers in the following rank, while the other hit a man three ranks farther up the marching column in the calf. He stumbled out of the line of march, hopping a couple of paces before falling to one knee. The century's chosen man, marching in his usual place at the column's rear, pointed at the treeline with his brass-knobbed pole and shouted a warning to his centurion.

'*Archers!*'

Julius reacted immediately, drawing his sword and pointing it at the trees.

'Buckets and boards! Get your bloody guard up!'

He turned to the leading century, gesturing urgently for Dubnus to take his men around to the right through the trees that ran almost to the side of the road as the forest's edge curved around from the barbarian archers' position.

'Dubnus, hook right! Get into the bastards!'

Another flight of missiles arced across the space between the forest and the road, hammering into shields hurriedly swung from their carrying positions to face the unexpected threat. Julius bellowed again, ignoring the arrows flicking past him.

'Fifth century, face the threat! Get ready to attack. The Ninth will attack into the trees to our right! At the march, advance!'

The troops obeyed the order without thought, their obedience drummed into them over long years of drill and practice fighting and reinforced by the shouts and pushes of their chosen man and his watch officer. The 5th Century advanced to their left into the scrub between road and forest, their shields raised against the continual harassing rain of arrows from the trees a hundred paces away, while the 9th Century to their right advanced briskly into the forest to their front in broken order, hunting through the trees for the rebel archers. Marcus, who had been marching alongside Dubnus, snatched a spear from the man closest to him and sprinted ahead of the advancing soldiers, outpacing even the fastest of them as he weaved around the massive oaks at a dead run, bursting through the scrubby bushes that dotted the gloomy forest floor.

The half-dozen Brigantian archers took fright in the face of the 5th Century's advance across the open ground in front of them, their attack only ever intended to harass the auxiliary soldiers rather than bring them to open battle, turning in their retreat to loose one last volley at the advancing Romans. As they turned back to run for the shelter of the deeper forest, Marcus, now a good twenty paces ahead of Dubnus and his men and still running hard, drew back his spear arm and fixed his gaze on the rearmost of the barbarians, slowing his run to a trot, and drawing back the spear until its razor-sharp iron head was level with his ear. He hurled the weapon with a power and artistry that made light of his sprint through the trees, his arm extended to follow the missile's trajectory to its target. Caught in the act of turning to run from the vengeful soldiers, the archer had only a split second's realisation, a fleeting glimpse of the weapon's blurred flight, before the spear arced down out of the trees and spitted him cleanly through the thigh. He toppled to the forest floor, his mouth gaping in a howl of agony as Marcus covered the remaining distance to stand over him with his sword drawn, watching the remaining tribesmen vanish into the forest's gloom as he sheathed the weapon. Julius and Dubnus joined him, his hands on his hips as he stared down at the fallen barbarian, apparently breathing normally in spite of his exertions.

'Nice throw, Marcus, that's worth a few cups of wine once we get to Arab Town. You didn't even hit the bone . . . '

The younger man scowled, stretching out his arm and spreading the fingers wide before bunching them into a fist and looking down at his knuckles, crisscrossed with scar tissue from his long years of tuition at the hands of his father's bodyguards.

'I must be losing my touch, Julius. I was aiming for the middle of his back.'

His brother officer laughed mirthlessly.

'And nevertheless, tragic though it is that you missed your mark by a foot with a spear slung on the run between trees, here we have that rarest of commodities . . . ' He extended an arm to gesture to the tribesman, still writhing with the pain of his wound. ' . . . a live barbarian captive. A bit soiled, I'll give you that, but in no real danger of dying any time soon and ripe for a few questions, I'd say.' He reached out and rapped on the spear's wooden shaft, then took a hold of it and twisted it sharply, rotating the wooden shaft inside the man's wound. The tribesman screamed again, louder than before, his eyes bulging with the effort wrung from his pain-racked body. The centurion smiled down at him. 'I thought that might hurt. Anything you feel like telling us?' The barbarian snarled back at him, spitting defiantly at his armoured chest. Julius smiled back even more broadly, looking down at the spittle dribbling down the shining metal rings. 'Oh, good, a challenge . . . '

Hearing a voice behind him he stood up, turning away from the fallen tribesman. Rufius had crossed the gap between the road and the forest's edge, and now stood staring into the shadows cast by the trees. He had picked up a fallen arrow and was examining the barbed head closely, talking in conversational tones to his comrades.

'One of ours, I'd say. That puts paid to the

story that they were all burned when we put the Noisy Valley stores to the torch. Just a shoot-and-run, do you think, or were they hoping to lure us into some nasty little ambush? That was the way in my day.'

Julius shrugged his indifference.

'Your day, Rufius? Well, my friend, these days it's just shoot-and-run. These are simple village boys, not tattooed Tava valley head jobs. I suppose it beats shooting at the squirrels. Casualties?'

The older man nodded, his face solemn.

'You've lost one man, he choked on his own blood before I could even get a bandage carrier to him, and you've one man with another one of these stuck in his leg. It'll come out easily enough once we get him to Arab Town.'

The centurion shook his head disgustedly, and then squatted back down next to his captive, batting away the man's hands from their ineffectual fretting at the spear wound and switching to the man's native language as he addressed the captive.

'I'd leave that well alone if I were you, it's going to hurt a lot more when it comes out.' He took a firm grip of the spear's shaft, the fallen tribesman's eyes slitting in expectation of the pain to come. 'And now, my lad, and without any further delay since we're in a hurry to get off down the road to collect some more soldiers, you can tell me which village you're from.'

The wounded man closed his eyes and shook his head, a tear trickling down his cheek. Julius slapped his face gently, shaking his head with mock sadness.

‘Come on, sonny, you know you’re going to tell me sooner or later, just cough it up now and save us both the unpleasantness.’

The tribesman shook his head grimly.

‘You’re going to kill me anyway. Just get it over with . . . ’

Marcus squatted down alongside Julius, his expert eye appraising the tribesman’s wound as he spoke.

‘He’s got a point.’

‘Piss off, Two Knives, I’m going to get the name of this stupid bastard’s village, and then . . . ’

‘And then you’re going to do what, exactly? Burn it to the ground? Kill every adult male? The place will probably be deserted once his mates get back there and tell their story. All we’ll ever achieve if we seek to punish these people for the crimes of a very few is turn more of them against us than ever attacked us in the first place.’

Julius stood, his face a picture of exasperation, one hand gesturing back to their captive.

‘So what do we do then, eh, Marcus? Just how do you propose to send these bastards the message that if they take us on they’ll end up regretting it?’

The younger man shrugged, pointing down at the wounded tribesman.

‘Kill him. Either that or get that spear out of his leg and get us back on the road. Just don’t fool yourself that if you kill him you’ll achieve anything other than to turn another dozen men from neutrals to enemies.’

The older man stared at him with a troubled expression.

'And what about the fact that he was part of an ambush that killed one of our men?'

Marcus nodded, extending a hand to indicate the tribesman's wound.

'He's got a spear through his leg. I'd say that's a decent down payment on what he'll have to suffer for the rest of his life. He'll probably never run again, he'll most likely walk with a limp . . . he'll pay for his stupidity over the next thirty years, but this way he's not a martyr for these fools to shout about, just a constant reminder of what happens when you cross the wrong people. Bandage carrier!' He reached out and pulled the weapon smoothly up through the horrified tribesman's thigh, easing its blade out of the wound's opening with delicate care and passing it to Dubnus. The wounded man's eyes rolled up as he lost consciousness, sagging back on to the hard ground. Marcus turned to the medic summoned by his call. 'Get that leg tied off, enough to stop the bleeding and keep him alive.' Wiping his hands on a handful of grass, the young officer turned back to his colleagues. 'There you go. He'll live, but he'll be crippled for the rest of his days, a burden on his tribe, and every time he walks past it'll send a powerful message to everyone around him. If you want to roll the dice with the big boys, you'd better be sure you can afford the stakes. Come on, let's put your casualties on a cart and get back on the road to Arab Town. I suddenly find myself in need of a drink.'

* * *

Night was falling across the fortified port of Arab Town by the time the Tungrian officers had their men bedded down for the night and were free to head for the officers' mess. The fort's looming stable blocks and barracks were silent silhouettes against the sunset's red glow, and only the port's pilot boat was anchored at the wooden pier that jutted out into the German sea, in stark contrast to the barely organised chaos that had greeted their previous visits during the summer to collect supplies shipped in from across the empire's northern provinces. Infantrymen and cavalrymen, their mounts, weapons, armour, boots, shields, supplies and more, had flowed through the port over the previous few weeks, drawn from legions and supply depots across the German frontier and beyond, as the Roman forces in Britannia scrambled to make good the disastrous losses incurred by the imperial 6th Legion at the battle of Lost Eagle. For the first time in all those weeks the fort's officers' mess was quiet, a relief from the hard drinking and inevitable boisterous behaviour of officers passing through to new roles with units in the field, determined to get thoroughly drunk one last time before months of enforced abstinence.

The Tungrian centurions had just settled down around the stove for the evening when the door opened to admit two officers, the newcomers shrugging off their cloaks and luxuriating for a moment in the room's warmth.

Rufius turned to greet them, frowning up from his chair.

'You two look familiar. Aren't you . . . ?'

The older of the two newcomers nodded.

'Second Tungrians. I'm Tertius, this is Appius.'

Rufius stood and offered his hand.

'I'm Rufius, formerly Sixth Legion and now an adopted member of the First Tungrian cohort. These cheeky young bastards have taken to calling me 'Grandfather'. This big arrogant specimen is Julius, or 'Latrine' to his men, for reasons I'll leave you to ponder, he commands the lead century, while this even bigger young lad is our newest centurion, Dubnus. The quiet man in the corner wearing, you'll note, two swords, is 'Two Knives'.'

Tertius narrowed his eyes.

''Two Knives'? Like the gladiators?'

'Just like the gladiators. Only faster. *Much* faster.'

Tertius raised an eyebrow.

'Now that I'd like to see.'

Rufius laughed grimly.

'You've missed the last performance, at least for a while. He only really waves them around at full speed when there's blood to be spilt, and we haven't seen much of that since Lost Eagle. Speaking of which . . . *Steward*! Wine for our friends here. You lads saved our bacon on that shit-spattered hillside, and we haven't forgotten it.'

The two newcomers pulled up chairs and made themselves comfortable, while the steward ferried cups of wine to the group.

'A toast.'

Tertius raised his cup.

'The lost eagle.'

They drank, and then Tertius wiped his mouth on his sleeve and spoke again.

'You know there's a hefty reward for the soldier that recovers the standard?'

Rufius nodded. Tertius took another mouthful of his wine.

'Aye. And we'll be out looking for the bloody thing soon enough. That, and the head of the idiot that lost it. Once we've collected our new prefect and legged it back to join the rest of the cohort we're slated for a tour up north to see what's going on along the main road to Three Mountains.'

Marcus Tribulus Corvus pulled a face and stared at the floor.

'What's the matter with your mate?'

Rufius took a sidelong glance at his companion.

'Not everyone has a bad opinion of the late Legatus Sollemnis. We were there when a nasty little shit by the name of Perennis sent the Sixth Legion into that ambush by lying through his teeth that the ground for their approach march was safe. He tried to kill our prefect too, except Dubnus here put his axe through the would-be executioner's spine and then shot the traitor off his horse at thirty paces. Beautiful piece of work, that shot . . . '

He darted a warning glance at Marcus, an imperceptible shake of his head, before turning back to the newcomers.

'Anyway, a new prefect? Where's he come from, to be coming ashore here?'

Tertius took another mouthful of wine.

'Germania, apparently. Supposed to be some kind of fire-eater from what we've heard, keen as black seed mustard apparently. We've come down the wall with two centuries to escort him back to join up with the cohort at The Rock before we go north. And you lads are here for reinforcements?'

Julius spoke up, his voice a deep rumble.

'Two centuries' worth of real Tungrians, trained, armed, armoured and ready to march. Just enough to get us back to something like full strength after the losses we took in that goat-fuck at Lost Eagle, and the only troops left in the port if I don't count a couple of centuries of Hamian fairies twanging their bows in the next barrack. We're lucky to be getting them, with so much competition for replacements, but our old prefect's commanding the Sixth Legion now, which counts for something. Grandfather and Two Knives have command of our two empty centuries, broken up to provide replacements to bring the other eight up to strength, and we've come to collect their replacement soldiers. Dubnus and I are along for the ride with our boys, just to make sure they got here unmolested. And just as well, given the fun we had on the way.'

Tertius nodded grimly.

'Barbarian bowmen, between Fine View and White Strength?'

'Yes. We lost one man and had another wounded. You?'

'Two wounded. Local boys showing off to each other, most likely. They know we've got better things to do than take the time required to catch them in the act. One of these days, though . . . '

He tipped the rest of the wine down his neck.

'My shout. More wine, Steward, and a beer for me. Make it a large one.'

An hour and several drinks later the Second Tungrian officers got to their feet. Appius, previously more or less silent, inclined his head in salute, his tongue clearly loosened by the wine.

'You'll have to excuse us, brothers; we have an appointment at the guest house with our new officer. Let's hope this one's a little more balanced than the previous idiot. That way he might get to live a bit longer.'

Even with the wine's effects, Rufius was instantly alert, despite his apparent torpor. He nudged Marcus's foot beneath the table to warn him, raising a curious eyebrow and smiling slyly up at the two men.

'We did hear the rumours. It's true, then? Prefect Bassus really stopped a friendly spear?'

Tertius grimaced, but his colleague Appius kept talking without any apparent concern.

'Well now, if you ask the question that way I've got no idea what happened. But if you were to speculate that Bassus had pissed off the wrong men one time too many, I'd have to agree that there's a certain kind of officer who takes a risk when he turns his back on his own men in a battle.

'Anyway, enough said. Good luck with your recruits. And watch out for those bloody archers.'

He scooped up his helmet and reached for his cloak, dragging it across the pile of garments and pulling loose the pin from Marcus's in the process. He bent and picked up the gold shield from the floor, giving its intricate workmanship an appreciative glance and turning it over and noting the words engraved on the obverse before he held it up with an apologetic face.

'Sorry, I've pulled this loose from someone's cloak.'

Marcus put a hand out with a tight smile and tucked the pin away in his pocket, ignoring a pointed look from Rufius.

Outside the mess, pulling his cloak tighter about him in the evening's cold as they headed for the guest house, Appius nudged his colleague.

'Did you see that quiet lad's sword? Not the long cavalry blade, the other one with the eagle's-head pommel? Prettier than a whore's make-up box, proper flash. I'll bet you he's the one they're saying got left a blade by the dead legatus, and you have to wonder why that would be, eh? And that cloak pin, that'd make big money from the right buyer, and it had an interesting inscription too. 'Keep warm, my son', and an aquila carved beneath the words. No way he's local, that's for certain — in fact I'll bet he's the same one that was supposed to be putting it to Bassus's wife before the lads in the Third Century perforated his back.'

Tertius shook his head, his face thoughtful.

'No idea. Not that I'd blame the boy if he was, there's no denying she's a tasty little piece. Right, here we are. Keep your mouth shut and let me do the talking.'

They entered the town's official guest house and were shown into the back room. A massively built man sat picking at the remains of a chicken in the light of several lamps, his thick brown beard slick with the bird's fat. He reached for a towel and wiped his hands and face.

'Sit down, gentlemen. Wine?'

Tertius took a chair, motioning to his colleague to do the same.

'Thank you, Prefect, a cup would be nice.'

The senior officer waited until the wine was poured and the housekeeper had withdrawn before speaking again, raising his cup in salute before drinking. His voice was hard edged, clearly accustomed to being heard without interruption.

'Second Tungrians, eh? I was told you're a battle-tested cohort. I was told that I'm lucky to be getting a cohort here, at this time, with the barbarians still in the field and plenty of glory left to be had. And I was told lots of things about the Second Tungrians that should make for an interesting discussion once we're north of the wall with some time to spare. In the meanwhile there are a few things I'd like to know.'

Tertius put his cup down and sat up straight.

'We'll do our best, Prefect . . . '

'Furius. Gracilus Furius. First things first. Cohort strength?'

'Seven hundred and twenty-four men fit for duty, sir.'

The prefect pursed his lips.

'Under strength, then. Casualties?'

'Yes, sir, all from the battle of Lost Eagle.'

'Almost a century. So, it's a good thing I've already found a century of prime replacements. Tungrians too.'

Tertius exchanged glances with Appius.

'That's good news, sir. I'd heard the only replacements left in town were already spoken for.'

Furius smirked at his circumspection.

'No need to be coy with me, Centurion, of course they're supposed to go to our sister cohort. I sought out the officer responsible for replacements and helped him to reconsider his priorities earlier this afternoon. He hummed and hawed a bit, but he soon changed his mind when he saw some coin.'

Tertius frowned unconsciously.

'There's a bit of a relationship between us and the First Cohort, Prefect. I'm not sure . . . '

'I think you're more than not sure, Centurion, you think that taking a century of replacements from under the First's noses would be unfortunate. Dishonourable, even?'

The centurion, sensing that a trap lay before him, trod carefully.

'Not at all, sir. All I was thinking was that the First Cohort is almost two hundred and fifty men down, that's all. Their first spear's going to be pretty unhappy if we have it away with half his replacements.'

Furius's face took on a sly look.

'You fought at the battle of the Lost Eagle, Centurion?'

'Yes, sir,'

'And that was where *my* cohort took the casualties for which we need these replacements?'

'Yes sir,'

'And, I've heard, it was only the intervention of the Second Cohort that saved the First from being overrun by barbarians?'

Tertius realised where the prefect was taking the discussion.

'Absolutely true, Prefect, we saved their skins all right. One of their centurions said as much to me not an hour ago. Of course, it was the First Cohort that did most of the damage to the barb . . . '

Furius spread his hands and shrugged.

'Well, *there* you are. We take a century's worth of damage saving our sister cohort from the mess they'd managed to get into, and they get all the replacements. That can hardly be right, now, can it? Eh, Centurion?'

Tertius knew which side to be on in this discussion.

'Of course not, sir. In which case we ought to be up and away no later than dawn, or run the risk of an unpleasant argument on the subject. I've met the officers who're here to collect those men, and I wouldn't want to get on the wrong end of their unhappiness.'

Furius smiled knowingly.

'Yes, I guessed as much. The replacements'

centurion has promised to have our century paraded and ready to go at first light, so let's get some sleep. Dismissed, gentlemen. Ah . . . one more question.'

The officers paused expectantly.

'Another story I've heard a few times is that there's a fugitive believed to be sheltering with one of the wall cohorts. Apparently this fellow is the last living member of a family that the emperor chose to liquidate, but his father sent him away to the northern frontier before the axe fell. There would be great imperial favour for the man that turned him in, perhaps a promotion. So spread the word, the man that identifies this traitor to me will be handsomely rewarded. Very handsomely.'

* * *

The First Tungrian officers rose early, and made the short walk to the transit barracks just as the sun was inching clear of the horizon. Expecting to find the barrack office empty, they were surprised to find the transit centurion already on duty. Rufius sized the man up with a swift glance, looking around the white-walled office with apparent indifference.

'Greetings, Centurion. We're here for two centuries of Tungrian infantry, reserved for collection by the First Tungrian cohort by order of Legatus Equitius, Sixth Imperial Legion. Point us at them and we'll get them off your ration strength.'

The transit officer was a sparsely haired man

of about forty, his uniform clearly legion issue. He rose from his chair with an apologetic expression and crossed the small room with two limping paces.

'I'm sorry, gentlemen; I have only the one century for you. There's a lot of demand for replacements, as I'm sure you'll be aware . . .'

He dried up under the stare of four suddenly very hostile men. Julius stepped in closer to him, raising a finger to silence his apology.

'We were here last night, Centurion, probably long after you'd gone to hide in your quarters. And we saw *two* centuries of prime infantry ready for collection. So how, I wonder, does that become one century overnight?'

He raised an eyebrow and waited for a response. The other man spread his hands helplessly.

'Another officer turned up an hour ago, a prefect with two centurions in tow. He gave me a direct order to sign him out a century of the Tungrians to replace battle losses, so I . . . I did.'

Rufius nudged Dubnus.

'Go on, lad, you know the routine.'

The powerfully built young centurion stepped past the transit officer, looking carefully at the wooden floorboards. Rufius spoke conversationally, his attention apparently focused on the barrack dimly visible through the office's open window in the early morning light.

'We know how it is, Centurion. You're in possession of one of the most valuable resources for a hundred miles and more. It must be quite a temptation when you're stuck here in this shitty little port with, what, five years left to serve? So when a senior officer turns up and offers you a combination of stick and carrot to sign him out a few dozen men, well, you find yourself wondering why you should end up with a load of grief when there's money to be made, don't you? This officer had a name, I presume?'

The transit officer watched Dubnus's progress round the office with increasing trepidation.

'He . . . ah . . . he signed as . . . '

He opened his record tablet with trembling fingers, scanning the words inscribed into the wax with a speed borne of fear.

' . . . as Prefect Furius, Second Tungrian cohort.'

Julius's scowl deepened.

'The bloody Second Cohort. I should have known it. This new prefect of theirs must be keen. Uncle Sextus will shit a cow when he finds out.'

'Found it!'

They turned to see Dubnus levering a loose floorboard away with his dagger. Throwing the wood to one side, he fished inside the cavity between floor and ground, pulling out a purse. He tossed it to Rufius, who hefted the small leather bag in his hand.

'Nice and heavy. Must be a decent enough sum. You know what they say, though — only take a bribe if the sum involved will compensate for the punishment you'll get for taking it. And in this case the punishment's going to be quite severe.'

'But I . . . '

Julius stepped forward, taking a handful of the wilting centurion's tunic in one meaty fist.

'No, I don't think so. 'But I . . . ' isn't going to be enough to get you out of this one. First off, you've pissed us off. We came here for two centuries to replace our losses from the battle of Lost Eagle. You heard about that one? You know, how one cohort was sent to take on the whole barbarian army. How that cohort held its line for an hour and more, and kept the blue-noses in place until the rest of the army turned up? Well?'

He prodded the centurion to get a response.

'Yes.'

'Good. And the bad news for you is that cohort was us. We all had good friends killed that day, and we're not in much of a mood to be messed about. Ever noticed how the road officers tend not to take their usual liberties with men who've recently seen combat? Ever wondered why?' He slapped the centurion twice, lazy blows that twisted the man's head to the left and right. 'Now you're about to find out. Second, our prefect that morning now commands Sixth Legion. You're still part of Sixth Legion, so when we report this balls-up to him, he'll likely have you dismissed the service. He hates this sort of corrupt behaviour. Third, my first spear is a right nasty bastard. He'll want to have you strangled with your own guts when he finds out he's been done over for a century of men he badly needs, men whose absence could place the entire cohort in peril.' He clenched his fist tighter, lifting the now terrified man on to his toes without any apparent effort. 'So, first we'll beat seven colours of shit out of you, take our one remaining century and leave, and in about a week or so you'll be a civilian, with no citizenship and no pension. And some time later, some time you'll never predict, the First Tungrian cohort will find you and leave you in a ditch with the life running out of you. It's nothing personal, it's just what you get for pissing off front-line troops. Dubnus, you can have this one.'

'The Hamians!'

The centurion's voice was little better than a squeak. Julius snorted his disdain.

'What about the Hamians? Useless bow-waving women. All they're good for is hunting game. There's a war on, in case you hadn't noticed. We need infantrymen, big lads with spears and shields to strengthen our line. Archers are no bloody use in an infantry cohort.'

He raised his meaty fist.

'No, mate, you're going to get what's coming your way.'

The other man gabbled desperately, staring helplessly at the poised fist.

'There's two centuries of them, two centuries. Take them and the Tungrians and that's two hundred and fifty men.'

Marcus spoke, having stood quietly in the background so far.

'So we could make a century of the best of them, dump the rest on the Second Cohort when we catch up with them and take back the century he sold them in return.'

Julius turned his head to look at the younger

man, keeping the transit officer clamped in place with seemingly effortless strength.

'Are you mad? There won't be a decent man among them. They'll be arse-poking, make-up-wearing faggots, the lot of them. All those easterners are, it's in the blood. They'll mince round the camp holding hands and tossing each other off in the bathhouse. Let's just . . . '

Marcus spoke over him with quiet assurance.

'I'll tell you what, Julius, Rufius gets the Tungrians and I'll take the Hamians as a double-strength century and weed out the weaklings for dumping on the Second Cohort when next we meet. Or shall we just go back to The Hill still one hundred and seventy men light?'

Julius sighed deeply, then turned back to the transit officer.

'It must be your lucky day. Here's the deal. We take the Tungrians, the Hamians, both centuries, mind, and the money. You keep your place here, and perhaps, just perhaps, we don't hunt you down and kill you. Deal?'

'Yes!'

He pushed the terrified centurion away, hard enough to bounce him off the office's wall.

'Right, Two Knives, you'd better go and get your men ready to move. Let's see just how bad this is going to be. Oh yes, and there's this . . . '

He turned back quickly, jabbing a fist into the transit officer's face and breaking his nose with an audible crack, then threw a right hook into the reeling man's jaw which dropped him dazed to the wooden floor.

'Prick.'

* * *

Marcus crossed from the transit office to the closest barrack and opened a door at random. Inside the barrack's stone-built cell, packed in like sardines on a market stall and dimly lit by the single small window through which the dawn's chill was seeping into the room, eight Hamians were waiting quietly, fully equipped and ready to march. Raising an intrigued eyebrow, he walked briskly up the line of eight-man rooms to the officers' quarters, rapped once on the door and walked in. The three olive-skinned men waiting for him snapped to attention, the tallest of them making direct eye contact in a way he guessed was designed to communicate status. He was well built, with wide-set brown eyes above a strong nose and a broad jaw, black hair cropped close to his scalp. Making the instant appraisal of all first meetings, Marcus was struck by the apparent unassuming confidence in the man's gaze, direct but without any challenge.

'At ease, gentlemen. Who's the ranking soldier here?'

The tall Hamian nodded briefly, keeping eye contact.

'I am, Centurion.'

'Your rank?'

'I am Acting Centurion Qadir ibn Jibran ibn Mus'ab, Centurion. I currently command both this century and the other, barracked across the way.'

Marcus nodded, looking at the other two men

with a raised eyebrow.

'These men are my seconds, Hashim and Jibril, Centurion.'

'I see. Very well, Acting Centurion, I am Marcus Tribulus Corvus, your new centurion. Your two centuries are to join the First Tungrian cohort as an over-strength century, as replacement for our losses in recent battle. You shall be my chosen man, and these two men your watch officers. You'll need two if you're to manage that many men. Perhaps it would be better if you were to provide your men with their commands for the time being, until I have the measure of their command of Latin?'

The Hamian nodded with an impressive imperturbability.

'Certainly, Centurion. Shall I parade the men? We are ready to march, as you may have seen.'

Marcus frowned.

'Yes. I'm sorry, your name again?'

'Please simply call me Qadir, Centurion.'

'Thank you. And why . . . why are you ready for the road, I mean? I expected you all still to be sleeping.'

Qadir smiled, placing both hands behind his back and bowing minutely.

'It was not hard to predict your arrival. The noise of the Tungrian century departing ensured that we were awake, and once it became clear to us that they had been bribed out of the transit officer it was easy enough to guess that we would be part of the compensation he would offer to you. I saw one of your colleagues checking the Tungrians last night, and he didn't look like a man who would take disappointment quietly. We have been here for three weeks now, watching other centuries arrive and leave, but now the barrel is clearly empty.'

Marcus fought the urge to smile.

'I see. Very well, Chosen Man Qadir, please parade the centuries for inspection.'

The big man nodded deferentially and spoke a few soft words to his comrades. They left the room in silence, leaving Marcus and Qadir alone in the quiet of the small room. The Hamian seemed content to wait for Marcus to speak first.

'How long have you been acting centurion, Qadir?'

'Six months, sir. And eight years before that as a soldier, watch officer and chosen man.'

Marcus raised an eyebrow.

'Eight years from recruitment to centurion? They must make officers very quickly wherever it is that you've come from. Either that or you're something special. I apologise for taking your command. You'll get it back soon enough, once we catch up with our sister cohort.'

'And exchange us for the men they stole this morning? I think that will take longer than you imagine, Centurion, and even when you do there will be another man posted to command my archers. Do not trouble yourself on my behalf. As long as I am with my people and have the strength to bend my bow I need nothing more.'

Marcus paced to the window, looking out into the grey dawn at the mustering Hamians.

'Archers. I'm afraid that archers are not what's needed now, not while there are barbarian warbands in the field.'

The other man appeared at his shoulder, his soft voice close to Marcus's ear.

'We had guessed as much. While we sat here and waited, centuries of men with heavy armour and spears were in and out in less than a day. It soon became clear enough to us that our having been sent here was a cruel mistake. Now that we are yours to command, it is my expectation that we will soon have heavier armour than this . . .' He fingered the thin rings of his light mail vest, drawing Marcus's attention to its insubstantial nature compared with his own mail, which was both longer and significantly heavier. ' . . . and spears of our own.'

Marcus nodded, his eyes fixed in appraisal of the soldiers parading outside the window. They were wiry for the most part, a few simply skinny, more bone and sinew than muscle, though they shared the broad powerful shoulders that defined their skill at arms. Their mail looked too flimsy to resist a determined spear or sword-thrust, their conical helmets lacked cheek guards, and their impractically light shields were circular rather than being shaped to fully protect a soldier's body. None of the equipment on show would act as adequate protection in a pitched battle.

'Can your men run?'

'If you mean over a distance, the answer is yes, Centurion. We are hunters, for the most part, used to covering ground in search of game. How they will perform weighed down with mail coats and heavy shields such as your men carry is another question. But I make one request of you, Centurion, and that is not to take their bows from them. To do so would be a grave mistake.'

Marcus turned to face the Hamian, his face creasing into a frown.

'As soon as I can manage it they'll be issued with a thigh-length coat of heavy ring mail capable of stopping a spear, a leather arming vest to wear underneath it and protect their skin from the mail's rings when that spear-thrust arrives, an infantry gladius, two spears, an infantry helmet and a full-length shield. All of which weighs more than you might imagine until the first time you put it all on. Then they'll have to march, or run, up to thirty miles a day once we're on campaign. The additional burden of a bow isn't going to help them cope with the load.'

Qadir spread his arms, palms upwards, and bowed, his eyes remaining fixed on Marcus's.

'I understand, Centurion, and I can see that you are right. And yet . . . ' He paused, searching for the right words to make his point without angering his new officer. ' . . . Centurion, to take their bows will be to take their souls. Each man has grown close to his weapon, over long years of practice. He has fired thousands of arrows in practice, until he can put an iron head into a target the size of a man's chest at one hundred paces, and can do this six times in one minute. The very core of what these men have learned over those years is that to hit the target time after time after time they must lose all awareness of themselves, simply focus on the centre of their target and become servant to the bow that seeks that target. These two centuries contain some of the best bowmen I have ever seen loose an arrow, capable of great accuracy with weapons they have come to love as dearly as their own children. And so I tell you, with very great respect to your rank and obvious character, that if these men lose their bows then they will also lose their hearts. And a century of men without heart . . . '

' . . . would be of little use to anyone?'

'Exactly so, Centurion. Exactly so. And now, with your forgiveness, perhaps I have embarrassed myself enough for one morning. Shall we review your new command, Centurion Corvus?'

Marcus inclined his head, gesturing for the Hamian to precede him through the quarters' low doorway. Outside, in the early morning chill, the two centuries were paraded along the barrack's frontage in a long double line. He walked along the length of both centuries, looking intently at the faces that stared fixedly to their front. Their eyes were bright enough, although their skin was sallow with lack of sunlight. Dubnus strode across from the transit office to join him, casting an unhappy glance down the line.

'Maponus help us. Two centuries of underweight bath dodgers whose only skill is hunting game for the pot. Quite how we're going to turn this lot into infantrymen is beyond me. Anyway, I've been thinking, you take the Tungrians and I'll have these. I can . . . '

He stopped talking as a smile spread across Marcus's face.

'Dubnus. *Brother*. I wouldn't have amounted to anything better than a rotting corpse in a ditch on the road south from Yew Grove without your help over the last few months. Nor can I pretend that I was responsible for turning the Ninth from a waste of rations to a fighting century, that was mostly you too. But trust me when I tell you this, these men will not respond to your style of leadership. They are lonely, frightened, but worst of all they feel worthless. They've sat here for the last month watching Gaulish farm boys in armour get snapped up like the last cake in the bakery while they, with all their abilities, are demeaned as incapable of fighting our war.'

His friend rolled his eyes.

'But they *are*! What are this lot going to do when a warband comes howling out of the forest? Run like fuck, I'd say!'

'I know. But there's something here I think we can use. Call it determination; call it desperation if you like. Whatever you call it, I think we can make a fighting unit from them. Quite what kind of fighting is still open to question . . . '

Dubnus gave him a long stare.

'They carry shields made out of wicker. They wear armour made with rings so thin it wouldn't stop a half-decent spear-thrust, no spears, no helmets to speak of, and a decent wind would carry half of them away. Just equipping them is going to be difficult enough, never mind what'll happen the first time they try to carry all that weight more than a few hundred paces. They could be a real problem in the field.'

Marcus nodded.

'Worse than not having a hundred and fifty replacements? Worse than not having two more centuries of men following our standard?'

Dubnus shook his head in weary resignation.

'I know better than to argue with you. Though I don't think your standard-bearer's going to see the funny side of this.'

* * *

Dubnus's and Julius's centuries were arrayed on the Arab Town parade ground, the soldiers' breath steaming in the grey dawn's chill as they waited for the command to head away down the road towards The Stronghold, five miles to the west. Morban and Antenoch, respectively the 8th Century's standard-bearer and Marcus's personal clerk, waited with equal impatience a small distance from Dubnus's 9th Century. Morban cast occasional dirty looks at the 9th's standard-bearer, and more particularly the standard held proudly in the younger man's hands.

'He isn't keeping that statue clean, the lazy bastard. I've got a good mind to go and take the bloody thing away from him.'

Antenoch gave the 9th Century's standard a sideways glance and shot the alleged offender a sympathetic glance, raising an eyebrow in commiseration and drawing a hurt rebuke from his friend.

'I saw that.'

The clerk shrugged his indifference, huddling deeper into his cloak.

'It looks fine to me. Anyway, leave the man alone, you grumpy bastard. I don't remember you cleaning it all that often either. You should worry more about helping Two Knives get a brand-new century ready to fight, and leave the Ninth to Dubnus now that he's their centurion. Hang on, here they come . . . '

The first of the replacement centuries appeared around the corner of Arab Town's bathhouse, its soldiers stepping out strongly under the close scrutiny of Tiberius Rufius and his newly acquired chosen man and watch officer. Morban's face split into a beaming smile.

'*Yes!* Look at that! Eighty sides of prime Tungrian beef. Look at the muscles on those boys! The Bear'll be after slipping a few of those lads into the Tenth to replace the axemen who fell at Lost Eagle.'

Antenoch nodded, keeping his eyes on the advancing century.

'Yes . . . Grandfather looks happy enough with his new men, doesn't he?'

Morban squinted at the advancing Rufius's grinning face, seeing the smile turn into a laugh as the veteran officer found him among the waiting soldiers.

'That isn't happy, that's pure piss-take. Look, he's pointing back down the road. What's he on about . . . ?'

Antenoch craned his neck to see over the marching troops.

'There's Two Knives, I can see his helmet's crest, but where the hell are his men? Hold on a moment . . . '

Realisation dawned upon him with a sickening thud.

'I can see their helmets, but only just. It's a century of fucking dwarves!'

Morban stood rooted to the ground as the first century marched past them and the second came into full view, his eyes widening with genuine horror. Rufius stopped alongside the staring pair, his face distorted with laughter.

'Oh, Morban . . . if only . . . you could see . . . your face!'

He staggered away, clutching his sides. A grim-faced Julius, marching alongside Marcus, gave him a dirty look as the front rank of the Hamians drew level with them and halted at Marcus's shouted command. He shook his head in disgust at the older man's uncontrollable laughter.

'I thought age blessed a man with wisdom as it took away his strength, but clearly not in your case, Tiberius Rufius. And what's *your* problem, Standard-bearer?'

Morban came to sudden indignant life.

'Rufius gets a century full of big strong lads, and we get a gang of . . . of . . . underfed Arab bow benders? What use are they going to be when the blue-noses come hammering at our shields? I . . . '

Marcus stepped between Julius and Morban, then bent to put his face an inch from the indignant standard-bearer's, his finger dimpling his mailed chest to emphasise his point. His voice was low but insistent, his face dark with anger.

'Be quiet and listen, *Statue Waver*. We've been bilked of a century by the bloody Second Cohort, who bribed them out from under our noses this morning. These men are the only troops left in the port, and probably the only ownerless soldiers in the whole of Britannia, so these are the troops we're taking home with us. We'll swap them with the Second at the first opportunity, you can be assured of that, but in the meantime you will treat them with the consideration due to the poor bastards. What's more, these 'underfed bow benders' speak Latin just as well as you do, in fact probably with a good deal more eloquence and a lot less profanity, and I doubt they're all that happy with your reaction. It isn't their fault they're stuck here, and if they're going to be a part of our cohort we'd better make them feel just a tiny bit welcomed. If you don't like that you can always go back to the Ninth, and I'll ask Dubnus for his new boy in return.'

Morban's indignation melted to anxious disbelief in a second.

'Not fair, Centurion, not fair at all. You know young Lupus ties me to you.'

Marcus kept his face stony, tipping his head towards the waiting Hamians with arched eyebrows.

'In which case you'd better get your head out of your backside and greet your new century. Chosen Man Qadir, allow me to introduce the Eighth Century's standard-bearer, Morban. He's a good man, if a little overfond of drink and whoring. Not to mention the occasional wager.

In fact, if Morban offers you odds on anything, the sun coming up in the morning, rain being wet, just anything, consider very carefully before putting your money down.'

Morban smirked just a little, his dignity sufficiently restored by his officer's carefully chosen insults, and stuck out a meaty paw to the tall Hamian chosen man.

'Welcome to the Eighth Century, Chosen.'

Qadir took the hand carefully, looking about him in mock incomprehension.

'My thanks, Standard-bearer, although I see only one other man besides yourself. Perhaps it would be more fitting if the Eighth Century were to welcome you?'

Rufius, having recovered from his earlier fit of laughter, slapped the stocky standard-bearer on the shoulder.

'He's got a point, Morban. If Antenoch's your century you'd best go and join these lads. I'm sure they'll follow your standard round if you're nice to them.'

Marcus nodded agreement.

'And if you want them to regard it as something more than your personal badge of office, perhaps you'd better give them a bit of education?'

The standard-bearer nodded, squared his shoulders and stepped out in front of the Hamians. The voice of Rufius's man was already ringing through the still morning air as he addressed the new 6th Century. He cleared his throat before shaking the century's standard at the wide-eyed archers.

'Eighth Century! I am your standard-bearer, Morban, and this is your standard. I am entrusted with carrying this symbol of our century, and with keeping it safe from any threat at the cost of my own life if all else fails . . . which means if you're all dead. You are collectively charged with a sacred duty to guard the standard, which is the heart and soul of our century, and to protect it during battle at any cost.'

He ignored Antenoch, who was making cross-eyed faces at him from behind Marcus.

'You will follow the instructions of our centurion, Marcus Tribulus Corvus, which I will repeat through movements of the standard for those of you who do not understand them. If I lean the standard to the left, we're turning left. To the right, we're turning right. If I dip the standard, we're starting the march, if I raise it we're stopping. If I dip it two times we're marching at the double, and if I reverse it we're retreating. My mate here . . . ' He nodded to the trumpeter alongside him, who promptly blushed scarlet. ' . . . will sound his horn when I'm about to issue an order with the standard, so pay attention and you'll always know what we're about to do.'

He paused for breath and stared at the men closest to him with a fierce intensity.

'In battle, this standard is your rallying point. If we advance, the standard will be close to the front of the century, and if we advance to the rear it will be with the century's rearmost troops. Where the shit flies the thickest, you will find me and this statue right behind you. And you will make us proud. Just don't let us down. Centurion?'

Marcus stepped out in front of the Hamians, nodding to Morban as the standard-bearer waddled back to join Antenoch.

'Soldiers, you may not be Tungrians, you may be what our esteemed standard-bearer calls 'bow benders', and I guarantee you that getting you ready for life in an infantry cohort is going to be a challenge for us all. However, and listen to me very carefully when I tell you this, because it means a lot to your new brothers-in-arms, all those difficulties mean nothing to me because you are now Tungrians. Let me say that again. You are now Tungrians.'

He paused, staring across the silent men, aware that Julius was standing just behind him and glaring at the wide-eyed Hamians with equal intensity.

'At the moment that means little enough to you. I'm just another officer spouting off about his cohort. But you will learn what it means to be one of us. And when you understand that, you will be one step closer to reaching the standards we will be expecting of you. Now, make ready to move. We're marching to Noisy Valley, and that's a marching distance of twenty-six miles, which at four miles an hour will take us about eight hours including rest stops. Easy enough work for a fully fit soldier carrying the light equipment you've been issued with. This is our first chance to see how you men measure up to our standards.'

* * *

Prefect Furius rode into The Rock's temporary camp in the middle of the afternoon with three centuries of soldiers marching easily at his back. Forewarned by a tent party of men sent running ahead for the last mile by Centurion Tertius, the cohort's first spear was waiting at the camp's entrance with his officers, ready to formally greet their new commander. He bellowed an order as the prefect's horse drew level with their small group, snapping the cohort's officers to attention. Furius dismounted, and a soldier assigned to the task ran forward and led the horse away.

The prefect looked about him, taking in the stone shell of the burned-out fort huddled under the wall's unbroken defence. The turf-walled camp alongside it was a picture of order, the lines of tents perfectly aligned and the men set to guard the turf walls alert and crisp in their movements. Finding nothing to excite comment, he turned to address the gathered officers.

'First Spear . . . ?'

'Neuto, sir.'

'A local name, First Spear?'

'A Tungrian name, Prefect. I was born in Gallia Belgica.'

Furius nodded.

'I rode through your capital, Tungrorum, on my way here. You must miss it.'

The first spear inclined his head.

'I do, sir, although it's a very long time since I saw the old place.'

'There are some men behind me who have

seen your settlement somewhat more recently. I have reinforcements for you from Tungria, a full century of freshly trained men.'

The first spear smiled thinly.

'So I see, Prefect. I must admit that I wasn't expecting such a welcome addition to our strength. Reinforcements have been hard to come by with six full legion cohorts needing replacement.'

The prefect smiled broadly, either ignoring or simply missing the slightly disapproving note in his senior centurion's voice, and spread his hands like a conjuror soliciting applause for his latest trick.

'Then it's a good thing for our cohort that I happened to be in the right place at the right time and with the right, ah . . . influence, shall we say? I suggest that we get these three centuries into quarters, and you and I can have a discussion as to how we're going to demonstrate some old-fashioned Roman military justice to this cohort. There's an officer-killer at large in this cohort, and we're going to find him and make him pay for his crime with his blood.'

He smiled into Neuto's suddenly expressionless face before turning to the men unloading his effects from the wagon behind them.

'And now, let's get my kit off that wagon and safely into my tent, shall we? Be careful with that jar, it contains enough naphtha to burn down a legion fortress!'

* * *

The Tungrians reached Noisy Valley shortly before dark that evening. Passing The Rock an hour before, Julius had shot a hard scowl at the smirking 2nd Tungrian soldiers standing guard at the entrance to their earth-walled marching camp. Pausing for a moment to allow Tiberius Rufius to catch up with him, he'd tipped his helmeted head to the 2nd Cohort men, his face sour with disgust.

'Look at those smug bastards. There's nothing those thieving arse bandits like better than to get one over on us, and there they are with a century that belongs to us happily camped fifty paces the other side of their turf wall.' He spat on the ground, his face hardening as the sentries nudged each other, clearly barely restraining themselves from hysterics as the Hamians hove into view. 'I'll fucking . . . '

Rufius restrained him with a hand on his arm, shaking his head in gentle admonishment.

'You'll only regret it. Their first spear will be forced to send you packing, and from what I've heard he's a good enough sort. And his prefect will probably send a complaint to Frontinius and make it all our fault . . . '

Julius shrugged off the older man's hand, but to the veteran centurion's relief simply stood and stared at the sentries until they decided that discretion was the better part of valour in the face of his obvious anger and slunk off behind the section of turf wall that masked the fort's entrance. Marcus strode past alongside his struggling men, a jaundiced glance at the fort's walls the only sign of his disgust.

‘See, young Marcus has it right. Save your anger for a time when it can be put to good use.’

The big man grunted, shaking his head as he turned back to the march.

‘I’ll have blood for this. Just not today . . . ’

The 6th Legion’s temporary headquarters was a sea of tents clustered around the partially rebuilt ruins of the northern command’s Noisy Valley supply depot. Rufius, having strolled back down the marching column to walk a while with Marcus and Qadir, wrinkled his nose. ‘This place still stinks of burnt wood, even now they’ve cleared away most of the wreckage. At least the Sixth is getting on with putting it back to the way it was.’

Despite the hour, the warm late summer air was filled with the sounds of hammering and sawing, as the legion’s troops laboured to restore the camp to its former magnificence from the burned-out shells of armouries and supply sheds torched to prevent their being looted by the triumphant barbarians three months before. The wooden bridge at the foot of the quarter-mile slope from the camp to the river had already been completely rebuilt, and the valley’s slopes on both sides of the fast-flowing River Tinea had been stripped of most of their remaining trees to supply wood for the reconstruction. The result was a bare landscape studded with tree stumps, their removal a low priority compared with the work of reconstruction, and across which half a dozen bonfires etched their sooty stains into the late afternoon sky as conscripted Brigantian labour collected and burned the unwanted debris left behind after the trees had been felled and cut up into usable sections by the legions' artisans. Marcus nodded distractedly, his attention focused on his men. The replacement Tungrians marching in front of them under Dubnus's command, accustomed to marching from their recent training, were still relatively fresh. By contrast, most of his Hamians looked fit to drop. They had taken almost all of the day to cover the distance from Arab Town, and the centurions' faces had grown darker by the hour as the archers struggled to maintain even the standard marching pace.

'Their feet must be as soft as babies' arses. Look, that poor bastard's got blood leaking out of his boots.' Julius pointed to a man in the front rank as they paraded the replacements on the Noisy Valley parade ground. Both of the archer's feet were visibly bleeding, the raw flesh visible between his boots' leather straps. 'This lot are going to need some serious sorting out before they can get back on the road. You go and chat up the legatus for any equipment he can spare; I'll get them into quarters and boots off.'

Marcus nodded unhappily, ordering Qadir to stay with his men and follow Julius's instructions. He presented himself in front of the rebuilt headquarters, one of the few buildings already completed by the repair gangs, greeting the duty centurion with the appropriate degree of respect the man would consider his due from an auxiliary centurion.

'Centurion Corvus of the First Tungrian

cohort, requesting an audience with Legatus Equitius.'

The legion officer leaned forward to put his face a foot from the younger man's, and stared down his nose disdainfully, his jaw jutting out between his helmet's gleaming cheek pieces.

'Requesting an audience with the legatus? And what makes you think the commander of Sixth *Victorious* has any time for you?'

Retaining his cool, Marcus returned the hostile stare with a calm regard.

'Mainly the fact that we stood together on a hillside quite recently, while a barbarian warband battered itself to pieces on our shields.' His eyes narrowed slightly as he leaned forward in turn to put his face inches from the centurion's. 'Which cohort, Centurion?'

'What?'

He repeated the question with deliberate and obvious patience.

'In which one of the Sixth Legion's cohorts do you serve, Centurion?'

The older man saw quickly enough which way the conversation was going, and his answer was a fraction less gruff.

'The Second.'

Marcus nodded, his eyes fixed coldly on the other man's.

'I thought so. You're a replacement, from Gaul or Germany, I suppose, and so you weren't here for the battle of Lost Eagle. But I was, and so was the legatus, or Prefect Equitius as I knew him at the time. I served with him after his promotion too, hunting *your* legion's lost eagle through the northern hills while you were still on the road to this place. So, Centurion, all things being equal, I expect the legatus will be happy enough to see me.'

He settled into a comfortable parade rest and waited, while the officer stamped away and the headquarters sentries smirked quietly under their helmets. A few minutes later a soldier came to the door to fetch him inside the imposing building, leading him to the legatus's office. Equitius was seated behind an impressive desk with a scroll open in front of him, one hand teasing at his thick brown beard as he read, but he got quickly to his feet when he saw the young officer and greeted him with a smile of genuine pleasure.

'Centurion Corvus, you are quite literally a sight for sore eyes. Quintus!'

A uniformed clerk appeared at the door from an anteroom.

'Legatus?'

'That's it for today, my eyes seem to be getting old before their time. Clear up those papers, we'll make a fresh start tomorrow morning. And have some wine sent in please.'

Papers cleared and wine poured, the legatus raised his cup to Marcus. 'Here's to you, young man, and your apparent continued anonymity. Your false identity seems to be holding up well enough so far, for all the fact that the name Marcus Valerius Aquila hasn't been entirely forgotten yet.'

Marcus nodded, sipping at his wine.

'And you're still in command of the Sixth

then, sir? There's no danger of the legion being cashiered for losing its eagle?'

Equitius frowned reflexively at the question.

'Oh yes, I believe there's been plenty of talk on the subject, but I think we're past the worst of it. No legion has been disbanded in over a hundred years, not since First *Germanica* and Sixteenth *Gallica* were broken up for joining the Batavian revolt back in the Emperor Vespasian's day. I'm told that some of the men around the throne were all for making an example of the Sixth, to 'put some backbone in the other legions', but we've been fortunate in having Avitus Macrinus in command in the absence of an effective governor. Not only did he rubbish the suggestion before it was even made, but he's also got enough influence in Rome to squash the idea flat. The Sixth Legion may have been humbled by the deceptions of a traitor, but we'll survive to take our revenge for the loss of our eagle the only way we know, on the battlefield.'

He tipped his cup back, savouring the wine for a moment.

'So anyway, 'Marcus Tribulus Corvus', what brings you to this gloomy supply dump when you could be enjoying life on The Hill, or else be out in the field hunting down our old friend Calgus? I'll warn you now that you won't sleep a minute past dawn for the hammering of the armourers. My idiot of a camp prefect set their new forges up right next door to the transit barracks.'

Marcus told him the story of their day, getting a smile for his impression of Morban's indignation on first seeing the Hamians.

'. . . and then ten miles later he's already trying to talk his way into my new chosen man's purse.'

Equitius nodded sagely.

'That sounds like the Morban I recall. How do you rate their chosen man?'

Marcus pulled a face.

'He's disappointed with his demotion, I'd say, but he's hiding it well enough. Almost inscrutably, in fact.'

'He's a politician, then?'

The younger man shook his head slowly.

'No, I'd say he's something better than that. Call it maturity, or call it simple acceptance, he'll serve happily enough until the time comes to take his position back.'

'When you reclaim your Tungrians from the Second cohort?'

'Something like that.'

Equitius raised an eyebrow, calling for his clerk again.

'Ah, Quintus, I'd like any information we have on the Second Tungrian cohort's new prefect, straight away please.'

The clerk saluted and left the room.

'One of the privileges of senior command, access to rather more information than I'm used to. Another cup of wine?'

The clerk returned five minutes later with a record scroll.

'Updated only today, sir. Prefect Furius has joined the Tungrians from the German frontier, from the First *Minervia* to be precise.'

'I see. Anything else?'

'No, sir, just the bare facts of his previous service. A spell with Twelfth *Thunderbolt* in Moesia some years ago, more recently six months with First *Minervia*, then over the sea to join us.'

'Thank you, Quintus, that will be all.'

The clerk withdrew, and the legatus raised an eyebrow.

'What my clerk is far too careful to say, at least in front of a man he doesn't know, is that serving six months with a legion before being pushed off into auxiliary service is something of a kick in the teeth for a gentleman. It certainly wouldn't have been a step for his former commanding officer to have taken lightly, given that Furius appears to have been sufficiently well connected to be favoured with a legion tribunate in the first place. And whether auxiliary or not, cohort commands weren't growing on trees when I was looking for mine, so he must still have influential friends given that he's probably been quite a naughty boy. He certainly must have some pull to have snagged a tribune's posting with First *Minervia* in the first place.' He gave Marcus a cautionary look. 'Mark my words, Centurion, the Second Cohort's new prefect might well have a colourful recent past, so I wouldn't bet on getting those troops back any time soon, not until both cohorts are in the same place as a sympathetic senior officer. So, let's get down to it, eh? You'll be keeping those archers for a while, so what do you need to get them into the field with a half-decent chance of survival?'

3

Later, in the evening's chill, Marcus left the headquarters and walked slowly through the flickering torchlight to the hospital. The soldier on guard duty saluted at the sight of his cross-crested helmet, and the young Roman returned the salute distractedly. Inside the building he paused for a long moment in a darkened corridor, lost in thought. Legatus Equitius had broached the subject of Felicia Clodia Drusilla with diplomatic care, mentioning as if in passing that the doctor, kept busier than ever she had been caring for a single cohort's medical needs now that she had several thousand men to look after, might appreciate a visit from an old friend.

'The legion's lucky that she was on hand to step in when her predecessor got himself killed on the road from the Yew Grove fortress. Luckier still that her father took the trouble to impart his surgical skills to her rather than abandoning her intellect to preparation for marriage and motherhood. I've requested a pair of replacement surgeons, of course, but there's no word on when they'll be forthcoming. Until then it's either the good lady or nothing. Not even the camp prefect can complain at her presence under those circumstances.'

While he had kept his face straight and his feelings to himself, in truth Marcus had thought of little else since their last meeting, or at least during those times when his mind had not been occupied by the duties of his command. Given both the circumstances of that brief encounter, and those of her husband's death, he had been prey to a host of doubts in the intervening weeks. And so the young centurion lurked in stealthy indecision. He and Felicia had briefly been close, but that was before . . .

'Centurion?' Marcus jerked out of his reverie, realising that he had been close to dozing in the quiet warmth of the hospital. An orderly stood before him with a dim lamp, the oil almost exhausted. 'Can I help you, sir? Do you require treatment?

'Marcus shook his head, removing his helmet. 'No, thank you, I have come to visit Doctor Clodia Drusilla. I'm told that she is here, and I would appreciate a moment of her time, if the hour is forgivable.'

'Yes, sir, I will pass your request on. Your name, Centurion?'

'Corvus. Just that.' He waited a moment, the fears of a thousand dismal reflections on their situation crowding back down on him. She must see that his life was not for her, she would have met another man, a safer man, she would be dismayed with his unheralded arrival, she . . .

'Marcus!' Felicia hurried down the corridor with her skirts flying, and wrapped her arms around him in a warm embrace that dispelled his fears in an instant. 'I've missed you! I'd almost given up on you as a lost cause, it's been so long. Come into my office.' She took his arm and drew him down the corridor, pulling him into the privacy of her room and closing the door before pressing him up against the wall in a long searching kiss. Breaking away after a long moment, she held him out at arm's length in the flickering lamplight, appraising him as if in comparison with her memories before poking his armoured chest. 'I'm sure I promised myself that you wouldn't be quite so sturdily dressed the next time we kissed. It's been so *long*, Marcus, I was sure you weren't coming back for me.' Her voice sounded small, almost lost, and her eyes moistened with repressed emotion.

He took both of her hands, her fingers warm between his. 'I'm sorry, I've been tied up patrolling the border area. The locals have reacted badly to not being liberated by their northern brothers, so they've taken to hit-and-run raids on Roman outposts and farms. The only way I might have seen you earlier would have been to get in the way of a blue-nose arrow. Besides, last time we met you were . . . ' He dried up, not wanting to say the words for fear of offending her.

Felicia sighed and shook her head, staring at the floor. 'I know, I was distant, and I've cursed myself a thousand times since. I suppose it was just a reaction to my husband's death . . . That and being told that he was killed by a wound in the back.'

Marcus trod carefully. Prefect Bassus had been stabbed in the back at the height of the pursuit that had followed the barbarian rout at the battle of Lost Eagle. He was widely reputed to have brought his death, presumably at the hands of his men, upon himself. His harsh leadership, combined with an inability to see his soldiers' growing anger with their treatment, had seemingly driven them to deal with him in the only way left open to them. 'You know he was . . . ?'

'A difficult man to like? Of course, who knew that better than I did? Why else would I have run away from him, although I thank the day I made that choice every time I pray to Fortuna. He didn't deserve to die that way, though . . . ' She was silent for a moment, her hands clenched in her lap. 'And I still feel guilty. When I heard he was dead my first reaction was joy, joy to be free of him, and to have my chance to be with you.' She turned her head away, staring into the room's shadowed corner. 'Nobody with a calling to healing should be able to take even the slightest pleasure in death, and he was still my husband. I felt so . . . ashamed of myself.'

Marcus put a finger to her chin and turned her face back to his own. 'He spoke to me on that bloody hill, when the Second Cohort pulled our chestnuts out of the fire at the last moment, before the barbarian charge, and I swear he knew what had happened between us, or at least guessed. He made it very clear that he was going to call me out after the battle, but I couldn't have fought him. I would have been forced to kill him, and that would have brought disaster on both of us. Whoever put that spear in his back saved me from taking my own life to avoid implicating us both, me for treason and you for adultery.' He paused for a moment to stare into her eyes. 'Anyway, he's gone. We can either decide to make the most of where we find ourselves, or just waste our lives worrying about our mutual guilt. I know which I prefer.'

She looked back up at him, her eyes soft in the lamplight, shrugging the sleeves of her tunic off her shoulders, so that the garment was held in place only by its friction with the slope of her breasts. 'And you'd like to know what my choice is? Why don't you lock that door and ask me properly?'

* * *

It was another two hours before Marcus made his way back to the transit barracks, bone weary and yet elated beyond expectation. Rufius looked up expectantly as he opened the door to the barrack the four centurions had agreed to share. Julius and Dubnus were already asleep in their bunks, huddled down into straw mattresses. 'Ah, so there you are. I had half a mind to call out the guard to look for you, it's been so long, but Julius convinced me that you were likely just guzzling down the legatus's Iberian red without concern for your elders and betters. Anyway, what have you been up to . . . you look like you're dead on your feet, but you don't smell of drink . . . '

The veteran centurion sniffed ostentatiously, his eyes widening as he did so. He leaned back in his chair and prodded the recumbent form behind him. 'Hey, Julius! Julius, wake up, man!'

Their brother officer woke with red-rimmed eyes, sat up, shot Marcus a glance and subsided back on to his bed. 'He's back. Big deal. Let me sleep, damn you.'

Rufius shook him by the shoulder. 'I think you're going to want to see this. Or rather, I think you're going to want to smell it.'

Julius sat back up with a frown, looked Marcus up and down and drew in a long breath through his nose. He stared at Marcus with a look of dawning amazement. 'Bugger me . . . '

Rufius snorted. 'I wouldn't turn over tonight or the horny young sod probably will.'

Julius tried again. 'You've . . . you've been . . . '

Marcus reddened, and Rufius pounced. 'Yes, he bloody well has. While we've been sat here worrying that some nasty little thief might have clouted him and left him for dead in the dark, he's been playing hide-the-cucumber. Not only that, but he hasn't even washed the lady's smell from his skin before coming back to gloat over us poor celibates. Didn't they teach you to go to the baths after a tumble, eh, boy, or least get a washcloth and a bucket and do your best with that?'

Marcus opened his mouth to retort, only to get Julius's cloth square in the face, still damp from his end-of-day wipe-down. 'Have one on me, lad. Just don't be settling down to sleep in here reeking like that or I'll be as stiff as a crowbar all bloody night. Go on, there's a bucket of water outside the door, go and wash it off like a decent comrade.' He stopped, caught off guard by the look on Marcus's face. 'Hang on, look at you. You look like every lovestruck prick I've ever had the misfortune to bunk with over the last twenty years, about as sharp as a ragman's donkey. You didn't even see that washcloth coming. I know who you've been with . . . what's her name, the doctor . . . '

Marcus turned for the door, the cloth dangling in one hand.

'Felicia. Her name is Felicia. And she promised to marry me.'

Julius and Rufius exchanged amazed stares, then Julius reached over to shake the only man in the room who was still asleep. 'Dubnus. *Dubnus!* You are not going to want to miss this.'

* * *

Calgus and his bodyguard left the warband's camp in the dawn's first light. They slipped away unnoticed, save for a few words with the men patrolling the camp's western face, men of the Selgovae tribe and still fiercely loyal to their tribal leader. Calgus whispered fiercely into the ear of the warrior commanding the watch on the camp's western wall.

'You've seen nothing all morning, Vallo, clear?'

The guard's leader, a grizzled and scar-faced veteran of two uprisings against the hated invaders, and fiercely loyal to Calgus, nodded impassively. He had been on guard the previous day, when the messenger he had been warned to expect had walked out of the forest from the west, stopping fifty paces from the camp's wall. When Vallo had gone forward to speak with him the northerner had simply uttered his message for Calgus and then turned impassively away, without any apparent regard for the dozen Selgovae warriors standing behind their leader. Now Vallo stood in front of his king, looking unhappily at the half-dozen men of Calgus's bodyguard as they clustered around their chieftain.

'We will keep silence, my lord. We will guard your tent, and tell any that ask that you are ill.' He leaned closer to Calgus, his voice tense for all the softness of the muttered whisper. 'But I do not like the risk you take in doing this.'

Calgus nodded and slapped the veteran's shoulder, looking round to ensure they remained unseen in the sleeping camp before replying in equally soft tones.

'I know. The Votadini will complain more loudly in my absence, and their king will continue his plotting, but this thing has to be done in absolute secrecy if it is to bring us the victory we need.'

'So you walk out into the forest with a handful of warriors. My lord, it is a mistake! It is the same mistake as when you were ambushed by the Romans when you went hunting. Your bodyguard all killed, and you spared only by the strength and speed of your sword arm?'

Calgus laughed softly, recalling his first encounter with the Roman traitor who had proved the key to their initial triumph over the Roman 6th Legion.

'Aye, there's a story. I'll recount it to you in full one night, when we've run the Romans off our land for good, but for now trust me when I tell you that this is a risk I cannot avoid. Not if I am to bring about the great victory we need to get their dirty feet off our land.'

The warrior bowed and stood aside, watching as the men of his chieftain's bodyguard ducked through the artfully concealed opening in the palisade that surrounded the camp and moved out into the trees ahead of the king, their spears ready to throw and their eyes on the forest about them. Turning back to his men, he gestured for them to continue their guard duty, looking across the camp long and hard to ensure that no early riser had spotted Calgus's quiet departure. When he turned back to the forest, the small group of men was already out of sight, hidden by the profusion of vegetation that flourished between the thick trunks of the oaks.

The small party made cautious progress through the silent forest, using a hunter's track through the dense undergrowth which had seen little recent use, to judge by the luxuriant foliage growing across it. They broke off the line of their march several times to wait quietly in the cover of the thick undergrowth, in hopes of surprising any attempt at following them through the forest's gloom. By midday they were crouched in the shelter of a fallen tree at the bottom of a valley about five miles from their camp.

'No, my lord, we are not followed.' The leader of the warlord's personal guard shook his head with absolute certainty, his voice pitched low enough that only Calgus could hear him. 'The forest is quiet, and anyone following us along these overgrown paths would be heard from two hundred paces.'

Calgus nodded his satisfaction.

'Good. Then I can push on without fear of being observed.'

The warrior pulled a face, looking around at the deep forest's confusion of trees and bushes.

'In all truth, my lord, I have a greater fear of what lies ahead of us than with what might or might not lie behind. What I have said is as true for us as for any man tracking us . . . '

Calgus nodded his understanding.

'I know. Once we start moving we'll be making as much noise as a herd of pigs on the hunt for nuts. But nevertheless I have to move on and take that risk. I have an appointment on the far side of this hill that I am unwilling to miss.'

'My lord.'

The bodyguard stood, gesturing to his comrades to prepare to renew their march. Calgus shook his head.

' 'I', not 'we'. This is a task that I must carry out alone, and you men must wait here for my return. While I'm away you can prepare torches, in case I'm later coming back over the hill than would be ideal, but you will under no circumstances attempt to follow me.'

'And if you don't return before dark?'

Calgus nodded.

'It's possible. In that case you are to build a large fire, and take turns in watching out for me, but you are still to stay here.'

He turned away and headed on up the hill,

pushing aside a branch that was overhanging the path.

'And if you still don't return, my lord? How long should we wait?'

Calgus paused for a moment, calling back over his shoulder.

'As long as it takes.'

He turned back to the path, muttering under his breath.

'Which, if I've misjudged my gamble, won't be very long. If I've got this one wrong we'll all be dead before dark falls.'

He climbed the hill with a hunter's caution, his eyes and ears straining for any hint of a presence in the trees around him, but neither saw nor heard anything to give him pause, continuing his careful ascent until he reached the top of the hill. Sliding into the shadow of a tree, he became absolutely still, so quiet that he could feel his own heart beating, and listened again. After a moment he caught a sound through the incessant drone of the forest's insects, only a faint fragment of noise, but enough to tell him that he was in the right place. As he eased back to his feet a spear slammed into the tree's trunk a foot from his face, stopping him dead as a warrior rose out of the foliage, another spear pointed straight at him, more men at his back. Each one of them was heavily tattooed, swirling blue patterns decorating their hands and faces. The king of the Selgovae raised his open hands, careful to make no move that might be interpreted as threatening.

'Well, that's the hardest part of the trick done;

I've found you without getting myself killed. Shall we go down the hill and see who's waiting for me at the bottom?'

The man behind the levelled spear scowled at him, gesturing his men forward.

'Take his weapons and tie his hands.'

He watched as the rebel leader was relieved of his sword and had his wrists tied together in front of him. Calgus's return stare remained steady throughout the swift process of disarmament and restraint.

'Do your people always treat invited guests in this way?'

The spearman snorted mirthless laughter.

'We are a long way from home, and the Hunting Hounds have learned the hard way to trust nobody until they are proved worthy of it. Bring him.'

* * *

Prefect Furius paraded the Second Tungrians after breakfast the next day, waiting next to his first spear as the cohort marched on to The Rock's parade ground. The older man spoke after a moment's silence.

'You intend going through with what we discussed?'

The prefect nodded confidently.

'Absolutely. I'll have Prefect Bassus's murderer underground before we leave here, that or the local crows will eat well for the next few days. My only concern about dealing with the matter today is that you haven't managed to find the bastard over the last two months.'

They stood in uncomfortable silence until the last century had marched on to the square, and the entire cohort was stood at attention. Furius strode out to face them, self-assured confidence in his authority apparent in his stride and bearing.

'Second Cohort . . . ' The ranks of troops waited expectantly to be ordered to stand at their ease. ' . . . normally I would order you to stand easy for my morning address, but this morning isn't normal, so you can all stay at attention. In point of fact, there hasn't been a normal day in this cohort since one of you put a spear through the spine of your last prefect.' If anyone had been dozing in the ranks before, it was certain that nobody was doing so now. 'Until now, nobody in this cohort has taken the trouble to find the man that killed Prefect Bassus. By rights he should long since have been avenged by the penalty that military law demands of his murderer — public execution. It seems, however, that this cohort is content to brush its problems under the mat. Until today, that is. Today, Second Tungrians, that failure to act will be rectified in the most public way possible. Before you leave this parade ground I will know who killed him. Either that, or you'll all rue the day you ever set eyes on him. I've sworn to Mars to take the murderer's life as revenge for Bassus's, sworn on an altar with witnesses and a noble sacrifice, with no way back from the promise. And I will, I promise you, exact revenge for him. How many more men die here alongside the prefect's killer depends entirely on you.'

He took a breath and looked across their packed ranks, playing the moment out, feeling the tension crackling through the men arrayed in front of him.

'Since I seem to be the only man seeking justice here, I'm going to need some help. I know that the first spear will stand alongside me, so now I want to know where the other officers stand. Any centurion that is willing to support justice for Prefect Bassus, stand forward three paces from your centuries.'

There was an instant ripple of movement, so fast that Furius suspected that his first spear had blown quietly in a few ears some time since he had first briefed the man as to what he intended. All ten of his officers stood forward of their men, having crossed, whether they realised it or not, their own personal Rubicons from which there would be no turning back.

'Very good. At least this cohort's officers recognise the enormity of the crime we're going to take retribution for. So, we have one man out of the eight hundred of you facing me to expose. What will it take to make that happen? I wonder. In fact, I've been thinking about it for the last five weeks, ever since the moment I found out about my new command, and the way in which it became available.' He paused for a moment, allowing a powerful silence to settle on the gathered soldiers. 'Some years ago I served in the Moesian border wars with the Twelfth *Thunderbolt*. There was a unit with true Roman discipline.' He stared across the cohort, sneering into his troops' collective wide-eyed stare.

'Yes, the Twelfth knew about crime and punishment, and any example of cowardice was met with the harshest of penalties. I'm tempted to follow their example, and decimate this cohort, literally to condemn one man in ten to death at the hands of his peers as punishment . . . ' Furius paused again, sweeping his gaze across the rows of stony faces. ' . . . but I realise that while that would be a fitting punishment, the odds of killing the murderer would be far too low to justify the lost fighting strength. So, I have decided on a different approach.

'You men are a disgrace, willing to allow the death of your commander to pass unpunished, and so I'm going to punish you collectively to the maximum extent I can without causing any loss of your fighting capability. As a result, the following punishments are effective immediately. First, you will all be fined an amount of pay equal to that which you have earned since Bassus's murder. On top of that, no further pay will be issued until his killer volunteers himself for punishment.' He waited for a moment, allowing the enormity of three months' lost pay to sink in. 'Second, if the killer is found, and justice granted to Prefect Bassus today, before the sun sets, I will commute that fine to one month's pay. And lastly, if the prefect's killer is not identified today, I will randomly select a man from each century for execution by his comrades. Execution which will be carried out without the use of any weapons other than your bare hands.'

He looked across their ranks, staring hard at faces whose gaze was locked firmly to the front, not daring to meet his eyes.

'You choose. I've got no orders other than to scout this area for barbarians, so we can stay here as long as you like while the man I'm looking for makes his mind up to come forward, just as long as you're all clear that every new day will start with each century choosing a soldier to be beaten to death . . . not to mention someone to do the dirty work. I'll be in my tent . . . '

* * *

The quartermaster's meaty hand made a loud thwack as he smacked it down on the counter. His pale eyes flicked between the two men on the other side of the desk, one hand distractedly smoothing his slicked-back hair.

'Are you pair mad? You pitch up as if you own the place, and then you offer to relieve me of two centuries' worth of equipment?' He glared across the wooden expanse at Marcus and Qadir. 'An officer fresh out of his napkin, and a chosen man in fancy dress with a bad suntan. Well, the pair of you can fuck right off.'

Marcus's face hardened, his well-being of the previous evening already forgotten.

'You're making a big mistake, storeman, I . . . '

The quartermaster's eyes widened.

'Storeman. Fucking storeman!? I eat storemen for breakfast. I shit storemen when I go to the latrine. You, boy, do not call me a storeman, you piece of auxiliary shit.'

Qadir raised an eyebrow at the tirade, and then turned his head minutely as if only very slightly surprised as Marcus put a hand to his sword. A voice from behind them pulled his attention away from the scene of impending violence. It was Rufius, speaking from the shadow of the store's doorway.

'I wouldn't if I were you, young Two Knives. I've known the big-mouthed idiot for longer than I care to remember and he's been the same for all those years, all piss and vinegar just as long as there's a nice wide counter between him and the men he's robbing. There's two ways we can do this. Either you can argue with him, show him your requisition all nice and official with all the right names and a pretty seal, and eventually jump the counter and offer him a new set of lumps in the time-honoured fashion, or I can simply remind him of one of life's oldest rules. I suggest we try it my way first, and if that fails you can have another go at doing it your way. Now, *Storeman* Brocchus, let's see how well you remember your old comrades, eh? Let me give you a clue. I retired from the legion after twenty-five years only eighteen months ago. No?'

Brocchus frowned with concentration, thrown off balance by the as yet unknown officer's supreme confidence.

'No? Here's another clue. I was the best first spear ever to grace the parade ground at Yew Grove. No? I thought not, you never did recognise quality in either supplies or soldiers.

One last clue, then. I never did tell anyone about you and that lady you used to see on the side, did I? Despite her being very close to a rather unpleasant centurion of our mutual acquaintance, a man who would bite your throat out if he ever even suspected you of diddling his woman.'

Brocchus recoiled from the counter with a look of combined amazement and horror. '*Tiberius Rufius?* But . . . '

Rufius walked out of the shadows, swept his helmet off and slapped it down on to the counter's surface, a wolfish grin painted across his face.

'I *know*! It's the sheer delight of seeing me again. I heard you shouting the odds like a stallholder's wife from outside and I thought, 'Bugger me, it's that old fool Brocchus giving out just like old times.''

'But you retired. I saw you go . . . '

Rufius grinned hugely, reaching across the counter to give the quartermaster's cheek a painful tweak.

'And now you see me back again, back in uniform . . . sorry, fancy dress . . . and having the best fun of my life. Yes, here I am again, with my mate here just out of his napkin and his over-tanned chosen man, and we're here to rob your stores of everything and anything of value to the hundred and sixty men standing outside that door. Not your legion issue, of course, no, we're looking for equipment fit for auxiliary *shit*, and I'm betting you've got enough hidden away back there for our purposes, given your love for squirrelling away anything and everything you might be able to sell.' He grinned widely at the quartermaster's amazed stare. 'And do you know just how much you can do to stop me? Given that we've got a signed requisition from the Sixth's legatus? A man who recently saw battle alongside myself and Napkin Boy here? And given that I know absolutely everything about your sordid little encounters with a certain officer's wife? Encounters I'm sure you'd prefer never got back to him? Nothing, eh, *Storeman*? So, muster your work dodgers and let's be about equipping a hundred and sixty brave men to go and stand between you and those nasty barbarians I'm sure you've heard so much about.'

The quartermaster paled, turned and fled back into the storehouse's gloom, calling for his men. Rufius smirked after him, raising a self-satisfied eyebrow at Marcus and Qadir.

'There you go, lads, definitive proof that it isn't who you know that matters, but who you know they've been shagging. Full infantry equipment for a double century of bow benders coming right up.'

* * *

If the 8th Century had made poor time the previous day, their progress with sore feet and their new burden of armour and weaponry made the previous efforts look sparkling. Qadir walked alongside Marcus as the Hamians struggled up a slight incline in the road from The Rock towards

Cauldron Fort, sweat beading his brow from both the warmth of the day and the weight of his new equipment. Each man was now shod with the standard heavy-soled combat boots, the hobnails lazily rapping out their laboured progress.

'This mail must be at least twice the weight of our previous shirts.'

Marcus smiled grimly back at him. 'Not to mention the arming vest, which you'll curse all day when it's this warm — until it saves your delicate skin from being cut by the rings when they stop a blade. Anyway, that's twenty pounds of heavy iron rings from neck to thigh, the best armour in the empire. Strong enough to stop arrow, sword or spear, just as long as a ring doesn't break or a rivet pop, and flexible too. The first time you see combat with the blue-noses you'll wish it was longer and thicker.'

'Blue-noses?'

'Yes. Our affectionate name for the tribes we're fighting. They have a tendency to paint themselves up for battle.' He raised an eyebrow at the Hamian's disbelieving smile. 'Oh, you can laugh now, but the first time you see a wall of screaming blue-painted lunatics charging at you you'll not be quite so amused.'

'I see. And the spear?'

'Six pounds each. You should be carrying two, but we decided that one would be enough, given you still have your bows. Before you ask, the sword weighs three pounds, the shield twelve, the helmet five, and there's another five pounds of kit on the carrying pole.'

'And you fight in this? I can barely walk for the weight.'

Marcus nodded. 'I know. The first week is the worst. Once your men get used to the extra weight they'll find they've grown muscle where there was little before. The . . . '

A scream from the century of Tungrians marching to their front snapped his attention to their ranks. A man had fallen out of the column, an arrow protruding from his thigh.

'Buckets and boards!' Dubnus's voice rang out in the sudden shocked silence, stirring the stunned troops into a flurry of movement as shields were pulled from the troops' backs, and helmets thrust over their heads. Marcus turned to his own men, his own order for increased protection dying in his throat. Qadir, his bow already in his hand, gestured with an open hand towards the distant treeline. 'With your permission? Before they realise what we are?'

Marcus nodded blankly, unprepared for the sudden turn of events. 'Be my guest.'

A half-dozen tribal bowmen were standing a few paces from the safety of the trees, ready to dart into their shelter just as they had during the outward march three days before. Nocking a wickedly barbed arrow to his weapon's bow-string, the Hamian effortlessly pulled the bow back to the limit of its ability to store the energy he was forcing into its stressed wood-and-bone frame. He took a moment longer to compose his shot, breathing in and half releasing the breath before loosing the arrow in a long shallow arc. As the arrow punched into his first target he was already nocking a second missile, sending it after the first before the barbarian had completed his nerveless slump to the ground, dropping the man standing alongside his first victim even as he gaped at his fallen comrade without quite comprehending what was happening. A third man fell as he started to shout a warning, and a fourth as the remaining tribesmen turned to run, the Hamian loosing his arrows with a speed and accuracy unlike any that Marcus had seen before. Morban, standing alongside him, gaped in astonishment. His mouth hung open unnoticed as the big Syrian's bow spat arrow after arrow at the now terrified barbarians.

Two men were left now, another shot dropping one of the pair as they sprinted for the trees in terror of the arrows that were killing them in remorseless succession. The last man reached the treeline and darted behind the trunk of a massive oak, peeping back out at the watching troops. Morban roared his approval, shaking the century's standard in triumph.

'Five men dead in twenty heartbeats! Cocidius's hairy nuts, but you're . . . '

He fell silent as the Hamian chosen man nocked a last arrow, ignoring the standard-bearer's noisy approval. Qadir waited for a long moment, holding another deep breath with his eye fixed on the distant tree, then loosed his last arrow just as the Briton looked out from his hiding place again, turning away to resling the weapon across his shoulder without any apparent interest in the shot's success. For a moment nothing happened, but then the last of the tribesmen staggered from his hiding place behind the oak with the last arrow protruding from his neck, and fell full length to the ground. Qadir turned to Marcus and repeated his small bow of the previous morning, hands open wide at his side.

Julius ran down the road towards them, a broad smile on his face. 'Bloody good work, that'll make the stupid young bastards think twice before any of them try that again. Let's get on the move again.'

Qadir inclined his head respectfully. 'I would, with your permission, Centurion, prefer to retrieve my spent arrows. And some of those men may not be dead . . . I think I can see one of them moving.'

Julius clapped him on the arm, pointing to the forest's edge, and the wounded barbarians. 'You're shit-hot with a bow, that's clear enough, but you still have a lot to learn about war here on the frontier. Those men you just put down can lie there and bleed to death for all I care. They might all die where they fell, or one or two of them might well make it back to their village. Either works well enough for us, since either way the message gets round the locals in double-quick time. Your arrows will give them pause for thought, and that's a price worth paying. Centurions, saddle your men up and get them moving!'

* * *

The exhausted Hamians trailed the other centuries on to The Hill's parade ground late that afternoon, wearily forming up for review alongside the replacement Tungrians as Acting Prefect Frontinius marched down from the fort.

Morban nudged Qadir in the ribs, muttering from the side of his mouth. 'Right, mate, that's First Spear Sextus Frontinius, or 'Uncle Sextus' when he's not within earshot. He's a decent enough officer, straight enough, and doesn't even mind being told when he's wrong as long as you don't rub it in. If he asks you a question don't try to be clever, just answer him and then shut up. If he wants to know more he'll ask you quick enough.'

Frontinius's step was lively enough but the waiting officers saw the obvious stiffness in his gait and exchanged meaningful glances.

'You can stop pulling faces at each other when you think I'm not looking. Yes, my bloody knee is still as stiff as a spear shaft and yes, it still hurts like buggery when I bend it first thing in the morning, and not much less at any other time. That's the price you pay for offering an easy target when there are blue-nose archers within bowshot. All of which is of far less importance than exactly what you've brought back from Arab Town. 'A double order of tunic lifters' was the term the officer of the guard used when he put his head round my office door five minutes ago . . . and it doesn't look like he was far off the mark, for all the nice new armour they're struggling to keep upright. So, who's going to enlighten me?'

Julius stepped forward, snapping a crisp salute before walking across to his superior, leaning close enough that his words would be for the first spear's ear alone.

'Our rules, Sextus?'

Frontinius shot him a penetrating stare, raising an eyebrow. 'Our rules? Twice in one year? This ought to be good . . . '

The centurion nodded to acknowledge his old friend and superior officer's point.

'Our rules, then. The Second Cohort has a new prefect, some hothead fresh from Germania with a point to prove. The bastard bribed the Arab Town replacements officer to let him walk off with one of our centuries, which left us with two choices, either to come back eighty men short, or to bring back enough of these Hamians to get us back to full strength.'

The first spear raised an eyebrow, looking out over the centuries paraded in front of him. 'And you went for numbers.'

'It wasn't my first choice. I'll live with it, seeing as we've got them re-equipped somewhat more like soldiers than dancing girls, and given that one of them killed a half-dozen of the local idiots on the way back, but left to me they'd still be sitting in Arab Town wondering why it's so cold in the middle of summer.'

'I see. We'll come back to the local idiots. So exactly whose first choice was it?'

'Our young gladiator, who else? Oh, I ought to mention that he's asked a certain lady doctor, recently widowed, if you get my drift, for her hand in marriage. Which, Cocidius the mighty hunter be forever mystified, she seems to have agreed to. You can expect the boy at your table one evening soon now asking for your formal permission.'

The first spear raised a sardonic eyebrow, shaking his head gently.

'That young man's been nothing but a source of entertainment ever since Prince Dubnus walked him through the gates, but let's concentrate on the Hamians for the time being. We'll worry about the marriage later. I presume he's intending to practise his transformation skills on his new century?'

Julius nodded sagely. 'Looks like it. I'm not sure that he understands the difference between what he managed with the Ninth Century and turning untrained men into soldiers, never mind untrained men quite so lacking in muscle. He did persuade Legatus Equitius to cough up the kit to make them look respectable, although they talked him into letting them keep their bows.'

'Hence the dead idiots?'

'Yes. Amazing shooting by their chosen man, too, he knocked over half a dozen of them in less time than it takes to tell the story. The fools never knew what hit them until it was too late. They were trying the usual shoot-and-run stuff — in fact they'd already hit us on the road east, killed one man and wounded another. We left him with Centurion Corvus's wife-to-be in the Noisy Valley base hospital.'

Frontinius snorted without mirth. 'So, the locals bit off more than they could chew? Good. Perhaps they'll think twice in future. So, these are useful tunic lifters then, despite appearances?'

Julius shook his head almost imperceptibly, his eyes lifted briefly to the sky in unspoken comment. 'They'll shoot well enough, but the rest of the picture's just one broken tile after another. They're nearly all twenty pounds underweight and a hand's length too short, they handle their weapons so badly the blue-noses will piss themselves laughing if we ever have to put them into a battle line, and their feet are as soft as silk. Or at least they were two days ago. Now they're just a bloody mess. Like I said, I'll live with it, and I'll give Two Knives all the help I can, but I think it's a lost cause. Two minutes of toe-to-toe with the locals will see half of them dead and the other half running.'

Frontinius nodded slowly, his eyes fixed on the Hamian ranks. 'I can see your point from here. On the other hand, we're likely to be back in the action before very long, and a double-strength century isn't a thing I can afford to turn my nose up at. Perhaps we need to allow Centurion Corvus the benefit of the doubt for a little while. Parade them properly.'

Julius spun away, bellowing for the four centuries to come to attention, and the two men waited for a long moment for the soldiers to settle down into immobility under the spirited goading of their watch officers. The Hamians, Frontinius noted, for all their obvious exhaustion, settled first and with a minimum of fuss. Nodding his satisfaction, the prefect paced out towards the Tungrian replacements and walked the front rank with questioning eyes. 'They still make big lads in Tungria, I see. Nice tidy equipment . . . you, air your iron.'

The soldier obediently unsheathed his sword, presenting the weapon's hilt to the officer.

'Clean, sharp, nice quality too. A good result, I'd say. This is your century, Centurion Rufius? Yes? You're a lucky man, although I'm not sure what you've done to deserve it. Now, let's have a look at our archers . . . '

He walked along the 8th Century's front rank, assessing their tired but erect stance. 'Nice armour. New swords and spears too. Well done, Centurion Corvus, good use of initiative to have Sixth Legion re-equip your men, although quite how you got equipment this tidy out of their stores is something of a mystery to me.'

Marcus met his questioning stare. 'I had a little help from Centurion Rufius, First Spear. Local knowledge still counts, apparently . . . '

'Good. Well done, Rufius, I'll buy you a cup of wine later on for saving our young colleague the trouble of going through that whole 'do you know who I am?' routine. This is your new chosen man, I presume, Centurion?'

'Chosen man Qadir, First Spear.'

'Thank you. Chosen, might I take a look at that bow?'

Qadir saluted smartly and handed him the weapon. Frontinius tested the bow's draw, grunting quietly with the effort, then handed it back.

'I hear that you killed half a dozen men with this earlier today?'

The chosen man nodded.

'Yes, First Spear.'

Frontinius handed the weapon back to him with a look of respect, then stepped up to address the century, raising his voice to be heard clearly. 'Soldiers of the Eighth Century, you may have been born and trained in Syria, but you are now part of the proudest and most respected auxiliary cohort on the northern frontier. The First Tungrians have faced battle in these hills many times and always come out on top. Always. We win, gentlemen, no matter the odds. We win, we bury our dead, we mourn and we move on. You will find your comrades hard bitten . . . uncompromising . . . and this may be offputting to you, but you will adapt to our way of going about our business. I suggest that you start adapting now, for I fear that your time to do so will be shorter than might have been ideal. Welcome to the war.'

* * *

The sun was close to the western horizon by the time the 2nd Cohort delivered forth Prefect Bassus's murderers. Respectfully summoned by First Spear Neuto, Furius strode out on to the parade ground, where the cohort had stood for most of the day. The soldiers were standing to attention, their faces fixed and sullen. Two soldiers stood out in front of the cohort's third century, half a dozen of the cohort's officers arrayed around them. Furius strolled up to the group, eyeing the pair carefully. Both men fixed their gazes on him, both wide eyed and pale with the gravity of their situation. The prefect turned to First Spear Neuto, gesturing to the men. 'So these are Prefect Bassus's murderers?'

Neuto nodded grimly.

'Yes, Prefect. Centurion Tertius commands their century. Centurion?'

Tertius stepped forward and saluted briskly.

'Soldiers Secundus and Aulus, Prefect. They have admitted to killing the prefect.'

Furius walked up to the pair, looking both men in the eyes for several seconds before speaking again. 'You both admit to the crime of murdering your commanding officer?'

Aulus said nothing, simply turning his bruised face away. Secundus nodded, his face a mask of contempt. 'I done the most of it. Put my spear through his bronze and his spine in one go and dropped the bastard face down. All he did . . . ' jerking his head towards the man standing alongside him ' . . . was take his iron to him once he was down. You want to take your revenge, you take it from me.'

'Why?' The soldier spat on the ground in front of the prefect's feet, sneering into his face. 'He wasn't an officer, nor a gentleman, he was just a right bastard. Punishments for this and punishments for that. Never a nice word for a good job, never a day off for the lads when we made him look good. I did it, but there was plenty more that wished they had. I never had to buy a drink for weeks that followed, not until they all started to worry about how revenge might be taken.'

Furius looked to Tertius with a raised eyebrow. The officer shook his head, never taking his eyes off the man in front of them as he spoke. 'Soldier

Secundus is an inveterate waster, Prefect. He drinks, he idles whenever he can, he whores. He's a good fighter, but he lacks discipline.'

'I see. And this one?'

Aulus's face was turned away from his officers, and his eyes turned to the ground as if to deny the weight of events now pressing down hard on him. Furius pulled his sword from its scabbard, putting the blade's point under the silent soldier's chin and forcing it round until they were face to face. The blade's tip dug into the soft flesh, starting a trickle of blood down the terrified man's neck. 'Why? Why attack your prefect when he was already dying?'

There was silence for a long moment before the soldier found his voice, quavering with desperation. 'I hated him. He had me flogged . . . '

Furius looked to Tertius for confirmation.

'Twice, Prefect. Ten lashes the first time, and twenty-five the second. Soldier Aulus is good for nothing, slovenly, lazy, not even a decent fighter. Prefect Bassus had hoped to knock some sense into him.'

Furius nodded, scowling into the soldier's face.

'And then there he was, helpless on the ground and you with a sword in your hand and your blood up from chasing barbarians, eh? What did you do?'

Aulus's eyes closed with the memory. 'I stabbed him in the neck. Just once. He didn't move, so I didn't do it again.'

Tears ran down his cheeks, provoking a weary sigh and a sad shake of the head from his centurion. 'You see the problem with the man, Prefect, he can't even make his confession like a man.'

Furius nodded decisively, then lunged forward without warning, burying the sword's point deep into the weeping soldier's throat, angling the blade upwards under the man's jaw. The man crumpled nervelessly, his blood spraying across both the officers' polished armour. Furius stepped back from the falling corpse, swinging the bloody blade back to point at the other man. 'I made it easy for your comrade here, because he was misguided and ineffectual in his complicity with your crime. You are the real murderer here, and for that you will pay a little more dearly than this simpleton did. Tie his hands!' He stepped back, the blooded sword still clamped in one hand. 'Second Tungrians! Hear my words . . . ' The cohort stood in absolute silence, every man straining to hear whatever their new officer was about to proclaim, their former disdain suddenly fascinated attention. The prefect pointed to the horizon, where the sun was dipping to almost touch the hills to their south and west. 'You have given your comrades up to justice in time to save yourselves two months' pay. This man's crime . . . ' he pointed to the corpse huddled on the ground in front of him ' . . . was to be weak, and to be in the wrong place at the wrong time. This man, on the other hand . . . ' he pointed the bloodied blade at Secundus ' . . . deserves the heaviest penalty I can award against him. Tomorrow morning he will be scourged, fifty lashes to be administered by the cohort's centurions. And then . . . ' He paused, smiling slightly with a clear relish for the sentence he was about to pass. ' . . . once the scourging has been completed to my satisfaction he will be crucified, and the cohort will parade past him to receive an example of the punishment to be expected for a crime of this severity. His legs will not be broken, since he does not deserve anything other than a slow and painful death.'

At the mention of crucifixion the cohort started visibly, and even Neuto's eyes widened as he stood behind his new commanding officer.

'I know that you will be wondering how I can order such a punishment. I know that it is more usual for the crime of murder to meet with death by beating with staves, to be administered by the killer's tent party, but this man will meet his fate like the criminal scum that he is.' He paused for a moment, jaw jutting, and stared out across the cohort's ranks in challenge. 'He will be guarded tonight by his own century. If he dies before the time I have appointed for him, or escapes in some amazing and unexpected manner, I will have that century's officer, chosen man and watch officer crucified in his place, and the rest of his century decimated, not once but three times. Thirty men will die tomorrow if this man fails to make his appointment with the hammer and nails for any reason.'

He turned to First Spear Neuto, inclining his head to indicate that the senior centurion should carry on, and then turned and walked back to his tent, the bloody gladius still held in his right hand.

Centurion Tertius turned to the first spear in amazement once the prefect was safely out of earshot. 'Crucifixion? First Spear, in Maponus's name . . . '

Neuto snapped at him, his tired face contorted with anger. 'Don't you *dare* bring shame on this cohort by appealing to the gods for the life of a senior officer's murderer, you fool! You told me you had no idea who killed Bassus, and I'll continue to believe that since you swore an oath, but that man dies tomorrow and that's an end to it.' He rubbed a hand over his face. 'In the meanwhile you can work off that bitterness by getting your man nicely secured against any unforeseen accidents. I expect you'll find your chosen man and watch officer more than happy to make sure nothing remiss happens to him. Then you can build me a cross. You'll find plenty of wood and nails in the remains of the fort. More importantly, we'll need something to hold your man upright tomorrow while he's being flogged.'

Tertius frowned, puzzlement written across his face. 'Upright? All the scourgings I've seen have only needed one thick post. You bend the victim over it and tie his hands and feet to keep him there while he's having his back opened up.'

The first spear rolled his eyes upwards. 'Yes. I *know*. And this one's going to be different. I want that idiot to be held upright while we're flogging him to death, *if* you take my point. So I want two posts set in the ground, tall enough to hold him up and wide enough to stretch him out standing up with ropes tied around his wrists. You can angle them forward just a little too; make sure he'll stay up even if he loses it halfway through. Angle them away from the parade ground, mind you. Dismissed.'

* * *

It was close to midnight before Tertius was done with his preparations for the next day. Labouring by torchlight, his men had set up two stout posts to hold the prisoner up during his ordeal the following day. Alongside the whipping posts they had erected a simple rough cross formed from two scorched wooden beams, one nailed horizontally across the top of the other once it had been sunk deep into the soil that underlaid the parade ground's thick gravel. Dismissing his work party to wash and find their beds, he walked exhaustedly to the tent inside which the century's watch officer sat patiently, showing no sign of weariness. 'I'll watch him for an hour. Go and get a wash and a bite to eat, he's not going anywhere.'

The man nodded his respect, his backward glances at the prisoner expressing with perfect eloquence what military discipline forbade him to say out loud.

The prisoner smirked at Tertius across the tent. 'That'll be him shitting roof tiles for the next hour. I'd bet you every denarius I have he'll go no farther than behind the nearest tent, if I hadn't already spent the lot on the Noisy Valley whores. That and if I weren't going to be flogged to ribbons and then nailed to a plank for the entertainment of the cohort in the morning.'

Tertius shook his head sadly. 'I could find it in my head to feel sorrow for you, brother, if only you had any idea why you speared the prefect. You didn't really know at the time, I seem to recall, and you still haven't got a clue today, do you?'

The condemned man shrugged under the heavy ropes securing him to the tent post. 'Not really. He was there, shouting the fucking odds, I had the spear . . . you know how it is . . . '

Tertius shook his head again. 'No, I really don't. Mother always wondered how on earth she produced two boys so very different . . . '

'I know. Just look at the state of you.'

Tertius laughed quietly, despite himself. 'You're going to die in horrible pain tomorrow, Secundus. Doesn't that dent your humour just a little?'

The other man shook his head. 'It'll be over soon enough, and I'll be on the other side of the river. So fuck 'em all.' He sized his brother up with an appraising glance. 'You've come to say goodbye. Consider it said. You've come to ask me if I'll take our secret with me to the grave. I will. You've done well for yourself, young 'un, better than I ever reckoned you would, you little bastard. Make an offering for me whenever there's an altar to Bacchus handy, there's a good lad.'

The centurion looked up, his eyes wet with tears. 'I didn't come to ask you to protect me. I came to tell you that I'll have revenge for you. You've earned a death sentence right enough, but not this way, not like a bloody barbarian slave. That bastard's got it coming, and I'll take his blood for doing this.'

His brother laughed without mirth, nodding approval. 'I expect you will, you've done everything else you ever set your mind to. Just don't end up tied to a tent post and waiting to be nailed up after you've done it. Now dry your eyes and share one last smile with me. You don't want to be caught crying over vermin like me.' He waited while the centurion wiped his eyes and face with the hem of his tunic. 'Now, before anyone else turns up, let's get one more thing agreed, eh?'

Tertius tilted his head in question. 'What?'

'Tomorrow. When the prefect hands the scourge round to the officers and invites you all to do your bit for military justice . . . ?'

The centurion took a long breath, composing himself. 'What?'

'Lay it on me like you've got a pair of swingers the size of apples, eh? No good my taking our little secret with me to the grave if you can't do your bit.'

* * *

Furius was relaxing in his tent with a beaker of wine when the tent flap opened and a centurion stepped through the gap, coming smartly to attention in front of the astonished Furius.

'What the bloody . . . '

'Centurion Appius reporting, Prefect.'

The prefect stared at the centurion, recognising him as one of the two officers sent to escort him from Arab Town to join the cohort.

'So it is. Is it usual in this cohort, Centurion, for individual officers to make their entrance to the prefect's tent late in the evening, and without any formal request relayed via their first spear?'

Appius shook his head, still staring straight ahead at the tent's far wall but without any of the nervousness that the prefect would have expected his admonishment to provoke in the man.

'No, sir. I am, however, responding to your request of a few days ago.'

'My request . . . ?'

'Yes, sir. Back in the guest house in Arab Town, you told us that any man that could point you at the fugitive that's reputed to be in hiding with one of the wall cohorts would be well rewarded.'

Furius smiled slowly.

'Indeed I did, Centurion . . . '

'Appius, sir.'

'Indeed I did, Appius. So what do you have for me?'

'There's a young lad serving as an officer with our sister cohort. Myself and Centurion Tertius met him in the Arab Town mess, before we came to meet you. He looks very . . . '

'Roman?'

'Yes sir, dark hair, brown eyes, and darker skin than we usually get round here unless the men have been shipped in from a lot farther south.

On top of which he wears a sword with an eagle's head as pretty as anything I've ever seen, beautifully engraved.'

He had meant to mention the cloak pin whose inscription he'd read at Arab Town, but the sceptical look on the prefect's face changed his mind.

'And you think he's the missing man, eh? Just because his eyes are brown and he has a nice sword?'

Again Appius didn't flinch from the harsh words.

'I didn't say I was sure he's the one, Prefect, but I do wonder what a young Roman would be doing in such a position. I believe it's more usually the case that young lads from the right background go to serve with the legions, prove themselves fit to command and end up as legion commanders . . . '

He stopped talking as he realised that an evil look had crept across the prefect's face. After a moment Furius realised that he was no longer speaking, and wrenched himself from his bitter reverie.

'What? Oh . . . yes. You're right, that is more usually the case. So why not bring this to me through the first spear? I shouldn't imagine he'd be very happy to discover you were here without his permission.'

Appius nodded, still apparently untroubled by the prefect's comments.

'Happy, sir? He'd have my balls off with a rusty dagger. I just thought, given that he's a good friend of the First Cohort's first spear . . . '

'That we ought to keep this discussion between us?' For the first time in the conversation the prefect smiled. 'Absolutely right, Centurion. In which case you'd best be on your way and come back when you've got some slightly better evidence to offer me, eh? And don't worry, man, I won't be letting on to dear old Neuto that we had this conversation. I don't intend to give either the fugitive, if that's what he is, or the men hiding him from justice, any warning that he's been uncovered. You find me the evidence and I'll do the rest. And I'll make sure you're well rewarded for your loyalty to the throne.'

* * *

The Tungrian officers gathered in The Hill's gloomy headquarters building for morning reports as usual just before dawn, the main hall's only illumination the torches burning along its cold stone walls. A hulking brown bearded centurion crossed the floor and clasped hands with Julius and Rufius before turning to Marcus, accentuating his welcome with a hearty slap of the young man's shoulder. 'Well, young Two Knives, I hear you've taken pity on us lonely men and recruited in a double century of Syrian girlie boys.'

Marcus nodded in mock resignation. 'It's true. I knew that if I returned with a century of infantrymen you'd be after me for your cut, so I settled for Hamian bow twangers instead. There are no axemen for you to be lusting after in the

Eighth Century, brother, you'll just have to pester Tiberius Rufius for your replacements.'

The 10th Century's centurion slapped his shoulder again, laughing easily in the quiet gloom. 'You cunning dog, you always were the smart one . . . ' He turned to Rufius, his hands spread in supplication. ' . . . and as he says, Grandfather, you do have a full-strength century of big strong lads. Surely you can spare me a few? Half a dozen would be a start, ten would be perfect. Will you help your brother?'

Rufius raised his hands defensively, backing off from the big man in apparent dismay. 'Oh no, it just isn't possible, Titus. You know I'd like to help you, but these new boys of mine are all well-educated and house-trained young men, drilled in the fine arts of infantry combat and military etiquette. I couldn't in good faith condemn any of them to descend to the degraded standards of behaviour your men have sunk to. I . . . '

'Attention!'

The gathered officers turned to face the door and snapped to attention. First Spear Frontinius had entered the room with the prefect following him.

'Brother officers, stand at ease. Make yourselves comfortable. I know that you're not used to seeing the prefect at morning reports, but we received a courier just before nightfall yesterday with the message we've all been waiting for. The new governor has taken command at Noisy Valley and his first order is for several cohorts, including ourselves, to march in and join up with the legions. As of now the war with the northern tribes is back on again, and there's still enough campaigning time left in the year for us to finish Calgus and his rabble off if they're unwise enough to offer us a straight fight.'

He paused for a moment, looking around his brother officers.

'We're ordered to report for attached duty with Sixth *Victorious* by dusk tomorrow night, which gives us one day for preparation and then a day's march to join the legion. You've got today to get your men and their gear ready for a good long stint in the field, so I suggest you make the most of that time and make sure we won't have anyone's boots falling to pieces or spearheads coming loose at the wrong moment. You, Centurion Corvus, had better start educating your Hamians as to just what it feels like when the blue-noses come knocking, and I think you'd better have some help with that, given the amount of time we've got. Prefect?'

The man waiting patiently behind him stepped out of the shadows.

'Gentlemen, for those of you that have been away putting down the Carvetii, my name is Gaius Rutilius Scaurus. My orders from the governor were quite straightforward, to get ready for a month's campaigning and bring my cohort across to join with the Sixth Legion by the end of tomorrow. Given the sparse nature of those orders there isn't all that much to be said on that particular subject, but I can give you an insight into this new governor. I believe that the last man to hold the post tended to take a back seat to the legion commanders when it came to setting the pace of operations. That will not be the case under Ulpius Marcellus, I can assure you. We'll soon be up in Calgus's face and looking to provoke him to come out of whatever hidey-hole he's hidden himself in and fight. I know this cohort has a proud reputation, and I know that reputation only got stronger given the fight you won against the odds earlier this summer. I think you can confidently expect the governor to be keen to make full use of your abilities, so make sure your men are ready for action, because make no mistake, gentlemen, it's coming your way. First Spear . . . ?'

Frontinius stepped forward.

'Thank you, Prefect. We parade at dawn as usual, full kit and marching order, please, both practice swords and iron to be worn. Today, my brothers, is going to be a long day for us all. Dismissed, gentlemen, with the exception of the following officers: Corvus, Julius, Rufius and Dubnus. I need a discussion with the four of you on the subject of getting our newest recruits ready to fight before this new governor puts us back into the war.'

* * *

The 2nd Tungrian cohort paraded soon after first light. Once the cohort had marched on to The Rock's parade ground, found their places under the grey sky and settled down, Prefect Furius walked out in front of them with a grim face. He nodded to Neuto, and the First Spear rapped out a crisp order.

'Bring out the prisoner!'

Soldier Secundus was marched on to the parade ground and tied to the whipping posts, his arms stretched tightly out to either side to keep him upright. Ropes strung between the posts at chest and groin level waited to catch his body when, as was usual with heavy floggings, he passed out with the pain and loss of blood. The men guarding him stripped away the loincloth that had been his only garment and stepped away from the whipping posts. Prefect Furius squinted across the parade ground at the posts, a note of uncertainty in his voice.

'An interesting arrangement, First Spear. Not exactly standard.'

Neuto nodded, shrugging.

'It's my usual method in these circumstances, Prefect. Once the scourging's well under way he'll faint away from loss of blood and pain, and I like to keep them on their feet. Keeps the blood in the body longer, and lets the troops see the mess we're making of the man. Sets an example, if you like.'

He watched the prefect carefully as the man raised an appreciative eyebrow.

'Good thinking, First Spear Neuto. Sets an example indeed.'

Neuto muttered a silent prayer of thanks to his gods, nodding his respect to the prefect with his face an inscrutable mask.

'Thank you, Prefect. Now, if you'll permit me . . . ?'

He walked out in front of the cohort, shouting

for the waiting men to come to attention.

'Second Cohort!' The silence while the soldiers waited for him to speak again was almost tangible. 'Second Cohort, you will this morning witness the execution of the man that murdered Prefect Bassus. Let this be an example to you of how we deal with criminals within our ranks.'

He walked grimly across to the helpless prisoner, readying himself to play his part as the first officer to wield the scourge, shaking its leather ropes loose with an impatient gesture before pulling his arm back in readiness for the first blow.

'*Hold!*'

Furius stepped forward, his hand outstretched.

'I think I'll take the first five, First Spear. You did the hard work yesterday in getting the fool to confess . . . '

He hefted the scourge for a moment, letting all gathered see him examine the braided ropes, jagged pieces of bone knotted into the leather at each finger-length from the handle, then flicked the whip high over his shoulder before delivering a fearsome blow across Secundus's back from right shoulder to left kidney. He struck again, aiming at the left shoulder to paint a rough cross of deeply scored wounds on the condemned soldier's back. Blood began to seep slowly down the valley of the man's spine. The third blow was delivered horizontally across the small of the prisoner's back, the prefect swinging his whole body into the whip's vicious strike. The fourth blow scourged his backside, clawing deep into the soft flesh of his buttocks, while the fifth was delivered with shocking power straight down the back of his head, ripping away lumps of hair and scalp. The last blow tore a moan of pain from the previously silent soldier.

Furius turned back to his suddenly wide-eyed troops, walking the few paces to the third century and handing the whip to Tertius. A soldier from a century to his left suddenly bent double and noisily puked his breakfast up on to the parade ground, momentarily unable to comply with his centurion's barked command to get back in the ranks.

'Five lashes per centurion, starting with the prisoner's own officer, and all to be delivered with the same force I've just demonstrated. Two to the back, one to the kidneys, one to the arse and one to the head. Any man going easy on this piece of shit at any time will be ordered to repeat the blow and be subjected to administrative punishment and loss of pay. I know that's five more than I ordered, but let's call it five more for luck, eh? Begin!'

Tertius stepped forward, the tremor in his right eye hidden from the watching soldiers by his helmet's brim, hesitating for a second that seemed to last a lifetime as he looked down at the scourge's bloody leather ropes. A piece of skin was caught on one of the whip's bone teeth, almost translucent in the early morning sun, and he bent to flick it away into the parade ground's dust.

'Go on, lad.'

The words, snarled through his brother's gritted teeth, snapped him back to the moment. He bent over the whip, readying himself to swing it back over his head for the first stroke, and muttered a reply that only his brother would hear.

'I'll be making a sacrifice in your memory, brother, but not to Bacchus. My offering will be to Nemesis.'

He arched his back to put the maximum possible power into the first stroke before swinging the bloody leather ropes across his brother's back, that part of him which quailed at the horrible damage wrought by the scourge's bone teeth buried deep beneath both the need for survival and the possibility of sparing his brother the cross's final indignity. Wielding the scourge with such power that his feet left the ground momentarily during each stroke, he hammered the whip's flailing tails into Secundus's body with all his strength. With the fifth blow delivered, raking as powerfully into the helpless body suspended in front of him as the first, Tertius turned back to the cohort with a stone face, seeing Neuto's nod of approval out of the corner of his eye as the first spear took the scourge from him.

As Tertius settled into the parade rest at the head of his century he saw the senior centurion deliver his first blow, grunting explosively with the force he put into the scourge's application. More than one of the whip's tails flew astray, their bone teeth flicking across the prisoner's throat unseen by most of the men on parade. As he watched his eyes narrowed with the realisation as to just why Neuto had bid him set up the unusual whipping posts. The first spear delivered the same blow to the other shoulder, and again the whip strayed fractionally in its path to rake across the helpless soldier's neck. The prefect stood contentedly to one side as the whip was passed to the next centurion with a few quiet words of encouragement from Neuto, his satisfaction evident as this officer also laid into the prisoner with all his strength. Again the first two strokes flicked around his brother's throat, and, watching the man's legs carefully, he saw a thin rivulet of blood twisting round the bared thigh. A sharp-eyed soldier to Tertius's right muttered a comment to his mate and he whirled round, rapping his vine stick across the man's arm with a meaningful stare.

'Silence in the ranks!'

After thirty or so lashes Secundus sank against the ropes stretched across his body, the agonising pain and blood loss robbing him of his ability to stay upright. The blood running down his neck no longer sheeted down his chest and legs to merge with that flowing from his ruined back, but now fell in a shower of heavy drops into the gravel a foot in front of his feet. Still the prefect did not seem to realise that the prisoner was now fighting for his very life, and the officers continued to take their turn with the scourge, now heavy with torn flesh and an accumulation of drying blood. The cohort's mood had subtly changed as the scene had played out in front of them, and as more of the soldiers had realised that their prefect was being robbed of his crucifixion with every heavy drop of blood that fell from their comrade's neck. Previously standing in sullen resignation, they now watched with hawk-eyed attention the vigour with which each centurion prosecuted his share of the flogging, realising with something approaching gratitude their officers' determination to kill the man with the whip, and spare him the cross's agonising asphyxiation. With the punishment's completion, the first spear stepped forward and put an expert finger to the motionless prisoner's bloody windpipe, pulling a face and turning back to the cohort with a shout for assistance.

'Bandage carrier!'

While the field medic fussed around the prisoner, seeking a pulse, the senior centurion grimaced to Furius.

'It happens sometimes. The Jews, I believe, limit the practice to forty lashes for fear of killing the offender . . . ' He paused as the bandage carrier turned and shook his head. ' . . . as seems to have been the case here. No matter, Prefect, justice has been done, and been seen to be done. We have a cross ready. Shall we nail him up and parade the men past his corpse?'

The prefect stared closely at his deputy for a moment, his eyes narrowed slightly in suspicion, but the first spear's return gaze was blameless. Furius nodded, his face sour.

'Indeed, First Spear. A shame to be robbed of the man's last agonised breaths, though . . . '

The wistful look on his face told Neuto everything he needed to know about his new commander.

4

The Tungrian cohort marched down the hill to the parade ground an hour after dawn with both purpose and trepidation. The troops were unusually quiet and orderly in the cold early light, reflecting soberly on orders that could see any or all of them dead inside the month. The prefect stood alongside First Spear Frontinius, watching the centuries march past, his German bodyguard close behind him. The red-haired giant, a full head taller than his master, had excited much comment in the cohort, both for the obvious strength in his heavily muscled and scarred body and as a result of his apparent unwillingness to speak to anyone save the prefect himself. More than one of the officers had greeted the man, to be met with no more than a respectful nod of his massive head. While there was nothing at which anyone could take offence, neither was there any hint that the man would be a source of either conversation or, more importantly to the cohort's soldiers, information.

'Your men look purposeful enough, First Spear, although I'd expected a little more . . . '

Prefect Scaurus paused for a moment, searching for the right word.

'Banter? Horseplay? Usually you'd have got it, they express themselves just like any other cohort on the frontier, but they know what's coming. We lost the best part of two centuries at

Lost Eagle, and they were probably assuming that it was too late in the year for any more serious campaigning.'

The prefect nodded his understanding.

'Nobody can say they haven't demonstrated their loyalty to the emperor this year. That's the problem with reputations, there's always someone that wants to see them demonstrated . . . '

Frontinius studied the younger man with a sideways glance as his new commander watched the centuries flowing out of the fort and down its paved road on to the wide parade ground. A head taller than the first spear, the prefect had a spare frame more suited to distance running than infantry combat, yet seemed to carry the weight of his armour and helmet easily enough.

'And speaking of reputations, you're still not sure what to make of what you see, eh, First Spear?'

Frontinius started at his prefect's comment, delivered in a level, almost bored tone without the younger man ever taking his eyes off the marching troops.

'I'm sorry, Prefect, I was just . . . '

'Relax. It would be a strange thing if you weren't still wondering what to expect from your new commander. Right about now I should probably be telling you what an experienced soldier I am, putting your mind at ease on the subject of whether I'm fit for command of your men. Am I right? After all, I've been here for a fortnight and never once even hinted at my experience beyond telling you what positions I've served in previously.'

Frontinius nodded grudgingly.

'It's often the case that a new commander will make a point of telling his officers about any fighting he's taken part in, although I don't really . . .'

He stopped talking as Scaurus turned to look at him with a half-smile playing on his lips.

'I know. You want to know my capabilities, but you don't want to overstep the mark in asking me to tell you where I've been and what I've done. Well, First Spear, let's have an agreement, shall we? I won't question you on the subject of your competence, other than wanting every last tiny detail about this cohort and this war from you, and in return you'll let me demonstrate the way I work by just watching me work. Whether you take that as a sign of strength or weakness doesn't really concern me very much, and we'll learn a good deal more about each other than we might by trotting out lists of achievements that either of us could have gilded or even plain fabricated for all the other man knows. Agreed?'

Frontinius held his return stare for a moment before nodding slowly.

'As you wish, Prefect.'

The cohort paraded, the ground's sandy surface grey in the dawn's weak light. Frontinius strode out in front of his eight hundred men, addressing them at a volume that made his words audible from one end of the parade to the other.

'Good morning, First Cohort. This is an important day. This day will live as long in your memories as that little skirmish with the blue-noses a few weeks ago.' He paused for a moment, watching the faces of those men in the ranks closest to him, their expressions betraying a mixture of faint amusement and sick apprehension. 'This is the day we go back to war. Now that we've got a new prefect and two centuries of replacements, we are considered ready to fight. Our orders are to march east and join up with the Sixth Legion for one last effort before the weather gets too cold for us to stay in the field. Soldiers, this cohort was the first one on the list when the governor was deciding which units to put alongside his legions in the line of battle. You are proven battle winners, and your reputation goes before you.'

He paused, searching the same faces and finding them mostly set with determination. Good enough. 'I know that you were hoping not to be called back into the war this year, but I also know that you are strong enough to give the emperor your best efforts for as long as it takes to finish this war, and put Calgus in chains and on his way to Rome. And now, before we start, let me introduce you to your new comrades. The Sixth Century, eighty home-grown Tungrian recruits to bolster our fighting strength, and the Eighth Century, a double-strength century of archers from Hamath in the province of Syria, far to the east of Rome. As of this moment they are fully fledged members of this cohort, and I expect them to be treated with the appropriate respect. It's obvious to all of you that the men of the Eighth Century are different to the troops that we usually encounter, but I don't expect that to make any difference to any soldier here. The first man in front of me at the punishment table for raising a hand to any of these men without very good reason will feel like he's been hit by a falling tree by the time I've finished with him.'

He paused for breath, raking the impassive troops with a hard stare.

'Nevertheless, our new Hamian comrades do present us with something of a problem in that they are unused to bearing the kind of weight that we routinely carry around on campaign. And so . . . ' He gestured to his officers, and then waited while Marcus, Dubnus, Rufius and Julius walked out in front of the cohort to join him. 'The Eighth Century will need help to achieve the same performance as the rest of you, and so I am therefore temporarily detaching these three centurions from their centuries, and giving them and Centurion Corvus forty men from the Eighth apiece to work with. With a little luck we'll have our new centuries ready for anything the blue-noses can throw at them by the time that we see action. Centurions, carry on with morning exercises.'

The four centurions quickly divided the 8th into four equal-sized groups, each of them pulling their temporary command into a tight huddle around them. Marcus, having retained Qadir in his party, spoke slowly, giving his chosen man time to translate his words for those men whose grasp of Latin was imperfect.

'You may be archers, but you're going to learn to fight as infantrymen and you're going to do it quickly. Whenever we have the opportunity, you will train as one century, but with frequent and close attention to your sword and shield drill. My brother officers and I will help you learn how to fight in practice combat with their centuries, but first we need you to grasp the basics. And the first basic is shield handling. You, come out in front with me.'

The wide-eyed Hamian stepped away from the comfortable anonymity of his place in the front rank, eyeing his new officer uncertainly and casting the occasional nervous glance at Qadir.

'Raise your shield until you can just see over the top. No, higher . . . that's right. Now, brace yourself, and remember that your shield is your only defence against the enemy's swords and spears. We'll worry about spears later, so let's see how you do against a trained swordsman. Antenoch?'

His clerk stepped forward, swinging a heavy wooden practice sword and smiling at the nervous archer in anticipation as he limbered up to fight. He held up the sword, making sure the Hamian got a good look at its scarred wooden blade.

'This is a practice sword. It's heavier than the real thing to help build strength in the sword arm, and that means it will make an almighty bang when it hits your shield. It will jar your shield arm, but if you drop the shield then the next thing you know you'll be face down with your guts hanging out. Ready?'

The Hamian managed a hesitant nod, triggering Antenoch's attack. Hammering at the man's shield with the heavy wooden sword, he beat back the panicking archer until the Hamian was almost on his knees, then thrust the blade over the top of his sinking shield to inflict a painful jab into the gap between his mail coat's neck and the rim of his helmet. He stepped back from his grimacing victim, watching the man rub the sore spot.

'You let the shield fall and opened yourself up for the kill. You're dead. Get back in ranks. You, come out here.'

Another man stepped out to face him, his face set in determination.

'Good, you look keen; let's see what you can do. Remember, keep that shield up.'

Ten seconds later the Hamian was on his back, cursing at the pain in his right ankle while Antenoch reached down to pull him back to his feet.

'That was better, but if an enemy sees that your shield is held too high he's likely to try to go under it and cut your feet off. You need to keep your eyes open, and drop your shield to stop his attack if necessary. Let's try that again.'

Qadir leaned across to Marcus.

'And if two men attack at the same time, one high and one low? Surely then the man is doomed?'

Marcus smiled without taking his eyes off Antenoch's demonstration.

'Not if he's in possession of the infantryman's two most important assets.'

The chosen man raised an eyebrow.

'And those are . . . ?'

Marcus lifted the ornately decorated gladius bequeathed to him by Legatus Sollemnis halfway out of its scabbard, the razor-edged blade gleaming in the weak morning sun.

'One of these, and those.'

He pointed at the gathered Hamians as they watched Antenoch's demonstration with wide eyes.

'Soldiers?'

Marcus shook his head.

'Not soldiers, Qadir, brothers. And all in good time.'

* * *

Calgus strolled out of his tent later that morning, having apparently spent the night there. In reality he had entered it less then five minutes before through an opening cut in the side facing the forest, having made the return journey through the forest by the light of torches carried by his bodyguard. His adviser Aed was waiting for him as summoned, and the old man looked up at his king with a calculating gaze, the slight wind ruffling his thin hair.

'My lord. I trust your venture into the forest met with acceptable results?'

Calgus nodded, looking out over the camp from their vantage point, the highest ground within the palisade wall.

'Oh yes, very acceptable once their initial caution was out of the way. When the time is right, our trap will spring shut on the legions with a finality that will remove the print of their boots from our soil for good. We will slaughter Romans in numbers not seen since their great German massacre, and after that disaster they've never attempted to colonise the lands beyond the Rhenus in all the one hundred and fifty years that have followed. I will make these lands as great a source of terror to the Romans as ever the forests of Germania were, and drive them back into their fortresses far to the south of their wall, never to return.'

The old man nodded, his soft voice expressing views intended for his king's ears alone.

'A glorious aim, my lord. Before that, however, you may have to consider dealing with King Brennus at some point in the near future. In your absence he has continued to spread discontent, and his defiance will inevitably encourage others to consider their obedience to you. Do we still need his people's spears in our strength, given your apparent success in bringing fresh support to our cause?'

Calgus nodded, looking down the slope to the Votadini section of the camp.

'I suppose not, given their continual agitation against me. But I cannot send them back to their land, my own warriors would start to question the need for them to remain were that many spears to walk away, and as for the other kings . . . '

Aed smiled thinly, his eyes bright with purpose.

'Perhaps there is an opportunity here? Were the Votadini to be caught in the open by our enemies they would undoubtedly be massacred to the last man. That would leave their king alone and isolated here, and his kingdom open for . . . *annexation*. If only we could find someone within their number with sufficient ambition to allow himself to be lured into such a mistake, it is quite possible that our enemy would remove the problem without ever dreaming of the service they would be performing for you.' He paused for a moment, his sly glance flicking to meet his king's amused stare. 'Perhaps you might cultivate King Brennus's nephew, Martos? My friends in their camp tell me that he longs to lead the tribe into battle at their head, and cover his roof beams with Roman heads.'

Calgus shook his head slowly, a smile spreading across his face as the audacity of the idea gripped his imagination.

'Gods, Aed, but you'll outdo me for ruthlessness any time you like. You advise me to send the Votadini to their deaths, murder their king and take his lands?'

Aed shrugged, his expression neutral.

'Sometimes large problems demand harsh solutions, my lord. The Votadini will be no worse off under your control than under Brennus, and there is no way you can trust the man. His behaviour shouts his defiance of your reign, and he has more men available than are camped here. If the warriors he has held back succeed in their search for the hostages, he will have us both at spear point five minutes after the news of their release reaches him. A change of leadership might bring some relief from his incessant complaining and scheming. I suspect that he is in contact with the Romans . . . '

Calgus laughed.

'I don't doubt he's in contact with them, or how could he have been so confident that my head would buy him peace with them? I don't think his men will find their kinfolk in a year of searching, and I don't believe that we can kill him and be sure that the act won't have repercussions beyond our control . . . but I take your point. He's a focus for discontent, and that can only get stronger once we join battle with the Romans and their lackeys. There is an idea I've been musing on these last few days, a way to bring the remaining legions north with a fury on them that will have their heads in our trap before they have the time to see it. Perhaps I might invite Brennus's nephew along to share the spoils?

* * *

The morning stayed dry, despite the gathering clouds threatening rain, and by the break for the midday ration Marcus reckoned that the Hamians had absorbed as much shield drill as they were going to for one day. Dubnus confirmed his view with a weary shake of his head.

'Their heads have gone to cabbage, it's all too much for them. I vote we get them out in the hills and get some air into their lungs.'

The other officers agreed, and once the midday ration was consumed the 8th was formed into column of march and headed off into the land to the wall's south. Initially setting a gentle pace, Marcus gradually increased his speed at the column's head until the Hamians were covering ground at something like the rate required to keep up with the rest of the cohort on the march. He turned and walked backwards for a moment, assessing their sweating, strained faces and painful gaits before calling across to Morban.

'Keep them moving, I'm going for a chat with Qadir.'

The chosen man was halfway down the column, encouraging a flagging man to keep up his pace. Marcus waved to Dubnus, pointing at the struggling archer, and his friend ran up the column with a barked command to keep moving.

'This man's finding it hard, and I need to talk with the chosen man. Can you help him along for a few minutes?'

Dubnus nodded, gesturing Qadir to surrender his place alongside the flagging archer, the man's eyes now rolling with desperation. The chosen man moved aside and in a second the massively built centurion was in his place, his mouth close to the struggler's ear.

'Are you finding this difficult?'

The man nodded.

'Would you like to stop?'

The Hamian nodded eagerly, his face lightening with the promise of relief. Marcus winced, knowing what was coming next as Dubnus sucked in a lungful of air and bellowed his response into the flagging soldier's ear.

'*Well, you fucking well can't stop, because if you do I'll put my boot up your arse to the third lace hole! You're in the field, your century's on the march, and you'll stop for nothing and nobody unless your officer says so! It's march or fucking die for you, sonny, and the rest of you, so forget that it hurts and focus on the man in front of you! If he can do it, so can you! You in the next rank, stop your fucking smirking unless you want to come for a private run with me and see how long you last, you bow-twanging ration thief!*'

Marcus shrugged at Qadir's raised eyebrows as they moved a few paces away from the marching column's path.

'He was my chosen man until recently, and he seems to have retained the non-commissioned officer's approach to motivation.'

Farther down the line Julius was giving another man the same treatment, his face contorted with apparent rage.

'*That pain you're feeling is weakness leaving your body, so stop your snivelling and march, you maggot! If you fall out of the line of march I will beat you back into it with my vine stick, and if that breaks I'll use the flat of my fucking sword! You can either march or choke, but whichever one it's going to be, fucking get on with it!*'

Qadir looked back for a long moment, and then turned back to his centurion with evident distaste.

'It is not my approach.'

Marcus shrugged, more than a little embarrassed at his chosen man's air of disappointment.

'I know, but given the time we have to make these men battle ready we're left with little alternative. You're going to have to harden your heart a little, Chosen, or your men aren't going to be ready when the time comes for them to march and fight with the rest of the cohort.'

The other man nodded unhappily as Marcus continued.

'Yesterday they finished a march that should have taken four hours in twice that time, and their feet were raw meat before they even started. If we take them into the field in this state they'll be a liability to the cohort, incapable of either marching or fighting. So I've got two choices, I either get them fit at a reasonable pace and give them time for their feet to recover, or I push them through their pain and get quicker results. And you and I *need* quicker results. Their feet will turn to leather quickly enough. But I need your help, I need you alongside me while I'm pushing them, so that they can see there's no way out of this nightmare except to give more of themselves than they knew they had in them.'

Qadir looked at him, a hint of disbelief in his face.

'And if they do not have any more of themselves to give?'

Marcus's smile was grim.

'Oh, they've got it, we all do. It just has to be pulled out of them. My friend Dubnus has one method, Rufius, Julius and I are all a little different in style, but we're all looking to get the same results. By the time we've finished with your men they'll march thirty miles in a day and still be singing their hearts out for the last mile. They'll stand in line and stop a barbarian charge with the rest of the cohort. I hope they'll still be archers, but they will be infantrymen, I promise you that.'

The century marched on for another twenty minutes until Marcus judged that they had reached the point he had agreed earlier with Julius. Morban gave the signal for the halt, reinforced by the century's trumpeter blasting out a single note.

'Rest break! Water only and leave your field rations alone!'

The Hamians sagged exhausted to the ground for the most part, and Marcus allowed them a few minutes of rest before gaining their attention with three raps of his practice sword on a soldier's shield.

'Eighth Century, there is something wrong here. Can anyone tell me what it is? No? A silver sestertius to the man that can tell me. Not you, Morban, you already know the answer.'

The Hamians stared at him and about them, searching with renewed interest.

'Anyone? No? The answer isn't out there, it's right in front of me.'

The Hamians stared at Marcus uncomprehendingly, as he hardened his voice with scorn.

'The second I called the rest halt you *soldiers* were on your backs without a care in the world. No guards posted, no one worried about anything beyond getting a gutful of water, and no concern for what might be over the next hill. Or waiting for you in that wood.'

He pointed at the treeline two hundred paces distant and blew his whistle in a shrill blast. Armed and armoured men emerged from the trees, forming into a battle line.

'Lucky for you that's only the Fifth Century, and not a blue-nose warband screaming for your blood. There are two lessons to be taken from this. One: you take your rest stops standing up from now on, and each tent party chooses a man to stand guard, with the specific duty of watching the ground around them for danger. Now, would anyone care to guess the second lesson?' The Hamians stared at him blankly, and a feeling of near-despair made the young centurion shake his head. 'The next lesson, gentlemen, is basic infantry fighting. In two minutes those soldiers are going to charge into our line in exactly the same way the blue-noses will once they get the chance. This is your chance to practice your shield drills from this morning. Form a line! *Move!*'

* * *

Later that evening, with the sun well beneath the horizon and the 8th Century nursing blisters and aches in their barrack, too tired on their return to the fort for there to be any point in archery practice, the centurions gathered for a cup of wine in The Hill's officers' mess. Marcus tipped his cup back and called for another with a speed that raised Rufius's eyebrows. Julius and Dubnus exchanged knowing glances, and Rufius tipped the cup towards him, ostentatiously staring into its emptiness.

'Anyone would think you'd had a hard day lad, rather than the gentle stroll round the hills that we enjoyed today. Or is there something on your mind, perhaps?'

Marcus blew a long breath out through his lips.

'What do you think? We march for Noisy Valley tomorrow, and we could be in action against the tribes a few days after that. How in Cocidius's name are we going to turn them into soldiers before they have to fight for their lives against men that have spent most of their lives getting ready to kill them?'

Julius shook his head, his scorn evident even through a mouthful of dried meat.

'One day and you're giving up? Just because my lads gave your boys a gentle spanking?'

Marcus closed his eyes at the memory. Julius's 5th Century had battered the 8th into submission in less than a minute despite being half their strength. The brutal simplicity of their assault had scattered the hapless Hamians like chaff, and their march back to The Hill had been a sombre plod conducted in resentful silence.

Rufius shook his head on the other side of the table.

'Our young friend's dismay is simply the result of inexperience.'

He put his cup down, placing both hands on the table's scarred surface.

'Marcus, have you ever taken a century of

recruits from raw to trained? Your exploits with the Ninth don't count. Your lads were already infantry trained, they just lacked the right leadership until you turned up. I don't doubt your ability to lead experienced soldiers, I'm just asking if you've ever been part of turning a collection of farm boys into infantrymen?'

Marcus shook his head slowly.

'I wasn't a guard officer for long enough . . . '

' . . . and the praetorians tend to take in men who've already had the rough edges hammered off them. You see, taking stupid lazy kids and turning them into fighting men is a bit of an art.'

Julius nodded sagely, and even Dubnus was giving the veteran centurion an approving look.

'You get them on the parade ground on their first day and you'd swear they didn't know left from right, much less which end of their new spear has the pointy iron thing attached. All you've got is eighty or so individuals, some stupid, some lazy, and all of them utterly clueless. As a legion centurion faced with that, all you've got to help you is a chosen man to push them around from behind and a watch officer who, if you're lucky, has trained recruits before. That and a few simple rules learned from older and possibly wiser men down the years of your service.'

Rufius raised an eyebrow to the other two, both of whom nodded sagely as he continued his lecture.

'There are only three tricks that a centurion has to perform to turn the average bunch of teenage idiots into trained troops, ready to try their hand against the barbarians. Number one is obvious — he has to drill them in the use of shield, sword and spear in every spare moment, until every possible move, attack or defend, is as natural to them as breathing. That way they'll do whatever he orders without even having to think about it. Number two, he has to get them fit, ready to run all day if that's what's needed, and he has to run alongside them every step of the way or lose their respect. But those are the easy bits, and without trick number three all you end up with is a bunch of fit idiots who know how to sling a spear but can't see any reason why they should.'

He paused for a drink, aware that every officer in the room was listening now, most of them with faint smiles. He gestured around the mess with his free hand.

'See, both young Caelius and that battered old bastard Otho both know what I mean. Trick number three is the most delicate and difficult trick a centurion ever gets to try. It isn't written down anywhere, because every one of us does it a different way, depending on our personal style and who we learned it from. For some officers it's the most natural thing in the world, others find it so difficult that they can never really get their recruits to swallow it. I know that I can do it, and every other man in this room knows the same or he wouldn't be here. I also know that your bow benders won't learn even the most basic moves properly unless we apply it to them good and hard. I can teach you how to do it if you'll let me . . . '

He paused, giving his friend a long stare.

'But?'

'You're a good man. Educated. Cultured. Yes, you're a trained gladiator and you've killed on the battlefield enough times to show you're a warrior. We all respect that, but . . . '

Marcus put his cup down, a note of irritation creeping into his voice.

'Go on.'

'It's simple enough. Trick number three is about being a bastard, that's the top and bottom of it. Your recruits have to know that given the slightest excuse you'll come down on them so hard they'll be reaching up to wipe their arses. And Marcus, I'm just not sure you've got enough bastard in you to turn these boys around, given the amount of time we've got.'

He glanced up as the mess door opened and a bulky figure ducked through it into the room.

'Oh, Cocidius help me, here comes the Bear for another try at lifting a tent party out of my century.'

* * *

The next morning dawned grey and damp, with an insidious drizzle that swirled in the fitful wind and found its way beneath the 8th's cloaks and into their armour even before the Bear's 10th Century had stamped down the line to their place at the far end of the cohort. Frontinius, who made a point of keeping his most likely replacement as first spear fully briefed at all times, walked alongside Julius's 5th Century as they marched down the fort's steep road to the parade ground, his conversation with his brother officer conducted in tones too quiet for the soldiers marching alongside them to overhear.

'So all in all you really don't know what to make of our new commander?'

The first spear nodded wryly.

'That's about the size of it. He hasn't given me any hint as to his previous experience beyond the positions he's held previously, which wouldn't worry me too much if his career wasn't quite so unusual.'

Julius glanced across at him.

'Unusual?'

'It didn't occur to me at first, but people like him, members of the equestrian class, they follow set paths through their lives. He was prefect of an auxiliary cohort over ten years ago by my reckoning, which would have made him about twenty-five, and that's younger than is usual for a first command. They're supposed to do a few years of public service to knock the rougher edges off them before they're let loose on the army. After that he was a tribune with Twelfth *Thunderbolt* during the war against the Quadi, and then again with the Fifth *Macedonica* fighting the Marcomanni. I reckon he would have completed that last stint a couple of years ago.'

'And after that . . . ?'

'Exactly. Nothing at all until he pops up here as an auxiliary prefect again. It's all wrong, Julius, he should have gone on from his tribunate to command a five-hundred-strong cavalry wing, and by now he should be commanding a full-strength wing like our old friend Licinius, either that or be retired to public service. Instead of which he seems to be going backwards. There are two good-sized questions about our new prefect that I'd like to hear the answers to — for a start, why has he been demoted from his last declared position back to command of an infantry cohort?'

Julius nodded his agreement.

'And what's he been doing for the last two years?'

'Exactly. Something doesn't add up here, and until I know the answers to those questions I'm not going to turn my back on the man.'

Julius grunted his agreement, then raised a crafty eyebrow.

'I meant to ask, have you had anyone in front of you asking for permission to marry since we got back from Arab Town?'

The first spear's face brightened.

'Funny you should ask, there was a young centurion in to see me only last night. Bright young lad, seems to have found a good woman, a widow, but young enough and with some skills that would make her a valuable person to have around the cohort. He made a persuasive case, for all that we're only days away from marching back into blue-nose territory and he might be dead in a week. Yes, we had a good chat on the subject.'

'And?'

Frontinius turned to face him, a mocking smile on his face.

'Our rules? Just Sextus and Julius, old mates that enlisted on the same day and have always reserved the right to ignore rank and speak our minds to one another.'

Julius nodded.

'Well, under normal conditions I would, as first spear, be forced to tell you that I must respect the confidential nature of the conversation. Under our rules, however, I can tell you . . . '

He paused for a moment, drawing out the silence as the 10th century marched past them.

'Yes?'

'To mind your own business, you nosy bugger!'

He stalked on to the parade ground with a grim smile at the weather and called for his centurions to brief their troops on the day's march to Noisy Valley. Marcus turned to face the Hamians, already looking bedraggled in the persistent drifting rain, and found that, unlike on the previous day, he was the sole object of their attention. One hundred and sixty pairs of eyes were fixed on him, their message a combination of anger and misery, and he paused for a long moment before speaking.

'Good morning, Eighth Century . . . ' He paused and smiled into their resentment. 'Today you see Britannia in all its true glory. We get weather like this roughly one day in every five, you'll be pleased to hear. Today we will be making the march to Noisy Valley, which will get you warmed up soon enough, but before we do let's consider yesterday. We marched fifteen miles at the standard campaign pace and nobody failed to finish . . . even if some of you needed some encouragement along the way.'

He waited for one of the sea of stony faces to crack. Nothing.

'Halfway through the march we conducted a surprise attack, which, unsurprisingly, didn't go very well. You were assaulted by a century of battle-hardened soldiers and you lost. Painfully. Some of you have bruises to show for that defeat, and you've all got sore feet. It's raining, you're cold, you're wet and you'd like nothing better than for me and my brother officers to drop dead on the spot. If you could stand here and look at yourselves with my eyes you'd see unhappy men, some of you angry, most of you just sullen. And let me tell you, let me *guarantee* you, it's going to get worse. Today we march to war.'

He glanced up the line, and saw that most of the cohort's centuries were already on the move back up the hill to the fort. Nodding to Qadir, he gestured for the 8th century to follow.

'Chosen, get them moving! Get some breakfast into them and make sure they're ready to march straight afterwards.'

Once the century was climbing back up the hill's steep slope he dropped back to Qadir's place at the column's rear.

'Good morning, Chosen.'

The big man inclined his head.

'Good morning, Centurion.'

'How does the day find our men?'

'Truthfully, Centurion?'

'Anything else would be to the detriment of us both.'

'Then truthfully, Centurion, they are tired, footsore and they long for anywhere other than this living hell.'

Marcus nodded, recalling Rufius's advice of the previous evening.

'Exactly as I would expect. And it's going to get worse for them before it gets better, I'm afraid. But I have only two choices, Chosen, one being to drive them through this hell while the other is to allow them to surrender to their pain and misery. No choice at all, really. They have to reach the infantryman's sad understanding of his plight since time began.'

'Which is, Centurion?'

'That there's something worse than pounding on down the road when your feet hurt, when the rain's bucketing down and there are still twenty miles to go before stopping to build a camp for the night. They have to understand that keeping going is much better than what will happen to them if they stop.'

Qadir marched on in silence for a moment before responding.

'And if you gain a century of infantrymen while losing their skills with the bow? We did not practise yesterday, and now we must march for most of the day.'

Marcus took a long moment to answer.

'In all truth, Qadir, I would take what this cohort so badly needs and count the loss as an acceptable price.'

'Acceptable for you. And for these men?'

'I would expect the loss to be devastating to them . . . '

'And you would be right.'

Marcus paused again, taking stock of the moment.

'Qadir, my brother officers tell me that in their experience we must take this century to its limits to find their motivation, and that without motivation they will never be ready for what awaits them to the north in time. If that happens then you and I might as well cut each of our men's throats now, and save the barbarians the trouble. If I'm going to make them into soldiers fit to march north past the wall and into enemy territory, then you and I must both be as one in our approach to their training.'

Qadir looked away from the line of their march for a moment, beads of water falling from his helmet as he strode along beside the 8th's last rank.

'I do not like the thought of descending to behaviour as base as that I have seen from your brother officers. I feel that it demeans these men, who have joined your army under such different circumstances to be used so . . . roughly, and in a cause for which they are simply not prepared. And yet . . . '

Marcus held his breath while the Hamian paused as if lost in thought.

' . . . and yet, I see that we are trapped in this terrible place. And so I will ally myself with you in using their methods to make my men fit to survive this coming journey into darkness.'

Marcus sighed audibly with relief.

'Qadir, I . . . '

'But there is a condition I must beg you to accept. Without it all is lost to these men, whether or not they become the soldiers you so crave them to be. I must insist that we find a way to give them time to practise with their bows each day.'

The young centurion nodded.

'I was just about to get to that.'

* * *

The cohort mustered on the parade ground again after breakfast, each century's tents, cooking gear and rations packed on to carts that would form part of the supply train, moving in the cohort's centre on the march. As the 8th Century marched down the hill to their place on the parade ground, Morban's usual place at their head was occupied by Antenoch, while the standard-bearer stood with his grandson Lupus at the fort's gate, hopping from foot to foot in his impatience.

'Where is the dozy old bag? The cohort will be leaving in a matter of minutes and I can't leave you here alone. Perhaps that idiot boy didn't deliver my message . . . '

A young woman came into view, running up the hill past the centuries making their way down to the parade ground. She saw the waiting standard-bearer and dashed up to him, breathlessly panting out her news. Morban listened for a moment, then left the weeping child in her company and hurried down to where Marcus stood in front of the 8th's men.

'Centurion, the boy's grandmother . . . '

Marcus listened for a moment, told the standard-bearer to take his place at the century's head and walked briskly to the first spear's review platform.

'Excuse me, First Spear.'

'Centurion?'

'We have a problem, sir. Morban's grandson was to stay with his grandmother in one of the local villages, but we've just had word that she's died overnight. There's no other family to leave him with, and as the son of a soldier . . . '

He left the sentence unfinished. Both men knew that the boy would be fair game for the locals without his last direct family member to keep them at bay. The threat of massive reprisals would ensure that nobody local was stupid enough to take fire or iron against the fort in their absence, but the victimisation or even the murder and quiet disposal of a soldier's child would be another matter entirely. Frontinius gave the matter less than a second's thought.

'Bring him with us to Noisy Valley. We'll find someone there to look after him while we go hunting barbarians in the hills.'

Morban nodded in quiet relief, pointing to the wagon bearing the century's equipment.

'Get on that cart, lad, sit still and don't touch anything. Thank you, Centurion, I couldn't have left the poor little sod here on his own.'

Marcus nodded, his mind elsewhere as the leading century started marching up the hill that separated the fort from the military road that ran to the east and west behind the line of the wall.

'We'll take him as far as Noisy Valley and no farther. I'm not risking him getting mixed up in a full-scale battle, and in the meantime you're responsible for his good behaviour. That means no wagering while he's around you, and no whoring either. Not that I expect you'll get much of a chance with several thousand legionaries ahead of you in the queue.'

* * *

The cohort arrived at the Noisy Valley fort late in the afternoon, and was directed into temporary defences thrown up alongside the partially rebuilt wooden fortress that dominated the main road to the north. They were camped alongside the 6th legion and several other cohorts from along the wall's length. As the Hamians gratefully slumped to the ground for a short rest before pitching their eight-man tents, Morban slapped the 8th century's trumpeter on the shoulder with his free hand.

'No digging for us tonight, my lad. Let's make a beeline for the vicus, or whatever the lazy bastards have rebuilt of it, see if we can't find a wet to wash the dust from our throats.'

Marcus put out a hand to detain him.

'Not so fast, Standard-bearer. First we need to make sure that our new troops get their tents pitched in such a way that the first gust of wind won't blow them away. After that I want an hour's practice with spears and shields, and after *that* they'll need to have the evening campaign routine explained to them. All of which means that you're going to be the busiest man in the century, and that's before you spend whatever time's necessary to look after your grandson.'

The 8th century exercised with their spears once their camp was set up, their efforts under the tuition of the four centurions watched with amusement by the rest of the cohort and with exasperation by the first spear, who called Marcus over to him after a few minutes standing in silence beside the exercise ground.

'Utter rubbish. You'll not get them slinging a spear straight in anything less than a month, and we'll be in action inside a week. Take their spears off them, and find a way to get them motivated to learn which end of their swords does the damage. If that demonstration's any guide we'll have to dump them on the Hamian cohort as replacements.'

The century lined up to hand their spears in to the quartermaster with broad smiles, although their relief was soon forgotten in the face of Marcus's grim-faced statement once they were back on the parade ground. Julius, Rufius and Dubnus stood behind him, their faces dark with anger at the implied criticism of their training methods, their harsh stares scouring the century's suddenly solemn ranks for any sign of levity.

'You've had your spears taken away because you were about as much use with them as a gang of vicus drunks. Some of you seem to regard that as a victory. Your officers, on the other hand, consider it something of a disgrace. Just to be clear, any attempt to provoke the removal of your swords and shields by means of such wilful underperformance will result instead in the loss of the only thing that seems to matter to you. If you fail to improve your collective performance with your remaining infantry weapons I will have no choice but to relieve you of your bows, and turn you over to the Sixth legion's camp prefect for general duties. You either make a bloody effort or you'll find yourselves cleaning out the latrines on a permanent basis.' He paused and scowled across the century's ranks, allowing the threat to sink in properly. 'So, sword drill, and I suggest you put some effort into it this time . . . '

Watching the 8th going through their paces again, Frontinius noticed Marcus nod to Qadir, motioning for the practice to continue before taking Antenoch and Morban to one side. He nudged the prefect's arm, pointing at the three figures as they limbered up for sparring.

'The centurion seems to have decided to work off his frustrations with a little swordplay. Watch carefully, he's quicker than greased weasel shit once he gets going.'

The two soldiers each took up a wooden practice sword, buckled their helmets tightly and raised their shields ready to fight. Marcus, who, as the prefect was intrigued to note, was wielding a second wooden sword instead of a shield, waited in almost perfect immobility while the two men approached him from either side with slow, careful steps, clearly intending to attack their officer in a pincer movement in the hope of overwhelming him. They paused in their advances for a moment, exchanged glances and then, in a sudden flurry of movement, both men struck, Antenoch stabbing his sword at his officer's chest while Morban swung his weapon in a vicious arc at his head.

Marcus parried the first attack while ducking under the second and shoulder-charging his standard-bearer's shield, the impact making the older man stagger back off balance and fall back on to the ground. With one assailant momentarily out of the fight, Marcus turned on Antenoch with a speed and purpose that immediately put the clerk on the defensive, hammering a blow into the edge of his clerk's raised shield with his left-hand weapon. As Antenoch compensated by pushing the shield round to his right, the young centurion feinted left then darted right, leaping into the air to jab his blade around the shield's edge and into the soft flesh of his neck, pulling the blow to avoid breaking the skin but still inflicting a painful scratch. He spun away from the cursing soldier, avoiding a wild swing from Morban by a hand's span as the standard-bearer charged back into the fight. The older man went for him with furious purpose, hacking wildly in the hope of overwhelming his defence, but Marcus simply stepped back out of range of a shield punch, parrying the blows until the short-lived power of the standard-bearer's attack had burned out. As the pace of his attacks slowed, the centurion took the attack back to him, disarming the sweating soldier with a deft slap to the wrist of his sword arm with the flat of his blade, which left the sword hanging uselessly from the standard-bearer's numb fingers. Morban stepped back and dropped the useless weapon, shaking his head to stop the fight. First Spear Frontinius raised a questioning eyebrow at his prefect.

'I told you he was good, didn't I?'

Scaurus nodded his agreement with his first spear, his eyes narrowed as he watched the young officer talking his men through the fight, pointing out the points at which he had ridden his advantage to beat them both.

'While I find myself forced to agree with you, First Spear, I'd still like to see him fight a real swordsman. No disrespect intended, you've built a fine cohort here, but your men are like most other soldiers, drilled to fight and kill from behind a line of shields and not to duel like that . . . '

'I'll fight him.'

First Spear Frontinius turned with surprise, his eyebrows raised as he looked from the prefect to his bodyguard, who had previously been as silent as always in his place at the senior officer's back.

'Did he just say what I thought he said?'

Scaurus nodded, his lips pursed in a slight smile.

'He doesn't say very much, but when he does it's invariably interesting. You want to spar with that officer?' The German nodded, and Scaurus turned back to Frontinius. 'With your permission, First Spear, I think your man would find Arminius here a worthy enough test of his mettle. Shall we pair them up and see what happens?'

Frontinius shrugged.

'This should be interesting. Centurion Corvus!'

The German strode out on to the parade ground, tossing aside his cloak and tunic to reveal a torso slabbed with muscle, his chest scarred in several places and, at the point where his arm and shoulder met, dimpled with the telltale pucker of an old arrow wound. He took a practice sword from Antenoch but disdained the proffered shield, reaching instead for Morban's blade. The standard-bearer gave up the weapon with raised eyebrows, walking around the towering bodyguard and muttering into Antenoch's ear.

'He fights Dimachaeri style too, eh? Fancy the odds?'

The clerk pursed his lips.

'Look at the bloody size of him, and the state of his body. That's a fighter if ever I saw one. I'll have five denarii on him.'

The two men squared up, their practice swords almost touching. The German kept his eyes locked on Marcus's and hefted the wooden weapons to take their balance, his grating voice loud in the parade ground's sudden hush as the sweating soldiers craned their necks to see what was happening.

'Ready?'

Marcus nodded, and the bodyguard went for him with a speed and grace that belied his size, forcing the young centurion backwards with a swift succession of attacking blows with both swords which looked, for a moment, likely to end in the Roman's painful defeat. Adjusting quickly to the other man's all-out style, and taking a perverse enjoyment in having his skills tested properly for the first time in months, Marcus began to match him blow for blow. Stabbing, parrying and hacking with a fluidity and skill close to matching the best the watching men had seen him muster with his blood up on the field of battle, he took the fight back to the German with single-minded intensity, pushing the bigger man back half a dozen steps with the ferocity of his counter-attack. The two men fought to and fro, all four of their swords ceaselessly hunting for an opening in the other's defence while continuously fending off the other's attacks. Stepping in close, his swords flung wide to deflect the Roman's blades, the German shaped to deliver a powerful head-butt to his opponent, but Marcus, trained from his youth by men experienced in the dirtier side of combat in Rome's savage arena fighting, saw the move coming and spun away, hooking the other man's leg with a swinging kick and putting him on his back. The German simply rolled backwards out of the fall, regained his feet with a broad grin and charged back in with both swords, putting Marcus back on the defensive once more.

The fight became steadily more physical, as both men sought to take an advantage that their mutual swordsmanship denied them both. Punching Marcus with a fierce blow from his muscular forearm, sending the younger man staggering back with stars flashing in his vision, Arminius shaped for the kill only to grimace with pain as the Roman, thoroughly enraged at the blow's force, danced back in and put a hobnailed boot into his knee. The two men separated for a moment and circled each other, each of them eyeing the other with a new wariness, searching the other's face for any sign of weakness. First spear and prefect shared a glance and nodded to each other.

'*Enough!*'

The prefect's shouted command hung in the air for a moment, neither man acknowledging the order until, with distinct reluctance, the German dropped first one and then the other of the practice swords. He held out a hand to Marcus, who dropped his own swords and took the offered clasp, wincing with the force of the German's grip. The previously blank-faced bodyguard was smiling slightly.

'You fight well, as well as anyone I've crossed swords with. I'll fight with you again.'

Marcus nodded.

'That was the best bout I've had since I left . . . home. You'll have to teach me a few of those moves.'

The bodyguard nodded, leaning in close to whisper in his ear.

'I was taught by a master swordsman. When the time is right I will share what I have learned with you.'

Prefect Scaurus and the first spear took their leave of the cohort once the soldiers had settled down to the evening meal. Frontinius left Julius in command, scowling darkly at the ground around their earth-banked defences.

'We'll move to full campaign routine, Centurion, double patrols and nobody allowed out of the camp without your express permission. The watchword is 'Lost', the response is 'Eagle'. We'll be back in a couple of hours if this commanders' conference goes to form, so make sure there's something warm left over for us when the rest of you have finished filling your faces.'

Inside the fortress's stone wall, blackened by smoke from its buildings' destruction by burning in the face of the warband's advance months before, the two men followed directions from the gate guard to find the headquarters. The prefect smiled wryly at the size of the new building.

'Typical legion thinking. If the eagle's going to live anywhere for a while it has to be housed in a building big enough for a cohort to bunk down in.

Inside the building they found two dozen or so senior officers waiting around in quiet conversation. Frontinius spoke quietly in his prefect's ear.

'No sign of the Second Cohort. Looks like we'll be hanging on to the Hamians for a while yet. Oh, here we go . . . '

From a side room a trio of men entered the praetorium, their polished breastplates shining in the torchlight. The oldest of them, a thin man with a grey beard, nodded briefly to Scaurus, while the 6th legion's legatus acknowledged his old friend and former first spear with a swift handshake, giving his successor a brief but openly curious stare. They walked briskly to the raised briefing podium, adorned with the 6th legion's bull emblem, and turned to face the collected officers. Frontinius whispered in his prefect's ear.

'I hear he eats bread shipped all the way from Rome, and that by the time it gets here it's so stale that he can't get much of it down him at a sitting because it cuts his gums up so badly.'

Scaurus smiled faintly, muttering out of the side of his mouth.

'That's how he stays so thin. He also writes out a dozen or so orders every night before he goes to sleep, and has the officer of the guard send them out to his legates and prefects at intervals through the night to foster the illusion that he never sleeps . . . '

The governor addressed the gathered officers in a clear, calm voice.

'Gentlemen, let me introduce myself. I am Ulpius Marcellus, former governor of Britannia now returned at the command of my emperor to put this wretched province straight again. For those of you that don't know them, these men are my legion commanders, Legatus Equitius commanding Sixth *Victorious*, and Legatus Macrinus commanding Twentieth *Valiant* and *Victorious*. I've sent Legatus Metellus back south with six cohorts of the Second *Augustan* to keep order on the western border, while the rest of his cohorts have been divided between the Sixth and the Twentieth. That gives us a pair of over-strength legions, and a total force of fifteen thousand legionaries. Add in your auxiliaries and we comfortably outnumber the strength that our spies tell us we can expect Calgus to put into the field.'

He paused, sweeping a piercing stare across the gathered officers.

'My predecessor seems to have spent altogether too much time in leisure, and nowhere near enough up here keeping tabs on the barbarians, as a result of which we find ourselves here today while *he* finds himself ordered back to Rome.'

He paused again, looking around his assembled officers.

'Where, gentlemen, he will find himself in a distinctly unhappy position — as might we all if we fail to put down this revolt quickly and without further serious loss. This isn't an emperor to take failure easily, gentlemen, not when Praetorian Prefect Perennis, who as some of you will know is the man standing behind the throne, discovers that his son was a casualty of the opening battle of the war. Failure is therefore not an acceptable option for any of us. These next few weeks before the winter starts to close in are going to be hard and dirty for all concerned, and by the end of this campaigning season I'm firmly expecting that we'll have this man Calgus's head, either on the end of a chain or in a jar headed for Rome by fast courier. Either will do. The only question that needs answering right now is how we're going to achieve that.'

He paused again, turning to his staff officer.

'Map.'

The map was unrolled and spread across the

table in front of the senior officers. Marcellus looked around the group gathered at the table.

'All told we have some twenty-two thousand spears to put into the field. Our intelligence, including information from some sources rather closer to Calgus than he could ever suspect, tells us that he has no more than fifteen thousand men at best, so once we get them to commit to a straight fight it'll be over quickly enough. However, and this is going to be the moot point of this campaign, any engagement with these barbarians must, *must*, take place on favourable ground.'

The officers round the table nodded solemnly. The battle of Lost Eagle and its grisly aftermath for both sides were still a raw memory for them all.

'We want Calgus to bring his fifteen thousand out on to open ground, give us time to get our twenty thousand into line and then mince his men up in the usual style. He, on the other hand, being a clever brute, wants us to advance eagerly on to ground of his choosing — forest, broken ground, anywhere that our tactics don't work half as well — and then set his dogs loose on us from several directions. We're going to be gathering round this table every night of the campaign, gentlemen, and I'm going to be expecting you to bring me every idea under the sun to make Calgus ignore his instincts and come out to meet us before the winter sets in, especially as he gets near the limits of his supplies. I have no intention of reporting back to the emperor that we've had to settle in for the winter without a victory, preferably one that ends this squalid little war here and now. So you'd all better get thinking.'

He pointed to the map, indicating Noisy Valley's position two miles south of the junction of the north road and the military road.

'So now we're ready to strike north up the main road and into the mountains to the north-east, such as they are. We suspect that Calgus has his warband camped somewhere around here, on the southern slopes of the range, hidden deep in the forests. Our first task is to find his warband, so there'll be a broad screen of cavalry out in front of the main force probing forward, seeking contact. Once we've got them located the next trick will be to either draw them out into the open or, if we can't manage that feat, fix them for long enough that Sixth and Twentieth legions can bring their strength to bear on their defences in a classic siege. While we're doing that we'll patrol aggressively to either flank just to make sure the locals keep their heads down and let us get on with it unmolested. That ought to give the auxiliary cohorts something to keep them out of mischief . . . '

5

The next day dawned brightly, and Calgus mustered the tribal leaders once the morning meal had been taken. The command had gone out for every man to be ready to march, with his war gear and a day's food, and there was a palpable tension in the air as the gathered chieftains watched him stalk into their midst, his bodyguards looking about them with poorly disguised anxiety at the hostile faces around them. Calgus turned to survey the scene, taking the measure of the men gathered at his command. The tribal leaders stood impassively for the most part, many of them with sour looks that told him they would rather be elsewhere; only the men of his own Selgovae tribe had raised a cheer when he entered their circle. The other tribes, he judged, had at last realised that a war fought in what appeared primarily to be his people's best interests would not necessarily be good for them.

'Brothers . . . ' Calgus paused, waiting for any reaction from the gathered mass of warriors, but none came. ' . . . you have delivered a hammer-blow to the men that seek to invade our land, subjugate our people and strip us of both our wealth and our dignity! We have already defeated one legion in battle, and forced the Romans to scrape up every spare soldier in the northern half of their empire in order to put their boot back on this province's throat. I know that some of you are saying that we have done little more than pull the tail of a dangerous beast, provoking it to strike back at us with all of its power . . . and in truth you are both right and wrong. Do the Romans still have three full legions in Britannia? Yes! Does the bulk of that strength lurk, waiting to strike out and crush us, and within two days' march of this encampment? Of course it does!' He had their attention now; he knew it even without staring round at the faces surrounding him.

'Ask yourselves, however, what would happen if we managed to repeat that trick, and crush another of their legions in the same way. What then, when there are no more replacement soldiers to be had?' He allowed the silence to build, looking around him with a broad grin, watching realisation starting to dawn on the men around him. 'Three legions, my brothers, that's all they have. There will be no further reinforcement from over the sea. If we break one more legion they will be unable to replace it, not now that every available man in the northern empire is already in this province. The Roman governor will be faced with a stark choice, to defend their wall with only two legions, and one of those needed in the south to keep the western tribes under control, or to retreat south by a hundred miles, and form a new line of defence based on the fortresses of Yew Grove and Fortress Deva. An indefensible line, with a mountain range running straight through the middle and the whole of the Brigantes tribe south of their wall suddenly liberated to join the rebellion and to double our strength in fighting men. The governor will try to hold on, to wait for eventual reinforcement rather than face the disgrace of abandoning a wall built by an emperor and making their defence of Britannia impossible. And he will be doomed to fail.'

Now was the critical moment in his oration, his chance to grab the men around him by the balls.

'My brothers, if we can just take down one of the legions facing us there will be no more reinforcement for their northern frontier, and their general will be forced to make the terrible choice I have described to you. And this whole country will fall to us like an apple whose time on the tree has come to its end. We will be free to take back the wealth they have stolen from us, free to travel wherever we wish without needing their permission. Free to live the way we choose, without their legions forever forcing us to live by their rules.' He waited for a moment, turning to look around his audience. Every man's eyes were locked on to him, and in each face he saw nothing like the apathy of five minutes before. *Nearly*.

'So, how do we destroy another legion? First, my brothers, we are going to anger the Romans, by taking our war to them in a way that they will neither predict nor be able to tolerate. Tonight will be a fat moon by which we will be able to make our way to their wall, and cross it undetected. Nightfall today will see us in position to strike at a border fort, to mount a swift and terrible attack that will destroy both fort and garrison, and by tomorrow evening we will have returned here in triumph. Of course, their cavalry will outpace the legions in the search for us as we retreat back here, they will find our trail and follow it here, bringing the legions in their wake, but that is exactly what we want them to do. When they think they have us trapped, that will be the moment for our greater trap to be sprung.'

'And this greater trap, Calgus. Just what would that consist of?'

The question came from Brennus. Of course.

'Powerful allies, King Brennus. Powerful enough to smash a legion with the shock of their attack, if that legion is stretched to besiege us here as I expect.'

Later, with his plan of attack reluctantly approved by the gathered tribal nobles, Calgus sought out Martos, King Brennus's nephew. Ignoring the hostile looks he was getting from the men around the young noble, he strode up to the man, stepping close to speak in quiet and measured tones.

'Prince Martos, I would like to speak with you in private for a moment, if you'll hear me?'

Martos, checking the edge of his sword with his thumb, nodded dourly.

'I will speak with you if that is your wish, Calgus. I may not agree with your methods, but I believe that we both want the same thing from these next few days.'

Indeed we do, mused Calgus inwardly as he extended an arm, inviting the Votadini prince to walk with him, but only one of us is going to live to enjoy it.

* * *

The sky clouded over in the early afternoon, and a thin drizzle contrived to insinuate itself into any and every place it could possibly reach. The Tungrians spent the day making sure that they were ready for another lengthy spell in the field, sharpening weapons and checking their equipment for any fault that might let them down on the march. The 8th Century spent the morning on the exercise field practising with swords and shields, every man paired with a veteran soldier from the cohort's other centuries and drilled time and time again in the simple disciplines of attack and defence.

Marcus walked among his allocated forty men with Qadir, gauging which of them might just be capable of standing in a battle line's front rank by watching the faces of the soldiers set to teach them their murderous trade.

'That one, training with the one-eyed soldier. Front rank.'

The imperturbable chosen man made a mark on his writing tablet and followed Marcus down the line. When they compared notes with Julius, Dubnus and Rufius, their combined findings made uncomfortable material for discussion with First Spear Frontinius when Marcus met up with him to discuss the morning session's results.

'I've got about a dozen men that I can put in

the front rank with a clear conscience, and another thirty or so with a fighting chance of surviving their first fight. After that it's a lottery, the rest of them are just so much padding . . . '

Frontinius nodded gravely.

'Work them harder. You've got a day, perhaps two.'

Soon after midday another cohort arrived at the fort, and was directed to establish their camp alongside the Tungrians. Once the soldiers realised the identity of the newcomers they quickly entered into the usual spirit of the two cohorts' encounters, exchanges of abuse quickly giving way to exchanges of news and gossip. Scaurus and Frontinius waited for the appropriate period of time, then made their way into the 2nd Tungrian cohort's camp and presented themselves at the command tent. Escorted inside, they found First Spear Neuto and Prefect Furius bent over an equipment list, working out what to raid the fort's stores for. Furius turned, and, recognising Scaurus with a heartbeat's pause that was imperceptible unless the watcher was looking for it, he took the offered hand and shook it vigorously.

'Rutilius Scaurus! I hear you've got the First Tungrians, and here I am with the Second Cohort! Just like old times with the good old Twelfth, eh? Here, meet my first spear, Neuto. Neuto, this is my old comrade Rutilius Scaurus, from my days in Germania with the Twelfth Legion. Scaurus and I were both thin-stripe tribunes with the legion when we were sent to root out the German tribes, both of us not much better than callow youths with no real idea of soldiering, and yet here we both are with independent commands to play with.'

The first spear gave Scaurus and Frontinius a look that spoke volumes for his relationship with his prefect, offering his hand to Scaurus before clasping Frontinius's and slapping him on the shoulder with his other hand. The two men were clearly glad to see each other, and at Neuto's suggestion they headed off to the fort's officers' mess to share information, and work out whether either could help the other with supplies or equipment. Outside the tent Neuto gave Frontinius a look that told him even more about Prefect Furius, his voice kept low but with a distinct edge of anger.

'I'm glad to see you, old comrade, although I wish it were under happier circumstances. Let's get a beaker of something warm inside us and I'll share my news with you . . . not all of it good.'

With the first spears' departure the two prefects stared at each other in a long moment of silence. Furius spoke first, his eyes suddenly hard as he faced his former comrade.

'Well, Gaius Rutilius Scaurus, it's been a long time since Moesia. What have you been up to for the last ten years?'

Scaurus shrugged.

'I stayed with the Twelfth for three years after you left to return to Rome, until we'd finished off the Quadi in fact. A year after that I was back to Moesia for the war with their neighbours the Marcomani, this time with the Fifth *Macedonica*, and now I've been sent here to help put down another barbarian uprising. I've spent the occasional few months in Rome to remind me why we fight, but mostly I've been in the field.'

'A warrior's life, then. Still dedicated to Mithras, eh? And yet here we both are, both of us with an equal status after all those years, despite my little slip at Thunderbolt Gorge. Don't you find that galling, eh, Scaurus? You toil away on the borders of the empire for a decade while I enjoy the comforts of home, then in six months I go from enforced retirement to command of a thousand-strong infantry cohort. Doesn't that rankle just a little?'

Scaurus shrugged, without any visible sign of concern.

'Not really. We come from different worlds, you and I, our families couldn't be much more different if we'd tried. I do what I do, and you . . . well, you do whatever it is that you do. Still fond of the odd crucifixion, are you?'

Furius nodded slowly.

'I'm still a firm believer in keeping discipline nice and taut, if that's what you're asking. While we were out over the wall I managed to find and punish the man that killed this cohort's previous prefect. I had him . . . '

'Whipped to death, from the rumours flying round the camp.'

Furius's voice took on a note of self-justification.

'He went on the cross as well.'

Scaurus shook his head gently.

'You crucified a dead man?'

Furius bristled, his temperature clearly rising.

'It served as an example.'

Scaurus kept a straight face, seeing the signs he had long ago learned to recognise in the other man's reddening features.

'I'm sure it did.'

* * *

Frontinius took a cautious sip at his broth, pursing his lips at the taste and putting the steaming beaker down as he passed judgement on his new prefect for Neuto's benefit.

'So at first I thought he was just another weak-chinned amateur like most of the idiots we get as prefects, but all in all I'd say he's probably going to be good enough, given his experience. Not that he's been very forthcoming about exactly what he's done in the last ten years, but he seems to have seen enough action to have knocked the corners off him, even if he won't talk about it. What about yours?'

The two first spears had found a quiet corner in the officers' mess and were sitting over their broth, waiting for it to cool slightly. The hot soup's steam rose into the room's chilly air as the steward laboured to get the fire properly lit. Frontinius had quickly recognised that his old friend needed to share his recent experiences with someone that he could trust. Having asked the question, he kept his mouth firmly shut in the hope of encouraging the 2nd Cohort's senior centurion to tell his story. Neuto grimaced, shaking his head as he spoke.

'At first I thought Furius might be a decent

replacement for Prefect Bassus. He's not short of money, that's clear. He's got a jar full of naphtha that he uses to light his brazier, just a small splash and the wood goes up like a grain store with the first spark from the flint, and that must have cost him a small fortune. He seemed to know what he was talking about too, he told a good story about his time in Moesia fighting some tribe or other, and he was brisk and businesslike in just about everything he did. 'Here,' I thought, 'is a man that I might be able to do business with. Perhaps not quite such a find as your last prefect — now *there* was an officer — but decent enough, nevertheless.'' He sipped at his broth. 'It took me about three days to get over that sadly mistaken first impression. First of all, he paraded the cohort at Red River and told them what a shower of bastards they were for killing Bassus, and how he was going to make them pay for it. Three months' pay forfeit for the entire cohort, reduced to one month if he got his man before dark the same day.'

Frontinius grimaced in turn.

'But he got his man, right? There's simply no way a full cohort is going to stand for losing that much money to protect one man. I'd say his tactics were spot on.'

Neuto shrugged, unwilling to cede the point his friend was making.

'Yes, he got his man, but . . . '

'Then you can't really argue too hard against his methods, can you? After all, whoever it was did kill a prefect, let's not forget that. Anybody I know?'

Neuto shook his head dismissively.

'No. Just some idiot soldier, a typical wooden-skulled headcase who acted on impulse and stuck his iron through Prefect Bassus's back simply because he didn't like the man. To make it worse, he was the older brother of one of my centurions. Something I was supposed not to know, and of course something I actually knew from about an hour after the younger brother joined up. Our new prefect had him crucified . . . '

Frontinius blew on his broth and took a mouthful.

'We heard. The cavalry lads were full of it when they pulled in last night. A little severe, for all that he killed an officer. I hear the man died on the whipping post?'

Neuto nodded, a small smile touching his lips.

'Yes. Prefect Furius made the mistake of ordering him to receive fifty lashes.'

'*Fifty*?'

'Exactly. He'd probably have died even if my officers hadn't contrived to open the poor bastard's throat with the scourge, after I'd had a few quiet words in the right ears, but I wasn't taking any chances. Then the idiot had him nailed up anyway.'

Frontinius grimaced again.

'I still couldn't argue that he's unfit for command. So what if he's a little free with the hammer and nails, the man had it coming to him, right?'

Neuto sat back, looking at his friend.

'I can live with the carpentry fixation, just

about, but he's just not very *good*. We were sent out to look for the blue-noses, a roving commission for a new prefect and the perfect chance for him to get used to his new command, right? I advised him to use the cavalry to screen our movements and seek out any signs of the warband . . . '

'And?'

Neuto's face wrinkled with disgust.

'He didn't allow them out of sight for the entire time we were out there. The man was in perpetual fear of bumping into a fight, and he said he wanted all his spears close to hand in case of a pitched battle. I tried to get across to him that four hundred horsemen weren't going to put any sizeable hole in a decent warband, and we'd be better finding them without being found ourselves, and then steering well clear, but he wasn't having any of it. No, we just blundered round the hills without a bloody clue, and for all I know the only thing that stopped the blue-nosed bastards from hacking us to bits was either simple dumb luck in that we missed them or else they were too busy laughing at us. And he's hardly walked a mile since he arrived, rides a horse alongside the cohort on the march like he's a legion tribune!'

He drained the beaker and slapped it down on the table with a calculating glance at Frontinius.

'I'll tell you what else, he's absolutely fixated with some fugitive that's evaded the imperial strangler. He's always on about it, how he'll pay a big reward to the man that finds him, how much prestige he'll get if he's the man to bring the fellow to justice. I ask you, how likely is it that some runaway aristo is going to be hiding up here with us, in the middle of twenty thousand Roman troops, eh?' He looked across the table at Frontinius, his eyes suddenly narrowed. 'Not even you could be that stupid, and you did some monumentally daft things when we were young recruits, as I recall . . . *eh, Sextus*?'

Frontinius's face froze into immobility.

'How long have you known?'

Neuto shook his head disbelievingly.

'Jupiter's *tits*, I prayed I was wrong! That bright young lad with the two swords?'

'The same. He's the one that found the supplies waiting for Calgus's western attack and burned them out back in the spring. Remember that? If not for him we'd have had ten thousand of the bastards at our backs as well as the warband to our front. The boy's good, Neuto, and I can't just abandon him now that he's made a place with the cohort. How did you work it out?'

His friend shook his head, taking another sip of his broth.

'I didn't. My *least* favourite centurion seems to have worked it out after meeting your man at Arab Town. These things have a habit of finding their way back to a man who keeps his ear to the ground, as well you know. Does your prefect . . . ? No, on second thoughts I'm better not knowing. Cocidius's sword and fucking spear, Sextus, how long do you think you can keep this quiet, now that we're tucked up close with half the bloody army? The next thing you'll know is Furius will be calling for the carpenters again, except this time it'll be you tied up ready for the scourge.'

Frontinius frowned.

'I've got an idea to get him out of the fort tonight, and tomorrow.'

'That's fine for today and tomorrow, but we're going to be in the field for weeks. Mark my words, Furius is offering a bag of gold to the man that unearths him; and rumour has it that one of my centurions is on the scent. Knowing the man in question, he'll be all over your cohort trying to get some proof. And if that bastard Furius gets a sniff of your boy he'll be dog meat inside a day. As will you.'

He sat back, shaking his head at his old friend. Frontinius nodded grimly.

'And that's my problem, and not one for you to get dragged into. Although I'd appreciate any warning you can give me, I guess it's for the best that we never had this conversation.'

Neuto nodded grimly.

'Agreed. Now, let's talk about the reinforcement century Prefect Furius seems to have procured out of the Arab Town docks for me.'

* * *

'No fucking way! Those men are mine and I'm keeping them.'

If the mood in Furius's tent had darkened with the departure of the first spears, it had turned distinctly ugly once Scaurus had raised the subject of the stolen century. He held a level gaze on Furius, watching his eyes intently.

'You knew very well that those troops were earmarked for my cohort, didn't you, Gracilus Furius? We're still significantly under strength, and yet you bribed them out from under our noses without a second thought. And now you tell me that you're going to hold on to them no matter what . . . '

Furius leaned back in his chair, a faint sneer playing across his face.

'That's right, and there's not much you can do to get them back. I've got a requisition document signed off by the replacements officer, all nicely legal, and the century in question is already distributed into my cohort. So, unless you've got some shiny new sponsor that I don't know about, you haven't even got the clout to take this up the ladder. You do know how I got this command, even after Thunderbolt Gorge and the best part of ten years of enjoying the pleasures of home, don't you? It was simple. I just asked my father to get me back into uniform. If you thought he was well connected ten years ago, well, you should see him now. He may be a wrinkled old bastard, but he's got more money than he knows what to do with. If he'd wanted to become a senator he only had to ask, he's got ten times the money required for the favour, and he knows where to spend it. That bread-nibbling beanpole Ulpius Marcellus is a friend of the family, and I can tell you what his reaction will be if you take the problem to him — he'll just laugh in your face. Senior officers like their commanders to show some initiative, or hadn't you heard? They find this sort of squabble amusing to watch but irritating to deal with, so you've got as much chance of getting that century back as you have of being promoted to legatus, you pipsqueak. Apart from that, you also got two centuries in the place of one. I'd say everyone should be happy.'

He smiled tightly, but the smile turned to a thin-lipped glare as Scaurus stared at him for a moment longer before speaking again, his direct gaze making the other man uneasy. This wasn't the sort of behaviour Furius remembered from their last spell as colleagues.

'If you're determined to do this, then so be it. Just don't be surprised if you end up regretting it. I believe you've regretted one or two things you've done recently, if the words I've heard are true.'

'Regret it, why am I going to . . . ?'

Scaurus got to his feet, ignoring the other man's spluttering.

'Thank you, Gracilus Furius, for your hospitality, and for the conversation.'

He turned to go. Furius caught his arm, his sense of superiority picked to threads by something for which he had no real concept.

'A moment, Rutilius Scaurus. I asked you a question, and you haven't answered me yet. Your sponsor? Who *is* your sponsor these days?'

Scaurus turned back, easily taking the other man's hand from his sleeve.

'You're right, I didn't answer you, did I?'

He turned away and walked out into the

drizzle, leaving Furius with a bemused, almost worried look as he watched his colleague walk away into the cold autumn afternoon. He stared about him until his gaze alighted on one of the soldiers standing guard.

'You, take a message to Centurion Appius. Tell him to report to me immediately.'

⋆ ⋆ ⋆

First Spear Frontinius hurried back to the cohort once his discussion with Neuto was done, and spent a few minutes talking urgently to Scaurus before going to look for the 8th Century. He found them marching wearily back on to the exercise field in readiness for another long session with their swords, and called Marcus and Dubnus to him with an urgent wave.

'A change of plan, Centurion Corvus, we need to get you out of camp. One of the Second Cohort centurions you met at Arab Town last week seems to have worked out who 'Centurion Corvus' really is, and I don't want you around when he comes looking for proof. The prefect of the Second Cohort is looking for you, and it won't take very much more deduction on his part to put us all in deeper water than we can swim in. Get your men some bread to eat and then take them out for some night familiarisation. You can take the Fifth Century with you, they're good at night work, and the prefect has asked me to send his man Arminius out with you as well. Apparently he grew up in the German forests, so he should be a handy man to have along for the night. This way we can show our Hamian brothers what it's like to patrol in the open countryside after dark, and as a side benefit I expect you'll be able to work out who among them is suitable to send out on listening patrols in future. Just get them out of the main gate as quickly as possible without making it look like you're in a hurry.'

The two centurions led their men north from the fort without fanfare, with the archers dressed in their heavy woollen cloaks to provide as much anonymity as possible, striking out from the north road into open country as soon as they were out of sight of the walls. They conferred for a moment, and then Dubnus went forward with a pair of tent parties to scout the ground in front of their line of march. The 5th Century men took turns to trot forward and then go to ground, searching their surroundings intently for any sign of the enemy. The remainder of the two centuries marched forward at a gentle pace behind the scouts, and Marcus was pleased to see that the Hamians were coping with the terrain well enough, even if many of them were still clearly footsore. The prefect's bodyguard strode forward in silence, always staying within a few feet of him, and Marcus quickly realised that his presence was more to do with his protection than any benefit the German might gain from the exercise.

Less than ten minutes after their departure Centurion Appius strolled into the 1st Cohort's lines. Promptly challenged by the guard sentries, and having asked to speak to one of the centurions he had met in Arab Town the previous week, he found himself staring into the barrel chest of an officer he had not previously met. Titus stared down at him with an unreadable expression for a moment before speaking, his voice a growling rumble.

'You're looking for one of my brother officers?'

Appius nodded, suddenly conscious of the fact that, even less than fifty paces from his own men, he was very much on another cohort's turf.

'I met some of your mates last week on the coast . . . I just thought I'd come and say hello to them again . . . '

He stopped speaking, aware that the giant standing in front of him was looking decidedly uninterested.

'They're out on detached duty. Come back another time. Bring a century of Tungrian infantry with you if you're hoping for any sort of welcome.'

The big man turned away, leaving Appius standing alone in front of two unfriendly-looking sentries. He turned away, inwardly cursing his luck. Furius had made it very clear that he expected quick results from him, given his certainty as to the young Roman centurion's real identity.

* * *

The Hamians and their escorts made steady progress across the open land to the fort's north-east, skirting round isolated copses and crossing the open farmland in a long column under a cloudless sky, their cloaks long since removed in the warm afternoon air. As the sun dipped towards the horizon the centurions called a halt, bringing their 250 men together in the cover of a large copse of oak trees. Marcus gathered them all in close so as to be heard without having to shout.

'We'll be staying out overnight, so you can eat half your bread now if you want to, but keep the other half for the morning. What we're going to do now is advance across the ground in front of us as quietly as possible, taking as much time as we need to make sure we do it silently. We're going to try to get within a hundred paces or so of one of the wall forts without being detected. As an incentive for you all, if we do manage to get in and out without being noticed you'll all get an afternoon's free time when we get back into camp, and I would imagine that those of you with bows would be welcome to join the Hamian cohort at shooting practice to find out if you still know how to use them. Eat your bread and take a rest, we'll be on the move again once the sun's below the horizon.'

The soldiers waited patiently, some of the men passing the time with quiet games of Odd or Even, while others simply talked softly among themselves. The older and more experienced soldiers rolled themselves up in their cloaks and slept, Dubnus among their number once he knew that Marcus had no intention of resting. Arminius lounged on the grass underneath a massive gnarled oak close to Marcus and Qadir, and listened in silence to their conversation until a lengthy pause developed. Both men turned to him in surprise as the previously taciturn German addressed the Hamian chosen man.

'You seem very much out of place here, Chosen Man, you and your men. Might I ask how you came to this province?'

Qadir shrugged in the early evening's half-light.

'There is very little to tell you, but I will share what there is. We were recruited from our home in the city of Hamath, which means 'fortress' in my native tongue, by the occupying troops of the Third *Gallica* legion. For some of us it was a choice between desperate hardship or imperial service; for others it was a simple desire to see the world beyond our limited experience . . . '

The German nodded knowingly.

'And for you?'

The big Hamian stared at him for a moment before answering.

'I committed a crime that would have seen me dead within a day, had I waited for what passes for justice in Hamath to catch up with me. I knew that once I was sworn to service I would be beyond the reach of my pursuers.'

He stared at the ground for a half-minute before continuing, both Marcus and Arminius respecting his reverie.

'Anyway, I am sure you both know that my people have a certain ability with the bow, and for as long as we have been subject to other nations we have provided their armies with archers. Many of us were already blessed with more than acceptable skill with the weapon, but our Roman instructors drilled us in one task and one task only; to hit a man-sized target at a distance of one hundred paces time after time. We would shoot hundreds of arrows a day, and do so day after day, until we could all put an arrow into a man at a distance of one hundred paces, no matter whether it was the first or the one hundred and first shot of the day. We developed the strength in our shoulders, punishing our muscles until they were strong enough to bend our bows hundreds of times a day, and our backs and bellies became hard, with ridges of muscles where soft flesh had been before. Finally, when we were deemed ready to serve the empire, we were marched north through a succession of countries, destined to serve on the frontier in Germania in a war with a vicious barbarian enemy, or so we were told. But by the time we arrived on the northern frontier the fighting with your people was already at an end, and we were put into service in hunting game to supplement the standard rations, rather than killing other men.'

He paused again, a half-smile on his face.

'Germania was very different, of course, with thick green forests and wide rivers, and quite unlike our home, but we came to relish the hunting in those happy days, when we were allowed to roam more or less as we wished in search of wild pigs and deer for the pot. It came to an end, of course, it was only ever an interlude in our path to this place. How could such a perfect existence last, when there is always a war somewhere on the edge of the empire that needs to be fed with men's lives? And so we moved north again, passed along the frontier from one fortress to another until we found ourselves on the shores of the German sea and ordered to take ship for the province of Britannia as reinforcements. Which is the reason why we came to be sitting in the barracks of a port called 'Arab Town' when the centurion here came looking for infantry soldiers, since when our very lives have been turned upside down. We are to become infantry, or to die in the attempt as seems more likely to me . . .'

Arminius nodded his thanks for the tale, quite unabashed at the Hamian's fatalistic view of his men's future.

'You are more fortunate than you know, Chosen Man Qadir, in that you have already avoided one long and brutal war. The peoples that lived north of the River Danubius, my people the Quadi among them, were strong and proud of their prowess with the sword and axe, strong enough to have put our Roman masters on their back foot for more than a year when the war began. We crossed the river in strength ten summers past, and defeated the Roman army that stood between us and their settlements in the shadow of the Alpes mountains. The Romans sent another army to put down our revolt once we had their main fortress besieged, but we defeated them in their turn, and took the fortress once the relief force was beaten. For a time we believed that we were invincible, but we had little enough time to enjoy the feeling, for the following year a mighty army drawn from legions across the whole of Europa forced us to retreat back into our own lands, and imposed a truce upon us that gave them time to gather yet more strength, in readiness to cross the river in their turn. Soon enough the Romans brought the war to our lands, hunting the tribes down one by one and taking bloody retribution for their earlier losses.'

He paused, taking a drink from his water skin.

'When they broke their truce and attacked into our tribal lands, claiming that we were giving aid to our neighbours the Marcomanni in their fight for survival, we knew that we would have to fight them to the death, either theirs or ours, and that no quarter would be asked or given by either side.

'And so it was, on a blindingly hot day at the height of the summer, that we lured the Twelfth legion, the Thunderbolt as they termed themselves, on to perfect ground, and sprang a trap that bottled them up in a rocky defile. We had them helpless, trapped under the full heat of the sun and without water. Oh yes, you smile now, thinking the lack of water a trivial thing, but they were desperate for it even before the sun was at its full height, and they had been marching most of the morning without reaching the stream around which we had based our trap. We charged into their line three times, and with each attack we killed and wounded more of their soldiers, and sapped the strength of those men left on their feet. After the third charge our leaders shouted that victory was inevitable, and that we would wait for the Romans to surrender once they succumbed to their thirst. Our warriors paraded up and down their line within a dozen paces, drinking water carried from the stream, pouring it over their heads to rub in their lack of anything to drink.

'As we waited for them to surrender, however, something strange started to happen in the sky over our heads. Clouds gathered, boiling up into huge thunderheads and darkening from white to a sullen grey in what seemed only a few minutes. Rather than release the rain that their appearance promised, they continued to grow and darken, turning an unnatural colour, blue-green, like a huge bruise on the heavens. It seemed as if the sun had fallen below the horizon, and so much light was blocked out that we could barely see the Romans as they stood and waited for our next attack. Then, without those warning rumbles a storm usually gives out, a mighty thunderbolt speared down from the clouds to shatter a tree not fifty paces from our line, instantly sending it up in a pillar of flame. The roar of thunder that accompanied it was instant, without any pause at all, and it battered at our ears so powerfully that some men were deafened by the noise. My own hearing was certainly affected, as if my head were wrapped in heavy wool.'

He paused, smiling wryly at Marcus.

'Now I am not, you must understand, a man given to what you Romans call 'superstition', but even I, I will admit, was taken aback by this sudden sign from the skies. My comrades were for the most part terrified out of their wits, and the Romans could not have failed to see our previously solid line disintegrate into chaos, even if they still lacked the energy to attack us. Moments later, though, while our warriors were still quailing at the flaming tree so close to our shields, and what it might mean, a rainstorm smashed down from the clouds gathered overhead. The rain lashed down so hard that it stung our skin, and the downpour was so fierce that trickles of water became busy streams in minutes.

'Of course, where we saw a dark omen the Romans, whose shields bore the thunderbolt their legion's name boasted, saw quite the opposite. Once they had collected enough of the falling rain to slake their thirsts they came at us like ghosts out of the storm, their faces painted with mud like the barbarians they called us. We saw their shields, every one emblazoned with the lightning bolt, loom out of the storm's murk and that was enough for most of us.' He shook his head sadly, his eyes misting over with the memory. 'We were broken men before ever the fight started. They put us to the sword, showing no mercy until we broke and ran for the hills. I ran with the rest, of course, not to do so would have meant dying without ever getting a chance to fight back, such was the panic around me, but when I got the chance I hid myself and waited for the Romans to pass. I meant to attack them without warning, and die with some pride, unlike my comrades, who were falling to their swords and spears without even turning to fight.

'It was a lost hope, of course. The second I leapt from cover I had half a dozen soldiers in my face, and I went down to a bash on the head from a man I never saw. That would have been it, except a young tribune stopped them from killing me, and claimed me as a slave. A tribune, as you may have guessed, by the name of Scaurus. He gave me a strange choice but a clever one, either to serve him as a bodyguard, and earn my freedom by saving his life and thus repaying my debt to him, or go back to my people in shame, my life forfeit, and forbidden to fight again for fear of the retribution of his god. He told me that when he realised that the legion's men were trapped, with many soldiers and even officers terrified for their lives, and knowing that they would all die without some divine intervention, he offered a prayer to Mithras. He told me that he offered to bring another man to his service for every remaining year of his life if the god would show his hand and provide some chance for the Romans to regain their natural ascendancy over us. It seemed to him that the words were barely out of his mouth when the clouds started to gather . . . I chose to serve him, of course, and so joining his service to Mithras was only right.' Marcus nodded his understanding.

'And in return you're training him to fight the way that you do?'

The German gave him a strange look, then nodded.

'Yes. And he's a quick student . . . And you, Centurion, will you share your story with us?'

Marcus looked across the clearing at Dubnus, asleep in his cloak on the grass.

'I cannot tell you much, or you will both be in as great a danger as my friend there. I will tell you that I hope for little more than you have both achieved, to find some measure of peace after the events that have conspired to bring me here. I crave the ability to turn my mind to the future, rather than brooding on the past and dreaming of revenge.'

Qadir nodded his head, looking squarely into his centurion's eyes.

'That is a wise desire, Centurion Corvus. The lust for revenge can take over a man's life, and come to master him until it drives him to the exclusion of all other cares, but I can counsel you from my own experience that it bears little fruit other than bitterness and destruction. When I took a man's life as recompense for my personal loss, I found little in the act to compensate me for the price I was to pay for that moment of bloodlust.'

Once the sky above them was darkening to purple Marcus roused his men, many of whom had taken the chance to get some sleep before the long night before them, and set them to making their silent approach to the wall's defenders. After a few minutes' progress across the open hillside he realised with a start that he could hear almost nothing from the troops behind him. Intrigued, he peeled away from the line of march and squatted in the grass, watching and listening as the soldiers moved slowly past him. After a moment's contemplation of his men he realised with an even greater surprise that the men making the more audible noise as they progressed up the hill were not the Hamians, but the 5th Century men who were supposed to be their teachers in the art of night patrolling. He got back to his feet when the column's rear passed him, dropping in alongside Qadir and speaking quietly in his ear.

'Your men seem to have the measure of this, Chosen.'

The other man smiled at him through the evening's gloom.

'No need to be quite so surprised, Centurion. I told you that we are hunters by training, and that we spent much time hunting in the forests of Germania. These men all know what it means for their stealth to be the difference between eating and going hungry. And now I suggest that you make a little noise and return to your place at the head of the column. These men won't stop advancing until you tell them to.'

* * *

By the time the sun had set, and the moon had risen to take its place over the empty countryside, the main barbarian strength was already south of the rampart. The warband had crossed the frontier undetected through an abandoned mile fort between The Rock and White Strength, flowing unhindered out into the open ground behind the wall. Scouts led the warband to within a mile of White Strength, with Calgus and his bodyguard following close behind. Apparently undetected, the barbarians deployed quietly into and through the silent pine forest that ran to within two hundred paces of the fort's southern gate, silently closing the noose on the 800-man garrison without betraying their presence so close to their enemy's main line of defence. Calgus squatted down on his haunches at the forest's edge and the main tribal leaders gathered around him, their differences forgotten in the wake of his speech that morning.

Once the morning's gathering had broken up, and the leaders had gone to prepare their men for the march, Calgus's adviser Aed had given him a curious sideways glance.

'So my lord, do you *really* believe that if we destroy one legion the Romans will inevitably lose their grip on this entire province?'

Calgus had laughed softly, keeping his voice low enough to prevent his bodyguard from overhearing.

'Those fools needed something to fight for, so I gave it to them. The theory's sound enough, though. If we could destroy a legion, or hit them both hard enough to send them running south licking their wounds, then we'd give their governor a choice to make that he can't get right, no matter whether he chooses to retreat to the south or hold the line of their wall. And to make that happen I need warriors with fire in their hearts, not just a collection of men yearning for home.'

Now he watched the Roman fort with a careful eye, seeing the torch flames fluttering in the breeze blowing across its high stone walls.

'Eight hundred men just there for the taking. I'd say ten thousand of us ought to be able to knock one little fort over without very much trouble. What matters most is how we use the garrison once they're defeated.' He turned to the tribal leaders clustered around him, looking for one man in particular. 'Martos, your uncle and I have disagreed as to the right way to finish this war, but you and I have the chance to put our people in such a position of strength that no Roman general will have the ability to defeat us. Will you put the Votadini tribe's warriors alongside our own in this battle?'

The Votadini prince nodded decisively.

'I will, Calgus. My people will fight the Romans to the limit of our abilities. Tell me what you need from me . . . '

Calgus clapped him on the shoulder.

'I need your men to help smash our way into the fort, of course, but I also have in mind a means of getting the Romans to come after us with a rage upon them that will lead them blindly into the trap I am building for them. It will be dirty work, but if you can make the picture I have in my mind become a reality then nothing will restrain them from their need for revenge, or the consequences of such blind fury. The honour of provoking these usurpers to make their greatest mistake will be yours . . . '

* * *

The first indication Marcus had that his men were not the only force abroad in the darkened forest was the suddenness with which the Hamian walking alongside him froze into immobility, putting a hand across his centurion's chest and hissing a soft warning. The men behind them went to ground without needing to be told, and for a second he was left marvelling at their discipline, until the man alongside him ruined his feeling of well-being in an instant with a quiet whisper in his ear.

'Other men in forest. Not Roman. Hear speaking.'

Dubnus appeared at his other shoulder, sufficiently alert not to speak. The Hamian reached across and nudged him, pointing out into the darkness and then waggling two fingers in front of him to indicate moving men, miming a man talking by opening and closing his fingers close to his mouth. Dubnus whispered a quiet question.

'How many?'

The Hamian pulled a face to show he was guessing, then pointed back up the column before raising ten fingers, closing his hands and then opening them again. Marcus and Dubnus exchanged glances, the latter whispering again with an edge of incredulity.

'Thousands of them?'

Marcus nodded, putting a cupped hand to his ear to indicate that they should listen. The sounds were quiet, muted to the edge of inaudibility by the forest's foliage, but they were unmistakable. An army was crossing the forest in front of them, the sounds of snapping twigs and guttural voices reaching them through the trees.

The two friends exchanged glances again, and then Marcus turned back to the Hamian alongside them, bending to whisper in his ear.

'Fetch Qadir. Quick and quiet.'

The man nodded and was gone, ghosting away back down the column without a sound. Dubnus leaned close and spoke quietly in his ear.

'They must be moving to attack White Strength.'

Qadir appeared beside them a moment later, his face still imperturbable in the moon's faint illumination. Marcus beckoned his head close before whispering to him.

'Your men seem to have the edge when it comes to silent movement in the dark. Do any of them have what it takes to kill in the dark? Do we have any thieves, or murderers? I need a few men that won't be afraid to put a knife in a barbarian's back, and won't waste any time staring at the corpse. Well?'

Qadir pondered for a moment, and then whispered an order to the man next to him, who vanished off into the darkness.

'I have sent him to find two men who are of the background you desire. They have reformed, saved by the discipline demanded by their bows, that and the worship of their goddess, and both have renounced their former crimes. As have I.'

Marcus grinned wolfishly, his teeth a pale white in the shadows.

'Then let's hope I can persuade the three of you to revive your former selves for a short while. Dubnus, you'd best gather a few of your best men. And you . . . '

He turned and spoke to Arminius, who was waiting in silence three paces behind him.

'You'd better come too. We're going hunting.'

* * *

Only minutes later, just as the guard mounted at all corners of White Strength was changing, the sentries posted to watch out over the wall to the north reported lights on the horizon in increasing numbers. The cohort's prefect ran to the watchtower and took the stairs two at a time, the unit's first spear close at his heels. They pushed aside the gaggle of soldiers watching the distant, flickering dots of light, and took stock of what little they could make out in the darkness.

'Shit.' The prefect turned to his senior centurion. 'It's a warband all right, there's nothing of ours that large that would be running around by torchlight in the dark, moon or no moon. The decision is ours; we either abandon the fort and head for Noisy Valley or stay here behind our walls and make a fight of it.'

The centurion, a leathery twenty-five-year veteran, with less than a month to his discharge under normal circumstances, spat expressively over the tower's parapet.

'I say we stand and fight. I've already supervised the reconstruction of this bloody fort once this year, and I'll be damned if I want to have to do it all over again. Besides, that lot might just be a diversion to persuade us to run for it. For all we know there's thousands more of the bastards already south of the wall, and waiting for us between here and the legions at the Valley.'

The prefect grimaced at the thought of his command caught on an open hillside in the dark by a warband of barbarian warriors raving for their heads.

'I agree. You get the cohort stood to, and I'll write a dispatch for the governor. With a bit of luck we can keep the buggers tied up for long enough to let him manoeuvre two legions into position for the kill. You never know, this could be the action that finishes the war.'

* * *

The Tungrian hunting party went forward in total silence, and again Marcus was struck by the way that Qadir and his Hamians seemed to ghost through the darkness with an almost total lack of sound. Within a dozen careful paces they had taken the lead, padding softly through the darkened forest ahead of the Tungrians with delicate care for twigs or branches underfoot, their footfalls muffled by the carpet of pine needles. Somewhere off to their right an owl screeched, and the party froze into immobility for a long moment before starting off down the gentle slope again. After a few minutes' more careful progress the leading man raised his hand to halt them, and Marcus eased forward to crouch next to him.

'Many men, close. We stay here, listen, watch. Any closer, we be prisoner.'

Marcus nodded, signalling to the other men to

hold fast. To their front the sounds of the warband were ever more apparent as the barbarian raiders gathered their strength to attack. Dubnus leaned in close to whisper in the man's ear.

'They're waiting for something.'

Seconds later a horse's scream of agony rang through the woods, answered almost immediately by a roar of triumph from the tribesmen. Dubnus nudged Marcus, putting his head close to his friend's ear.

'Dispatch riders, most likely. The warband were waiting to capture the message for help. Those poor bastards are in for it now.'

Marcus nodded in response to his friend's bald statement.

'Stay here, I'm going forward for a look.'

Without allowing any time for argument he wormed forward on his stomach, crawling fifty paces or so until he reached a fallen tree. Where the tree's roots had been ripped from the soil by its fall, a wide plug of dry earth still clinging to their tangles, a dark hole had been formed between the trunk and the bowl-like depression left in the ground. He slithered silently into the gap, covering his head with his cloak and looking out at the ground on the other side of the fallen tree. The clearing before him was almost empty, with a knot of warriors dragging three struggling men across the needle-strewn forest floor. As he watched them the barbarians, a dozen strong, manhandled the trussed Romans to their feet and quickly lashed them to trees before cutting away their clothes to leave them naked and shivering in the cool night air. With a sick certainty Marcus watched as one of their captors unsheathed a knife, its polished blade a pale bar of moonlight in his hand, and stepped up to one of the captives. He thrust the blade deep into the captive's thigh without any warning, wringing a reluctant snarl of pain from the helpless man before pulling the bloodied knife free and dragging its blade across the man's eyes. If the man's first cry had been born of physical distress, torn reluctantly from him by the sudden unexpected pain, the scream that echoed through the forest as he was blinded was a howl of agonised despair.

* * *

With the dispatch riders away towards the south-west, the soldiers manning the fort's ramparts waited anxiously. The first spear watched impassively as the torches drew closer, counting under his breath. He stared ruminatively at the flickering lights, muttering to himself.

'Two hundred or so. Hardly seems enough for a full-sized warband. Say there's one torch for every ten of the bastards, that's more like . . . '

A shout from the fort's southern wall spun him round, staring out into the darkness. In the deep shadow of the woods to the fort's south, where the faint moonlight was unable to provide any illumination, a spark of light was bobbing along the line of trees. Every few seconds a new light would kindle in its wake, until the wood was alive with light. The first spear hurried down the tower's steps into the fort's bustle, calling the officers to him. They gathered to find him grim faced, one hand reflexively gripping the hilt of his gladius.

'We've been fooled. There's a warband in the woods to the south and it looks like they're getting ready to storm the gates . . . '

He issued a crisp stream of orders, sending a century to man the fort's south-facing wall, splitting another to guard those parts of the east and west walls to the south of the point where the fort's defences met the wall's line, and took the calculated risk of leaving only one more to man the fort's northern side. The prefect stood alongside him as, gathering the other three centuries to the southern gate's double arch, he arrayed the nervous soldiers on all three sides of the fort's most vulnerable point. The veteran officer shook his head ruefully.

'It's quite simple really, Prefect, they showed us the torches to the north to flush us out. The man leading that collection of savages out there knew that one of two things had to happen once we saw what looked like movement in strength to the north — either the full cohort retreating to the south, or our messengers heading for Noisy Valley. Either would be an acceptable result for the man commanding that warband, since all he ever had to do to bottle us up in this trap was kill our only means of getting a message through to the heavy boys. With our messengers almost certainly taken there's no way for the legions to know he's got our nuts between the bricks, and without the legions there'll be no escape for us. He's got the rest of the night to chop a way in through one of the gates, most likely this one, since the other three are all on the other side of the wall . . . ' He pointed to the twin south gates, their thick timbers reinforced with three heavy oak bracing bars apiece. 'It looks tough enough now, but they'll be hacking down a tree out there right now and getting it ready to swing at those doors. No gate can take that sort of treatment for long.'

The prefect frowned, weighing up their options.

'If their main strength is to the south surely we could still run to the east on the northern side of the wall. Standing orders specifically instruct all fort commanders not to waste lives defending fixed positions.'

The senior centurion rubbed a hand across his tired face, blinking away his fatigue.

'In the darkness, and with two or three thousand of them waiting out there to the north? I'd say we're better off taking our chances here, Prefect . . . ' He turned to the men gathered around the gate, raising his voice to make sure they all heard him. Men leaned out over the rampart's internal wall, keen to hear the man who ran their small world speak.

'Well now, my brothers, here's the thing. Those blue-faced bastards have pulled a nice little trick, got men to the south of us as well as the north. They're between us and Noisy Valley, so they're probably already carving up the messengers we sent that way. If you listen carefully you'll hear them screaming, most likely — it's what they always do with captives, partly to get the piss running down our legs and partly because, well, that's just what they do.'

He paused for a moment, looking around at the soldiers' serious faces in the flickering torchlight.

'This only ends one of two ways, gentlemen. Either we hold them off for long enough that the legions at Noisy Valley can get here and save our arses, or those barbarian bum-fuckers will manage to bludgeon their way in here, which is more than likely, and then try to overwhelm us in nasty, dirty street fighting. They have the advantage of numbers; we have discipline and superior equipment and training on our side. You all know the drills, all you have to do is follow them and we have a decent chance of getting out of the other side of this night with our heads still on our shoulders.'

He pointed up at the walls.

'Soldiers on the rampart, you'll have men with ladders looking to swarm up on to the walls. Your first priority is to push the ladders clear, and dump the bastards into the ditch, but watch out, they'll have archers behind them shooting at anything that moves. Any man that gets his feet on to the fighting surface is your number-one target, and you take him down with spear, sword or your teeth and nails if that's all you've got left.'

He took a breath, casting a jaundiced eye over the men standing around him, many of them looming over his stocky frame.

'Soldiers in the streets, once I've finished this

little speech you'll form a wall of men, from one side of the street to the other, and on all three sides of the gate. This is going to be street fighting, my lads, so no throwing your spears this time, I want ten blue-nose dead for every spear, not just one. Front rankers, tonight we fight in the old-fashioned style, spears held underarm and thrust up into bellies and throats from behind your shields. None of that overarm nonsense, you'll just open yourself up to a sword in your armpit. Rear rankers, if you can reach, you can go in overarm, but be careful not to stick it through your mate's ear. It may not endear you to him . . . '

The soldiers smiled wanly at the tired old joke, appreciating his effort under the circumstances.

'If you lose your spear, air your iron and take it to them in the usual way, short thrusts, throat, thighs or guts, it doesn't matter which, open your man up and step back to let him bleed to death. Nothing fancy, and no heroics. Rear rankers! If the man in front of you goes down, his place is yours, so don't wait to be asked. Jump in there and fight like you've got a pair, because if the line breaks you'll be the first one looking down the shaft of a barbarian spear that's scraping your spine.'

He looked around him, taking the measure of his men. In the moment of silence he distinctly heard a distant wail of agony from the treeline. As he had grimly predicted, the barbarians were torturing the captured messengers, using their screams of pain to send a message back to the fort's garrison.

'One more thing! You lot look like you'll run like frightened children the second that gate gets smashed in. It's simple enough! If we fight well enough to hold them off until dawn then we get to live, or at least some of us will. If there's anyone here that can't take a joke, well, it's a bit late to wish you hadn't joined. So let's give these blue-faced sheep-shaggers something to think about. You lot sing well enough when there's nothing at stake, let's see if you can belt it out when the blue-noses might have your heads off within the hour! Who'll start us off . . . ?'

A man on the wall above responded first, his voice ringing out clearly above the rattle of equipment from the street below.

'*The centurion took a message to the general's villa where . . .*'

The response from the cohort's men was instantaneous. They roared into the song, lifting the hair on the first spear's neck.

> ' . . . *he was greeted by the great man's wife, in face and body fair, Having given her the tablet he bowed and turned to leave, But found the lady's gentle hand had gripped him by the sleeve.*'

'Amazing . . . ' The senior centurion turned to find the prefect standing behind him. He leaned in close, shouting into his subordinate's ear as the second verse began, 'You've just told them that this is going to be the goat-fuck to end all goat-fucks, and they burst into song at the first opportunity. Perhaps we'll get away with this after all?'

The veteran officer nodded, leaning over to shout his own response over the cohort's enthusiasm.

'Perhaps. The song gives them something familiar to hang on to. Let's just pray they're still singing that loudly in an hour. And let's hope we can find the right god to ask for that small favour.'

* * *

Marcus hadn't waited to witness any more of the barbarians' torture of their prisoners, but headed back up the slope as fast as he could without making a noise that might betray him to the tribesmen. He looked around at the small group of soldiers, his face rigid with rage and his voice a furious whispered growl.

'They're torturing the message riders we heard them capture. There are twelve of the bastards, and eight of us. If they manage to warn their comrades that we're here then we'll probably all die to the last man, both centuries, but if we don't do *something* then those three men are going to die after several hours of that agony. Who's with me?'

Qadir drew his dagger from its sheath, holding it up to the moonlight.

'I'll come with you. We'll all come.'

Dubnus nodded.

'We've got three archers, so that's two shots apiece and six men down before they know what's happening and another six for the five of us. Seems fair enough.'

They crawled down the slope in silence, gritting their teeth to ignore the shouted pleas for mercy and screams of pain, as the barbarians were clearly warming to their role of making the message riders' torture painfully obvious to the men defending the fort. When they reached the fallen tree, Marcus set Qadir and his three bowmen along its length and ordered them to keep their heads down until he gave the signal, then led the remaining 5th Century men away in a low crawl to the right. The scene was now lit by several torches set in the ground around the trees to which the prisoners were tied, and the Tungrians took special care as they crawled slowly around the clearing's edge until they were between the scene of torture and the warband, then huddled for a last whispered briefing from Marcus.

'When I give the order, the Hamians will put two arrows into the air apiece. If we wait for them to stop shooting we'll likely be too late to avoid one or more of the survivors making a break into the forest, and if that happens we'll have minutes before there are hundreds of men combing these woods for us. So I've got a better idea . . .'

The barbarians were gathered around the last of the three message riders to have retained his consciousness, however much he might have preferred to have slipped into the merciful oblivion that had claimed his colleagues. Their hands bloody from their torment of the other two men, they were competing to see which of them could wring the loudest scream from their helpless prisoner, and were watching one of their number as he probed inexpertly at the root of the man's penis with his knife when a call from behind alerted them to the presence of newcomers.

'Who the *fuck* are you?'

The tallest of them strode out from the group with a swagger, backing up his challenge with his obvious bulk, while his comrades turned to back him up and crowded in behind him. The newcomers, four men huddled into their cloaks for warmth, stopped just inside the clearing's edge, the largest of them calling out a reply in their own language.

'We are sent by Calgus to help you.'

The torturer's leader stepped closer to them, waving them away dismissively.

'We have no need of help. Go back to the fight, if you have the balls for it . . . '

He stopped in his tracks as a series of muffled thumps reached his ears, turning back to see one of his men down and another two staggering away. As he stared uncomprehendingly another three of the torturers jerked with the impact of the unseen arrows hammering into their unprotected bodies. The newcomers dropped their cloaks to reveal their armour and weapons, and sprang forward with their swords ready to fight, but the barbarian had already realised his peril and turned away from their threat, sprinting for the clearing's far side and gathering his strength to hurdle the fallen tree that lay across his path, seeking escape into the night in search of help. A shadowy figure rose from the ground in front of him, sharp iron glittering in the moonlight, and the tribesman ripped his sword from its scabbard as he used the tree's trunk as a springboard for his attack, leaping at the other man with the blade held ready to strike. His opponent snarled and bounded forward to meet his charge, swinging his sword in an arc of razor-sharp iron.

Marcus ran toward the prisoners with both swords drawn, butchering a tribesman who turned to face him with a brutal hack of his spatha which cleaved the man's body from shoulder to breastbone before kicking him off the blade and turning in search of a fresh target for his rage. Another man ran for the forest behind the trees to which the prisoners were bound, but made barely a dozen paces before an enraged Scarface ran him down and sank his gladius between the fleeing tribesman's shoulders, while Dubnus charged into a pair of hapless barbarians with the heavy axe that was his habitual night patrol weapon. Smashing the butt of the axe's heavy wooden handle into the face of the nearest man and breaking his jaw with an audible crack, he dodged to the right to avoid a sword-blow from the other, cleaving his attacker's arm clean off at the elbow with a swing of the heavy blade. Spinning through a full circle, he lopped off the stricken barbarian's head and then swung the axe blade high before hacking it down into the reeling victim of his butt stroke, chopping his head almost in two and killing him instantly. He ripped the axe blade from the dead man's head as the one-eyed soldier known to his mates as Cyclops dragged the last man's body across the clearing and dropped it on to the ground next to them.

Marcus walked across to a writhing tribesman, the man's hands fretting at the arrow buried in his back, and dispatched him with a swift stab of his gladius, then looked over the corpses of the dead tribesmen and frowned.

'There were a dozen of them, I see only eleven dead men.'

Dubnus pointed at the fallen tree.

'One of them ran that way. Go and see for yourself.'

The barbarian group's leader was laying spread-eagled a dozen paces beyond the tree, while the three Hamians stood solemnly around him. Seeing their centurion approaching, they moved away to allow Marcus to view the body. The man's corpse was almost headless, only his neck and lower jaw remaining attached. A gout of blood had exploded down his chest, glistening black in the moonlight, and the rest of his head lay in the pine needles half a dozen paces from the rest of him.

'How did you . . . '

Qadir pointed silently to a dark figure standing in the shadows behind them.

Marcus nodded to Arminius and then turned back to the prisoners, still tied to their trees. Even the man that was still conscious was babbling meaningless gibberish at his rescuers, and the other two men were simply lolling against their ropes with no sign that they would regain consciousness any time soon. The barbarians had tortured them beyond their endurance, using their knives to ensure that the Romans would never be able to walk or use their hands again. The two unconscious men had endured the brutal ruin of their sexual organs, and all three had suffered dozens of knife cuts. The ground around the two unconscious men was sticky with their drying blood, and its coppery stench filled the air around them. Cyclops spat on the ground, shaking his head.

'We're too bloody late. They'd have been peeling the poor fuckers soon enough. All we've done is saved them from any more of these animals' fun.' He hefted his sword and stepped closer to the nearest of the three mutilated men. 'Best I do this quickly, young sirs . . . '

Marcus shook his head and pushed the blade aside.

'You're right, there's no way we can take them with us, but if there's a need to finish them off I'll not let another man do my job for me. Dubnus, take the men back to the century and I'll join you once I've seen these men across the river.'

His friend nodded and gathered the Tungrians, disappearing quickly and quietly back up the slope and into the darkened ranks of trees. Marcus sheathed his spatha, hefting the gladius and putting the short blade's point against the first man's ribs, angling it ready for the mercy stroke. A thought struck him, and he turned away to search the barbarians' bodies until he found a purse full of Roman coin on the big man that Arminius had beheaded. Taking three coins before discarding the purse, he moved quickly, pushing one of them into the unconscious man's mouth before repositioning the gladius.

'Go to your gods, my friend.'

He stabbed the sword through the message rider's ribs, expertly putting it through the man's failing heart and killing him instantly. A thin wash of blood trickled down the man's chest, testament to the amount he had already lost under the barbarians' knives, and he died with no more than an almost silent last exhalation of breath. Marcus moved to the second man, but found his skin cold and his eyes empty. He pushed a coin into the man's mouth, then looked across at the last of them to find the captive's eyes locked on the gladius in his hand.

'*Take me . . . with you.*'

Marcus shook his head sadly, hefting the sword as he spoke.

'The barbarians have left you a wreck, friend, severed your hamstrings and cut off your thumbs. Even if I could carry you to safety you'll never walk or hold a sword again. Better to die here with some dignity.'

A tear trickled down the message rider's cheek.

'*Make it qui . . .* '

He grunted with pain as Marcus struck fast and without warning, slamming the gladius into his chest and twisting it to make sure of the kill. The dying man's eyes stared into his own for a long moment, then rolled upwards as his spirit left him. Marcus stood in silence for a second before tucking the last of the three coins into the dead man's mouth and wiping and sheathing his sword. A voice from the shadows at the edge of the clearing spun him round, hands reaching for his swords.

'You are a good man, Centurion Corvus. Not many men would have taken the time to find coin and see these men safely across the river.'

Arminius stepped out of the gloom, his face sombre in the presence of the dead messengers.

'An unhappy passing, but you gave it all the dignity that was to be had. And now . . . '

He gestured up through the trees to where the two centuries would be waiting for them. Marcus nodded, but turned back towards the doomed fort.

'We should leave before we're discovered, I know. But I have to see it . . . '

The German nodded.

'Quietly, then. We go as far as the forest edge. Any closer and we may find ourselves in the same trouble as these poor bastards.'

6

The duty officer at Fine View fort, seven miles to the east of White Strength, frowned with concentration as he leaned out over the fort's western parapet, turning his head slightly in the hope of reducing the wind's whine as it ruffled the crest of his helmet.

'You're sure you heard a trumpet?'

His watch officer shifted uncomfortably.

'Certain, Centurion. It was the lad here that heard it first . . .'

He gestured to a soldier so young that his face was not yet darkened by any trace of a beard.

'I can still hear it, sir. Listen, there it goes again!'

The centurion grimaced, screwing his face up in concentration. There it was . . . just . . . barely audible over the wind's gentle moan.

'Fuck me, they're blowing the alarm signal. You, run for the first spear, tell him that White Strength is under attack!'

In the five minutes that it took for the senior centurion to make his way to the fort's rampart the distant trumpet calls had stopped. He stood on the wall and stared out to the west.

'The Frisians are in the shit, from the sound of it.' The first spear turned to his prefect. 'I doubt we'll need to evacuate before dawn, they'll be too busy trying to fight their way into the Strength, but you'd best order the preparations. We'll have to get word to Noisy Valley, though; they won't be seeing or hearing any of this given the lie of the land.'

His superior nodded and went to find his dispatch riders. The three men were waiting by their quarters, dressed and ready to ride.

'Well predicted, gentlemen. There seems to be some kind of attack going in at White Strength and we're going to need you to ride for Noisy Valley and get the legions into the fight.'

The small group's commander, a young decurion temporarily detached from the Petriana cavalry wing, his aristocratic bearing confirmed by the thin purple stripe decorating the sleeves of his tunic where they protruded from beneath his bronze breastplate, nodded his understanding.

'Yes, Prefect. I'll send these two east and then south, there's no way they'll get through to the west.'

The cohort's commander raised an eyebrow.

'Not riding out yourself, Decurion?'

The young man smiled easily, pulling on his helmet and fastening the strap tightly under his chin.

'Oh yes, sir, I'm riding, just not to the east. I said these two wouldn't make it, but then neither of them's riding my horse.'

His superior stepped closer, looking the decurion up and down.

'Are you completely fucking mad, young man? If you ride to the west those bastards will have you dangling by your ankles with your balls in your mouth before sunrise.'

The cavalryman smiled again, his eyes steady on the prefect's.

'It will take until well after daybreak for these two to get through to Noisy Valley, by which time White Strength will be finished and those barbarians might well be knocking at your door too, eh, Prefect? I can probably make the ride in about two hours, and with a bit of luck the blue-noses won't know I'm coming until I'm past them.'

The prefect nodded slowly, putting out a hand.

'My apologies, Cornelius Felix, I'd taken you for something of a fop. If you get away with this you'll have a place in the histories for centuries to come.'

The younger man took his hand, then tapped the hilt of his sword, the torchlight glinting off its gold and silver decoration.

'And if I don't, at least I'll go down fighting. Mind you, I won't be the blue-noses' biggest problem if they catch up with us. Have you *seen* the chaos Hades can cause when the wicked bugger starts kicking?'

* * *

The defence of White Strength had begun well enough for the garrison's men. They had waited under cover of the fort's walls until the attacking barbarians had carried their improvised battering ram up to the gates, by means of ropes tied around the stripped trunk sufficiently loosely to allow them to be lifted. With the ram directly beneath them, ready to be swung at the gates, they had rained a hail of heavy stones down on to the heads of the men swinging the tree trunk. Dozens of the tribesmen had fallen under the barrage, and when more of them had rallied to the faltering attack, a shower of oil heated to the point of boiling by fires built into the fort's walls had sent them away in screaming agony. For a few minutes it had seemed that the barbarian onslaught would fail, but a fresh group of attackers had quickly discovered that the gate's initial defence had all but exhausted the supply of both stones and oil, and had set to swinging the heavy ram with gusto, while archers peppered the rampart above their comrades with arrows as soon as any of the defenders showed themselves. Even as the left-hand door of the twin archways started to disintegrate under the ram's crunching impacts, and the soldiers waiting in the streets below shifted nervously in their defensive lines around the point of attack with their shields held up against the rain of arrows coming over the southern wall, warning shouts rang out from the fort's northern side.

The first spear ran from his place behind the centuries waiting around the straining gate, his view of the fort's northern side blocked by the buildings between him and the source of the sudden commotion. As his field of view to the fort's northern wall opened up he stopped and stared, aghast at what he was seeing. Along the fort's thinly manned north wall barbarian warriors were climbing over the parapet from what appeared to be a dozen siege ladders. The outnumbered defenders were fighting back bravely enough, their swords flickering in the moonlight as they struggled to hold back the tide of attackers, but there was already a knot of tribesmen holding out against attacks from both sides of the fort's north-west corner, and more warriors climbing over the wall behind them with every passing second. Turning to shout to the nearest of his officers, the first spear's eye was caught by a flicker of light in the sky above the north wall. In a flurry of flame a shower of fire arrows arced in over the fort's defences, the missiles impacting in showers of sparks across its northern side. While most of the arrows would strike the buildings' tiled roofs or the paved streets, a few, he knew from grim experience, would inevitably hit the wooden frames around which the barrack blocks were built. Another volley of blazing arrows hammered down into the fort, breaking the spell that had frozen him in place for a moment. He spun back to bellow an order at the men waiting for orders on the walls to east and west.

'*Fourth Century, get your arses on to the north wall and throw those bastards back where they came from!*'

As the century hurried along the fort's walls to confront the new threat, he stalked back to the men clustered around the gate, putting the fire attack to the back of his mind. He hooked a thumb back over his shoulder towards the growing flames, shouting to the prefect over the fire's crackling and popping.

'Fire arrows from the north. We'll have to let

the old place burn, we've got no men to spare to fight it. All we have to do is keep the cohort alive through the night, nothing else matters. We've rebuilt the barracks once this summer already; we can do it again just as long as we can survive until morning. Besides, at least we get to fight in the warm for a while . . .'

The southern gateway's left-hand arch, sorely tested by repeated blows from the barbarians' improvised ram, burst open with a weary groan of tearing timbers. The doorway stood open to the darkness beyond, but for a moment there was no flood of attackers through the ruined defences, rather a moment's unnatural quiet as both attackers and defenders gathered themselves for the fight. In that brief instant of peace the shouts and screams from the north wall seemed like no more than the rumour of a distant battle, disconnected from the havoc about to break on the grim-faced centuries clustered ready to defend their tiny world. A soldier in the front rank hawked loudly and then spat on the ground in front of the defenders, shouting a challenge into the night.

'*Come on, then, you blue-nosed sheep-fuckers! Let's be having you!*'

As if the barbarians outside the gate had been waiting for the challenge, and as the echoes of his shout died away, a wave of tribesmen stormed through the opened gateway and threw themselves on to the defenders' shields. Other men hacked away the bracing that was keeping the right-hand door secure. The second arch was open within a minute, despite the high price in blood the defenders made the men fighting to open it pay for the privilege. Hacking at the soldiers with their long swords, the barbarians made easy targets for the expertly wielded spears striking into their mass from all three sides of the gate. Their first attack foundered in a welter of dead and dying men, as wounded and dying warriors staggered away from the Roman line in sprays of their own blood.

The prefect shouted encouragement into his senior centurion's ear.

'We're holding them!'

The veteran officer grimaced, ducking as an arrow struck his helmet and clattered to the ground.

'Early days, Prefect, early days. I'm going up to the north wall, see if we've . . . '

A shout from the fort's south wall, almost directly above them, made them both crane their necks. Fresh enemy warriors were climbing over the southern defences, gaining footholds on the wall all the more easily in the absence of the men sent to repel the attack on the fort's north side. Their archers filled the air to either side of them with flying iron to impede the defenders' attempts to get at their ladder. A soldier fell from the parapet with an arrow lodged in his throat, thumping heavily to the cobbles beside the officers. In the space of a minute there were fifty men on the wall's broad fighting platform and the defending soldiers were clearly already on the back foot. They were fighting not so much to evict attackers but simply to hold their ground against the inexorable build-up of warriors now pouring over the southern wall in three places. As the officers watched helplessly, one of the barbarians slung his spear down into the defenders' ranks with a triumphant shout, piercing a defenceless soldier's neck from back to front and dropping him like a sack of beans in a fountain of his own blood.

The first spear shouted into his superior's ear to be heard above the clamour of combat.

'They've got the fucking walls. We either pull back or stay here and let them shower us with iron until we're too weak to resist.'

The other man nodded his understanding.

'Fall back, there's no choice.'

His subordinate grimaced, waving a hand at the scene before them.

'A fighting retreat. With the enemy coming on like vicus drunks. This is going to be fun . . . '

He bellowed above the fight's noise, keeping a wary eye on the barbarian warriors gathering on the wall above him.

'*Centurions, to me*!'

⋆ ⋆ ⋆

Cornelius Felix rode west at a measured pace, using the light from the moon overhead to follow the road to the west as it ran parallel to the south of the wall. The big horse beneath him was skittish, unaccustomed to working in the dark, and its ears pricked forward and twitched at every tiny noise. After several miles the road climbed a gentle ridge, providing him with a good view of the neighbouring fort, seemingly afloat in the sea of torchlight from the surrounding attackers. The black stallion beneath him pawed at the ground impatiently, made nervous by the darkness and clearly eager to run. White Strength fort seemed adrift in a sea of flames, from both the blazing buildings within the walls and the hundreds of blazing torches clustered around them. As he watched, a volley of fire arrows arced over the fort's walls. In the night's quiet air, the wind having fallen away to nothing for a moment, he could just make out the distant sound of singing. He listened for a moment, then muttered quietly to himself as he spurred the horse on down the track.

'Well, if you men have still got the balls to sing a marching song with that many blue-noses battering at your gates, I'm sure I've got enough to make one quick run past you. Come on, Hades, you cantankerous bastard, let's go for a gallop and see where it gets us.'

He urged the horse forward, using the reins to hold the big animal's speed down to a fast trot as they closed the gap to the embattled fort, all the while calculating when to unleash the power rippling through the horse's flesh beneath him. With half a mile left to run he bent to speak into the horse's ear.

'Right then, my lad, if there was ever a time for you to prove you're not just an evil sod that likes biting grooms, this is it!'

He touched his spurs to the horse's flanks again, easing his tight grip on the reins to allow Hades to gradually accelerate his pace until they were cantering nicely and then, when it seemed impossible for them to go unnoticed for another second by the mob of tribesmen now swarming around and into the fort, he kicked the big horse's flanks hard and bellowed encouragement. Clamping his thighs to the animal's flanks he rose slightly from the saddle as the stallion responded with an exhilarating acceleration to its full speed, a bounding gallop that catapulted horse and rider along the stretch of road that ran past the fort's southern walls.

They were spotted almost immediately, guttural warning cries alerting the archers closest to the big horse's path, who swung to fire the next volley of fire arrows not into the burning fort, but at the unknown rider flying past them faster than most of them had ever seen a horse move. Most of the arrows flew too high, archers accustomed to shooting over the fort's wall failing to adjust their aim sufficiently, but one flaming shaft streaked in low, shooting across the horse's nose with barely a hand's span to spare, and the big animal baulked for a moment. Fighting the momentarily terrified beast for control, Felix jabbed his spurs into its flanks with savage intent, firing the animal across the firelit ground in a foam-mouthed charge, both horse and rider intent on nothing more than escaping the rain of fire arrows. One missile hissed unseen past the decurion's head and another rebounded from his helmet, the incendiary weapons now replaced by the evilly barbed iron-headed hunting arrows that the archers intended showering on to the defenceless garrison once their stock of fire arrows was exhausted. The horse lurched in mid-stride as a dart buried itself deep in its shoulder, lunging sideways away from the source of the pain until the decurion pulled it back straight. Despite the arrow's impact the beast charged on, if anything made faster by the wound's pain. A final flurry of arrows whipped past the fleeing horseman, and the last of them found its mark, punching up into his unprotected armpit as he leaned forward over the horse's neck, and nearly unseating him with the impact. Almost insensible with the enervating shock, Felix slumped across the galloping horse's neck and hung on to its mane with the last of his strength, as the pair were swallowed up by the surrounding darkness.

The big horse slowed, feeling its rider's weight across its heavy neck, and turned its head to look at the decurion through the delicately decorated armour that covered its long nose and eyes. The officer rallied his strength, his entire right side numb with the pain of the arrow's protrusion up under his arm and only his good arm's grip on the reins keeping him from slipping from the saddle. A figure loomed out of the darkness and the wounded horse reared its head in surprise, only to find its movement restrained by a strong grip on its bridle. Cornelius Felix reached left handed for the hilt of his sword, but found his hand restrained by a strong grip that the pain of his wound left him powerless to resist. He slumped on to the horse's neck, hanging on for dear life as the animal reluctantly followed its unknown captors into the forest's moonless gloom.

* * *

In the burning fortress the Frisian cohort had retreated from their walls, those men not already felled by barbarian arrows and spears fighting their way back into the fort's centre to mount a desperate last defence against attackers now railing at their shields from all sides. For every warrior that fell to their spears another two implacable enemies came through the gates, and when the barbarians had gained first a foothold on, and then control of, the fort's south wall, and began to shower the troops with spears from above, the first spear had had no choice but to order a retreat. Fighting his way back through the tight streets with his men, he had been one of the first to fall to his knees with an arrow buried in his calf, decapitated an instant later by the barbarians pressing hard against the retreating troops.

Bereft of their leader, the auxiliaries had fought on under the prefect's command, the senior officer donning a soldier's helmet and shield to take his place in the line, but now they were being steadily ground down by the ceaseless attacks coming from all sides as they consolidated into an increasingly beleaguered defensive square at the fort's heart, in front of the burning headquarters.

'Barely two hundred of us still standing now.'

A panting centurion, the last officer still fighting other than the prefect himself, gave his superior a weary look and nodded agreement. The prefect grimaced from the pain of flesh wounds in his right thigh and arm, baring his teeth in a snarl of frustration.

'We fight on. There's still a chance that the legions at Noisy Valley have got wind of this. If they moved out an hour ago they could be here in minutes . . . ' The centurion's face was blank with battle shock, his eyes alone betraying the combination of hope and disbelief that flickered in his otherwise reeling mind. 'So we fight on. My turn in the line, I think, you take a moment to get your breath back. If I go down then it'll be up to you to rally these men, and to hold on as long as you can.'

The centurion nodded, raising his sword in salute as the prefect, his teeth bared in a snarl of defiance, stepped into the square's thinning line one last time, parrying a barbarian spear-thrust with his borrowed shield before gutting the weapon's owner with a blow that would have made the dead first spear nod with quiet admiration. The cohort's remnant fought on in silent exhaustion, their meagre perimeter shrinking by the minute as the barbarians crowded in, eager to kill before the fight ended. The officer parried another attack, shouting above the barbarians' clamour to his men.

'One last song, lads, show these bastards we're not done yet! 'The General's Wife'!'

He led the song off, smiling grimly as the soldiers responded to the familiar words of the first verse, their voices momentarily drowning out the guttural cries of the tribesmen baying for their blood. The cohort's remnant fought on with desperate purpose, hemmed in by the press of their enemies as the barbarians remorselessly tightened their grip on the remaining defenders. The centurion straightened his helmet and stepped into the line alongside his prefect, filling his lungs to belt out the song's last verse.

> '*Our hero like a gentleman inclined his head once more, And wondering who was booked in next he headed for the door, On leaving the house to his surprise he found an impatient queue, His chosen man, watch officer and his clerical writer too!*'

The two men shared a moment of unspoken understanding, the fact of their vastly different origins rendered meaningless by desperate circumstance. The prefect tipped his head to the centurion, lifting his shield a fraction as the barbarians massed just beyond sword-reach and readied themselves for their final assault. A voice rang out above the warband's baying clamour, and the tribesmen fell silent. From behind the barbarian line the voice called again, this time speaking perfect Latin, to the prefect's astonishment.

'Soldiers of Rome, I am Calgus, Lord of the Northern Tribes. I have taken your messengers, burned out your fort, and reduced your strength to a shadow of its former pride with only a small portion of my army. Your position is hopeless, and in a few minutes you will all be dead, or dying in ways that will make you beg for death. If you surrender now, you can spare yourself such indignity. You have fought well against impossible odds, but there will be no rescue for you. No word of this dirty little battle will have reached your legions yet, they still lie asleep behind their walls at Noisy Valley, and you truly are alone in the dark. Surrender to me, soldiers, and renounce your service of the empire and I guarantee you will not die here . . . '

Prefect and centurion shared another glance, the senior officer raising a questioning eyebrow, his grim amusement obvious. There was no way that the surrender of a Roman of the equestrian class, so obviously advertised by his purple-edged tunic, would be greeted with anything other than protracted torture from which his eventual death would be a welcome relief. The centurion spat on the blood-slickened cobbles, then called back to the unseen speaker.

'You bastards just want some prisoners to make sport with. We'll not die now, I'll give you that, but you'll drag us away to the hills for a more leisurely game than you'll get here. If I'm going to die then it'll be with a sword in my hand, and with as many of you dead as I can manage before you put me down, not with my dick sawed off and my eyes pulled out in some forest clearing. Now fight or fuck off, before the legions turn up and bend you over for a good shagging, you blue-nosed turd punchers!'

The prefect nodded his respect, looking around at his men and raising his voice to be heard in turn.

'Well said, Centurion. Let's show this barbarian scum how Roman soldiers fight to the bitter end.'

Calgus spoke again, his voice light with amusement.

'Very well. If death is what you desire, I shall grant your wish.'

His voice hardened as he barked out an order in his native language, the waiting warriors pressing forward to swing their swords down on to the tightly packed soldiers, while others thrust their spears into the gaps opened as the defenders lifted their shields to fend off the fierce sword-blows.

* * *

Calgus stood in the ruins of the shattered fort, pulling his cloak over his face against the reek of smoking timbers. His bodyguard had spread out round him, stabbing down into the fallen auxiliary troops whose corpses still littered the narrow streets of White Strength to ensure that none of the fallen soldiers was faking death. The combined stench of burnt wood, blood and faeces was overpowering even through the cloak's rough material, the bodies of the defeated Romans littering the ground in increasingly tight circles centred on the piled corpses of their last stand. The Votadini warriors he had put at the front of the assault were busy taking heads and searching for booty, but Martos spotted Calgus and called his men to attend their leader. They stood and gathered around him, bloodied but proud of their victory. Calgus stared around him with evident pride.

'Warriors, you have struck a huge blow at our

enemy! A whole cohort of their traitors torn to pieces! Another of their forts made useless to them, and another piece of their defences burned out. Mark my words, the soldiers to the east of this place will be clenching their arses when they see the smoke from this victory rising into the sky come the dawn!'

He pulled his sword from his hip and punched it into the air.

'*Victory!*'

The warriors gathered around him echoed the shout in a mighty roar. He sheathed the blade, clasping arms with Martos.

'Well done, Prince Martos, well done indeed. Your men have proved themselves, despite the mutterings of some of the men around my council fire. The Votadini will be in the front rank of the great plan that will have these Roman bastards off our land for good, and you, my friend, are going to be the man your people will praise for your victory. All that remains now is for you to complete the job, as we discussed. I'll leave a small party of my men to guide you back to the forest when you're done . . . and be assured, you're part of my plans for the future of this country once we've smashed their remaining strength.'

Martos nodded his gratitude, turning to encourage his men in their last grisly task. Calgus moved away with a quiet smile of satisfaction, heading for the fort's gates and the road back to the warband's forest encampment. At the gates a single figure detached itself from the shadows and stood waiting for him. The man was reed thin, with only a short sword to burden him.

'My lord.'

'You know what to do. Don't fail me.'

⋆ ⋆ ⋆

The gate guards standing guard duty on Noisy Valley's northern gate tumbled sleepily out of the warmth of their guardhouse, their haste encouraged by their centurion's shouts and liberally applied vine stick as he chivvied them up on to the fort's wooden walls.

'Get your fucking helmets on and get ready to fight, there's something coming down the road! You, go and get the first spear! *Run!*'

The sounds were distant, sometimes lost in the wind, but distinctive enough, boots and hoofs clattering on the road's paving stones. The soldiers peered out anxiously over their shields, hefting their spears and looking for something to throw them at. The centurion strained to make out more detail in the uncertain light of the torches fixed over the wall's parapet.

'They're ours! Get the gate open and get them inside!'

Two hundred men and more clattered through the briefly opened gates, their centurion raising a weary hand to the guard century's officer, who was staring at the arrow protruding from the right flank of the horse he was leading. The horse's rider was apparently more dead than alive, slumped unconscious in the saddle with his dangling right arm black with blood. The centurion spoke with quiet authority, watching as his exhausted men marched into the safety of the fort's walls.

'Good morning, Centurion, I'm Tribulus Corvus, centurion, First Tungrian cohort. White Strength fort has been attacked by a force I estimate to be several thousand strong. The barbarians were shooting fire arrows and had broken through the gate when I last saw it . . . '

The unconscious rider groaned softly, his arm dripping blood on to the road's surface.

'Mars, look at all that blood, it's a wonder you got him this far.' The guard centurion turned away, barking orders at his men. 'Bandage carrier, get something round that arrow and put some pressure on it or he'll be dead before we get him to the hospital. Chosen, you look after this lot, I'd better get the first spear and the prefect out of their beds. The war's back on again!'

* * *

The eastern sky was showing the first signs of the dawn's onset by the time the toiling Votadini tribesmen had completed their grisly task, and the tribes' warriors were eager for the command to run for the forest's safety. A trio of Selgovae warriors stood ready to guide them, their leader a painfully thin man clearly well accustomed to covering ground at speed. Martos strode over to the man, gesturing with a hand to the north.

'Our task is complete. Now we must make haste, before their cavalry find us here.'

The leader of the guides nodded respectfully.

'Then follow me, my lord, and I will lead you as instructed by my lord Calgus.'

The warriors ran for a short time to the west, until they reached the gate through which they had breached the wall hours previously, then spilled through the small opening and headed north in a long column, following the bobbing torches carried by their guides. As the night lightened to reveal a thick blanket of early morning mist, making the direction of their travel almost impossible to discern, Martos ran forward to join the guides. They were jogging easily, he noted, where his own men, their energy nearly exhausted by the harrowing battle for the fort, were staggering along in their wake, barely managing to keep up with the easy pace being set for them.

'You're sure you know we're on the right track? I can't tell where we are.'

The lead guide nodded confidently.

'We planned for this, my lord; I've left marks to guide our steps. About another fifteen miles, I'd say.'

Satisfied, the young chieftain dropped back to give his men the news, but as the column of men ground their way towards safety he still frequently stared out into the impenetrable murk, visibly unhappy at his lack of control of their situation. At length the guides indicated that the warband should stop for a rest break. The Votadini warriors gratefully fell out of the line of march and sat down in the pale shadows of the trees that lined the rough track they were following, chests heaving for breath as they tipped the last of their drinking water down parched throats. The Selgovae guides stayed on their feet, their leader pacing cautiously forward into the still-thick mist while his comrades stared back down the column's length with faces set in stoic immobility. One of the tribe's family chieftains limped tiredly up the column after a few minutes, an older man walking respectfully behind him.

'My man here reckons we're off our path, my lord.'

Martos raised an eyebrow, gesturing to the mist around them. Behind him, unnoticed by the resting warriors, the two remaining guides exchanged significant glances and began to step carefully backwards into the mist, keeping their gazes fixed on the tribal leader's back.

'And how can he tell, in this?'

The peasant warrior came forward, bowing his respect. His hair was grey, and his features seamed with lines, but his eyes were bright with intelligence.

'Lord, I grew up on this ground many years ago. I know my own country, lord, and I just sat down by a tree I used to climb as a lad. I know every inch of that tree, and I . . . '

'Yes. You know where we are. So where are we?'

'If we're heading back to the forest we came from, I'd say we're too far to the west, my lord, ten miles too far.'

Martos frowned, turning to the place where the guides had stood a moment before, only to find it empty. The sound of mocking laughter sounded from the mist, and his clan leader stared angrily into the mist beside him, a hand clenched on his sword's hilt.

'We're betrayed, my lord. Those Selgovae bastards have led us out to the west, not to the north. They've hung us out for the Roman cavalry to find out here. The second this mist lifts we'll stand out like ticks on an ox's back, and we're probably only ten miles from their camp.'

Martos spat his disgust into the dirt.

'Aye, and our people are exhausted. It will take us all day to reach the forest in this state . . . '

The older tribesman stepped forward, his head still inclined respectfully.

'If I may, my lord, I know of somewhere we might find a hiding place, less than a mile from here. If their first sweep misses us, perhaps we'll be able to reach the forest tonight.'

Martos nodded unhappily.

'It's not much of an option, but it's probably the best chance we've got. And if we do reach the forest I'll hunt Calgus down and carve him to ribbons for this.'

* * *

Calgus arrived back in the barbarian camp in the middle of the afternoon, riding in at the head of his bodyguard, having left the rest of the warband marching in his wake. Aed was waiting for him at the camp's gateway, falling in alongside the barbarian leader as he jumped down from his horse.

'Success, my lord?'

'Complete success. As we discussed it, both the Roman garrison and the Votadini dealt with.'

'King Brennus has been asking for news of his men since sunrise. I think he may have realised just how vulnerable he is with his warriors out of the camp.'

Calgus drew his sword, an angry scowl twisting his face.

'I'll bring him *news*, once my men have ripped through his bodyguard. I'll take that sour old bastard by the throat and tell him how I've left his men for the Romans to make sport with. Then I'll take my knife and carve out his . . . '

Aed put a cautionary hand on his master's arm.

'It *might* be better, my lord, if the king were to be unmarked when the remaining nobles see his body? You can claim that his bodyguard attacked you when they realised their king was dead, and if there's no sign of violence you can argue with a straight face that he died a natural death, and that their attack and subsequent deaths were a tragic misunderstanding. He was an old man, after all . . . '

Calgus nodded grimly, turning for the short walk uphill to the king's tent and gesturing for his men to follow him.

'I'll smother the old bastard, then. It's time to make King Brennus regret the day he ever questioned my judgement . . . '

* * *

The 20th Legion returned an hour before dusk, the troops solemn in their unaccustomed silence, and the 6th came through the gates as the sun dipped to kiss the horizon, two auxiliary cohorts in column with them. First Spear Frontinius watched the sullen-faced legionaries march tiredly through the gates.

The two legions had headed north with swift and brutal efficiency just before dawn, the leading cohorts pounding out through the gates at the double march less than half an hour after the arrival of the Tungrians. Ordered to make their maximum speed to the embattled fort, and to engage and destroy any barbarian forces they encountered, the legionaries had sallied without their packs and carrying poles to let them sustain the punishing double march for as long as required, taking their bread and water ration on the move to save precious time. The auxiliaries had been left to guard the fortress for the few hours that the legions were in the field, while the army's two cavalry wings had ridden out shortly afterwards to scout beyond the wall, and seek any sign of where the barbarian warband might be hiding in the wake of the attack on White Strength.

The first spear watched the returning soldiers for long enough to identify the auxiliaries marching alongside them.

'The Vangione and Cugerni cohorts. That's Fine View and Aelian Bridge evacuated, then, but no Frisians . . . Julius, call a centurions' conference and brief our brother officers that we'll be on the road at first light tomorrow.

Anyone that needs anything to be ready for war had better get their shit in a pile double quick. If I'm any judge of men those lads have seen something that they didn't like very much, and I don't think our new governor's the type to let an atrocity go unanswered. And send a runner to the prefect. Now that the eagles have come back to roost we'll be called to a senior officers' briefing soon enough, I expect.'

They were. As ordered, the auxiliary cohort prefects gathered in the fort's headquarters, where the grim-faced governor and his legates were waiting for them, both men's cloaks and boots still spattered with mud. Once the officers were settled in the chairs set out for them the governor stood, his face more stony than usual.

'You'll be aware that White Strength was attacked last night, and that both legions went forward at full strength to attempt the garrison's relief. What you don't know is what they found when we got to the fort. Legatus Equitius, you were leading, you'd best tell it.'

The Tungrians' former prefect rose, looking across the gathered prefects and first spears with a bleak stare.

'We advanced on White Strength in haste, but with three cohorts abreast where possible, a front broad enough to hold the barbarians if they chose to attack us out of the ruins of the fort. We could see the flames from three miles out, probably past their worst but still licking at the sky. We crested the last ridge and I ordered a halt, and a deployment to battle formation. The ground around the fort was teeming with lights, hundreds of torches, which we mistakenly assumed was the warband waiting patiently for us to arrive. Twentieth Legion deployed to support us, and to refuse any attack from either flank, and then I ordered the Sixth forward in a deliberate attack, slow enough to detect any traps or ambush. The way down to face them was clear of anything that might have obstructed our advance, or any sign of hostile intent, and I was soon pretty sure that there were no tribesmen waiting for me at White Strength, although that didn't explain the torches still burning around the fort . . . ' He paused for a moment, rubbing his tired face with one hand.

'I rode forward to join the lead centuries, curious to understand the point of the display. We were perhaps three hundred paces from the fort when I guessed the truth of the matter, and half that when I realised with a sick heart that my suspicion was justified.'

The officers leaned forward to hear his voice as it sank close to the point of inaudibility with the memory's apparent power. 'The torches on which we were advancing were not, you might have guessed by now, simple brands left burning to guide us to the scene of the Frisian cohort's massacre. They were human bodies . . . ' The legatus shook his head with the memory. ' . . . human bodies, stripped and then impaled on wooden stakes, painted with pitch and set on fire. An entire five-hundred-man cohort slaughtered and then used as a demonstration of our enemy's appalling brutality in victory.'

He fell silent for a moment, staring at his

boots, then spoke again, turning to the governor and inclining his head respectfully. 'Believe me, sir, when I tell you that there's no desire in my head to tell you how we should fight, but be assured that my legion will be eager for blood when we face these bastards across a battlefield. Sixth Legion has sworn to Mars Cocidius and Jupiter that we will take these men down whenever and wherever the opportunity presents itself.'

Legatus Macrinus stepped forward, his face dark with a thunderous rage.

'As has the Twentieth.'

The governor took the floor, looking across his gathered officers and taking stock of their facial expressions and body language.

'So, gentlemen, our enemy has raised the stakes quite dramatically. In the space of a day he has confirmed that his army is still in the field, he has destroyed an entire cohort and burned out yet another wall fort. He has our men desperate for the chance to slip their collars and run wild at his warriors. As a statement of intent it's dramatic enough, but as a device to tempt us off our own ground, and away from the strengths that will win us this war, it's masterful.' He looked around the briefing, seeing thoughtful looks start to take hold among his subordinates. 'We will find that warband, and we will take their heads and leave the remainder for the crows, that I promise you, but we'll do these things in our usual disciplined manner. There will be no rash gestures, not by our soldiers and most certainly not by anyone in this room. Any man here that breaks this rule, or even connives at its circumvention, will be stripped of his rank and sent back to Rome for punishment. Are we clear?'

The officers nodded soberly, recognising the truth in Ulpius Marcellus's harsh words.

'Good. Make sure that message reaches all corners of your commands, along with this. I will sacrifice to the gods alongside them in thanks for bloody revenge when we find and flatten this gang of savages under our hobnailed boots, but that victory will be gained in the tried and tested way, fighting in line and taking our enemies' lives while offering none of our own in return. That's all . . . '

A flurry of activity in the headquarters' entrance hall turned the assembled officers' heads. A familiar figure strode into the room, his ornate helmet held under one arm. His age-lined, hawkish features were alive with the joy of the moment, a man in his prime doing what he loved most. He walked quickly to the front of the room, snapping off a salute to the governor and nodding to his friend Equitius.

'Tribune Licinius? I presume the Petriana wing has news for us, given your unexpected entrance?'

Licinius nodded confidently.

'Governor, my men remain in the field, standing guard around a detachment of the enemy who seem to have lost their way. There are fifteen hundred of them, more or less, camped in an old hill fort less then ten miles away from here as the crow flies. We came upon them in the late afternoon, as we patrolled back towards the wall. We must have been in too much of a hurry when we passed them on the way out, but they're bottled up well enough for now, I had the horns blown long and hard enough to bring the Augustan wing to join us, so we ought to be able to keep them there overnight.'

The governor looked to his legates.

'Well, gentlemen, perhaps our prayers are answered.'

Equitius frowned.

'I can see no good reason for any barbarian to be anywhere other than tucked up safely in whatever hide they've built in the deep forest, well to the north. Taking up a position so close to the wall is tantamount to suicide . . . or sacrifice.'

'You suspect a trap?'

Equitius nodded, looking to his fellow legatus for support.

'There's something not right with this. No leader in his right mind would choose to put his men in such a trap unless he expected to have his chestnuts pulled out of the fire. My instinct is to take this gift, but to make very sure that we screen the attacking force with overwhelming strength, just in case these trapped men are bait in a larger plan.'

Ulpius Marcellus nodded decisively.

'I agree. Let's grind these unfortunates into mince, gentlemen, and give our men something to cheer about.'

* * *

Frontinius walked back to the Tungrians' section of the camp deep in thought, his mind dwelling on the slaughter inflicted on the Frisian cohort, men he had soldiered alongside for half of his life. The mood in the cohort's lines was more anger than sorrow, attitudes hardening as the manner of their comrades' slaughter and the defilement of their corpses sank in. The news that a woman had been killed in the fort's vicus the previous evening, raped and then strangled in the opinion of Clodia Drusilla, barely merited a mention in their conversations alongside the enormity of this latest barbarian atrocity. Julius was waiting for him in the command tent, pacing impatiently around the small space with a hand on his sword.

'We're marching in the morning, yes?'

The first spear nodded, dropping his helmet on the table.

'Yes. We've got an appointment to destroy a warband that the Petriana have bottled up north of the wall, unless they've allowed the barbarians to slip away in the meantime. We'll not be back in camp until we've found Calgus and taken our iron to him and his murdering savages, I'd say. The next few days are going to be more than exciting enough for a pair of old soldiers like you and me. And now I'd better go and make sure that Morban's found someone to look after his grandson. The last thing we want is for the poor sod to be worrying about the boy when things are getting hectic.'

* * *

The army marched soon after dawn the following day, each of the two legions supplemented by auxiliary cohorts to make up two forces ten thousand men strong, each with the legion's cavalry thrown out in front of them to provide a screen against the threat of a barbarian ambush. The 20th Legion turned east a mile south of the wall, shaking out on to a wide front and heading for the charred wreckage of White Strength, while the 6th Legion and its supporting cohorts, including both the 1st and 2nd Tungrians, headed on north through the gate where the road met the wall. Scaurus had briefed his officers fully, making clear their part in the next day's plan.

'The governor's decided to clear the ground to the north and south of the wall before we strike out into enemy territory. He wants to be sure that our supply line back to the Valley stays open while we dig Calgus out of the hills, so we have to make sure there are no nasty surprises waiting to jump out behind us once we've marched north. We're also to deal with the warband that the Petriana have trapped about ten miles north of here, although there's still no clear reason why they'd be camped out in such a dangerous spot. So ourselves and the Second Cohort, and the Cugerni, will go north of the wall with Sixth Legion, turn east once we're clear of the forest and sweep the ground in front of the wall. When we reach the spot where the warband's waiting for us we'll split into two groups, one under Tribune Antonius to attack the hill fort and another led by the legatus to form a defensive line to the north and make sure nobody tries to interfere.'

After the briefing he'd spoken with Frontinius, outlining his plan for the next day.

'I've suggested to Legatus Equitius that we take the lead once we're through the wall gate, and peel off a century to have a quiet wander through the forest and look for any sign of the enemy before meeting the rest of the cohort on the far side. That will get Centurion Corvus safely out of the public eye for another few hours. His men are supposed to be hunters — let's allow them to do something they ought to be good at.'

Once the Tungrians were well clear of the wall gate Frontinius stepped clear of the column and waved back in the pre-agreed signal. At Marcus's command the 8th Century peeled off the line of march and stepped on to the twenty-pace strip of ground dividing the road from the forest, cleared of any vegetation to prevent an attacker from falling on marching troops without any warning. The Hamians stood and watched as the column ground past them up the road, the auxiliary cohorts followed by a seemingly endless stream of legion centuries, their layered plate armour marking the difference between them and the auxiliaries that led the column.

'Your men seem alert enough.'

Marcus turned to find the German, Arminius, at his shoulder, his eyes on the Hamians as they took their short rest break. Casting a careful eye over his men, Marcus was surprised to note that one man in every tent party was watching the forest's dark wall intently, and ignoring the legion's parade up the road.

'Yes, they seem to have absorbed their lesson about keeping watch well enough.'

He stared into the forest, pleased to see that the ground cover between the looming oaks was light enough for his men to pick their way through it with relative ease. At his command, the century shook out into a long line, with ten feet between each man, and at Qadir's shouted signal they stepped off into the forest to the east of the road with their shields unslung and swords held ready to fight. Once they were fifty paces or so into the forest each man was as good as alone in the gloomy light that managed to penetrate the thick overhead cover, the mass of vegetation all around them dulling the faint sounds of their passage to near-inaudibility. Scouting through the forest with the apparently instinctive caution that had so surprised Marcus the previous night, they hunted through the shadows for an hour before low whistles passed down the line summoned him to the scene of a discovery. Several men were gathered around a patch of scorched earth. Marcus took one look and spoke quietly to his soldiers.

'You four, all-round defence, ten paces out, and keep your eyes on the trees and your mouths shut. And *listen*. If a rabbit has a noisy bowel movement anywhere within a mile of here I want to know about it. You and you, signal the century to gather here. *Quietly*.'

He turned back to the object of their interest

to find Arminius squatting down alongside the burnt earth, poking at the ash with his finger.

'These ashes are cold, but recent. And it's a big fire, enough for twenty to thirty men.'

Marcus waited until the century were gathered around him, their faces both eager and nervous with the discovery.

'I want a search of the area around this fire, fingertips in the grass, knives in the soil. Thirty-odd barbarians don't camp out without leaving some clue as to who they were. And do it in silence, no talking. Raise a hand if you find anything.'

Qadir quickly organised the troops to form a search line and sweep across the area around the fire's black scar on their hands and knees, searching the ground in front of them with their fingers and probing the soil with their daggers for any small item that might have been dropped and trodden into the earth. After ten minutes a soldier put his hand in the air, his find carried across to Marcus by one of the watch officers. The man held out his hand, showing off a small piece of silver that the centurion took from his palm.

'Jewellery. Very pretty. Someone's going to be annoyed when he finds this missing from around his neck.'

A replica axe head, crudely fashioned but still recognisable for what it represented, sat on his palm. He showed Qadir the find.

'Seen anything like this before?'

His deputy shook his head, staring blankly at the glinting pendant.

'I have.'

The two men turned to find Arminius staring at the tiny silver ornament, his face creased in concern.

7

It was mid-morning by the time that Felicia was ready to remove the arrow from the wounded cavalry officer. She stood over her patient, his eyes slitted in a deathly pale face as he clung to consciousness with a tenacity that gave her hope for his survival, despite the blood-crusted arrow protruding from his armpit.

'Decurion? Decurion, can you hear me?'

The exhausted officer's eyes flickered in her direction, his mouth opening fractionally in a hoarse whisper.

'I hear you.' He swallowed painfully, licking his lips.

Felicia knelt by the bed, taking one ice-cold hand in both of her own.

'My horse . . . ?'

She smiled despite her concern.

'Your horse, Cornelius Felix, bit two men and kicked several more black and blue while they were getting the arrow out of him, but I'm told he's happily chewing his way through the fort's stock of barley even as we speak. And as for *you*, Decurion, you have a barbarian arrow deep in your left armpit. It seems to have missed your lung, and more importantly the artery that runs through your shoulder down your arm, but it must come out immediately. I need to clean out your wound and prevent the onset of sepsis. You've lost too much blood already, and you'll lose more while I remove the arrow, but to leave it there will probably kill you anyway . . . '

His lips moved again, the smile touching his eyes this time.

'Get the blasted thing out now, eh?'

She nodded mutely.

'Do it, but promise me . . . '

'Yes?'

'If the arm has to come off . . . ?'

'Yes?'

'Just kill me. I can't ride that monster Hades one-handed . . . '

Shaking her head sadly, she gently squeezed the cavalryman's right hand.

'My oath forbids me any such act. We'll just have to make sure this stays attached to you. Now drink this . . . '

She put a beaker to his lips and patiently tipped the drink into his mouth in small sips.

'What is it . . . ?'

'A mixture of wine, honey and the dried and powdered sap of the poppy flower. It will make you drowsy, or possibly even put you to sleep given the amount of blood you've lost. What I have to do to you now is going to hurt considerably more than the pain you're in at the moment.'

The doctor waited for a few minutes, noting the soldier's gradually slower breathing as the drug took effect.

'He's asleep. Let's move him to the table. You have to keep his arm absolutely as it is now, straight out from his body. We have no idea what the arrowhead might be touching in there . . . '

She supervised the orderlies as they carried the decurion from his bloodstained bed to the operating table, where so many men had laid in recent months, their wounds open to her gentle, skilful fingers. The table's surface was criss-crossed with the scars inflicted by her knives and saws, marks left from those occasions when she had decided that the removal of a limb was a safer alternative than risking the onset of gangrene in a shattered arm or leg. The wood's grain was rubbed smooth by the incessant scrubbing she insisted on to remove each successive man's blood from the surface before the next soldier was laid out for her attention.

'Keep his arm steady . . . that's it. Now get him on to the table.'

With the unconscious man's body arranged to her satisfaction, his arm held firmly at right angles from his body by one of the orderlies, she surveyed the wound carefully, noting the blood still leaking from the arrow's wicked puncture. Stepping away from the table, she studied her instruments for a moment before selecting a pair of polished concave bronze blades, one with a blunt curved end, the other with small hooks at its end. Turning to her helpers, she addressed the man standing ready to help her by the unconscious patient's head.

'So, what do we know about arrow wounds, Orderly Julius?'

'Doctor, the arrow is often barbed and will cause more damage during removal due to further tearing of the flesh inside the wound.'

'And so the usual method for the removal of

such an arrow is . . . ?'

'To push the arrow's head out of the body through a second wound opened for the purpose, when this can be achieved without risk. This allows the arrow to be broken in half and safely removed.'

'And given this arrow's location?'

'It would be impossible to make a second opening. The arrow must be withdrawn through the original wound.'

She smiled encouragement.

'Good. Have you carried out this procedure before?'

'No, Doctor, I have not.'

'Very well, you shall have your first opportunity shortly. From the look of the wound this is a broad-headed arrow, with only two barbs, and not one of ours. We can be thankful for that small mercy, can we not, Julius?'

The orderly responded dutifully.

'Certainly, Doctor. A flat-bladed arrow opens a pocket-shaped wound, which will close itself well enough as a result of the flesh swelling in response to the arrow's intrusion. A wound made by the three-bladed arrowheads used by our archers will not close, however, and requires much more attention during recovery.'

'And . . . ?'

'And . . . it has three barbs . . . ?'

'Rather than two. Exactly. So, back to this particular patient. Our decurion's arrow's upper blade and barb may be close to the large blood vessel that runs along the shoulder and down into the arm, and if we snag that vessel with the uppermost barb we will have a dead man on this table inside a minute or so. I'm going to use these . . . ' She lifted the bronze blades to display them to the two men. ' . . . to prevent that from happening. These two items are called a dioclean cyathiscus, because their use was invented by the Greek Diocles.'

She bent over the patient, sliding the first blade into the wound, probing gently for the arrowhead.

'There it is. Now I'm pushing the blade up and over the barb. It's smooth and blunt, so there shouldn't be a risk to the blood vessel. That's it . . . now there's a tiny hole in the top of the blade, which I'm going to engage with the point of the barb . . . got it. That barb is now harmless to the patient. Now the other blade goes in . . . see? I engage the tiny hooks over the first blade, like so . . . and I can now pull the arrow from the wound, with the second blade both providing the traction and keeping the first blade in place over the barb. That's the worst part over with, and not too much more blood spilt either.'

She looked at Julius.

'There's another set of blades over there, go and get them. We've managed to protect the blood vessel, so now it's your turn to make the other barb safe.'

The arrow was out of the wound a minute later, the orderly having made a decent fist of engaging its other barb before ceding control of the extraction to Felicia. She drew the vicious iron blade smoothly and slowly from its incision, looking critically at the missile before putting it to one side.

'There's a memento for our cavalryman when he wakes up. Now for this wound.'

She explored the wound carefully with blunt-nosed forceps, pulling out a scrap of cloth from deep inside the decurion's armpit and holding it up for the orderlies to see.

'See, a fragment of his tunic, punched into the wound by the force of the arrow's impact. We must never leave such an object inside a wound, it will cause sepsis, possibly gross infection, and frequently end in the death of our patient. Especially a man as weak as this from loss of blood. So, Orderly Julius, what does Celsus advise us to do now?'

The orderly looked up for a second, remembering his long hours of reading the textbooks that Felicia had lent to him.

'Doctor, we must pack the wound with lint soaked in vinegar to stop the bleeding, and pure honeycomb to assist the healing.'

'Correct. And the vinegar will also help to prevent infection of the wound. How long do you think we should wait before sewing up the wound?'

The man's face reddened.

'In truth, Doctor, I do not know.'

She smiled.

'And you will not guess, which does you credit. We'll make a medic of you yet, Julius. The answer is that we will decrease the size of the wound's packing with every change, which will be twice a day, until we can see that the flesh inside is healthy in colour and feel, and that the interior of the wound is closing. Only then can we safely close the wound. Well done, colleagues, I do believe that this man will live to fight another day.'

* * *

The 8th scouted through the forest without any further result for the next three hours, emerging out of the trees and into the bright daylight at midday, more or less. The soldiers took their meal in the shelter of the forest's edge and then slung their pack poles over their shoulders, heading for the meeting point that had been agreed at a brisk march. They saw no sign of any enemy during their ten-mile trek across the rolling country north of the wall, and overhauled the legion after an hour's progress.

The auxiliary cohorts were out front, sweeping forward on a broad front behind a cavalry screen provided by the 6th Legion's cavalrymen. The legion itself remained in column of march, albeit that their pace was slowed to accommodate the auxiliaries' cautious progress. The 8th Century marched up the column's length, steadfastly ignoring the inevitable barrage of insults thrown at their backs by the legionaries, and Marcus snapped off smart salutes to each cohort's first spear in turn. As they passed the column's head, past the thicket of standards that led the legion on the march, a single horseman rode out alongside them, his horse trotting easily alongside the running soldiers. Marcus had recognised his former prefect the moment his horse had peeled away from the legion's officers, and his salute was accompanied by a smile of genuine pleasure. Equitius leaned down from his saddle, throwing him a return salute.

'Centurion. I saw the colour of your men's shields and guessed that you might be Tungrians. I'll assume that you've been undertaking some private scouting mission for Prefect Scaurus, to judge from the haste with which you're tearing off into the distance.'

Marcus stepped closer to the horse, almost rubbing his armoured shoulder against its flank as he lowered his voice to ensure privacy.

'We've been scouting the ground to the north of the north road crossroads, Legatus, and keeping out of the way, if you know what I mean . . . '

Equitius nodded sagely.

'A good choice by your prefect, given the continued interest in your possible whereabouts. And . . . ?'

Marcus handed him the tiny pendant, waiting as the other man turned it over in his hand.

'A piece of barbarian jewellery. It means nothing to me . . . '

The centurion took the piece back, dropping it into the pouch on his belt.

'Nor to me, Legatus, but Prefect Scaurus's bodyguard tells us he's seen another exactly the same north of the wall. Far to the north . . . '

Equitius nodded again, a new understanding dawning in his eyes.

'I see. Well, in that case I won't detain you. I'd

imagine that your prefect will know well enough what to make of this interesting snippet of intelligence without my interference, given his experience. Gentlemen . . .'

He gestured to the land beyond the legion's lead cohort.

'Your comrades are out there, about a mile in front of us. They shouldn't be too hard to find, they're the fellows poking their spears into every bush on a two-mile front.'

As chance would have it, the first unit the century encountered was the 2nd Tungrian cohort. Mindful of the warnings not to advertise his presence, Marcus felt a frisson of uncertainty as he looked for an officer to ask where the first cohort might be found. The centurion he approached, rendered anonymous by the stark lines of his helmet's cheek guards, took one look and grinned triumphantly.

'I remember you, we've met before! You're . . . Two Knives, that's it!'

* * *

The Tungrians built a hurried camp alongside the 2nd Cohort, the Cugerni cohort from Aelian Bridge and three cohorts of the 6th Legion. The turf walls were raised quickly, and to a foot less than the regulation height since the prefects wanted their men to be fresh for the fight. First Spear Frontinius sent his men to dinner once their section of the rampart was complete. Marcus sat with Qadir and Antenoch, the latter casting dark stares at a chastened Lupus, who had been discovered, hungry and thirsty, beneath a tent on the century's wagon.

'The little bastard must have sneaked himself on to the cart when we were getting ready to pull out from Noisy Valley.' The clerk's exasperation with the child's desperation to be with the century had been all too evident, as had Morban's mortification when his presence had been discovered. Lupus had still been wet eyed an hour after his discovery, as the two men had taken turns to tell him just how stupid he was.

'I caught the little sod grinning to himself when he thought no one was looking,' Morban had confided to Marcus, 'so I clipped his ear again to teach the cheeky bugger a lesson.'

The child was sitting solemn faced between Antenoch and Qadir, the object of great curiosity for the rest of the century, who kept wandering past in ones and twos until their attention became tiresome, and their centurion ordered them into their tents.

'There's no way to get him back to the Valley,' Marcus had told a tight-lipped Antenoch, 'you'll just have to keep an eye on him.'

'And when we run into the blue-noses?'

'He'll just have to hide somewhere.'

The clerk had shrugged angrily, dragging the protesting child to his tent by one ear with dark threats of fearsome retribution for any further infringement of the rules laid down for him. First Spear Frontinius, surprisingly enough, had been more relaxed on the subject than anyone else in the boy's chain of command. Sitting at his meal with Julius, he had shrugged when the subject was raised.

'What can we do about it now? Nothing. The lad's going to end up as a soldier in any case, he's just getting an earlier start than the rest of us. Anyway, he'll be safe enough for tonight at least. I doubt that anyone's going to be bothering us with the rest of the Sixth less than two miles to the north and in a particularly bad temper, given that we get to take revenge for the Frisians while they get to stand guard.'

Julius smiled sourly.

'I'll happily swap, if that'll make them happier. Most of them are replacements for the men that died at Lost Eagle, and we've already seen one decent fight this summer . . . '

Frontinius laughed quietly.

'It doesn't work that way, though, does it? We're blooded, as are the boys from the Sixth who'll be fighting alongside us. Legatus Equitius has put the first team into this fight, so it's up to us to justify his confidence.'

Julius shook his head, squinting into the setting sun's dying rays.

'Just as long as the bloody Sixth's cohorts actually come to the fight.' He stretched his massive frame, tired from the day's march. 'So what did young Corvus find in the woods that was so significant?'

Frontinius shook his head.

'No idea. Some piece of jewellery or other. The prefect took one look and went into a huddle with his man the German. He's gone over to the Sixth's main body for a chat with the legatus, so doubtless we'll find out soon enough. Anyway, off to dinner with you, and then get your lads' heads down for the night. We'll be up before dawn, and I want everyone nice and fresh.'

In the quiet time after dinner, as the troops made their last preparations for battle before turning in for the night, a strange officer appeared in the Tungrian lines. Following directions from the patrolling sentries, he made his way to the 8th Century's row of tents and sought out Marcus. The two men stood talking in the camp's torchlight for a few minutes, then clasped their arms before the stranger turned to head back to his own part of the camp. The young centurion watched him go for a moment, then walked across to the 1st Century's section of the camp, seeking out the first spear with a worried look on his face. Frontinius listened impassively to his story, then sent for Julius.

'You met a pair of Second Cohort centurions at Arab Town, when you went to pick up our replacements?'

Julius scratched his head, still itching after a full day beneath his crested helmet.

'Decent enough lads, as I recall. Tertius and . . .'

'Appius.'

'Yes, that's it. Our brother officer Marcus has just had a visit from Tertius. They met on the march today, by pure good fortune. Tertius wanted to warn Marcus that the Second Cohort's prefect is convinced he's the son of a disgraced Roman senator, and that he's recruited this Appius to find him and deliver proof of his whereabouts. The Bear told me that he was around our lines at Noisy Valley only a few minutes after I sent the Eighth out on night exercise.'

Julius frowned, shaking his head at the apparent inevitability of the net closing around them.

'After which Prefect Furius will denounce the fugitive, take the credit for his discovery, and do his level best to have us all nailed up alongside Two Knives?'

Frontinius nodded.

'Exactly. From what I've heard he might even have a go at sticking it to Prefect Scaurus.'

Julius frowned.

'Why would this Tertius be so keen to tell us this? Surely he'd be better off just keeping his mouth shut?'

Frontinius acknowledged the point, reaching for his helmet and vine stick.

'It's a longer story than we've got time for now. Suffice to say that Centurion Tertius has quite a good reason not to be all that fond of his new prefect. I'm off to the Sixth Legion's lines now, there's a command conference. We'll finish this discussion later, but for the time being let's keep Centurion Corvus under as much cover as possible.'

* * *

The detachment's senior officers gathered in the command tent, waiting for Tribune Antonius to make his entrance. The auxiliary cohorts' prefects and first spears rubbed shoulders with three hard-faced legion senior centurions and a pair of junior tribunes, the latters' equestrian status clear from the thin purple strip on both men's tunics. Antonius entered the tent a moment later, and every eye was upon the senior tribune as he walked to the briefing table to announce his intended plan of attack. He stepped up to the table, pointing to the rough map sketched on its surface and speaking in a clear, confident voice.

'This ought to be straightforward enough, I should think. There are reported to be about fifteen hundred of them camped on that hill. They know we're here, so they will be ready, but they probably haven't eaten all day and they've already fought one pitched battle. With six cohorts we outnumber them by nearly three to one, so good enough odds for an assault, I'd say. Nothing too fancy, unless anyone's got any better ideas — we simply break in, we put them to the sword, and Calgus has one less warband to play with.'

He paused, looking around the tent at the gathered officers.

'I'm reminded that it's usual for auxiliary cohort commanders to be offered the first crack at the enemy in this sort of situation.' I'll bet he's been reminded of that old tradition, mused Frontinius inwardly. In fact I'll bet he had a queue of centurions falling over each other to remind him of it. 'So, gentlemen, it's up to you. Will the Tungrians and Cugerni lead the line for this action?'

Prefect Furius stepped forward, nodding decisively, to the amazement of the other two prefects and their first spears. Neuto's face froze into immobility, only his eyes betraying his surprise.

'Yes, Tribune, I think you'll find that we're more than up to the task. I propose that we make up the first wave, and that your legion infantry be kept in close reserve, ready to assist us if the going gets difficult.'

Antonius nodded approvingly, a brief smile twitching his lips.

'Well said, Prefect Furius, excellent spirit. Very well, I suggest that you take some time between the three of you to lay out your battle plan. The Sixth Legion will back you up in whatever you decide. Thank you, gentlemen.'

Outside the tent a thin-lipped Scaurus put a hand on Furius's arm, his anger clearly boiling over.

'Next time you decide to do something that stupid I'd appreciate some bloody warning!'

Furius bristled indignantly, and the Cugerni prefect walked away a few paces, studiously ignoring the two men as the 2nd Tungrians' prefect pointed a finger at his colleague.

'*Stupid?* I think you should explain yourself, Rutilius Scaurus.'

Scaurus held his ground, his voice lowered to avoid the words carrying back into the command tent.

'When Antonius offered us first place in the line he was simply doing what the legions always do, putting dispensable auxiliaries to his front to soak up the worst of the casualties, but what you offered him went a long way beyond that. You've just let him off the hook for this battle's conduct, and given him a cast-iron excuse for holding his cohorts back as long as he likes. We're not four thousand men attacking fifteen hundred any more, in fact we're not much better than evenly matched unless Antonius throws his men in alongside us, and he won't do that until we've already got the barbarians beaten. So we'd better do some quick thinking as to how this battle's going to be fought, because I don't think a frontal assault is going to be good enough.' He caught the lurking Cugerni prefect's eye and raised his voice. 'I suggest you both come to my tent in an hour.'

He summoned Frontinius with a jerk of the head and stalked away, his mind working fast, heading back to his own cohort's lines and talking as he walked.

'So you've got another chance at glory, First Spear Frontinius. We're to assault the hill fort with the other auxiliary cohorts while the Sixth Legion sits on its backside and watches us go about it. I'd imagine that young Antonius couldn't have imagined a better result if he'd tried.'

The First Spear shook his head in disbelief.

'We get to attack a barbarian warband uphill, into prepared defences, while the legion cohorts sit and laugh at us from behind their shields. We might win, but it'll be a bloody victory. I'd take Lost Eagle over the goat-fuck this could turn into if Cocidius decides we've had enough divine favour for one lifetime.'

Scaurus nodded.

'Unless we can turn their flank, and avoid a frontal attack, I'm forced to agree with you.'

Frontinius snorted.

'Turn their flank? Unlikely, since they're defending a circular position.'

They walked into the prefect's tent, and Scaurus slumped into a chair, gesturing the first spear into the other.

'I take your point. Talk me through it, then. You're the leader of this particular warband. How do you go about defending yourself when the Romans come to play?'

Frontinius scratched a circle in the tent's dirt floor.

'They'll assume that we're coming from the south, since they know well enough that we're camped here. They've not had the time to put up any kind of palisade, so if it was me in command of that rabble I'd line them up behind the southern side of the earth rampart, ready to fight but safe from any artillery we might have with us. Then I'd post a few men on top of the wall, perhaps four or five each to north, south, east and west, to watch for our approach. He knows that a force this size can't approach silently, so a few men with sharp eyes and ears ought to be enough to warn him of an advance from any direction. After that it'd be simple enough to move his force around the wall to match our point of attack. And, when we do show our hands, he's got time to get any field defences he's prepared into place, sharpened stakes, tribuli, that sort of thing. If we had any sense we'd just sit back and wait for them to give up for lack of food and water.'

'And if we split our forces?'

'He splits his, and the basic problem remains unchanged.'

Scaurus nodded slowly.

'So the watchers on the wall are the key. If they fail to give a warning, the warband remains oriented on our most likely line of advance.'

Frontinius glanced across at him sharply.

'*Yes?*'

'Well . . . I was just thinking about the Eighth Century . . . '

Frontinius nodded unhappily.

'So was I. We've got a problem with Centurion Corvus's visibility already, and I suspect your idea's about to make it worse.'

Five minutes later the two men walked into the 8th Century's section of the camp and sought out Marcus, quickly outlining the prefect's idea to the young centurion.

'Could it work?'

Marcus nodded slowly.

'I think so, Prefect. There's a man who'll have a better judgement than mine, though.'

He called for Qadir. The chosen man mulled the idea for a moment, and then he too nodded.

'Yes, we can do this. But not wearing armour.'

He held up a hand to silence the first spear's reaction.

'Please believe me, First Spear Frontinius, we can only perform this task if all conditions are right. We must be in position at exactly the right moment, when the rising sun lights up the men on the earth wall. We must reach that position completely undetected, or we will lose the element of surprise. And to do this we must not be burdened with your heavy mail shirts, helmets and shields. It would be impossible for us to make a silent approach carrying all that weight, and your plan, Prefect, depends on our being as silent as a fox hunting across the desert at night.'

Frontinius pulled a sceptical face.

'And if the barbarians discover you? What will you do against hundreds of them without your equipment?'

The tall chosen man returned his stare without blinking for several seconds.

'First Spear, in the Eighth Century you have one hundred and sixty of the best archers in the world at your command. Every one of us is capable of putting three arrows into a man-sized target at one hundred paces in less time than it would take a man to run the distance. It would be a brave warrior that could run into that.'

The prefect looked at Marcus questioningly.

'Do you agree?'

'Yes, sir. I suggest we wear our cloaks to cover up our tunics, but otherwise it should work well enough . . . if we can deal with their flank sentries undetected.'

Scaurus took a deep breath.

'In that case, First Spear, I suggest we go and speak to my fellow prefects. Although whether Gracilus Furius will appreciate our pulling his balls out of the fire is debatable.'

As it happened, both Furius and the Cugerni

prefect agreed with the plan readily enough, while Tribune Antonius picked a piece of lint from the broad senatorial stripe that decorated the right shoulder of his tunic and smiled in quiet amusement at the contrast between this quiet acceptance and the man's bluster of an hour before. He dismissed the officers to their preparations with a last quiet word of encouragement.

'Well, gentlemen, you'd better go and warn your centurions that tomorrow starts early and will end in victory. I'm looking forward to seeing the cohorts that won us the battle of the Lost Eagle in action again.'

* * *

Appius waited until well after dark before leaving his tent, with both cohorts bedded down for the night and the sentries' attention turned mainly outside the marching fort's earth wall. Dressed in his dark leggings and tunic, and keeping to the shadows, he made swift and silent progress through the camp and into the 1st Cohort's lines, slipping from the shadow of one tent to the next with a careful eye open for the patrolling soldiers, all the time keeping the other closed to protect it from the torches providing patchy illumination for the rows of tents. Within minutes he had found the tents housing the Hamians, slinking noiselessly up their line until he reached the spot where he estimated the centurion's tent would be positioned. Worming his way round the tent, he lifted the front flap fractionally, peeking into the darkened interior with the previously closed eye wide open. A single body was lying rolled up in a blanket, a centurion's helmet laid alongside the bed with a vine stick next to it. He slipped quietly inside the tent and across the grass floor to the neatly folded pile of clothes that awaited the young officer's wakening, ignoring the wooden chest at Marcus's feet for fear of a noisy hinge waking the sleeping man.

Running his hands across the garments, he encountered a hard object, the prick of a pin to his finger telling him that it was the cloak pin he had picked up from the floor of the Arab Town officers' mess. He pulled the metal disc from its hiding place beneath the man's cloak and grinned to himself in triumph, slipping it into his pocket and moving silently back to the tent's entrance. Opening the flap a fraction, he froze into immobility as a patrolling sentry padded past, the man's attention clearly elsewhere since the slight movement went unnoticed. When the soldier was twenty paces farther down the line of tents the intruder slipped out of the small opening, leaving the sleeping centurion none the wiser as to his presence.

* * *

The cohorts mustered for their short march to the hill fort an hour before first light, hundreds of torches blazing out into the darkness. Marcus walked with Qadir as the chosen man checked his men's equipment in the flickering light, watching as the Hamian and his watch officer took each man's bow in turn and tested its draw.

'It is customary,' the big man had told him. 'They expect us to examine every man's bow before we use them in battle. If I were to ignore the ritual they would fear some form of bad luck befalling them. Besides, better for a man's bowstring to part here than in the heat of battle.'

Dubnus walked down to the 8th's place at the rear of the Tungrians' column, smiling grimly at the sight of Marcus in his cloak, the heavy wool held closed with a borrowed bronze pin. He glanced at Antenoch, noting the clerk's sombre demeanour.

'What's wrong with him? Don't tell me he's getting nervy before a fight for the first time in his life?'

His friend frowned in the flickering torchlight.

'No, nothing like that. My cloak pin's gone missing and he's blaming himself. I've told him it's my fault, it probably fell off last night, so it'll either be trampled into the mud or safely tucked away in some lucky soldier's pack.'

His friend grimaced his sympathy.

'Everyone in the cohort knows it's yours, so if it's found it'll come back. And besides, you're better off with that bronze pin this particular morning. It's just a shame you've no armour underneath the cloak.'

Marcus returned the smile with a raised eyebrow and lifted the heavy wool to reveal his mail shirt.

'We haven't all given up on the virtues of a good strong defence. Once the blue-noses realise what's happening they'll come across that fort like a pack of dogs after raw meat, and someone's going to have to deal with the men that dodge our arrows.'

His former chosen man nodded solemnly.

'We'll be with you as quickly as possible.'

Marcus tapped the hilts of his swords.

'And until then I'll be getting some practice with these. Just don't take too long.'

He shook hands with Morban, detailed by the first spear to remain behind and look after Lupus, much to his disgust. Frontinius had ignored his protests, waving him away dismissively.

'It's not as if a standard's going to make much difference in this instance, and you should have made sure he was being cared for. Grin and bear it, Standard-bearer, because it isn't going to change.'

The auxiliary cohorts led the column out of their temporary camp in a blaze of torchlight, making their way across the intervening ground between the marching camp and the hill fort at a brisk pace. The 8th Century, dressed in their dark cloaks and without armour or shields, slipped in quietly behind the last of the three auxiliary cohorts, keeping back far enough to be sure that the torchlight would not betray their presence to any lurking scouts. Marcus and Qadir watched from the darkness behind their comrades as the cohorts paraded for the assault before the hill fort's southern rampart, the centurions marshalling their men with bellowed orders.

'Is it always this way? They're making enough noise to summon the dead from their resting places.'

Marcus shook his head despite the darkness.

'No, they're making a special effort to get noticed. Once the warband have taken the bait we can get moving.'

They waited for a long moment before Qadir tugged at his centurion's sleeve, pointing as vague figures appeared on the wall in the pale golden light of the cohorts' torches.

'There. On the wall! There must be hundreds of them.'

Marcus strained his eyes, watching as men appeared along the length of the fort's southern rampart.

'Yes, and there will be many more hidden behind the wall. A target for every arrow we have and more besides. Follow me!'

Marcus led the 8th away into the deeper darkness, scouting away to the west around the fort's curving earth wall, moving slowly to ensure that the century stayed together as they crossed the rough ground. When he judged the distance they had moved away from the main force was sufficient he stopped the advance with a soft command to Qadir, and the Hamians settled down to wait for the dawn. In the distance they could clearly hear the sounds of men being prepared for a fight, shouts of command and the occasional blare of a trumpeter's horn, all the while answered by the harsh cries of the barbarians waiting for them. Qadir spoke quietly into his ear.

'There must be thousands of the savages, to judge from their noise. If this goes badly then ours will not be the only lives lost this day. I have read about assaults on defended positions like this, and I fear your friends will pay a steep price to take that ground.'

Marcus nodded into the darkness, his face grim as he searched the invisible horizon for any sign of the coming dawn.

'We'd best not miss the mark, then.'

In the space of two minutes a subtle difference in the sky above the fort's earth wall became clear to the waiting soldiers, the beginnings of a gentle change of hue in the night sky to the east. Within another five minutes the first real hint of dawn tinged the slowly retreating darkness with a faint pink hue. Marcus stared intently up the slope, sensing Qadir doing the same at his shoulder without having to look round.

'There.'

He followed the other man's pointing arm, seeing a silhouette against the faint glow.

'And another.'

The shape of a shaggy-haired warrior moved across the dawn's faint glow as he crossed the earth wall's surface to speak with the first man spotted. They stood facing the south, ignoring their guard duty to focus on the likely point of attack. Qadir murmured quietly into Marcus's ear.

'We are still deep in darkness down here, so they see nothing and neglect their given task. They speak of the fight to come at their front gate, and perhaps their desire to be part of that, rather than this less than noble duty. Either that or they wonder if they might still slip away into the dawn unnoticed . . . '

Marcus nodded again.

'Can your men take them down with this much light?'

Even in the gloom he saw the white of his chosen man's teeth bared in a fierce smile.

'We can, but we need better light for the next task. Besides, I expected more than these two. A short while longer would be wise, I think?'

Marcus whispered agreement, and the two men waited while the glow of the eastern horizon slowly brightened. He was on the verge of ordering the attack when another silhouette climbed up the fort's slope, seeming to rise up out of the earth in front of them, and joined the other two men, now clearly outlined against a pink dawn sky.

'He must have been at the foot of the slope, perhaps praying silently to his gods?'

Marcus snorted mirthlessly.

'Emptying his bowels, more likely. It's time. Another five minutes and they'll have enough light to see us. Antenoch, stay here to guide the Ninth Century to us once the excitement starts. I don't want to risk them missing their way in the dark and leaving us without any means of fighting back if the barbarians get past our arrows.'

Qadir nodded, muttering a quiet command to the dozen archers he had picked out for this critical first task. Still indistinct to Marcus's eyes, their capes merging with the fort's deep shadow, they nocked arrows to their bows and took up the first slack. Marcus nodded to his chosen man.

'Now.'

Pulling back their bowstrings until the weapons made tiny creaking sounds under the strain, the archers made the last adjustments to their points of aim, waiting for Qadir's command. The chosen man paused for a long breath to allow them to settle, then hissed a terse command. The barbarian sentries staggered under the impact of a dozen arrows, all three slumping to the ground as the humming note of the bowstrings died away, hopefully unheard from within the fort. Marcus drew his cavalry sword and bounded forward up the slope, reaching the top in thirty seconds of scrambling climb, then dropped on to his chest and hugged the earth wall's parapet alongside the fallen barbarians. One of the men was quietly choking on his own blood in the dawn's silence, his bubbling breaths silenced by a swift stroke of the blade across his throat.

From the wall's vantage point the enemy camp was laid out beneath him, their fires still burning across the area enclosed by the circular rampart. In the dawn's pale light, with the sun still below the forested horizon, the mass of the enemy gathered 250 paces away on the slope of the hill fort's southern wall was an indistinct seething wall of shaggy warriors baying for blood. Only the warband's front rank was standing on the earth wall's parapet, presumably to protect the remainder of the warband against the possibility that the legion artillery's bolt throwers might yet make an unwelcome appearance. The remainder were gathered in the southern rampart's protection for the time being. Marcus could clearly hear the shouts of their leaders, building their men up for the bloodletting to come and obviously determined to make the invaders pay dearly for every foot gained. Scanning the wall to the east and south, he quickly spotted the expected groups of sentries still watching the ground to their front, clearly still unaware of the threat to their rear. Crawling back to the edge of the rampart, he beckoned Qadir and his selected archers to join him, muttering into the big man's ear.

'I need you to take down the other two groups of sentries . . . '

He pointed out the fresh targets to Qadir, who swiftly detailed a target to each of his men.

' . . . but two arrows each may not be enough for a silent kill. I suggest you bring up the rest of the century, and have them ready to start shooting the second the sentries are down.'

Qadir nodded, and waved the rest of the century forward to just below the rampart's lip. Grim faced, they nocked arrows and held their bows pointing downwards, ready to lift, draw and shoot. Marcus looked at Qadir one last time.

'Ready?'

The chosen man nodded.

'Shoot.'

Qadir jerked a hand forward to unleash his picked marksmen's arrows. The sentries fell under the Hamians' volley, one man clearly attempting to call out a warning despite his wounds, but the clamour of both the waiting cohorts and the warband's imprecations drowned out his efforts long enough for another arrow to slam into his back and drop him face down on to the wall's dried mud. As the sentries fell the remainder of the 8th's men scrambled up the last few paces of climb, quickly forming two lines with their bows held ready to shoot, every one of them now staring at Qadir in readiness for his order. Without waiting for permission, Qadir spread his arms to indicate that the whole century was to shoot, then pivoted to point at the mass of warriors unwittingly waiting under the threat of their bows.

The Hamians' first volley of arrows arced down on to the unsuspecting barbarians out of the dark western sky. Dozens of men fell, some dead before they hit the ground but most of them screaming out their sudden agony as the barbed iron slammed deep into their heads, necks and chests. Even as the first victims reeled under the shock of impact another volley punched down into their ranks, taking a fresh toll of their strength as the archers' still uncomprehending victims fell with blood frothing from their horrific wounds. Marcus grinned wolfishly, pointing at the enemy warriors with his cavalry sword.

'Keep them shooting! Pour it on!'

Qadir nodded without taking his eyes off the target as he nocked another arrow and sent it into the warband's screaming mass, shouting to his men to rain arrows on to the still-defenceless barbarians. Marcus's eyes sought and found the 8th's trumpeter.

'*Sound the advance. Blow, man, blow!*'

As the sweet notes of the call to advance sounded above the warband's howls, he drew his short gladius and held it alongside the longer cavalry weapon, testing the weight and balance of the blades in readiness for what he knew must come soon enough. Already the warband's rear ranks were struggling to regain some semblance of order, those men with shields sheltering behind them as best they could while fighting their way through the human wreckage of the 8th's stricken victims. A lone warrior broke away from the pack and sprinted towards the archers with his shield held close to his body, followed over the next few seconds by several more, the men's swords glinting in the dawn's pale light as they charged across the gap between the Hamians and their targets in a growing tide of fury. Marcus turned back to find Qadir still pulling arrows from his quiver and loosing them into the warband with impressive speed.

'Keep shooting! I'll deal with anyone that gets through!'

The chosen man nodded grimly, lowering his bow a fraction to shoot an arrow into the legs of the closest barbarian before shouting a command over his shoulder.

'Front rank, target the runners. Rear rank, keep shooting!'

As Marcus watched, his swords raised in their familiar stance with the blade points level, the front rank took aim at their attackers and loosed a volley of arrows that dropped half of them with head and leg injuries. A warrior who had been brave enough to attack without the protection of a shield reeled under the impact of half a dozen arrows and toppled to the ground without ever breaking stride, his legs kicking even as he sprawled full length in blood-slickened grass. Even with half the century now focused on their defence, they were still shooting hundreds of arrows into the defenceless warband every minute, giving the cohorts priceless moments of opportunity to smash through their defence of the hill fort's walls.

'*You!*'

The trumpeter jerked his eyes from the charging barbarians and on to his centurion with a guilty start.

'Keep sounding the advance. If they break through to the archers you will drop that horn, pull your sword and defend them to the death.'

The other man nodded jerkily, putting the trumpet back to his lips and drawing breath. Marcus turned back to their attackers, judging that the survivors had closed to within thirty paces. He shouted over his shoulder to Qadir over the trumpeter's renewed efforts, readying himself for the first clash.

'I'm going down on to the dance floor to try my luck. Try not to shoot me!'

'*What?*'

The chosen man paused in mid-shot as his centurion stepped down the earth wall and out into the space between the front rank and the charging barbarians, fewer with each volley that ripped at their tattered ranks but gathering strength with every second as more men fought their way out of the warband's milling chaos to run towards the 8th's position on the earth wall. He drew the arrow back to the limit of the weapon's capacity, forcing his strength into its stressed wood-and-bone frame, waited a second to allow his target to run on to the point of aim, then loosed the missile into the warrior's face at less then twenty paces, skimming the arrow's point across the top of the barbarian's shield and squarely through one eye socket. The tribesman spun to the ground with the arrow's immense impact, only half of the shaft protruding from his otherwise undamaged face.

Marcus forced his fascinated attention from Qadir's victim to the next-closest attacker, watching as two, then three arrows slammed into the man's shield, heavy iron heads punching through the layered wood with ease at such close range. The warrior's arm was probably pinned to his board by at least one of the arrows, his blood flowing down the inner bowl, but from the wide-eyed rage contorting the man's features it wasn't going to hamper the damage he would do if he fought his way through to the Hamians. Another arrow slammed through the attacker's calf but he staggered on, charging towards the centurion with his long sword sweeping down in a vicious blow at the unshielded officer.

Marcus stepped to one side with an easy grace, caught the barbarian's blade with his own long-bladed spatha and steered it away to his right, pushing his attacker's right arm across his body to open up his unshielded right side before stepping in fast, hooking his short-bladed gladius round to punch hard into the warrior's ribs, then straightening to shrug the grievously wounded man off his blade. Another man charged in to attack him from the left, too close for Marcus to reorient himself in time but giving him enough time to see the pair of arrows protruding from the warrior's left shoulder. The limb would be pinned in place by the arrows' unyielding intrusion, useless for anything better than holding the man's shield in place. Diving to the ground, he scythed the spatha in under the shield's immobile defence, severed the warrior's calf muscle and rolled back on to his feet, leaving the staggering cripple to the Hamians' bows.

A flight of arrows whipped past Marcus and into the oncoming barbarians, close enough that he heard the breathy whistle of the closest as it flicked past his ear. Several more tribesmen went down with wounds to their heads and legs, but enough had survived to narrow his eyes in calculation as to which would be his next combat. The two leading runners made his mind up for him, drawn to his cross-crested helmet's dull shine in the early morning sun, one of the pair a split second in front of his companion with his eyes fixed wide in the fierce joy of combat. Marcus's thrown gladius spun one precisely judged revolution through the dawn's chill air before embedding itself in his throat and dropping him choking into the dew-soaked grass. Parrying the other man's sword blow with the blade of his spatha, the centurion dropped to one knee to grasp his fallen comrade's long sword by its carved bone hilt, lifting it to deflect the warrior's next attack before jabbing the spatha's blade up into his attacker's jaw. After an instant of resistance the blade penetrated the roof of the barbarian's mouth and sank deep into his brain. He staggered backwards out of the combat, his eyes rolling up as he sagged lifelessly to the ground.

Recovering his footing, Marcus saw a trio of warriors closing on him fast, and beyond them another half-dozen advancing with their shields raised, and realised with a sickening lurch that he had allowed the heady exhilaration of combat to put him in extreme danger. A fresh wave of energy washed through the young officer as he steadied himself to meet the threat, his vision seeming to narrow and darken slightly as his body fed every usable drop of blood to his muscles. Nostrils flaring to suck in air, he rose on to the balls of his feet as if preparing to dance as the first three men charged in to attack.

The leading warrior made a straightforward lunge with his long sword, his eyes widening comically as Marcus smashed the blade aside with his left-hand sword, then thrust the other into his thigh, shifting his weight on to the weapon to force it through the heavy muscles and out of the man's leg in a shower of blood from the severed artery.

As the wounded man screamed in sudden pain, staggering where he stood with one leg unable to support his weight, Marcus hacked the spatha into the face of the warrior to his right so fast that it was all the man could do to parry the blow upwards, leaving himself open to a brutally powerful half-fist that ruptured his throat and dropped him choking to the ground. Marcus hacked at his first victim's head with his spatha, gripping the sword buried in his leg and kicking the grievously injured warrior backwards to impede the last of the three from bringing his weapon to bear, tearing it free as the barbarian fell away from him. He ducked reflexively as the last man's sword hacked through the air where his head had been, but before he could move to either attack or defend an arrow flicked over his shoulder and buried itself deep in the barbarian's ribs, the shock dumping the man on to his backside with eyes slitted against the pain.

Stepping swiftly back from the fallen warriors, wary of a last desperate knife-thrust from one of the wounded, he eyed the next wave of attackers with cold calculation. Where there had been half a dozen only four remained, and two of them were limping from arrow wounds, but they were still advancing towards him with their shields raised to deflect the continual flicker of Hamian arrows, others following close behind.

'You might be better off behind this.'

A shield slid into place across his body, a strong arm holding the heavy wooden board rock steady. Marcus didn't need to look around to know who the newcomer was.

'No, brother, you'll need it more than me.'

Dubnus chuckled darkly in his ear.

'Me? I've got another somewhere. Ah, here it is.'

Marcus looked round to see a soldier move into position alongside the 5th's centurion, putting his shield across Dubnus's body in turn.

'Well met, Scarface, although you might be better using that board for your own defence.'

The veteran soldier shook his head solemnly.

'Can't do that, sir. We look after our officers in the Fifth Century, as well you know, both past and present. And besides . . . '

Marcus grinned wearily, the fierce heat of combat seeping out of his body.

'I know, you've got a friend or two on the way.'

More of the 5th's men were pouring over the earth wall, ducking through the still-firing archers to take their place in the shield wall. The four-man group of barbarians stopped advancing a dozen feet from the century's quickly forming line of shields as the numbers facing them tripled in less than ten seconds, then started to back away as the full 5th Century mustered in front of the Hamians, rapping their shields with their spears and shouting insults at the unnerved barbarians. Marcus spoke without taking his eyes off the scene to their front.

'This could still get ugly if that lot decide to come at us in strength.'

He turned back to find Qadir on the wall above him.

'Qadir! Shoot everything you've got left into the warband!'

The 8th's rate of fire increased, the tired

archers giving the last of their trembling arm strength to rain their remaining arrows on to the wavering warband. With a triumphant bray of trumpets the hill fort's southern rampart was suddenly crested by familiar figures, the shields and helmets unmistakably Roman as the auxiliary cohorts fought their way into the demoralised defence.

'Qadir! Cease firing on the warband. Self-defence only!'

Even as the bows fell quiet, their little part of the battlefield suddenly silent without the incessant twanging of bowstrings, the depleted warband broke under a savage frontal assault, hundreds of men streaming away from the ill-matched fight across ground carpeted with the bodies of the dead and wounded. For a moment it appeared as if the remnant of the warband would escape, at least as far as the cavalrymen patrolling beyond the fort's earth walls, but as the Tungrians watched, the hill fort's rim was suddenly lined with the silhouettes of hundreds of soldiers, waiting grimly for the tribesmen to attempt a breakout, their spears held ready to throw.

'Sixth Legion.'

Dubnus nodded grim assent to Marcus's statement.

'And about bloody time. Seems we're taking prisoners after all.'

The routed tribesmen, helpless in the face of such overwhelming force, threw down their weapons and stood helpless under the legionaries' spears.

* * *

Legatus Equitius came forward with the remainder of the legion later that morning, keen to understand just why the warband had been camped in so precarious a position. He found the detachment in high spirits, and his senior tribune delighted with the result. Antonius led him across the ground over which the cohorts had trampled earlier that day, up the hill fort's slope and down into its bowl. As they crested the slope the scale of the slaughter became apparent. Legionaries were toiling to stack the barbarian dead on one side of the fort, while the wounded were squatting and lying in even greater numbers on the other. Equitius stopped to survey the scene.

'How many of them did you kill?'

'Four hundred and seventy-odd dead, nearly twice as many wounded.'

'And our losses?'

The tribune's smile told him most of the story before he even opened his mouth to reply.

'Thirty-four dead, sixty-two wounded and a dozen of them likely to be dead before nightfall.'

Equitius stopped walking and turned to face the tribune, his eyebrows raised.

'You killed and wounded twelve hundred barbarians for the loss of less than fifty men? I would have expected a nought on the end of our side of that tally. How did you manage it?'

Antonius smiled modestly.

'I deployed the auxiliaries in front of our own men and assaulted the barbarians in the usual manner, with one small variation. The Tungrian cohort has a double-strength century of archers, and I . . . '

Understanding dawned on Equitius.

'Ah . . . I see. The Tungrian archers. Let's have a look at the wounded, shall we?'

They crossed the fort's bowl and Equitius's bodyguard fanned out with their swords drawn and shields ready, their centurion walking forward with his vine stick under one arm in an obvious show of bravado. The wounded had, for the most part, one feature in common. The legatus favoured his deputy with a knowing smile.

'Horrible things, iron-headed arrows, when you're not wearing armour and a decent helmet, but lethal if you're caught in the open without a nice thick shield. A sound idea, Antonius, very fine work. Clearly you've been hiding your talents from me these last few months . . . eh?'

Antonius thought quickly.

'I can't take all the credit, Legatus. It was Prefect Scaurus that first mentioned the existence of his archers to me . . . '

Equitius smiled easily.

'Quite right, Tribune, credit where it's due.'

'I stationed men all around the fort once the fight was properly started, took almost three hundred prisoners.'

'You took prisoners?'

The tribune gave his superior a careful glance.

'I thought you'd want to know what they were doing here, so I took the liberty . . . '

Equitius nodded his agreement.

'Where are they?

'I've got a couple of centuries guarding them back at the camp, sir. I thought it best to separate them from their wounded, given that we're treating them in the usual manner.'

Equitius nodded again.

'Battlefield rules?'

'Yes, sir. The senior centurions are making the assessments. Given that we've got such a small number of wounded the legion medics are getting plenty of arrow removal practice on the easier cases, but anyone that won't be able to walk away from here is being taken over the fort's wall and put to the sword.'

Equitius shrugged, watching another seriously wounded man being carried up the earth wall by a pair of legionaries.

'They're all going to die, whether now or later. And now I'd best get over to your camp.'

'Yes, sir. You'll be wanting to question their leader?'

'You got their chieftain alive? Well, well, Tribune. In the words of a legatus I served under on the German border, it's as good to be lucky as it is to be good. And you, young man, having called down the iron rain on these poor fools and still pulled their leader unharmed from the wreckage, you can truly consider yourself to be a lucky man. Yes, I very much want to meet the murdering bastard, but before I do I've a more important appointment to keep.'

* * *

Equitius strode into Scaurus's tent fifteen minutes later to find prefect and first spear waiting for him.

'Gentlemen . . . you knew I was coming?'

The prefect smiled tightly, tapping his right ear.

'It's not hard to guess when a senior officer is likely to appear through the tent flap when one can hear a succession of centurions shouting at their men to stand to attention, all the time getting steadily closer. It was either going to be you, Legatus, or the governor. And Ulpius Marcellus isn't one for venturing out into the camp.'

The legatus smiled wryly.

'Very clever. Nearly as clever as that trick you pulled on those poor barbarians you had young Tribulus Corvus and his Syrians use for target practice this morning. My broad stripe had a decent go at taking credit for the idea, cheeky young sod, but it was pretty evident he wouldn't even have known you had any archers on the payroll, much less that they're led by a man who can't be allowed out into the countryside without him finding some novel way of bringing death to the blue-noses . . . '

He caught the look in Scaurus's eye.

'You look less than happy, Prefect. Am I to presume . . . ?'

'That I'm aware of your little secret with regard to my officer, Legatus? That I have already sought to minimise his exposure to those people likely to be looking for him? Or, perhaps, that I'm just a little concerned that this latest success, necessary though it was for the survival of my command, will bring the interest of the wrong people down on us all like flies on fresh shit. That would be 'yes' to all three. Sir.'

Equitius turned away, hiding a momentary smile.

'So you've already taken young Corvus under your wing, eh, Prefect? And why would that be, when everyone from the governor down tells me that you're as straight as the road from Dark Pool to the banks of the River Abus? You're supposed to be imperial through and through, Prefect, so why dirty your hands with our fugitive's sordid scrabblings to avoid justice, eh?'

Scaurus put both hands on his hips. His tongue played on his bottom lip as he judged the right answer to give to a man who was, for all the tension in the air, still his superior.

'Why, Legatus? Because I see myself in him, and if you want to see behind that statement you'll be a long time waiting. That and the persuasive case my first spear made for the man's capacity for battle. He's . . . '

' . . . simply worth saving, eh, Prefect? Those were the words that came to me when I asked myself what in Hades I was doing sheltering him from the throne's hunting dogs while I was in your shoes. But now we have a larger problem than our own ability to combine our obedience to the empire with loyalty to our ideals, do we not?'

Scaurus nodded unhappily.

'Indeed we do. There's a man less than two hundred paces from here who hates my guts with a passion I doubt either of you can comprehend, and who has a very good idea that Tribulus Corvus has found refuge with this cohort. I can assure you that for all the imperial favour that unearthing such a fugitive would bring him, it would give him nowhere near as much enjoyment as seeing me unmasked as his protector.'

* * *

The cohort awoke to mist and drizzle the next morning, took a hasty breakfast and prepared to stand to in the grey morning light. Marcus dressed in his tent attended by Antenoch and a sleepy Lupus, tucking his tunic into his woollen campaign trousers. The garment was a comfort permitted by the first spear only when the cohort was in the field late in the campaign season, a time of the year known for its wind and sudden rain.

'I'll never get used to wearing these blasted itchy things. All those years reading that trousers are the mark of the barbarian, and suddenly I can't go outdoors in anything other than high summer — or whatever passes for summer here — without them.'

Antenoch muttered his response into the pile of his officer's equipment.

'I can see how your delicate legs would enjoy the protection, Centurion. Would you like the leg wrappings too?'

A look passed between them, and Marcus snorted gently, a half-smile creasing his face.

'Don't mock the afflicted, Clerk, and pass me those socks and my boots.'

He tugged the heavy woollen socks into place, tucking their open ends under his feet as he laced up his polished hobnailed boots. Streaks of mud decorated their gleaming leather, betraying the lack of any attention the previous evening.

'We'll move this morning.' Antenoch brushed an errant horsehair back into place in Marcus's helmet crest and placed it on his bedroll. 'You don't get this many troops in one place without the boys in bronze wanting to march them aimlessly round the countryside. It's their way of convincing themselves that they're doing something meaningful.'

Marcus pulled on his padded leather arming vest, meant to protect the wearer's flesh from being cut by his mail's rings if they were struck by sword or spear, carefully pulling it straight to ensure that it wouldn't wrinkle and chafe under the armour.

'There's still a warband out there, or perhaps you'd forgotten that? We'll be advancing to make contact with the enemy.'

His clerk snorted.

'I'll put down ten to your five that our glorious leaders don't have the first clue where the blue-noses are hiding. 'Somewhere in the forests to the north-east' is about the limit of their intelligence, so once again we'll get to go and find them the hard way under the pretence of scouting to the flanks. Lupus, help me with the centurion's mail.'

He lifted the heavy mail shirt over Marcus's

head and pulled it down on to the leather arming vest while Lupus pulled the mail's hem down his thighs to ensure its close fit to his shoulders. Antenoch rubbed a finger at the rings across one shoulder, holding his hand out to the child.

'Dirty. You were supposed to brush and polish this shirt before bed last night, you idle little bugger. You want me to send the centurion on parade in dirty armour?'

He reached for the soft brush and set about the rings with vigour, the swift strokes shaking the uncomplaining Marcus from side to side as he raised an eyebrow at an unabashed Lupus. Antenoch clipped the back of the child's head with his open palm.

'You leave this dirty another night this month and you can kiss your purse money goodbye . . . what's that?'

Starting guiltily, the red-faced boy repeated his muttered comment aloud.

'I said there's nothing to spend it on anyway.'

Antenoch snorted.

'Welcome to my army, you dozy little sod. Of course there's nothing to spend it on, this is a fighting cohort on campaign, not a tour of the wall's honey-cake stalls. And while we're at it I can see mud spots on those boots. The centurion can see them too, but he's too polite to mention it . . . '

He shot a hand out and grabbed the boy's ear, twisting it painfully and pulling the child close to his face.

'You can consider this your administrative punishment. Next time it'll be loss of pay and privileges for you, my lad. Now off with you and find your grandad, make sure he's ready for parade and bring him here.'

Lupus ran from the tent clutching his reddened ear. Marcus raised an eyebrow.

'Pass my belt and baldrics. You're too hard on the boy.'

Antenoch shrugged, passing over Marcus's officer's heavy belt and sword harnesses.

'And you're all too soft on him. You're too nice, Morban's too busy being his grandfather and the rest of the troops treat him more like a mascot than a kid with a need for discipline. Someone's got to act like a father for him, and in the absence of anyone else . . . '

He raised an eyebrow at Marcus, inviting further comment, but none was forthcoming. After an uncomfortable pause the officer held out a hand.

'Helmet, please. Thank you.'

The centurion pulled his helmet on, tightening the leather chin strap and looking around him.

'Looking for this?'

Antenoch held out the thick knobbly vine stick, and Marcus took it, rotating it unconsciously until his thumb found its accustomed resting place in a small indentation.

'You're right, as it happens. We do spoil the boy in our own ways. I suppose we're all trying to compensate him for the roll of the dice he's had to endure in the last few months. I take your point, though, and I'll try to be a bit more like an officer with him, and a bit less like . . . '

He fell silent, and Antenoch nodded his

understanding, his face softening.

'His older brother? Don't change a thing, Centurion, I'll make sure that the troops give him a bit of a harder time, starting with that old bugger Morban. You just teach him how to throw iron around the way that you do, and leave the tough stuff to the rest of us.'

Marcus nodded, his eyes momentarily far away, then gathered himself and turned, stepping out into the morning's murk, calling for Qadir. Antenoch turned his attentions to packing away the centurion's gear, muttering quietly in the tent's silence.

'No, don't change a thing, Centurion. Being his older brother might help keep you the right side of sane, given all that's happened in the last few months.'

8

Late in the afternoon of the day after the battle of the hill fort the 20th Legion rejoined the 6th, having completed their sweep of the ground to the south of the wall, bringing with them the governor and his staff. Shortly after their arrival the Votadini chieftain was escorted into the governor's presence by the leader of Equitius's bodyguard, a pair of soldiers with drawn swords guarding against the unlikely chance of his being able to shed the coils of thick rope that bound him so tightly it was all he could do to walk unaided. His face was badly bruised, testament to the harsh treatment he had received from his guards since being captured, men incensed by the massacre of the Frisian cohort. Ulpius Marcellus raised an eyebrow at Equitius.

'Do we really need the swords, Legatus? Even ignoring my unlikely contribution, there are two legates, half a dozen prefects and the same number of tribunes facing this one prisoner, who, I am forced to note, is trussed up with enough rope to restrain a prize-winning ox. What are your men going to do, cut his throat if he hops towards me in a threatening manner?'

Equitius nodded his agreement, making a subtle gesture to his stony-faced guard commander, who, with a look that spoke volumes, ordered the two soldiers out of the tent. The governor leaned closer to the helpless prisoner.

'That's better. Who can focus when there's sharpened iron six inches from the back of his neck, eh? So, whatever your name is, do you speak any Latin?'

The prisoner nodded, his battered face defiant.

'I am Martos, sister's son to King Brennus of the Votadini, and I speak your language well enough. In the time before this war my tribe was a friend to your people.'

Ulpius Marcellus leant back in his chair, resting his chin on his hand.

'Yes, I know. I was governor of this country for four years, and I came to know your tribal king Brennus tolerably well. You'll probably be aware that we're still in communication with him, of a sort, and that we've offered him peace if he can deliver us this upstart Calgus in return. I would have thought that a decent enough bargain, but now I find your people implicated in a fresh atrocity against our forces. I know you took part in the attack on White Strength, so don't think to attempt to mislead me on the subject.'

He stared unblinkingly at the prisoner, whose shoulders slumped at the accusation.

'We fought at White Strength. Calgus . . . he . . . '

'Lied to you? Made you believe that you could succeed your uncle under his guidance, that you would be a strong man if you helped him to victory?'

Martos nodded, his eyes on the ground.

'So your men led the attack on the fort, am I right?'

Another nod.

'And how many of your warriors died breaking into the fort and putting the garrison to the sword? Five hundred?'

The reply was almost a whisper.

'More. Probably twice that many . . . '

Legatus Macrinus spoke up.

'With your permission, Governor? You're telling us that you sacrificed nearly half your strength to buy this Calgus a victory, and that in return he had you and your men dumped right in the path of our cavalry response? You want us to believe that he'd be willing to throw away so much of his strength to achieve a meaningless tactical victory and then pull the fangs from what was left of an unreliable ally's dissent? He'd have to be mad to be so profligate with his strength, unless . . . '

Martos lifted his gaze to meet the Roman's, his confidence returning.

'Yes. Unless he has more strength than you're aware of. Spare my life and I will tell you everything I know. Kill me, and I will take secrets to my grave that might cost you this war.'

The governor scoffed, waving away the suggestion.

'Spare your life? When I can interrogate any number of your men and discover everything I need to know without having to consort with a man that put an entire cohort of good men to the sword and then desecrated their corpses? Why don't you just ask me to name you emperor?'

Martos kept his gaze fixed on the governor.

'I was close to Calgus for long enough to know more about his schemes than he was willing to reveal to me. I overheard snatches of conversation I was never meant to witness, and I saw things that were meant to stay between Calgus and the men close to him. And I'll make you one firm vow. If you free me, and enough of my people to stand around me in battle, I will hunt down Calgus for you and bring you his head. I will swear an oath to any god you care to name to take vengeance for the lies and disaster that he has brought down on my people.'

Ulpius Marcellus thought for a moment, his eyes narrowed.

'Have this man taken away, Legatus. I think any debate on the subject should be private.'

The stony-faced centurion marched the bound prisoner from the tent, leaving the Romans looking at each other. Equitius broke the silence, shaking his head gently with wonder.

'I met Calgus, just before they attacked my cohort at Lost Eagle, and I knew then that he was a cunning bastard, but this is simply beyond my understanding. Leading an entire tribe's remaining strength into our path to cement his power over the others, that's more than just a bold step. Who's to say there isn't more in his plan that we have yet to discover the hard way? Another Lost Eagle might cost us this war, possibly even this province, we all know that.'

The governor raised an eyebrow.

'Are you suggesting that we do as this murdering barbarian requests, Legatus? Give the man his freedom and let him vanish into the depths of the wild country, escaping the justice that should already have his head on a stake outside this tent?'

Prefect Scaurus spoke into the silence that followed, his voice quiet and yet clear, demanding to be heard despite the absence of drama in his tone.

'Considering what the Votadini have been through, it's at least worthy of consideration, Governor.' He continued, not waiting for permission. 'Let's say they lost a thousand men at White Strength. We killed another five hundred or so breaking into the hill fort, and there's probably the same number of wounded that won't fight again for a few months, even if they weren't badly enough hurt to rate the legion's gladius solution. What does that leave, two hundred warriors? Two hundred and fifty? Calgus has already betrayed Martos once, so if he were to come back from the dead with that small a force I'd say the odds are excellent that the 'Lord of the Northern Tribes', having already told his men some story or other about how the Votadini have betrayed them all, will have his men put them to the iron without a second thought.'

He stood silently for a moment, allowing his words to sink in.

'There's another point worth considering as well, Governor. Before the war, the land between the two walls was divided roughly into two parts, not equal, but very distinct nonetheless. To the west, living under the control of thousands of our troops, were the Selgovae, Novantae and

Damnonii, forever testing our strength with ambushes and skirmishes. A posting up the north road was no cause for celebration for any soldier I ever discussed the matter with. To the east, on the other hand, were the Votadini. Compare and contrast, gentlemen. There were no forts on their territory, no requirement to control the tribe's gatherings, and no need to tie down thousands of our men in static positions that would make them a target for every disaffected young blood with a point to prove. I think the main question should be how we want this land of theirs to be governed after the war. Do we want to put four or five thousand more troops on to Votadini land, with all of the problems we always had with the western tribes, or would we prefer to take things back to the way they were . . . ?'

The governor nodded, glancing at his legates for their opinion.

'Your point, Prefect, is well made. I can take quick and satisfying revenge on this man and the survivors of his warband, such as they are . . . or I can play the politician and spare him, with his support and friendship the price I exact in return. Opinions?'

Scaurus glanced around him, taking the measure of his seniors' reaction. Apart from Furius's grim face, most of the men in the room looked thoughtful. The 20th Legion's legatus spoke up, his lips pursed.

'I dislike the idea of allowing this man his freedom, when he should by rights cough out his last breaths on a cross, but . . . ' He shrugged, shooting an appraising glance at Scaurus. ' . . . the prefect does makes a persuasive case. I would recommend a subtly different approach, however. Reprieve the man by all means, but don't allow him to run free. In fact, I say we keep him close. His men will make excellent guides as we push northwards into the hills, and when the time comes you can slip their collars and send them after Calgus when he least expects it. In fact, once he's unburdened himself of these hints and whispers he says he can recount to us, I commend you to put his men under the stewardship of young Scaurus here. He can worry about liberating his kingdom once Calgus's head is on the pole in place of his own.'

* * *

Scaurus hadn't seen his first spear so much as irritated during their brief association, so the experience of triggering incandescent anger in the man engendered something between exhilaration and genuine fear.

'I don't give a *fuck* what the governor said!' Frontinius put his pointed index finger squarely in his superior's face, his hold on a temper of glacial slowness but volcanic ferocity completely lost. '*You* can tell *him* that there is *no fucking way* that an assorted collection of barbarian murderers are going to find a place in *my* cohort!'

Scaurus raised an eyebrow, apparently hugely amused by the other man's rage.

'That's odd, First Spear, I could have sworn it was mine?'

Frontinius ignored the wry question, too far gone in his uncontrollable anger.

'Those bastards should all have been beheaded the second it was proved they took part in the White Strength massacre. That they're still breathing is bad enough, but for the senior soldier in the whole of Britannia to ask us to take them on . . . ' He spread his hands wide, frustration written across his face. What does he think we are? What does he think I am? I served with their first spear, he was a soldier with this cohort for a couple of years until the Frisians needed some replacements . . . '

Scaurus shook his head decisively, one word rapping out across his subordinate's diatribe.

'*Enough!*'

The senior centurion raised his head at the sudden harshness in his superior's tone, finding the prefect's face set with an implacability equal to his own. He drew breath to speak, but the words were unformed when Scaurus moved from his place by the tent's field table, putting his face uncomfortably close to the first spear's, features set in a snarl of anger the match of his subordinate's and more.

'I said '*enough*', and you'd better appreciate something that you might not have been faced with for a while, First Spear. I am your fucking superior *OFFICER*!' Frontinius flinched at the sudden venom in his superior's voice. 'When I give you an order, you may seek to debate its merits, you may tell me that you don't especially like it, but you will carry it out as completely and effectively as if it were you own idea. And for my part, while I will listen to your views, both seek and respect your opinions, I will eventually issue commands that I believe to be correct given my understanding of the overall situation. Which may well surpass *yours*. As for your questions, let me sum it up for you by answering just one of them: what does the governor think you are? The governor thinks you're a soldier of Rome, sworn to follow the instructions of your superiors, no matter what you may think of those orders.'

His voice softened slightly.

'The governor, Sextus Frontinius, believes you to be a professional, a career soldier with the ability to bury your distaste for this order and ensure that your people bury theirs alongside it. We've been chosen quite deliberately for this duty, First Spear, and it's a responsibility I neither can nor would seek to avoid. What's left of the Votadini warband marches with us when we leave here tomorrow, whether *we* like it or not.'

* * *

The Tungrians paraded the next morning with more than one man staring open mouthed at the motley collection of Votadini warriors drawn up in three rough lines alongside their prefect and first spear. Soldiers nudged each other in the ranks and shared whispered speculation as to the reasons why the survivors of the battle of the hill fort might be parading in front of them.

'Perhaps we're going to put them to the sword? You know, for White Strength?'

Morban turned a withering glare on the 8th Century's trumpeter.

'Do they look like they're ready to be slaughtered, you prick? They're all armed, for a start.'

A man in the century's front rank spoke up in the silence that followed.

'Perhaps they join cohort? Like us?'

Morban spluttered with poorly restrained mirth, his gaze fixed on the barbarians.

'Oh, fuck me, *that's* even better. Yes, that's right, we're going to take a pack of untrained murdering barbarian halfwits into an infantry cohort. Why didn't I think of it sooner! Tell you what, Ahmad, or whatever your name is, I'll give you twenty to one on that . . . no, fuck it, I'll make that fifty.'

'I take bet, Standard-bearer. One-denarius stake.'

'Easy money.'

The trumpeter, still red faced from his earlier rebuff, opened his mouth to speak.

'And no, you fucking can't have some of that. Now shut it, Uncle Sextus is about to let us in on what's going on.'

* * *

The Tungrian cohorts marched to the south-west along the line of the foothills for the first two hours after breaking camp and wading across the ford, a dozen message riders from the Petriana wing walking their horses alongside the marching soldiers. The Votadini warriors, almost two hundred and fifty men strong, walked to either side of the lead century, their leader silent and uncommunicative in their midst. The Tungrians and their new comrades eyed each other unhappily from time to time, neither side capable of trusting the other given their recent history. As the day wore on towards mid-morning the troops started to sweat under their heavy cloaks, and the order was given for both cloaks and helmets to be removed, and the latter to be hung around their necks.

'Take your cloak off, boy, roll it up and put it in your pack. Let the wind get to your skin and you'll soon be comfortable again.'

Lupus followed Antenoch's example, watching as the clerk bundled his own cloak into his pack, ready to be hoisted on to his carrying pole once the rest stop was done.

'Antenoch . . . ?'

'Yes?'

'Why can't I have a sword?'

'You've got a sword. What's that in your belt?'

The boy frowned.

'Not a wooden sword. A real one.'

Glaring a warning at the nearest soldiers, Antenoch unsheathed his gladius and handed it to the child, handle first.

'Take a grip of that. No, don't wave the bloody thing around, just hold it for a moment . . . See, heavy, isn't it?'

The boy shrugged, his eyes fixed on the weapon's blade as it weaved unsteadily in his hand.

'Not really. I could carry it. Everyone else has got one.'

'Well . . . '

'What if we're attacked? How am I supposed to fight without a sword?'

The clerk looked to the sky, seeking inspiration that clearly wasn't coming. An 8th Century soldier nudged him, quietly displaying a short dagger under the cover of his cloak and raising an eyebrow. Antenoch frowned, raised an eyebrow of his own and tilted his head to the child. The Hamian nodded encouragingly.

'How much?'

'To you, ten denarii. To the boy, is gift.'

Lupus watched the two men uncomprehendingly.

'A gift?' Antenoch's eyes narrowed. 'Why. You fancy him or something?'

The other man laughed.

'No, I do not like boys. Is simply gift. You were never boy, eh? You never wanted knife, shiny and sharp?'

Antenoch held his stare for a moment, then shouted up the length of the century's column of relaxing men.

'*Morban!*'

The standard-bearer stayed seated at the century's head, raising his head.

'*What?*'

'*You all right if Lupus has a knife?*'

The answer took a split second's thought.

'*How much?*'

Antenoch rolled his eyes, muttering to himself.

'Fuck me, not 'do you think he's old enough?',

but 'how much?'. That's our Morban . . . *It's a gift!*'

'*'Course he can, if it's free! Don't ask stupid questions!*'

Antenoch rolled his eyes at the Hamian, muttering a quiet insult.

'Tight-arse.'

He turned back to the boy, who, having realised the subject of the discussion, was wide eyed with anticipation, the sword dangling forgotten in his hands.

'I'll tell you what, young Lupus, I'll make you a deal . . . Here, give me that back.'

The child reluctantly held the gladius out, watching hungrily as it slid back into Antenoch's scabbard.

'Here's the deal. You keep the centurion's boots gleaming, no mud marks, and you polish his armour every night without fail, and you get to hold on to this.'

He took the dagger from the Hamian and held it up for the child to see. Sliding the small blade from its sheath, he put a finger gingerly to the blade's silver line as it flashed in the morning's brightness.

'Cocidius, but it's sharp!'

The weapon's donor smiled happily.

'No point in blunt knife. No point, see?'

The Briton raised both eyebrows in protest.

'Yes, thank you for proving conclusively that the old ones are indeed the old ones. So, boy, the knife stays yours just as long as you do your jobs properly. The first time I find either his boots or armour — including his helmet — dirty when we're dressing him in the morning, the knife goes straight back to . . . what's your name?'

The Hamian bowed his head in greeting, touching a hand to his forehead.

'I am Hamid.'

'To your new uncle Hamid. Deal?'

'Yes!'

'Good. Put the sheath on your belt, like this . . . see?'

The child stared happily at the knife resting at his hip, putting one hand on the handle in a self-conscious pose.

'Never mind posing for the sculptor, say thanks to Uncle Hamid here for being so generous.'

The Hamian struggled to stay upright as Lupus wrapped his arms round his neck.

'Thanks, Uncle Hamid!'

'Now, off with you up the column. Go and show your grandad your new weapon. Oh . . . '

He arrested the child's departure with a swift grab at his belt.

'And one more thing. No messing about with it, right? No throwing it, no cutting your initials into trees and no trying to cut your hair either. I catch you mucking about with that, or hear about it from anyone else, you'll lose the knife and you won't get it back. You want to be a soldier, you'd better learn to behave like one. Go!'

Lupus ran happily up the century's length, shouting to his grandfather. Antenoch settled back on his elbows, puffing out a sigh and shaking his head slightly with a half-smile.

‘I don’t know where the child’s energy comes from.’

He held out a hand to the Hamian.

‘Thanks, Hamid, that was decent of you.’

The other man shrugged.

‘He good boy. We all been young, wanted knife. He been unlucky, we hear. Give him little happiness, eh?’

Antenoch nodded.

‘Besides, his grandfather foolish enough to make me large bet this morning. He already paid for knife.’

‘Ah, that was you, was it? Well, it was still kind of you. Here . . . ’

He delved into his bag and pulled out a small paper parcel, passing it over to the Hamian.

‘I was saving this to share with the boy later, but I think he’d rather have the knife.’

‘Cake?’

‘Honey cake. Good too, go on, get it down your neck before we’re on the move again. I can’t see the boys in the shiny armour waiting very long before getting us on our feet again, the morning’s too good to waste when there’s still a long way to go to the river.’

Farther up the column the barbarian warriors were sitting in a tight group close to Dubnus’s 9th Century, the two groups exchanging wary glances. After a few minutes Dubnus sighed, told his chosen man to keep an eye on things and got to his feet, walking across to the Votadini group. Hundreds of soldiers watched his move with mixed feelings, one of them nudging his mate and pointing at the young centurion.

'Fuck me, the prince is going for a chat with them.'

Frontinius overheard the comment and swivelled from his discussion with Scaurus, taking in his centurion's approach to the diminished warband's leader. Standing in front of the squatting Votadini nobleman, he put out a hand.

'You must be Martos. My name is Dubnus, formerly a prince of the Brigantes people and now a soldier of Rome. If we are to walk these hills in company we might as well be on speaking terms . . . '

The words hung in the air for a long moment, as Martos looked the centurion up and down with blank-faced neutrality before returning his gaze to the outstretched hand.

'Well, Dubnus, former prince of the Brigantes . . . '

He took the offered hand, using it to pull himself to his feet. Face to face the two men were well matched, both powerfully muscled from years of wielding their heavy weapons, their faces dark from the continual exposure to the elements and their stances confident in their ability to best any man put in front of them.

' . . . it seems we have something in common, you and I, for I am a former prince of the Votadini, now reduced to running with the very wolves we sought to drive from our land.'

He stared hard at the centurion, waiting for any sign of offence. To his surprise Dubnus merely smiled grimly.

'Oh yes, I know *that* feeling. And yet I have

made my peace with these people, and turned my sword arm to their purpose. Will you walk alongside me when we rejoin the march? Perhaps we can offer each other some conversation of interest?'

Martos nodded slowly.

'I will. I might better understand what put you in that uniform.'

Frontinius watched as the two men nodded to each other and returned to their respective sides of the divide between the Tungrians and Votadini.

'Of all my officers, it would be Dubnus to make the first move . . . '

He turned to find Scaurus with a quizzical look on his face.

'I'm forgetting, you don't know the man. The centurion in question was tribal nobility south of the wall before he joined the cohort. Perhaps he understands what your man Martos is feeling in this situation better than the man himself.'

'And perhaps we start to see the method in our governor's apparent madness, eh, First Spear?'

Frontinius snorted and turned away, calling the cohort back on to its feet for the march, but Scaurus had seen the thoughtful look on his face, and stood waiting for the march to resume with a quiet smile.

* * *

The two cohorts marched at the standard campaign pace for most of the morning, skirting along the edge of the mountains in bright sunshine. From their path along the mountains' outskirts, two and three hundred feet above the plain, they could see the main body of the army. The two legions were marching alongside the river as it snaked across the valley, and a mile beyond their columns the two cohorts thrown out as guards on the right flank clung to the low slopes of the hills to the south. Dubnus and Martos walked together between the 9th Century and the Votadini remnant, deep in conversation. Speaking in their own language, their initial diffidence had quickly been forgotten as the barriers of their respective causes fell under their mutual curiosity.

'So I had little choice. Once my father was gone I knew that going back to my own people would see me dead inside a day. Besides, he made me swear to go to the Romans as he lay dying . . . '

Martos nodded solemnly.

'Such an oath cannot be denied once made.'

'Aye. It was hard for me here at first, even if Uncle Sextus . . . ' He caught the Briton's uncomprehending frown, 'Sorry, First Spear Frontinius, only he was a centurion at the time, had made a promise to my father to take me in. The men that commanded this cohort then did all they could to break me.' He smiled. 'The formal beatings never really bothered me, and they stopped the informal beatings after I got tired of defending myself and put three men in the fort's hospital for a month. After that things just settled down, and we all got used to each other. Mind you, I still wouldn't be an officer today if it weren't for a Ro . . . for a man that joined us a few months ago. But that's another story. And you, how do you come to be walking into danger alongside us, instead of waiting for us with your comrades?'

Martos recounted the story of his desire to supplant his uncle the king, and the subsequent betrayal by Calgus, his voice bitter with the recent memory.

'I was a fool, and nothing less. I should have stood by my king, but my head was turned by Calgus and his promises that I would return to my tribal lands in victory, and as his closest ally.' His voice fell, the words so soft that Dubnus strained to hear them. 'I wanted to be king, and all I achieved was the massacre of my warriors and the destruction of our family. My king is probably dead by now, and Calgus will send one of his trusted men north to rule my kingdom. My children will be put to death and my woman will either be killed or more likely made a toy for the new leader's men.'

He stared out over the plain below them in silence for a moment before speaking again, his voice stronger.

'All these things will happen, there's no way to prevent them, but I tell you this, Centurion Dubnus, I will have revenge on that slimy piece of shit that calls himself 'Lord of the Northern Tribes'. I will twist his guts in my hand and tear them from his body, and I will fill his clever mouth with his torn manhood before I allow him to die. Either that, or I will die with my sword thick with his men's blood. I have sworn this, and my warriors have sworn to follow me to either victory or death.'

Dubnus smiled darkly.

'And such an oath cannot be denied, once made. I wish you well in your quest for revenge, and given the chance I would count myself honoured to fight alongside you. I too have a score to settle with Calgus.'

The other man gave him a scornful look.

'You think we'll be allowed to fight in your line? I doubt it, Centurion, our ways are too different, and I doubt that we're trusted even half well enough for such an *honour*.'

Dubnus nodded, ignoring the bitter tone in the other man's voice.

'True enough, but we're not like them.' He pointed down at the two legions grinding their way across the plain below them. 'They fight in a ponderous fashion, much as they move across the land, their movements cautious and measured, always seeking to bring their swords and shields to bear on the right ground. We, on the other hand, are faster across ground, and while we can fight their way we can also take our iron to the enemy with speed and stealth. Your chance to fight alongside us may come sooner than you think . . . '

* * *

After the midday rest stop, Tribune Scaurus and the first spear walked down the cohort to meet up with Furius and Neuto at the head of the second cohort.

'The Votadini say it's time to turn north and get up the mountain a fair way if we're going to keep scouting along the mountain flanks. Apparently we'll have to cross the Red River about ten miles from here, and the only good ford is above a waterfall up in the hills.'

Furius grimaced.

'I still don't like following these savages off into the wild. For all we know there's a fucking great warband waiting for us up there. We'll be cut off from the main body, probably out of sight too . . . '

Scaurus nodded in apparent sympathy.

'I know. If it's any consolation I don't think these men will lead us astray. Their hunger for revenge on Calgus is too strong.'

Furius snorted.

'A view based on your long experience of dealing with the locals, eh, Rutilius Scaurus?'

Scaurus leaned closer to Furius, lowering his voice.

'You know, Gracilus Furius, one of these days you're going to make one thoughtless remark too many for your own good. As it happens, I do know much more about this country and its people than most people appreciate, and while there are some very good reasons why I intend keeping it that way, I'm happy to tell you this; in my opinion Martos doesn't intend us ill. Call it instinct, or call it the very simple fact that he has the strongest possible motivation for guiding us to the right place — either way I don't think he'll be selling us out. So I suggest that we show some balls and get on with it, before our subordinates start wondering if we're just a little bit lacking in eagerness to do our jobs.'

He turned away without waiting for an answer from his astonished colleague.

'First Spear Frontinius, let's have the first Tungrian back on their feet and ready to march, please. We'll camp beside this ford for the night and head off into the wild tomorrow morning.'

* * *

The afternoon's march was harder on the troops than the morning's progress, the late summer sun beating down on them without interruption, and by the time the river came into view their tunics were wet with sweat beneath their mail armour. Frontinius knew that every man in the cohort was looking at the clear cold water flowing down from the mountains above them with something close to desperation. He paraded them with their backs to the water, raising his voice to be heard above the river's rippling cascade down its rocky bed, and the thunder of its fifty-foot drop over the falls a hundred paces farther downstream. The 2nd Cohort formed up alongside them, their first spear gesturing to him to brief both cohorts as to their previously agreed course of action.

'First and Second cohorts, you will dump your kit in the places where your tents will be pitched once the wall's built. You can have a drink from your water bottles if you've got any left, and then get on with building the turf wall. If you have no water left . . . ' He paused to gauge how many of them were straining to hear the next words. ' . . . then you are an idiot and will go thirsty until the wall is up to the satisfaction of myself and my brother officers. Each cohort will build one long and two short sides to the camp, and link up in the standard two-cohort pattern. Lots have been drawn, and the guard centuries will be the Third and Eighth centuries of both cohorts.'

Which was fortunate, given that the Hamians still had little talent for cutting turf to the right dimensions or placing it to form a strong wall, and were little better than porters for the cut turf.

'When the turf wall is complete both cohorts will use the river to wash, two centuries at a time, in strict lottery order and for the length of a five-hundred count. The guard centuries will patrol the area to ensure that we don't get any nasty surprises, and will wash and eat last. All centurions to First Spear Neuto for camp layout and guard duties. Centurions Tertius and Corvus, to me, please. Soldiers, to your duties!'

The parade broke up into the usual purposeful chaos of camp-building, the centuries streaming away to their allotted sections of the earth wall. Marcus told his men to wait where they stood, and hurried across to the first spear, who was giving instructions to a pair of message riders who were to ride out and find the legions, and deliver the customary report as to the cohorts' position to the governor. The two centurions nodded their greeting to each other as Frontinius turned back to them.

'This country should be empty of any

barbarian forces, since we're supposed to have them penned up to the north-east, but you can consider me as sceptical as ever when it comes to the words 'should be'. So, centurions, you're going to scout the vicinity and tell me what you can see. Tertius, you're going to take your boys across the river and see what's over the next hill. Cautiously, though, I don't want to advertise that we're here. Centurion Corvus, you can do some climbing too. Go to the top of that hill behind us and take a good look around. Dismissed.'

The two centurions saluted, shared another brief nod and headed away to their men. Gathering the 8th, Marcus pointed up the hill to the camp's west, its slopes rising steeply from the riverbank to a rounded summit high above the ford.

'We're going up there. Chosen, we'll leave our shields here with a tent party to watch over them. Tell them I want every one of them washed clean by the time we come down again, just in case they think they've drawn easy duty.'

The century started to climb, at first grumbling quietly at the renewed exercise but then, as the view below them expanded with their progress up the slope, and as the cooling breeze dried their sweat, with less complaining and more chatter about what they could see from their elevated viewpoint. After a few minutes of climbing Marcus stopped for a moment, taking a deep breath to slow down his racing heart. Qadir, following close behind him, took the opportunity to pause in his turn.

'This is harder work than I expected.'

Marcus nodded, pointing down at the marching camp.

'Yes, but look at the view. See, there's my old century toiling away at the ankle-breaker.'

'Ankle . . . breaker?'

'Sorry, I don't suppose you're familiar with our terms. It's a ditch that is dug all the way around a marching camp, if time allows, and the spoil is thrown to the inside of the ditch to form the basis for the turf wall. It's called the ankle-breaker because the sides are cut straight, and at least two feet deep. If you fall into it in the darkness you'll almost certainly break your ankle. We haven't bothered with it until now, not with two legions within earshot, but now that we're well and truly alone out here it's a necessity.'

His chosen man nodded, gazing down at the labouring troops.

'I see. And you know they are your former troops because . . . ?'

'Ah, that's easy. I can see Dubnus striding round and shouting at the idlers. There, see? Add to that the fact that there seem to be a gang of barbarians carrying turf for him . . . '

Qadir nodded.

'Should we perhaps resume our climb? Some of the men are already close to the top.'

Marcus turned back to look up the hill.

'Gods below, you lot might not like marching, but give you a peak to climb . . . '

The view from the top of the hill was worth the climb. Down in the valley below they could see some of Tertius's men working their way up the hill on the far side of the river, while other tent parties had split off to left and right to follow the line of the river to north and south. The marching camp was already half built, its wall casting an appreciable shadow in the late afternoon sunshine. The land was pretty much bare of any vegetation bigger than small bushes except for a number of trees scattered down both banks of the Red River to the south of the falls. To the north and west were rolling hilltops of much the same height, although a succession of gradually higher peaks rose towards the highest of all, a good ten miles distant. To the east, the southern slope of the hill facing the ford ended abruptly in a near-vertical drop.

'That's interesting.' Marcus pointed down at the river. 'See, there's a shelf of hard rock running through the hillside, that's what makes the waterfall so tall. This side of the river it's hidden under the ground, but on the other side of the river it's been uncovered.' He stared down at the seam of rock running away into the distance. To the south of the outcrop was gently sloping land seamed by tributary streams of the Red. 'You know, that makes the riverbank below the falls much easier to defend. It would take a good while to get a body of men down that rock face to the far bank, it's steep enough to make for a slow climb, and far too tall to jump.'

'Yes, but look over there.'

Marcus followed Qadir's pointing finger. Off to the east, almost at the limit of visibility, a line of smoke was rising from a valley three or four peaks away.

'Might that be the barbarian camp?'

Marcus nodded.

'I'd guess so. And if we can see that . . . '

They turned to the south-east, taking in the view down the Red River's valley. Far away, down on the flat land out of the hills' undulations, they could see the occasional flash of sun on polished metal.

'The legions. They'll be camping for the night too, probably busy doing exactly the same as us. Hacking out a marching camp and dreaming of a dip in the river.'

'Yes. Unaware that up here there are two cohorts who have already washed their sweaty backsides in the water that will flow past them in an hour's time.'

Marcus laughed at him, unable to contain his amusement at the Hamian's turn of phrase.

'If I didn't know better, Chosen Man Qadir, I'd say that you've spent too much time consorting with Morban of late. 'Washed their sweaty backsides . . . ?''

Qadir grimaced.

'It's inevitable. You should hear some of the things that our men have started coming out with.'

⋆ ⋆ ⋆

First Spear Frontinius caught Tertius watching him again as they reached the crest of the valley's eastern slope. The 2nd Cohort centurion had been shooting him surreptitious glances ever since the first spear had declared his intention to join them in fording the river and exploring the ground on the other side. The river's fast-flowing water had been delightfully cold, cooling and refreshing the troops of Tertius's century and breathing fresh vigour into their tired bodies as they waded across the calf-deep stream.

'Amazing what a bit of running water will do for a man, eh, Tertius? Ten minutes ago this lot were puffing and groaning at the thought of more marching, and now they're off up the hill like fourteen-year-olds on a promise.'

Tertius answered with a non-committal grunt, continuing his climb up the valley's side. The first spear smiled to himself. This was a game he played with loaded dice.

'So tell me, Centurion, since we've not met before, how long have you served with the Second Tungrians?'

The other man took a long moment to answer, his tone cautious.

'Thirteen years, First Spear. I joined a year after the cohort moved to Fair Meadow.'

'Local boy?'

Tertius's reserve was still evident in the guarded tones of his reply.

'Not really. My father was a centurion with the Twentieth Legion, he retired to Veteran's Hill with my mother before I was born.'

Another officer that had settled down with a girl from a fortress vicus, Frontinius mused, a marriage of convenience for both parties. An older man with money and influence, but lacking a companion with whom to share his retirement, and a woman past her youth and staring into the abyss of approaching middle age, with soldiers' money getting harder to come by as her looks started to fade. She would have provided him with company and comfort in return for respectability and security. A new start in one of the veterans' colony towns was the usual way to provide suitable anonymity to such a union.

'A soldier's son, then. He must have told you a good number of tales about his time following the eagle. The Twentieth was heavily involved in putting down the last bit of local stupidity, back in the sixties.'

Tertius smiled.

'That he did. I grew up with the old man's stories, that and his mates forever showing up to sit round and relive their glory days . . . '

'And so you ended up on the wall, eager to make him proud.'

'He died five years ago, before I made centurion. It was his last ambition to see me with a vine stick in my hands, but making it to officer rank takes the time it takes . . . for most of us.'

The last comment was added in a tone so quiet that Frontinius half wondered whether he had imagined it. He pushed on, as the men in front of them turned up the slope towards the saddle, the lower ridge between two hills.

'You have a good first spear, one of the best. And how's that new tribune shaping up . . . Furius, isn't it?'

Tertius grimaced slightly, although it could have been the effort they were now having to put into climbing the valley's side.

'Tribune Furius is a strong man, First Spear. He does what he thinks is right, and allows the consequences to fall out as they will.'

Frontinius snorted.

'Don't I know it! I've a double century of archers to prove that. I hear he's a man with a taste for the crucifix as well.'

Tertius looked startled, his mouth working without anything coming out, the sudden reminder of his brother turning the words to dust in his mouth. Frontinius ploughed on in a gentler tone, recognising the emotion washing over the centurion.

'I heard about your man falling foul of him, and the way that Neuto and the rest of you spared him the indignity of the nails. I would have done the same in my colleague's place.'

Tertius took a moment to reply, his eyes moist as he stared out across the rolling hills.

'All I can tell you, First Spear, is that if there's an irregularity to be found, anything this tribune can turn to his own advantage, he will find it and he *will* use it.'

He turned to face Frontinius for a moment, taking a deep breath of the cool breeze.

'Anyone with a secret to hide would be better off somewhere else . . . '

Frontinius nodded his understanding, then clapped a hand on the centurion's shoulder.

'Well then, Centurion, let's get to the top of this pimple and see what we can see. Look, the Eighth Century have already got to the top of their hill.'

* * *

'So then he as good as told me that Furius already knows about young Corvus, and advised me to move the lad or risk discovery. He was less subtle with Marcus yesterday . . . '

Tribune Scaurus took a sip from the single cup of wine to which he had rationed himself for the night before replying. The first spear had come to his tent soon after the evening meal was finished, and double-strength sentries had been posted both around the marching camp and as listening patrols out across the river.

'Which means not only that Furius has a pretty fair idea that Corvus is not what he seems, but he's not doing all that good a job of keeping the fact to himself. So, First Spear, what to do?'

Frontinius scowled darkly into his own cup.

'Not as simple as you might think, Tribune. The boy's a member of the cohort now, not the friendless fugitive he was six months ago. He's fought and killed alongside these men, formed the kind of bond that sometimes takes a lifetime. The Ninth Century would fight to the death for him, almost to a man, and my centurions count him as a brother. If we send him away to uncertainty, even with the best intentions, we'll have a very unhappy cohort on our hands, I can promise you that.'

'And yet if we keep him here, and that meathead Furius denounces us to Ulpius Marcellus, neither of us is going to see many more sunsets. And don't forget that there are at least two senior officers embroiled in this nasty little affair, both your former tribune and tribune Licinius. I can think of half a dozen heads that will end up on stakes if this goes public. No, he has to disappear into thin air, and it has to happen soon. Once we're south of the wall again, the same day we pass through the north road gate, he has to vanish, and take his doctor with him or she'll be the next subject of Furius's ill intentions.'

Frontinius nodded sadly.

'I'd hoped that we could keep him here a while longer, and that the excitement would die down and allow him to settle and make a new life. If any man has earned some peace then that young man is a decent enough candidate.'

Scaurus tipped the rest of the cup down his throat.

'And you, of all people, First Spear, are well placed to know just how unfair life is. As it happens I have an idea that might just keep the lad alive for long enough that he gets to enjoy a little of the peace you describe, and his woman too, but it requires him to leave this cohort at the first opportunity. Preferably with 'killed in action' noted against his name in the pay records. It's either that, or watch your command be torn apart around you while Furius has a cross built for you. It may not be much of a choice, but it's the only one you've got. Oh, and by the way . . . '

He pointed a finger at the view through the tent's open end. In the 9th Century's lines the Tungrians and Votadini were indulging in a temporary weapons swap. The soldiers were hefting the barbarians' heavy swords above their heads, marvelling at the strength required to make more than a couple of the chopping attacks the long blades were made for, while the tribesmen were laughing at them from behind a row of borrowed shields, grimacing through the gaps between the shields and the brow pieces of the helmets they had donned to complete their impersonation.

'Amazing, isn't it, how quickly fighting men find the things that make them the same, and learn to ignore the things that make them different?'

* * *

Dubnus strolled into the 8th Century's section of the camp an hour later, Martos walking alongside him with a hand unconsciously resting on the hilt of his sword. The Hamians were already asleep in their tents, exhausted by the day's march, but, as the young centurion had expected, Marcus was still wide awake, discussing possible tactics for the next day with Qadir and his watch officers. All four men were wearing their heavy woollen cloaks, in contrast to the two Britons, who seemed not to notice the evening's chill. Marcus stood, clasping hands with Dubnus and turning to regard Martos steadily, his expression neutral.

'Martos, this is my brother-in-arms Marcus. Marcus, this is Martos, a prince of the Votadini tribe, now our ally and, as of today, my friend.'

Marcus nodded his greeting, extending a

hand. Martos took it, sustaining the grip for a moment.

'Your hand is cold, Marcus. That, and your face, tells me that you were not born in this land.'

Marcus nodded.

'I was born in Rome, and lived there for most of my life. This may be a pleasant evening to you, but I'm used to warmer.'

'And your soldiers?'

Marcus smiled, extending a hand to Qadir, who took his cue to bow his head slightly.

'My chosen man can speak for himself, but since his homeland is even warmer than my own, you can probably draw your own conclusions.'

The Briton looked at the Hamians bleakly for a long moment before speaking again.

'I asked Dubnus to show me the men who broke my warriors' will in the battle for the hill fort. I was curious to meet the soldiers who rained death on to my people, to look into their eyes and see what kind of men they were. I expected cold-hearted killers, and yet, as with the other men of your cohort, find only ordinary men like my own. If anything, your men look even more out of place here than mine.'

Qadir stood, offering his hand to the Briton.

'I must ask your forgiveness, Prince Martos. My men have been trained for years to regard their targets as simply that . . . targets. I am not proud that we killed so many of your warriors, although I am in honesty pleased that they managed their first battle as well as they did. Please accept my sympathy for your losses.'

Martos nodded, his eyes locked on the big Hamian.

'My heart is still bleeding for the men that have preceded me across the river, and I have hardened it for revenge on my enemies, but I cannot number you among them for simply fighting as you have been trained.'

His eyes flicked on to Marcus, narrowing with curiosity.

'A few among my men, warriors that managed to fight their way clear of the slaughter you called down upon us, speak of a lone officer who stood against a dozen of them two and three at a time. This man, they say, fought with two swords, and possessed both speed and skill they have not seen before . . . ' He looked at the Roman expectantly, gesturing to the two swords at his sides. 'This man was you?'

Marcus smiled.

'My archers are new to this style of fighting, and to war itself, and even a few of your warriors would have put them to flight in minutes. I had no choice except to get out in front of them.'

The Briton surprised him by bowing slightly.

'Necessity or not, you have the respect of my tribe. To stand alone against so many angry men will have taken great bravery . . . '

'Either that, or he's had the sense knocked out of him by too many blows to the head.'

Martos tossed his head back and laughed uproariously at Dubnus's jibe.

'That's good, I'll tell my warriors that the man who bested several of their number single handed was punch drunk at the time.' He put a hand on Marcus's shoulder, his focus on the Roman intent. 'It's a good thing I didn't manage to get free of the press of my men, or I too would probably have ended up face down under your blades. I look forward to the opportunity to wield my own sword at your side, now that fate sees us both looking for the chance to take the same man's head. And now, new friend Dubnus, I'd better get back to my men before they grow restive.'

Dubnus turned to follow him, raising a fist to Marcus for a tap in parting and nodding to Qadir. The chosen man watched the two men walk away towards the 9th Century's tents.

'They have a different approach to life, these Britons. In my country a man in his position would take his first opportunity to put a knife between your ribs, and mine too in all probability.'

Marcus pursed his lips, considering the point.

'I can't say that it would be any different in mine. And yet to all appearances the man's happy to treat the whole thing as water under the bridge. Let's hope he feels the same way when we're toe to toe with his former allies.'

* * *

The next morning started out fine enough, the cohorts' stand-to, their breakfast and preparations for the march illuminated by the early morning's soft red light. The supply carts were to be left in the marching camp's shelter for the day, each man carrying a double ration in his pack in case, as seemed likely, they were unable to return to the camp that evening. Morban, freed from his duties minding Lupus by Antenoch's reluctant agreement to remain at the ford with the boy and a tent party of men to guard the supply wagons, stared sourly into the sky above the hill to their east, nudging the 8th's trumpeter with an elbow.

'Red sky . . . '

The youth followed his pointing arm.

'And?'

The standard-bearer raised his eyebrows despairingly, looking around at the equally uncomprehending Hamians.

'Fuck me backwards, you really don't have a clue, do you. Didn't your dad ever tell you what happens when the sky's that colour?'

'What colour? Pink?'

'Don't get funny with me, you little prick. 'Red sky in the morning, soldier's warning'? No? Never mind, just make sure that your cloak's packed at the top of your gear, you're going to be wanting it out before the midday stop.'

As it happened, and as the trumpeter took great pains to point out to him at the midday ration break, the day stayed clear and bright all morning as the two cohorts slogged across the largely treeless hills and valleys. Nevertheless, dark clouds were indeed building up behind them in the south-west. Eventually, after the fifth or sixth comment at the expense of his weather-forecasting abilities, Morban judged that the moment had come.

'Very good, smart-arse, if you're so confident

that it's not going to rain, how about a small wager. Or are you only brave after the event?'

The cohorts moved on again a few minutes later, the Votadini reckoning that they were only a few miles from the warband's presumed stronghold. Scaurus and Furius, in a spirit of some reconciliation after their falling-out the previous day, agreed that their respective units would switch their cohorts' modus operandi from the march to a more tactical approach. Frontinius gathered his centurions, a note of quiet satisfaction in his voice.

'Right, we're now officially the point of the spear. The First Cohort takes the lead from now. So, it's quiet routine from here, brothers, no trumpets, no singing. We advance at the walk rather than the march and I want eyes on the horizon to all sides at all times. Dubnus, you've got the scout century so you'd better get your idle bastards to start justifying their boasting and get right out front. I want you as far out as you can get without being out of sight, and I want every blade of grass turned over for signs of the enemy. They're somewhere out there, probably lying in wait for the legions, and our job is to find them without being spotted. If you do find them, you make the signal; you pull your horns in and wait for me to come forward to join you. No heroics. And yes, you can take your new friend with you just as long as you don't let him any farther forward than you, and the rest of his men stay well back. This advance will be scouted exclusively by Roman forces from this moment.'

The 9th went forward in the manner they had

perfected in the previous months, individual tent parties scouting forward in complete silence and communicating with Dubnus by hand signals. They advanced cautiously across the hilltop's broad expanse, every seam and fold in the otherwise bare ground explored carefully by the advancing soldiers. An hour later, with dark clouds gathering overhead, the leading tent party probed cautiously into a copse half a mile in front of the cohort's advance. The soldier Scarface motioned to his mates to stay where they were at the trees' edge, and raised his spear ready to throw as he slid noiselessly into the copse, weaving carefully around the gnarled trunks of the clustered oaks. The veteran soldier sniffed the air with a furrowed brow, then silently laid his spear and shield down on the grass to ease his stealthy movement through the trees, drawing his sword and once more motioning for his troops to hold their positions. Advancing cautiously around the rock outcrop that dominated the thin collection of trees and scrub, his sword held ready to fight, he froze into perfect immobility.

In front of him, with his back turned to the wide-eyed scout, a barbarian warrior was squatting with his breeches around his ankles, grunting quietly in an apparently fruitless act of defecation. Inching forward, his attention locked on to the back of the barbarian's head for any sign that his lurking presence had been detected, Scarface stalked the tribesman with his sword raised until he was less than a foot from the man's oblivious back, hardly daring to breathe for fear of alerting his target. He paused for a moment, unconsciously rehearsing with tiny movements of his hands before taking a decisive step forward and wrapping a big hand across the barbarian's face, stifling his surprised exclamation and pulling his head back to open his throat to the sword's blade. Ignoring the blood sluicing from the massive wound opened across the barbarian's neck as the man tottered to his feet, Scarface stepped back to reverse his grip on the sword's hilt before pivoting forward on one muscular thigh to punch the point into the dying man's back and through his heart, dropping him lifeless on to the grass. Sheathing the bloody blade, he grabbed the dead man's corpse by the arms and weaved back through the trees the way he had entered the copse.

Dubnus ran forward to meet the eight men struggling back towards him, Martos and his four-man bodyguard running alongside him. The soldiers were gathered in a tight group as they came to meet him, apparently weighed down by something large and heavy. As he reached them they dropped their burden to the ground and stepped aside, revealing the dead barbarian warrior with his throat ripped wide open and a gout of blood down his chest. The dead man's eyes were bulging in testament to his last frantic struggles. Scarface stepped forward, still breathing heavily from his retreat pulling the man's dead weight.

'He was in the trees. I caught him with his back to me, so I cut his fucking throat to stop him shouting out to his mates and then put my iron through his back. We grabbed him and got him out of there before anyone noticed, but they'll be looking for him soon enough . . . '

Dubnus looked more closely at the dead man.

'So why are his trousers round his knees?'

The veteran's expression was a study in pained explanation.

'Because, Centurion, he was trying to have a shit when I did him. Why do you think I've got the bloody stuff all over my feet? Seems my iron unstoppered his arse better than all the grunting he was doing while I crept up on him.'

The young centurion shook his head in disbelief, looking at Martos with a raised eyebrow. The other man returned the gaze, his face set grimly.

'This is worse than I expected. We've thrown a stone into a wasp's nest, and we have only a matter of minutes before the swarm is upon us.'

Dubnus nodded, drawing his sword and hacking off the dead man's head, picking it up by the mane of greasy hair and turning back to Scarface.

'Did you actually see any more of them?'

The veteran shook his head, but his expression spoke volumes.

'No, but as I was stalking this boy I could smell wood smoke, and plenty of it. Could be a dozen of them, could be the entire bloody valley full for all I know.'

'Cocidius help us. Given that the warband's supposed to be five miles farther east, and given *that* . . . ' The young centurion pointed to the severed head staring slackly back at them.

' . . . I'd say we're in deeper shit than what you've had sprayed on your boots.' He pointed to one of the younger soldiers. 'You, boy, you fancy yourself a runner, so you take this and you leg it back to the first spear as fast as you can go . . . ' He pushed the barbarian's severed head into the soldier's hands. ' . . . and you tell the first spear there's a camp over the hill, cooking fires lit, strength unknown, and make sure he gets to see *that*. He'll know what to do.'

He turned to his men as the runner bounded away.

'Right, one man runs to each tent party and tells them to get back here, quiet over quick, mind you, and save their wind. I reckon we've got a long run ahead of us.'

9

By chance, it was Rufius's century that the runner reached first, and the veteran took one wide-eyed look at his grisly trophy before grabbing it from him and running back up the cohort's column with a speed that belied his years. Finding the senior officers watching the 9th Century's stealthy but hasty retreat with professional concern, he held out the dead barbarian's head to his first spear, too breathless to speak. To his surprise, Scaurus was the first to speak.

'Gods below, he's a Venico!'

Furius wrinkled his brow.

'He's another dead barbarian, that's what he is. Why so . . . '

Frontinius, having stared for a long, silent moment at the dead man's head, at the face decorated with swirling blue tattoos, spoke over him as if not even aware that a superior officer was speaking.

'How far is it back to last night's campsite would you say, Centurion Rufius?'

'Ten miles, give or take, First Spear.'

He nodded, and then turned to Scaurus.

'You're right, of course, that is indeed a barbarian of quite another tribe to those we *thought* we were facing. If Calgus has managed to achieve what this looks like, then we're on very dangerous ground indeed.'

'And you recommend . . . ?'

'That we get both cohorts turned around and running for their lives. In very short order this man's mates are going to miss him, look for him and fail to find him, at which point they'll come over that hill. The second they realise we're here we'll have a full warband at our heels. I'd get the message riders away to the legions too, tell them that we'll be holding the line of the Red River at the waterfall ford.'

Prefect Furius's frown deepened.

'Not so fast, First Spear. We find a single barbarian several miles from our objective and we're going to take to our heels for fear of the rest of the warband coming to find him? This is probably just a stray hunter, or . . . '

Rufius spoke out, having regained his wind from his run up the hill.

'With respect, Prefect, that's no stray. I've fought these bastards in the hills to the north of the River Tava, and those tattoos tell me he's a warrior. And the scout century reported wood smoke, cooking fires most likely.'

Scaurus nodded decisively.

'Enough chat.' He raised a hand to silence his open-mouthed colleague. '*No*, Gracilus Furius, one moment. First Spear Frontinius, get the First Cohort turned round and headed for the ford. I'd recommend the double march, but that's for your discretion. I'll have a quiet word with my colleague while you get them moving.'

Frontinius saluted and turned away, then stopped and half turned back.

'One problem, Prefect. The Eighth Century

won't sustain the double for more than a couple of miles, and I can't risk three other officers to chivvy them along under these circumstances.'

'I know. Tell Centurion Corvus that he's on his own, free to make his way back to the ford by any route he sees fit, but we can't wait for him. Now, my colleague . . . '

He led a protesting Furius away, ignoring the curious glances the message riders were giving the two of them as they waited for their instructions.

'Come over here and listen to what I have to say. No, just for once, *just* this once, listen to another man's opinion before shouting your own from the rooftops.' The other man's spluttering protests ran dry under his level stare, replaced by a thin-lipped glare as Scaurus spoke quickly, and with a hard edge in his voice that his colleague had not heard before.

'That dead man belonged to a tribe we call the Venicones. In their own language they call themselves the 'Hunting Hounds'. And if we think we've had a rough war this far, then I can tell you it's about to get worse. *Much* worse. They live beyond the Antonine Wall and their men are tattooed, wearing their warpaint all the time and not just when the mood takes them. There are thousands of them, and they live to raid, and burn, and most of all to kill their enemies in cruel and barbarous ways. They have an utter disregard for danger, and a burning desire to see us dead. All of us.'

Furius had quickly lost any hint of his previous bluster, his eyes flicking nervously to the 1st Cohort which had now turned around and was heading back across the hill's empty expanse at the double march. Scaurus continued to speak as he tightened his helmet strap ready for the march.

'You want to know how I know this? You've doubtless heard about the Antonine Wall, and how we decided to abandon it, purely to shorten lines of supply back to Yew Grove and Fortress Deva. All of which was a carefully concocted fiction. There were nineteen forts on the northern wall, more than we have on the current border, yet guarding a frontier less than half the length. It was perfect, less than forty miles to defend, easy to build a concentration of troops that would intimidate the locals into peace.' He snorted. 'I've read the governor's report scrolls from the period, and they were genuinely terrifying. Those inked-up bastards burned out more than half of the forts at one time or another, killing thousands of men before we decided to cut our losses and leave them well alone. So, colleague Furius, when whoever's camped over that hill comes looking and finds our tracks beaten into the grass, I want to be as far along the march back to the Red River as possible. You can stay if you like, but I guarantee that the last few minutes of your life will be more exciting than you would have wished.'

He turned to go and Furius recovered his wits, putting a hand on his sleeve and blurting out a question. His voice quavered slightly, and his gaze flicked to left and right, like that of a man seeking a means of escape.

‘Surely the governor would want us to hold our ground? Shouldn’t we . . . ’

Scaurus turned back to his brother officer, a softer look on his face than the hard-eyed stare he’d fixed on the other man a moment before.

‘It’s all right, Furius, I was there at Thunderbolt Gorge, remember? I know what you’re going through, because I was there the last time it happened to you. And no, there’s nothing to be gained from making a stand here except a quick and unpleasant death. The governor put us out here to make sure that nobody gets to swing a hook into the legions’ left flank when they go in to dig Calgus out from his hidey-hole, agreed? Which, you might have guessed, is exactly the reason that these barbarian maniacs are lurking out here. They won’t have come south looking for a fight in anything less than full strength, so unless we manage to alert Ulpius Marcellus to their presence, he’ll find that even two over-strength legions are not really any match for thirty thousand or more angry barbarians driving in hard from two or three different directions. Unless we manage to warn him what’s waiting out here we’ll end up with Calgus in possession of every bloody eagle in Britannia, the country aflame and probably lost for good. I suggest that you get your men moving, *Prefect*.’

* * *

Marcus and Qadir watched as the 1st Cohort’s centuries ground past them, the soldiers too busy gulping air to shout the usual insults at the Hamians. Indeed, he wondered whether he detected a hint of sympathy in the glances that the labouring troops were shooting at them as they left the 8th Century toiling along in their wake. His discussion with the first spear had been both brief and bleak.

'I can't leave anyone to help you, my main priority now is to get the cohort back to the ford and ready to fight off the Venicones when they come swarming across the Red. You'll have to make your own way back and join up with us when you can. My advice would be not to push your boys too hard, and make sure they're ready to use their bows on anything that catches up with you. It won't be much use having the ability to hit a man at a hundred paces if you're too winded to pull the arrow back.'

He'd slapped Marcus on the shoulder, wished him good luck and marched off at the head of the cohort. Prefect Scaurus had done much the same a few minutes later, having the good grace to look a little guilty at leaving the Hamians to fend for themselves.

'It will rain soon.'

Qadir stared skywards as they marched, watching the heavy grey clouds hanging over them, a slight green tinge hinting at the downpour lurking within their dark, looming bulk. Marcus looked upwards briefly, then shot a glance back over his shoulder, past the rapidly closing 2nd Cohort at the hill behind them.

'Let's hope so. A decent downpour might give us the chance to get back to the ford before the

Venicones catch us out here and . . . '

With a brilliant flash a lightning bolt crackled between cloud and ground a mile or so distant, a crashing boom loud enough to wake the dead rolling over the marching Hamians a few seconds later. Marcus tapped Qadir on the arm, shouting over the thunder's reverberation.

'Keep them moving, in fact push them up to a hundred and twenty paces a minute. If they get to brooding about what's behind them they'll be more likely to get twitchy, so let's give them something else to think about.'

The 2nd Cohort thundered past at the double march, their glowering prefect sneering across at the single labouring century from his horse. Behind them, appearing over the hill in their wake, came half a dozen horsemen. Marcus shouted to Qadir, pointing back at the barbarian riders.

'Have the men ready to shoot, but keep their bows hidden until the moment comes. I want them nice and close before we show our hand, so wait for my signal.'

The chosen man dropped back down the column and spoke quietly with the archers as he went, his hands emphasising his orders. The horsemen closed steadily on the century's rear, stringing arrows to their own bows in anticipation of ranging alongside the century and shooting into their helpless mass, further slowing their retreat.

'Qadir, chisel tips! Get ready!'

The chosen man nodded, unslinging his own bow under the cover of his men's rank's and reaching back to pull one of a few flat-headed arrows from the quiver hung over his shoulder, locating the arrow by a small protrusion on its base. The horsemen rode up alongside the century, their loose formation opening up as they prepared to start shooting, no more than thirty paces from the Hamians.

'Qadir, *now*!'

At his chosen man's shouted command the archers stopped marching, swivelled to face the horsemen and lifted their bows to shoot, the riders' proximity making their marks laughably easy. Their broad-headed arrows flicked across the gap, punching into the horses' sides with savage power, and the animals screamed as the chisel-tipped arrows did what they were specifically designed to do. The flat-headed arrows' horrific power punched chunks of ribcage snapped free by their impact deep into the animals' bodies, crushing their lungs and internal organs and inflicting fatal wounds on the hapless beasts. Their riders were pitched from their saddles by the sudden collapse of their horses, struggling back to their feet only to find themselves facing a line of bows that riddled them with arrows in seconds. The few horses that didn't fall immediately struggled away in obvious difficulty, the arrows protruding from their sides slick with frothy blood spouting from their punctured lungs, and their riders made easy targets for the arrows that dropped them from their dying mounts. Inside seconds the pursuit had gone from easy chase to bloody ruin, a single rider-less horse trotting slowly out of arrow range before slumping to its knees, unable to rise as its blood sluiced from three deep chest wounds.

'Keep moving!' Marcus pointed impatiently at the next hill, waving the 8th Century forward. 'Morban, a hundred and twenty a minute. Let's get out of here.'

The 8th Century ground on up the slope, the 2nd Cohort already over the top and on their way down the other side. There were still, Marcus reckoned, another three valleys between them and the ford, a good two hours' marching even in good weather.

With a gentle patter the long-awaited rain started to fall, the initial shower intensifying quickly until the Hamians were marching through a downpour, their bows quickly hidden from the rain in oiled goatskin bags. At the top of the slope Marcus stopped, letting the century continue past him as he squinted back through the rain. On the crest of the valley's far slope a mile or so distant, their numbers made uncertain by the shifting curtains of rain, a mass of warriors were crossing the summit and starting to pour down the hill. They would catch his men in much less than half an hour, he guessed. He turned back to find his century's ordered line of march suddenly disintegrating into chaos as a hundred and more barbarians charged out of the rain to their front.

* * *

The 1st Cohort reached the Red River's ford by mid-afternoon, exhausted soldiers splashing their way through water already a good six inches deeper than had been the case that morning, the rain beating off their helmets with increasing vigour as the last centuries staggered up the Red's western bank. One tired Tungrian slipped into the rushing water, and for a moment it was touch and go as to whether he would find his feet again or be washed downriver and over the falls on to the rocks below. It was a mark of their physical exhaustion that not a single soldier took the chance to poke fun when he rose out of the river's icy grip, water streaming from his helmet, and made the bank in a flurry of limbs. First Spear Frontinius greeted each century that crossed with the same greeting.

'Fill your water bottles! Get any food you've got down your necks and get ready to stand to. Centurions, to me . . . '

When the officers were all gathered, bedraggled and mudstained, he laid out his proposal for the defence.

'We've no choice but to make our stand here, it's the only defensive position for miles. It'll be dark in about six hours, so we'll have to hold them off that long unless the rain gets heavier and makes the ford impassable. We'll hold the riverbank unless anyone's got any better ideas, two-man depth and four-hundred . . . three-hundred-and-twenty-man width, that should be plenty to stop them getting any foothold on this side. We'll build an earth wall on the riverbank, use the turfs from the marching camp, then fight with spears, not swords, and keep them down in the water and at the mercy of the cold and the current. One tent party per century to set up the tents as cover for the wounded, the rest of the cohort to build that wall as fast as possible. And be careful to leave a gap for the Second Cohort to cross through. Tribune, anything to add?'

Scaurus shook his head, clearly still exhausted after the punishing pace of their march.

'Anyone else got a question? Centurion Rufius, is this about the Eighth Century?'

Rufius nodded tensely.

'Yes, First Spear, I request permission to take a small party back out and look for the Eighth.'

'Denied, Centurion, and you too, Julius, before you ask. The Eighth will have to take their chances. Get to work! Dubnus, you left here this morning with two centuries' worth of Votadini but I don't see them now. I don't suppose you could enlighten me as to where they are?'

Dubnus grimaced, waving an arm back across the river.

'Martos wasn't about to leave the Eighth on their own to be slaughtered, First Spear, he said there were too many good men to leave to the Venicones.'

'And he wasn't about to ask me for permission to leave the cohort either, I suppose?'

Dubnus nodded tiredly.

'For what it's worth, I think he'll be back, and hopefully with the Eighth following him.'

'For what it's worth, Centurion, I hope you're right.'

The 2nd Cohort struggled across the ford fifteen minutes later, and Neuto found Frontinius supervising the building of the earth rampart along the ford's western bank, pointing critically at the way the soldiers were stacking their turfs.

'Not too close to the water, or it'll be washed away if there's much more rainfall farther up the valley. Like this . . . see? Now carry on, only faster.'

He turned to face Neuto, shaking the mud from his hands.

'Glad you could join us. All present?'

The other man nodded dourly, shaking droplets off the brim of his helmet.

'We lost a few that couldn't take the pace, they'll be dead by now, but the rest all got here. The last we saw of your boys they were shooting holes in the Venicone horse scouts, but then the rain came down like the sky was falling and we lost any sight of them.'

Frontinius nodded, his expression forcedly neutral.

'Now you're in we can close the wall. I doubt we'll get it more than three feet high before they're crossing the river but even that should be enough. Now, let's discuss what your boys can add to the defence . . . '

Scaurus had greeted Furius as his horse climbed from the river, taking a grip of the animal's bridle and leading it away from the soldiers toiling to fortify the Red's treacherously slippery bank in the pounding rain. Arminius followed the two men as Scaurus took his colleague far enough from the troops that their privacy was guaranteed, turning his back on the officers to face the river and ensure that no one tried to interrupt them. Furius climbed stiffly down from the exhausted animal and turned to face Scaurus, but before he had time to say anything the other man forestalled him by raising a hand to silence whatever it was he had been about to say.

'I'm taking command, Gracilus Furius. I'm sorry, but there's no way to sugar-coat it so we're best getting it out of the way here and now.'

Furius's eyes widened with anger.

'You're *taking* command? By what authority . . . '

Scaurus smiled grimly, shaking his head in quiet amusement. 'It's always about power and rank with you, isn't it, Furius? By Ulpius Marcellus's authority, who else could give it to me? I was sent north on a scouting mission before he was even formally appointed, when it was clear to everyone but the last governor that the northern tribes were ready to boil over. Of course, it had all gone to ratshit by the time I got here, but that didn't make my job any less valid, just a damn sight more dangerous . . . '

Furius interrupted impatiently.

'So fucking what?! You've no more right to . . . '

'*Shut up*.'

Furius's head jerked back as if he'd been struck, and before he had any chance to regain his composure he found Scaurus's face close to his own, his eyes suddenly slitted with anger in a face white with suppressed anger, and his voice a furious monotone.

'One more word from you and I'll take my sword to you. I know you, Gracilus Furius, I know what you're capable of, on and *off* the battlefield. You're the big man in camp all right, all spunk and swagger when there's a condemned man to nail to a cross or some helpless girl to terrorise, but I stood next to you that day at Thunderbolt Gorge and watched you change from a self-assured bully to a snivelling coward in the time it took for you to decide that we were all going to die. If you think I'm going to let you anywhere near those soldiers once there are ten thousand Venicones on the far bank of that river, and all of them screaming for the chance to carve our balls off, you'd best think back to just how much leadership you gave your cohort that day. If you stay here alongside me and keep your mouth shut, then assuming we're not all dead before nightfall I'll see that you get a share of whatever good news comes our way before you're sent home. But if you make one squeak or squeal that might sap these men's capacity to resist, those tattooed bastards will be practising their knife work on your bloody corpse.' He raised his voice, ignoring the open-mouthed Furius. 'Thank you, Arminius, I'll have the scroll now please.'

Frontinius and Neuto turned to face Scaurus as he walked up to them, the German at his shoulder holding a message cylinder with its wax seal still intact. Scaurus held out his hand and took it from him, gesturing to it as he addressed the two men. Scaurus nodded to both men.

'Gentlemen, this scroll contains some very explicit instructions from the governor as to the limits of my authority, which, for the avoidance of doubt, are just about non-existent unless and until I'm talking to a legatus. I'm taking command of this defence in order to ensure that there are no unfortunate misunderstandings on my colleague Furius's behalf. We stand here, gentlemen, and we either hold this position or we go down fighting.'

He stared at his subordinates, waiting for any comment. Neuto scratched under his helmet's left cheek guard before replying, his face impassive.

'And about time too, if you were to ask me. Let's get on with it.'

* * *

The Venicones arrived on the far bank half an hour later, at first in a trickle down the eastern slope of the Red River's valley but soon in greater numbers, until the eastern bank of the river was thronged with warriors. A few were waving heads and Roman helmets at the defenders, but given the rain it was impossible to make out any detail. Julius and Rufius stood and watched them, desperate to know whether Marcus had fallen victim to the barbarians.

'Could be our boy, but then again . . . '

Tiberius Rufius turned away, sickened at the sight of what might be his friend's severed head.

'If it was him, then at least it was probably quick.'

Rufius nodded, acknowledging Julius's point.

'I'll give you that. If I'd known that those bloody archers would lead to this I'd have . . . '

'You'd have what? Stopped him from adopting them? Made sure that the prefect made a point of dumping them on that prick Furius? Nothing you or I, or even the first spear, could have done would have prevented what's happened, and what is simply *is*. Now, if you don't want to make your exit the same way that poor bastard did, *whoever* he is, then get your shit in a pile and get ready to defend this piece of riverbank.'

Rufius nodded again, breathed deeply and then held a hand out to his friend.

'I'll see you when this squalid little fight's done, either here or in Hades.'

The 1st Cohort were drawn up behind the freshly built wall in battle order, their shields running with water as the rain showed no sign of abating. Each man in the front rank held a spear ready to use, while the men in the rank behind held three apiece, each with the front ranker's spare and his own pair, ready to hold the soldier to their front in place on the slippery ground with a steady grip on his belt.

'When they come across the river, the front rank will ready spears for defence. Take your spears to them while they're climbing out of the water. Do *not* wait for them to get to the top of the rampart.'

Dubnus was ranging along the rear of the 9th Century, bellowing out his last instructions to the soldiers waiting tensely for the fight to begin.

'Keep your wits about you and your shields ready, and watch out for their swords.'

Scarface tested his footing behind the turf wall's modest defence, seeking a firm footing before the fighting began. He muttered quietly to his neighbour, tipping his head to indicate their centurion.

'I'm not sure what's worse, that lot over the river shouting the odds or having him strutting up and down like he's an officer or something.'

The other man nodded, spitting morosely into the river's fast-flowing water.

'Yeah. Was better when we had our young gentleman to tell us what to do, an' he was stood behind us with the big stick. Don't suppose we'll be seeing Two Knives again, though . . . '

Scarface nodded morosely before looking back over his shoulder.

'You, rear rank, you'll have to keep a better grip of my belt than that unless you want me in the river with those tattooed bastards.'

Across the river, after the expected period of time for orders to work their way down to the family groups that made up the warband, the Venicones stopped milling about and advanced into the river with fresh purpose. The water reached almost to their knees, reducing their progress to a slow walk as they fought against the Red's continual efforts to pull them off their feet. The waiting Tungrians settled down behind their shields, crouching into their shelter as the stronger Venico warriors began hurling their spears, for the most part futilely, although one lucky throw toppled a 3rd Century soldier across the rampart with his throat torn open.

The barbarians advanced through the freezing river's flow to the western riverbank and began their assault in earnest, attempting to climb the earth wall and get to close quarters where their swords could come into play. Hopelessly disadvantaged by the turf rampart, losing the ability to use either spear or sword against the defenders as they climbed out of the water, they were easy meat for the Tungrians' spear-thrusts. Within half a minute blood clouded the river's water, as dozens of men fell back from the attack with horrific upper-body wounds inflicted by the darting spearheads that struck repeatedly into their ranks. A warrior might fight on for a short time with a single wound, but with hundreds of spears thrusting at the attackers ten or twelve times a minute the slaughter was more than the Venicones could sustain. A horn blew and the remaining attackers withdrew past their dead and dying comrades, shouting insults and threats at the impassive soldiers. Scarface took a deep breath, wiping the blood from his face where it had sprayed after his spear had pierced deep into a Venico warrior's chest. He spat over the rampart into the river's torrent, watching the surviving barbarians straggling back to the far bank.

'Easy enough. I did for five of the fuckers without ever even seeing a blade, never mind using my shield. They can keep doing that as long as they like . . . '

On the eastern hillside, in a position chosen to allow the senior officers to see over the 1st Cohort, and with uninterrupted views to both north and south, the two cohorts' tribunes and first spears watched as the Venico warriors backed away from the earth rampart. First Spear

Frontinius curled his lip dismissively, pulling unconsciously on his moustache.

'That was a diversion, and not much more by my reckoning. There are men moving along the bank in both directions. Let's hope your men up and downriver are up to the task, Prefect Furius.'

The bands of warriors dispatched along the Red's banks moved quickly, the northern group climbing the gentle slope until the wide expanse of the ford gave way to the steeper and narrower banks of the river where it ran through the softer rock that had once overlain the ford's granite shelf. Higher they climbed, seeking a narrow point at which to wade or jump the river and thus reach the western bank unopposed. To the south another warband headed downriver, skirting round the falls by way of a slow, steep climb down the sloping rock face before jogging downstream in search of their own crossing point. Frontinius watched them go, his eyes narrowed in calculation as he stared into the rain, the downpour slowing as the clouds above them started to lift.

'The rain's stopping. Which means we'll only have a few hours before the ford reduces in speed and depth enough for them to rush us in real numbers.'

Three hundred paces upriver the northern warband had found what they were looking for, a narrowing in the stream caused by the presence of a huge boulder buried deeply in the eastern bank. The massive, ancient rock reduced the river's width to less than a running man's jump, if well judged. Half a dozen men stepped back and ran at the jump, vaulting off the boulder and landing, in all but one case, squarely on the far bank. The one exception missed the bank's edge by six inches, floundered and was swept away downstream in an instant by the fast-moving stream.

The remaining warriors turned to signal to their comrades, and went down under a volley of spears from the nearest 2nd Cohort century as they advanced out of the thinning rain. The soldiers rushed to the bank and formed a hasty line, meeting the next wave of warriors with spear points that dumped every man unceremoniously into the Red to be washed back downstream to the ford in clouds of their own blood. The centurion gestured to his men, half of them forming a defensive line while the rest set to work behind them with their turf-cutting spades to open a gap which, when cut through to the river's bank, would widen the river sufficiently to make the leap impossible. Without the cover afforded by the rain the 2nd Cohort's dispositions were now becoming clear, several centuries stepped up the western bank in ambush positions for just such an eventuality. Scaurus watched as the 2nd Cohort men toiled at the riverbank, his face thoughtful.

'They'll get no joy that way, the river's moving far too quickly. It's a crossing downstream from the falls that worries me — the flow might be slow enough for them to find a way across somewhere down there.'

Frontinius grimaced into the gentle drizzle that still drifted in the air.

'I could send more men down there . . . '

'Yes, but we need to keep the whole length of the river defended as well as possible. Weaken the section upstream of the falls and they'll find a way across there instead. We'll just have to make the best of what we have.'

He looked to the south again, but the Venico warriors that had gone south down the Red's eastern bank were now invisible in the afternoon's murk, a thick mist replacing the rain as the day's warmth steamed moisture out of the sodden ground.

⋆ ⋆ ⋆

The 8th Century and Martos's warriors lay soaked, muddy and bedraggled against the northern bank of a small stream, a tributary of the Red that ran in the shadow of the long rocky shelf scarring the hillside to the east of the falls. With his feet in the fast-flowing water Marcus peeped over the bank's crest, just able to make out the figures of the Venicones as they hunted down the Red's eastern bank less than two hundred paces away. Within a minute, he realised, they would draw level with the stream's entrance into the river, and have clear line of sight to the 8th's hiding place. He looked up and down the line of his men, gesturing them to stay prone against the mud. A single warrior moved into view, his presence almost ghostly in the curtains of mist hanging in the muggy afternoon air. The man stood slightly crouched, scouting the path for the warband behind him, his head cocked to one side as he listened for any threat, then slowly moved on down the river's bank. Another man followed, then more, these warriors less alert than their scout.

'How could he not see us?'

Martos answered his quiet question in an equally low voice.

'Mist. Mud. Luck . . . '

'They're looking for a way across the river.'

'Yes. Did you see their axes? They will look for a tree to drop across the river, then call the warband down here and seek to cross it in stealth. Your people will have centuries posted along the bank, but with this mist . . . '

He shook his head, and Marcus understood his frustration. With such restricted visibility such a breach of the cohorts' defences might go unnoticed long enough to allow a build-up of warriors on the far bank too strong to be contained.

'There were only thirty of them by my count.'

Marcus turned to face the Votadini leader.

'You propose to attack them?'

Martos pursed his lips, his gaze steady.

'In this mist they will not see us until we are almost on top of them.'

'And if there are more following?'

'Then we will make a brave stand until your men's arrows are spent. We cannot stand by while these men breach your defences undetected.'

Marcus nodded.

'You're right. Let's get into them before any more of them climb down the outcrop and pitch up here.'

Martos clapped him on the shoulder.

'That's the way. My men will go first, and take down those few, and I suggest your men take our northern flank, get their bows uncased now that the rain has stopped and be ready to shoot. The next few minutes will be exciting for us all.'

* * *

The Venico scouts had ghosted noiselessly through the shifting curtains of mist for half a mile down the Red River's course before they found what they had been sent to look for, a pair of trees at the river's edge which could, with the right felling, be dropped neatly on to the far bank and so form a makeshift bridge. Sending a man back to call for reinforcement, the warband's leader ordered his four best axemen to set about the trees' thick trunks, watching with satisfaction as they hammered deep notches into the wood, their cuts perfectly placed to put the trees' leafy tops on to the eastern bank as they fell. The river's far bank was wreathed in mist that was rising from the saturated ground under the sun's heat as the rain clouds temporarily cleared, and the sound of their axes was muffled by the murk to the degree that he doubted anyone more than a couple of hundred paces away would have any clue as to the threat they would shortly pose to the Roman right flank.

With a creaking tear the first tree fell exactly as required, its leafy branches easily reaching the far bank. The tree's massive trunk stretched out into the misty air above the swollen river, an immovable bridge into the heart of the Roman defence. A moment later the second tree fell, bouncing off the trunk of its companion and coming to rest tidily alongside it. A man grunted behind him, and the chieftain turned to find one of his men on his knees with a spear protruding from his chest. Even as he took in the scene, a dozen indistinct figures charged out of the mist, mud-coated wraiths wielding long swords and butchering his unsuspecting men. Even as they realised they were under attack the Venico warriors hesitated for fateful seconds at the sight of the men running at them, long haired and clad in clothing identical to their own, and their weapons equally familiar. The Venico leader's realisation that these were not his own people came to him far too late, as he saw that the mud-smeared man shaping to attack him was not only wielding two swords, one long, one short, but was wearing a Roman centurion's helmet. The attacker brushed his sword aside with one blade, then punched the other into his chest so quickly that he hardly saw it coming. Even as he gaped at the sudden shocking pain, the mud-coated warrior drove the other sword under his ribs before ripping both blades free and shouldering him aside to fall dying on the muddy ground. As his life slipped away from him he saw a tall and muscular warrior walk up to the Roman, slapping him on the back in congratulation.

'A good kill, Centurion.'

Marcus nodded, watching the Venico leader's

glassy eyes lose their final spark as the man's spirit left him.

'The poor bastard didn't realise what was going on, not until he felt my iron in his heart.'

He shook himself free from the moment of reverie, calling out to his men, still hidden in the mist.

'Eighth Century, to me, quickly now!' His men hurried from their hiding place to join him, clustering round their officer with the air of lost children. Martos smiled around him, recognising the Hamians' fear of such an unexpected and desperate circumstance.

'That was our turn to do the killing, little brothers, but yours will come soon enough. Make your hearts hard, as they were at the hill fort, for you will soon be killing your enemies again. This I can promise you.'

The archers stared back at him without comprehension, their eyes wide at the sight of the bodies of the Venico warriors, and Marcus realised with a start that his men, for all the slaughter they had wreaked on Martos's warband days before, had not yet been face to face with the human debris of battle. He clapped his hands to get their attention.

'Eighth Century, the time has come for your greatest test. At the end of this day you'll all be able to hold your heads up among the soldiers of our cohort as warriors. Now, follow me across this makeshift bridge, and once you're across unpack your bows and get ready to shoot. Nobody looses an arrow without my command, because Martos and his men will be following us across. Martos, bring your men over as quickly as you can, there'll be more of them along.'

He nodded to the Briton, and then clambered nimbly on to and along the trunk of one of the fallen trees with Morban following closely behind him. Jumping down on to the Red's western bank, he turned back to wave the 8th Century across. Shapes were forming in the mist in front of him, soldiers drawn by the sound of the tree's fall advancing to attack with their spears ready, and Marcus threw himself to the ground, pulling the standard-bearer down with him, knowing that the first spears would be thrown at chest height.

'Roman soldiers! Eighth Century, First Tungrians!'

A soldier loomed out of the mist, his spear held low and ready to thrust, and Marcus called out again, his voice tight with urgency.

'*Roman soldiers!*'

The spear's point stopped an inch from his throat, and the soldier behind it braced the weapon, ready to drive it home.

'Get up.'

Marcus climbed to his feet, wiping a fresh coating of mud from his face.

'I'm Corvus, centurion of the Eighth Century, First Cohort. Those men across the river . . . '

The soldier turned away.

'Centurion Appius!'

His officer came forward to the riverbank, took one look at Marcus and shouted for his chosen man. He turned back to the Roman with a wry smile.

'Well now, look at *you*, Centurion Two Knives. There's me looking all over for you, and then just when I'm least expecting it the gods drop you out of the sky, or so it seems. We'll have to . . . '

Marcus interrupted him with a dismissive shake of his head.

'No time. We can discuss whatever it is you want from me later, but for now my century is across the river, waiting to cross!'

Appius nodded.

'We'll talk later, then. Chosen!'

Appius's second-in-command got the Hamians moving across the tree trunks, while the two centurions considered the threat to the cohorts' defences. Marcus pointed into the mist towards the outcrop, hidden in the rolling mist.

'They sent a runner back to the warband. We killed the rest of them, but he was gone too quickly. As long as it takes to get back to the ford and back again, then we'll be knee deep in barbarians. Speaking of which, there are friendly locals on the other side too, so you'd better pass the word for your men to hold on to their spears until they hear the command to throw . . . '

Antenoch dropped from the tree's curved surface, saluting both officers.

'Centurion Corvus, there are warriors climbing down the rocks, we can hear them.'

Marcus turned to the other centurion.

'We've got five minutes, no more, and there'll be hundreds of them fighting us for this piece of riverbank. My archers can hold them off for a time, but we need to destroy these trees.'

Appius's men took guard around the tree's impromptu bridge while the Hamians, the last men of the 8th Century still crossing, took their positions up and downstream, readying their bows to shoot. The first of the Votadini came across the bridge at something close to a run, the urgency of the situation telling in the speed with which the warriors crossed, one or two coming perilously close to falling into the Red. Martos, the last man across, walked across the impromptu bridge at a more dignified pace, pointing back across the river.

'They're close, I could hear them shouting to each other. They'll be trying to cross in less than a minute, and nothing short of burning these trees out will keep them at bay, if that were even possible.'

Appius snapped his fingers, turning to Marcus with a new light in his eyes.

'Fire! That's it! I know a man that keeps a ready supply. Keep them busy, eh, Two Knives? You're in charge here until I get back!'

Marcus caught his arm as he turned to go.

'Take our Votadini allies with you, there's no way they can stay here.' He turned to Martos, offering the Votadini warrior his hand. 'Thank you for staying back to lead us to safety, we would have been found and slaughtered without your guidance. Follow this officer and he will lead you to the main body. You'll be better off there, safe from the risk that some idiot will take you for a Venico . . . '

Martos nodded, taking the offered hand before beckoning his men to follow him, then ran north along the riverbank behind Appius, heading for the ford.

Marcus called Qadir to his side.

'Right, Chosen, I suggest that you get your men ready to start shooting. There are no friendlies left to cross the bridge. Aimed shots only and no volleys, we need to make every arrow count.'

The shouts of the approaching Venicones were audible over the river's babble now. Their excitement turned to anger as they encountered the bodies of their comrades. In the mist wreathing the Red's far bank they milled around for a moment and then, goaded by their leaders, started their assault. Leaping on to the fallen tree with swords and spears ready to fight, they advanced along its length, hideously vulnerable targets for the waiting bows. The Hamian archers picked them off with lethal precision, dropping the warriors into the river's fast-moving water with their blood spraying from two or three arrow wounds apiece.

As the skirmish played out before him, Marcus was looking not to the barbarians his men were killing by the numbers, but to those on the bank behind them, their number swelling by the minute as more of the warband struggled down the outcrop and ran to join their comrades. Still calculating the odds, he staggered back as an arrow punched into the mail armour covering his chest, the missile dropping to the damp grass with its energy dissipated against the stout iron rings. Another arrow flicked off Morban's helmet, and the standard-bearer ducked for cover behind the Hamian line with an unaccustomed agility.

'Archers! Target the far bank with volleys.'

He smiled grimly as the Hamians loosed a volley of arrows across the river which resulted in a chorus of groans and screams from the warriors milling about on the far bank, recognising the tactics being employed by whoever was in command on the far side. In an instant, whether deliberately or not, the game had been changed. Forced to fire en masse in order to kill or suppress the barbarian archers, the Hamians would run through their remaining arrows in minutes, rather than the much longer time possible if they were required only to pick off single targets.

While the first volley tore into the mass of barbarians lining the far bank, sending most of them to earth, the second and third found far fewer targets as a result.

'Cease volleys! Aimed shots only!'

And probably a tenth of their stock of arrows were expended in less than half a minute. An astute leader on the far bank might reckon it worth the loss to throw his men back on to their feet to make the Romans run through their arrows, and remove the threat to their crossing at the cost of a few hundred lives. Without the threat of the archers, and with their bowmen to keep the defenders' heads down, whoever was leading the men on the far bank would be able to mass twenty or thirty men on the trees' broad trunks, ready to rush into their midst with hundreds more at their back. A few well-picked men with their feet on the western bank might occupy the defenders for long enough for their fellow warriors to reinforce them and secure the tiny bridgehead, allowing the trickle to become a flood. The warriors were on their feet again quickly enough once the iron rain no longer fell among them, barbarian arrows once more flicking through the ranks of the Hamian and Tungrian defenders.

'Volleys!'

Another three volleys were loosed to good effect, another tenth of their arrows gone. The situation was descending into a straight trade-off, bodies for arrows, and with sick certainty Marcus watched as the warriors rose again, some with more than one arrow wound.

'Qadir!'

The chosen man hurried across to him, keeping low as barbarian arrows resumed their irregular but potentially lethal hail.

'How many arrows do we have left?'

The big man grimaced.

'Perhaps fifteen per man.'

They had enough arrows for five more rounds of their deadly game, perhaps seven or eight if he restricted them to two shots each time. Ten minutes' worth, and no more.

'Aimed shots only. No more volleys. Tell your men I want no wasted arrows.' He turned to the other century's chosen man and watch officer, shaking his head in apology. 'Sorry, gentlemen, your boys will have to take their chances with the barbarian archers. If I keep firing volleys to make them keep their heads down I'll be out of arrows in less time than it'll take for reinforcements to arrive.'

An ugly thought occurred to him.

'Could either of you throw a spear across the river?'

The men looked at each other, then at the river, calculating the distance. The chosen man nodded slowly, his eyes still calculating the throw.

'Not sure that I could, but I've got plenty of big strong boys that would make it easily . . . '

Marcus motioned to Qadir, signalling a withdrawal.

'Get them back ten paces, Qadir, we're in spear range. I suggest you do the same, Cho . . . '

The instruction died in his throat as he turned away from his men, the iron head and ash shaft of a Venico spear hissing past his face close enough that he felt the wind of its passing on his cheek. The other century's chosen man jerked backwards a pace as the spear, having missed its target by the merest fraction, buried itself in his throat and took his life as compensation. Another half-dozen men were hit as they retreated from the river's bank, two of them Hamians. While the first archer's mail coat saved him from any harm worse than a severe bruise, the second man hit was less lucky, and went down with a spear through his back as his mail's rings parted under the weapon's impact. Qadir ran forward and grabbed the fallen Hamian by the collar of his ring mail, snatching up his shield and raising it against further attack as he dragged him back to safety. Marcus knelt by the man's head and put a finger to his throat.

'He's dead.'

The men of the 8th watched him lying motionless in the mud with what the young centurion momentarily took for numb detachment, until he realised that the dead man was the first casualty the century had suffered since his assumption of command. Marcus and Qadir stood behind their men, watching as the Hamians systematically shot down any man that set foot on the fallen tree trunks, steadily depleting their remaining arrows.

'They're manoeuvring us neatly into position to be mobbed once we've run out of arrows and shot back whatever they've shot at us. We can't defend the bank, they'll just shower us with spears and bleed us dry, and that means they can throw men across until they've built enough strength to roll us over. Make sure every arrow finds a target . . . '

He stalked away, forcing himself to ignore the arrows aimed at his distinctive helmet as he approached the 2nd Cohort soldiers cowering behind their shields. With their chosen man dead the century was leaderless, at least until Appius returned from whatever task he had decided would provide an answer to the fallen trees' threat.

'Watch officer and standard-bearer, to me!'

A pair of soldiers detached themselves from the century, using their shields for protection against the intermittent barbarian arrows. Marcus hefted the shield he had picked up from beside the dead chosen man, and ducked into its cover.

'With your chosen man dead you're the only leadership left for your men.'

The two men regarded him unhappily. Content to enforce their officer's discipline, and to organise the more mundane duties of the century, neither looked particularly eager to assume the burden of command. He stepped in closer to the pair, leaning to put his face only inches from theirs and to allow him to speak more quietly, but with an unmistakable edge to his voice.

'I can see that you don't like the idea, but you have no choice in the matter. Without your leadership these men will break and run once my archers run out of arrows, and the barbarians will come across that bridge with their tails up and looking for the revenge on us for all the men we've killed here. And if your men run, if *you* let that happen, they will be hacked to pieces inside five minutes. As will we all. Within half an hour every man in both cohorts will either be running for their lives or have their guts laid out for inspection. So, gentlemen, what will it be? Death, or glory?' The two soldiers looked at each other, each of them seeing his own uncertainty mirrored in the other's face. Marcus changed tack, reaching for humour where the plain facts weren't succeeding. 'You're both scared shitless, right?'

They nodded reluctantly, the standard-bearer cracking the thinnest of smiles as he spoke.

'I'll probably manage one good shit once those

bastards are across the river.'

Marcus sighed gently, thanking his gods for the soldier's unfailing gift of humour in the darkest situations. He looked quickly to Qadir, who held up a hand with the five digits splayed out. Five arrows per man, perhaps three more minutes.

'I'll let you into a secret, then. I've just led these lads, all scared out of their wits by those headhunting bastards, through rain and mud and blood to get across the river in one piece. All that time, hiding up hills and in ditches, and I've been busting for a good long sit-down all that time.' The two men goggled at him. An officer, and clearly a nicely brought-up boy too, telling them that he needed the latrine? 'And if I can hold on to my arse all afternoon on the wrong side of the river with that lot running around, then I'm sure that you two can give me a few minutes of leadership for these poor buggers. So here's the deal. You take four tent parties each, and you deploy them to either side of my lads, one left, one right . . . '

His plan explained, he hurried back to his century, drawing his cavalry sword and praying for both men to find their courage when the time came.

'How many left?'

'One or two arrows apiece.'

He took a deep breath.

'Eighth Century, every man without any arrows remaining, raise your right hand.'

Two dozen or so hands went up. When another dozen barbarians had been toppled from the tree trunks he shouted again.

'If you're out of arrows, right hand up and keep it up!'

About sixty this time. Looking back into the mist he could see nothing, no sign of reinforcement. That they would have to fight hand to hand was now inevitable. That there was only one way that they could fight successfully, and even then only for a very limited time, seemed equally likely.

'Eighth Century, those of you with arrows, keep shooting, but listen to me! When you run out of arrows put your arm in the air. When enough men have run out, I will give the order to draw swords. If you're still shooting, put your bow down and air your blade. Pick your shield up and form a line, two men deep just as we trained you.'

More hands went up in the air, until about ninety per cent of his men were no longer able to shoot at the attacking Venicones.

'Draw your swords!'

The remaining archers stood, and with the rasp of metal on metal the century drew their swords and jostled into something approaching the standard defensive formation, twenty paces or so from the riverbank. The Venicones were already crossing the trees in numbers, perhaps a dozen men now visible on the western bank. Marcus muttered under his breath, judging the right moment to commit his men.

'Mithras forgive me sending these innocents to face those animals.' He drew breath and bellowed in his best parade ground roar. 'Eighth

Century! At the walk! Advance!'

For an awful moment nothing happened, as the archers struggled to digest the terrible novelty of their situation. From his place behind the century Qadir suddenly roared a command, his voice unrecognisable compared to his usual mannered speech.

'*FORWARD!*'

Where the formal command had failed to galvanise the Hamians, the sudden bellow from their rear set them moving. Crouching behind their shields like terrified recruits faced with their first practice battle perhaps, but nevertheless advancing on the baying tribesmen. Marcus shot a surprised look at Qadir, and was amazed at the fierce stare he received in return as his chosen man spoke, his voice an angry snarl.

'They're dead, whether they attack or simply stand and wait for it to happen. They might as well go to meet their goddess with their dignity intact.'

Marcus nodded, stepping forward to stay close to the rear rank, pushing at their backs with the dead chosen man's long wooden pole as Qadir followed suit with his own. The bellowing Venicones were less than ten paces away, hammering swords against their small shields to raise a din calculated to stand off the numerically superior Roman force while more men crossed the river behind them. Qadir's voice boomed out over the tumult again.

'Forward! Board and swords, gut the bastards!'

The Hamians edged forward, their reluctance

to take the fight to the wild-eyed warriors railing at them painfully obvious. The Venico tribesmen's confidence visibly grew as they took in their opponents' clear desire to be somewhere else, half a dozen of them stepping boldly across the slowly narrowing gap to hammer at the archers' shields with their long swords. One of them, his confidence in the face of such poor opposition clearly sky high, angled his sword down over a shield in a powerful thrust, putting the blade's tip through the throat of the man behind it. The dying Hamian convulsed with the wound's shock, his struggles disrupting the century's line of shields and encouraging another tribesman to step in and attempt a kill. The blade flashed down in a vicious arc, missing its intended target by a hair's breadth but, more critically, scaring the wits out of the men to either side and suddenly, decisively, splitting the century into two distinct halves separated by a two-foot gap. Unless it was closed at once the tribesmen would be in there, hacking furiously to either side and in all likelihood shattering the 8th's already fragile confidence completely. Marcus dropped the wooden pole, drawing his spatha with a flourish and reaching for the hilt of his gladius in readiness to throw himself into the gap, but as he pulled the short sword from its scabbard and steeled himself to fight he was elbowed aside by a bulky figure.

'*Syria!*'

Qadir had snatched up a shield and beaten him to it, leaving him standing impotently with both swords ready to fight, but without any means of getting at the Venicones hammering at the shield wall behind which he was trapped. Watching helplessly and aghast at his chosen man's likely fate, he was amazed to see the previously placid Hamian bury his sword deep in the closest tribesman's guts, then kick him off the blade while parrying an attack from his left with an almost dismissive flick of his borrowed shield. He swung the blade, already running red with blood, backhanded, hacking into another man's neck and almost severing his victim's head from its shoulders with the force of the blow. A spray of hot blood showered the front rankers around him, its coppery stink filling the air.

'*Deasura!*'

The scream came not from the near-berserk Qadir, but from one of the archers standing close to him, and like the clap of thunder that presages the full fury of a gathering storm, it galvanised the Hamians to sudden, almost unbelievable action. In the space of a heartbeat their blood was up in a way that Marcus would never have predicted, most of the front rank screaming their defiance and, amazingly, gloriously, actually fighting back with their previously useless swords. Not all of their thrusts were anywhere near a target, but within the space of ten seconds there were half a dozen more dead and dying tribesmen at their feet for the loss of one man, who charged out of the line in the full grip of his newly discovered bloodlust, and died quickly and messily once separated from the protection of the century's line of shields. The century had been transformed from hapless terror to clumsy but effective attack by Qadir's sudden lunge into their front rank, and with their blood up the Hamians showed no sign of backing off their intended prey.

Thinking quickly, Marcus abandoned his original plan and gestured to the 2nd Cohort watch officers to hold their ground, then ran to the end of the 8th's line, bellowing down its length to get his men's attention.

'Eighth Century!'

A brief, somehow unnatural quiet fell across the tiny battlefield, the remaining Venicones' attention grabbed by his appearance at the end of the Roman line just as much as that of his own men.

'Eighth Century, advance to the riverbank!'

A pair of barbarian warriors, one lean and sinewy with a pair of throwing spears and a small hand shield, the other a giant of a man with a six-foot-long broadsword, broke from the knot of surviving warriors and sprinted across the narrow gap towards him with furious purpose. Allowing no time for the Hamians to respond, Marcus stepped forward purposefully to meet their charge, ducking and twisting under the first of the thin man's spears as it hissed past his head. Taking the spearman for his first target, given the lanky warrior's two-pace lead on his larger companion, he slapped the man's shield with his extended spatha before spinning in a lightning-fast full circle to the spearman's right. The unexpected move put the barbarian between him and the broadsword's greater threat, and Marcus scythed the long cavalry sword round in a long arc that ended in the spearman's unprotected flank. The devastating backhanded spatha cut open his side beneath his ribcage to his spine. The grievously wounded warrior dropped his shield with a howl of agony, his bowels voiding themselves in a stinking rush as he tottered on legs turned to jelly by the wound's fearful pain.

Shifting his balance swiftly from his bent left leg, Marcus sprang upright, kicking the grievously wounded warrior on to his comrade even as the other man drew his massive sword back, only to be thrown off balance as the dying spearman flew backwards into him. Without hesitation Marcus stepped in fast and thrust the spatha's three-foot length through the dying spearman's body and into the swordsman's guts, letting go of the sword's hilt and raising the gladius over his head. He flashed the blade down to point at the frozen Venicones, snarling at the Hamians behind him.

'*To the riverbank! No prisoners!*'

The archers swept forward with the irresistible force of an incoming tide, gladius blades licking in and out of their line in silver and red flashes as they put the suddenly terrified tribesmen to the sword. The Venicone warriors that remained either went down fighting against impossible odds or broke and ran for the fallen trees' bridge to the eastern bank. Barely a dozen escaped the Hamians' onslaught, two of them tripping in their haste to cross the river and falling into the fast-moving flow, washed away into the mist in seconds.

The Hamians, left in gloriously undisputed possession of the riverbank, were suddenly exhausted as the brief, exhilarating combat rage washed out of their bodies. More than one man found himself yawning uncontrollably where he had felt godlike power only a moment before.

'Now I see why you people speak of battle the way you do . . . '

Marcus turned from wrenching his spatha from the bodies of the two Venicone warriors to find Qadir standing at his shoulder, his sword and shield hanging loosely by his sides. This was the Qadir he had grown accustomed to, once more quietly spoken and considered.

'It was quite amazing. One moment I was watching my men suffer at the hands of those barbarians, the next . . . '

He ran out of words, a small tremor in the corner of one eye evidencing his sudden exhaustion. Marcus slapped his shoulder hard, a blow calculated to sting.

'The next minute, brother, the animal in you found his release. You took your iron to the men that were killing your men and you fought like a demon. Don't try to rationalise your rage, recognise it for what it was, and what it will be again, if need be. Old Julius had better watch out, you could give him more than a run for his money. Oh yes, one more thing. *Deasura?*'

Qadir nodded.

'She is Atargatis, our goddess. In battle we call on her as the Dea Syria . . . '

A sudden yelp from the riverbank had them both ducking for cover, Marcus from long practice, Qadir with a certain self-consciousness but no less speed. A flight of arrows from across the river slammed into the slumping archers, dropping one man choking with a barb in his mouth and wounding several others in arm and leg, beyond the protection of their ring mail. The 8th shuffled backwards out of the heavy rain of arrows, each man's shield studded with feathered shafts by the time they had gained the safety of their previous position, all but invisible to the barbarian archers. Qadir stalked away up the line, counting under his breath and shaking his head sadly on his return.

'How many?'

The chosen man's reply was delivered in a downcast tone.

'One hundred and forty-three men capable of fighting. We have eight dead, including the men we left by the river, and the rest are wounded in varying ways. Some of them will live . . . if we can get medical attention.'

Marcus shook his head.

'Little chance of that, I'm afraid. The nearest real medic is miles away, with the legions. We're more likely to see the Venicones face to face again. And soon.'

10

The two prefects and their first spears were standing on the hillside behind the 1st Cohort's defence of the ford, watching the Venicone warriors on the far bank as they stood immobile in silent ranks, eerily quiet as they waited behind the mist's diaphanous veil.

'They can't ford the river here, not while it's flowing this fast and not with our spears waiting for them, and they can't cross up or downstream because we've got men waiting for them there too. What else can they do but wait?'

Frontinius fell silent for a moment as he stared down at the silent tribesmen massed on the river's far bank, then turned to his opposite number.

'How many of them would you say there are down there?'

The 2nd's Cohort's first spear pursed his lips.

'I can see . . . four, perhaps five thousand of them or so. Why, are you wondering where the rest are?'

Frontinius nodded slowly.

'So am I. That many of them just don't seem enough for their leaders to have made the gamble to throw their lot in with Calgus. I would have been expecting ten thousand at the very l . . . hang on, what's that?'

A body of barbarian warriors was advancing quickly into view up the Red's western bank, running ten paces behind a single man with his sword drawn, and for a moment the watching officers believed that some great catastrophe had occurred farther to the south and the Venicones were upon them. Then, even as Frontinius opened his mouth to start shouting orders, he found Neuto's hand on his arm in unexpected restraint.

'Hold up, that's my man Appius leading them in! Those blue-noses must be your tame Votadini.'

Frontinius narrowed his eyes and peered down at the newcomers.

'You're right. Coming with me?'

Neuto nodded tersely, and Frontinius turned to the prefects, saluting quickly.

'Excuse us, gentlemen.'

The two men bounded down the hill, Frontinius favouring his bad leg, meeting Appius at the bottom. The panting officer gasped out a brief account of the 8th's crossing of the Red, beckoning Martos forward to join them. The Votadini leader stepped up, nodding his respect to the officers while Appius eased himself out of their field of view, then turned and slipped unnoticed away to the rear.

'Your officer has his men in good order, but he told me to warn you that they will only hold for as long as they have arrows to shoot. You must take reinforcements to them, or the Venicones will cross the river and sweep your men away.'

Frontinius turned to Neuto.

'Three centuries?'

His colleague thought for a moment.

'Four, I'd say. We have no idea what we might be running into.'

Frontinius turned to the 1st Cohort's line along the riverbank, shouting to his officers.

'Centurions Julius, Dubnus, Rufius and Titus, to me, and bring your centuries with you! Quickly!

'The rest of you, take a wider spacing and keep your guard up. There's no telling when that lot might choose to start shooting arrows at you. Otho, you have command here until I get back, take your instruction from the prefect.'

He turned back to Martos, pointing to the hill behind them.

'You've done well, but this is our fight now. Stay here, and keep out of the way unless you don't have a choice.'

The officers marched off to get the 1st Cohort's centuries moving, and Martos spoke to the men gathered around him without taking his eyes off their retreating backs.

'So, do we stay here and wait for something to happen as instructed, or do we go with them and *make* it happen?'

His one surviving chieftain stepped forward.

'We should go and find a fight, my lord, although we may be mistaken for the Venicones in this mist.'

Martos nodded grimly.

'It's a risk I'll take. We fight.'

On the hill above them Furius and Scaurus stood in uncomfortable silence, watching as the four centuries disengaged from their defensive line and hastily formed a column of march. A movement below them caught Scaurus's eye, and he nudged Furius, pointing down at the running man.

'It's that officer of yours again. Appius, is it? But why's he carrying a torch at this time of day . . . and what's in that jar?'

Prefect Furius stiffened, recognising the bright red pot . . .

'Jar? Gods below, that's my bloody naphtha!'

⋆ ⋆ ⋆

On the riverbank downstream the Hamians waited nervously, watching as the Venicone warriors once more built up their strength on the Red's western bank in ones and twos, crossing the bridge in safety now that their opponents' arrows were exhausted, the Hamians having shot back the scattering of barbarian arrows they had scavenged from the ground around them. Marcus and Qadir stared into the mist, spotting figures moving on the other bank, but they were too far back from the river to be sure, given the mist's obstruction. Morban joined them, his standard held in one hand as he stared across the river's thirty-foot width.

'What's happening over there? It looks like . . . '

Marcus nodded.

'Like a body of men passing to the south. A lot of men.

Sounds like it too, from the little I can hear with this mist deadening everything. Nothing we can do about it, though, so I don't intend giving it very much thought.'

Qadir shivered. His battle rage had long since burned out, leaving him damp and tired.

'There must be sixty or seventy of them now. Should we attack again?'

Marcus shook his head, his gaze fixed on the gathering tribesmen huddling defiantly around the fallen trees' branches.

'Soon. I want more of them across the river before we go again.'

'More?'

'More. If we attack too soon their archers will pepper us as we close for the fight, but if there are enough of them across the river their view will be blocked. Besides, we were successful last time mainly as a result of your heroics. This time we're going to do it my way.'

He looked to either side of the Hamian line to check that the Tungrian century was still in position, the soldiers prone on the damp ground and therefore effectively invisible in the mist. The barbarians continued to cross the river until he judged that there were enough of them on the western bank for his purpose. He stepped forward, raising his sword to get the Hamians' attention.

'Eighth Century. You've done it once, you can do it again. To the river!'

The Hamians went forward without bravado, but steadily enough, while the Venicones waited for their attack with grim faces, aware from the corpses clustered around them that the previous fight had gone against them. When the archers had advanced into sword-reach the barbarians began their furious assault in near-silence. They were fighting for their lives, hacking brutally at the Hamians' shields and helmets, and for a moment, as first one and then another of the men close to him reeled from the fight with horrific head wounds, Marcus wondered whether he'd left it too late to make the attack. The century held its ground, though, fighting back with the grim resolve of men that knew they lacked any other option, however terrifying the disfiguring injuries of their comrades. It was time for the other century to play their part.

'Eighth Century, at the walk, pull back! Morban, as we discussed it . . . '

He exchanged a glance with Qadir, both of their faces taut with the moment's uncertainty. If the century had mastered the idea of the fighting retreat they would pull off the simple trick he had planned for the barbarians, if not then the plan would most likely turn into a bloody rout. Slowly, almost reluctantly, they retreated at the pace the standard-bearer was dictating, Qadir's long pole held across their backs to keep them steady. As the Hamians pulled back from the barbarian warriors their unbroken wall of shields and readied swords kept the Venicones, advancing in their wake, firmly at bay. For thirty steady paces the Hamians pulled back, their pace remaining even and their attention focused on the warriors to their front. Nearly . . . Marcus glanced quickly to his left, looking for the watch officer he needed to be waiting there. The 2nd Cohort man, now on his feet and waiting for the signal, caught his eye through the mist and raised his sword to show that he was ready. Looking to the right, he found the standard-bearer equally ready to fight.

'Eighth Century, stand fast!'

It was the pivotal moment. Would the Hamians be capable of halting their retreat, however measured? Qadir's bellow rasped out along the wavering line.

'Hold them! Deasura!'

The response was immediate, a stiffening of backs and a shouted response.

'Deasura!'

The Hamians stopped in their tracks, catching the advancing Venicones off guard as they blundered on to the waiting swords. Recoiling from the shock of the suddenly stiffened Roman defence, they presented the opportunity Marcus had been waiting for.

'Tungrians, attack!'

The 2nd Cohort centuries rose from the mist-covered ground to either side of the barbarians, still unnoticed by the tribesmen. The watch officer to Marcus's left spat on the wet grass, hefting his broad-bladed thrusting spear and muttering encouragement to the men alongside him.

'Come on, then, my lads, if these puny little bastards can show the blue-noses the colour of their guts I don't see any reason why we shouldn't have some fun too. *Advance!*'

Four tent parties to either side, the Tungrians advanced swiftly from their hiding places, driving hard into the flanks of the Venicones with their spears. Some of the enemy warriors fell without ever seeing their attackers, others turned to face dim figures half seen in the mist and went down under their attack without ever raising their swords in defence. Turning to face the unexpected attack from their right, the beleaguered warriors offered an undefended target to the four tent parties still waiting unseen to their left. Rising out of the mist, they too tore into the unprotected flank presented to them, spears flashing from their line of shields to spill yet more Venico blood. Caught between the two attacks, and with the Hamians' line of shields obdurate to their front, the tribesmen fought and died where they stood, the slaughter complete in less than a minute. Panting from their exertion, the watch officers found Marcus and saluted, both men's armour sprayed with blood from the massacre.

'What now, sir?'

'Take your men and . . . '

His attention faltered as a light grew in the mist to their left, swelling from a glow to a point of fire in seconds. Appius ran out of the mist, his blazing torch casting shadows across the waiting soldiers. Breathing hard, he stopped running and arched his body backwards to ease the pain in his sides.

'Take this . . . '

He passed the torch to Marcus, hefting the jar as he sucked air into his lungs to speak again.

'Naphtha . . . belongs to our prefect . . . magic stuff . . . you just . . . put a splash . . . on a fire . . . then set . . . a spark . . . to it . . . burns lovely. We empty this . . . on that tree . . . it'll burn like . . . year-old firewood. I'll do the pouring . . . you throw the torch on . . . once I'm clear.'

The two officers moved forward, accompanied by two tent parties of Tungrians, who hunted down the few tribesmen lurking in the mist close to the riverbank. Gulping another deep breath into his heaving chest, the Tungrian centurion unstoppered the heavy jar and stepped into the foliage, pouring splashes of the pungent fluid over the branches. With the trees' topmost foliage ready to burn, he stepped away, putting a hand up to Marcus to forestall any move to throw the torch into the fume laden air.

'Plenty left. Let's do this properly.'

Stepping through the spread of branches to the river's bank he poured more naphtha over the lower branches, emptying the jar with a last flourish and dropping it into the mass of leaves. Turning to leave, he staggered as if he had tripped, putting a hand into the naphtha-soaked foliage to stop himself from pitching on to his face. As he straightened up from his crouching position, the arrow which had struck him protruding from his neck and a look of disbelief on his face, a volley of spears arced low across the river, one of them punching through his armoured back and dropping him face down across the tree's leafy mass. Raising his head with agonised slowness, he lifted an arm, beckoning feebly to the waiting soldiers. The standard-bearer started forward, but found his arm gripped by the stony-faced centurion.

'That isn't what he's asking for.'

The fallen officer waved again, pointing feebly at the tree's pale foliage. A pair of tribesmen mounted the trunk, ignoring the reek of naphtha as they scurried across the river to reach him. The dying man's head and helmet would make a mighty prize. Marcus lifted the torch, offering it to the watch officer and standard-bearer.

'He's got an arrow through his neck and a spear in his back, and those blue-nosed bastards will have his head off before he dies unless we do something. *This* is what he wants. He's your officer, do either of you want to . . . ?'

Both men shook their heads.

'In that case may Mithras forgive me for sending him a warrior in such circumstances . . . '

He threw the torch into the trees' mass of fading greenery. As the flaming stave hit the fallen tree's branches the naphtha ignited with a heavy thump, shooting a ball of fire unlike anything that any of the men present had ever witnessed high into the misty air. Appius reared up out of the flames with one fist held high, then sank slowly back into their grip. Somewhere in the blaze something exploded, presumably the jar, and a fresh gout of flame bloomed briefly in the branches, already well alight. The barbarians who had crossed the river to take the dying centurion's head dived from the burning trees into the river, their hair and clothes burning, and the mist around the violent blaze vanished in seconds, vaporised by the intense heat.

With a clear view over the river for the first time, Marcus's eyes widened at the sight of hundreds of Venicone warriors, more than could ever have made their way down the rocky path alongside the falls. He turned to speak to Qadir and saw movement out of the corner of his eye. Pointing, he bellowed the only warning that the two centuries were going to get, ripping his spatha from its scabbard.

'*Venicones!*'

The warriors came out of the mist to the Romans' rear, over one hundred strong, their swords flashing orange in the fire's flickering light, and fell on the Hamians with savage war cries. Caught unawares, the archers dithered for a moment, dying by the dozen as the barbarians hacked and thrust at their unprepared line. Marcus bellowed a desperate order, knowing that his command was seconds away from rout and slaughter.

'*Turn and fight! Fight or die!*'

With thirty-odd men having been felled by the sudden attack, the men not already dead or dying lifted their shields into a rough wall and momentarily halted the slaughter. Marcus bellowed an order at the Tungrians, pointing with his sword to emphasise the urgency in his voice.

'*Flanks!*'

The two men nodded and ordered their men, waiting behind the Hamians, to run to either side of their wavering line, temporarily preventing the barbarians from overlapping their defence. Qadir walked down the decimated Hamian line's rear, bending to shout into his centurion's ear over the guttural cries of their attackers.

'They must have a crossing point somewhere downstream!'

Marcus nodded grimly, his swords held ready by his sides.

'Nothing we can do about that. Our only hope now is that the fire attracts some attention . . . '

A soldier in front of the two men spun on his feet and dropped with his throat opened and fountaining blood, and Marcus stepped into the gap before his chosen man had the chance. He battered away the killer's bloodied sword with his gladius, thrusting the spatha's point into his throat. Another warrior stepped into the fight and swung his sword up for a downstroke, opening himself up long enough for Marcus to take a fast step forward and whip a booted foot into his groin. Doubled over with the pain, the swordsman was an easy kill as the young Roman hacked hard at the man's bowed head, chopping into his skull and dropping him to the sodden turf.

Around him his century was slowly, remorselessly being taken to pieces, a continual stream of Venicone warriors strengthening their attackers as they hacked and chopped at the Hamians. The Tungrians alongside them were suffering equally, and Marcus guessed that he had less than half his original number of men facing perhaps twice as many of the enemy. He parried a Venicone spear with his gladius, killing the man wielding it and then the men to either side with swift, economical attacks that seemed to happen with unconscious volition, his mind focused more on their predicament than the fight. The man next to him went down with a spear thrust through his mouth, choking on the blood that was gushing down his windpipe with a horrible gurgle, and Qadir stepped in alongside him, scowling over his shield at the odds they were facing. As the two men shared a momentary glance, preparing to die where they stood, a shout rang out over the din of their doomed fight.

'Tungria! *Tungriaaaa!*'

With a start Marcus realised that there were helmeted heads looming over the barbarian left flank, big men, their faces contorted with rage as they hammered into the abruptly wrongfooted Venicones, their axes rising and falling in arcs of bright silver and sprays of blood. The Bear's 10th Century had discarded their shields to a man and were wielding their weapons like barbarian berserkers, each man painting himself with blood from head to toe as they raved at the Venicone warriors like men possessed.

'Eighth Century, attack. Attack!'

The remaining Hamians responded to Qadir's exhortation like punch-drunk boxers, their sword-thrusts no better than a reflex reaction to the bellowed command. Hardly a man put his blade to his intended target but, with Titus's men to their flank and rear in full battle rage, and the soldiers to their front seemingly intent on revenge where a moment before they had been all but out of the fight, the Venicones were unable to offer resistance. They turned and fled, still dying under the Tungrian axes, running wildly in all directions to escape their implacable enemies. The Hamians stood in their uneven line, unable to offer pursuit as the barbarians ran, able only to watch hollow eyed as another Tungrian century appeared out of the mist. Julius and Frontinius hurried to the 8th's line, seeking Marcus. He saluted, aware that he was trembling on the edge of exhaustion. The first spear clapped a hand to his young officer's shoulder in delight, ignoring the blood that stained his armour.

'It's good to see you, Centurion, we'd written you off hours ago. Your situation?'

Marcus pulled his helmet off, dragging a bloody hand through his sweat-soaked hair.

'First Spear, the Eighth Century and our Second Cohort colleagues here have held this crossing since we used it to reach this side of the river. As you can see it's now useless, thanks to the bravery of Centurion Appius.'

He told the story of their defence of the crossing point in swift, economical terms.

Frontinius nodded approvingly at the short tale's end, turning to the two centuries' remnants and raising his voice to make himself heard.

'Well done, all of you, very well done. I'd say you've more than played your part today. Centurion Corvus, take your men back to the ford. You can stand guard at the camp in case any of those tattooed bastards get past us.' He turned to Julius, pointing south into the mist. 'Centurion Julius, take all four centuries south down the riverbank and find their other crossing point, and quickly. That can only have been a probe, and wherever it is they're crossing they'll still be putting men across the river. We can't afford for them to build their strength up. Whatever they're using to get across, make it unusable and then form a stop line in case they've already got more men across than we know about. I think a few of them got past us, but all they'll find is the rest of our two cohorts. Now, Centurion Corvus, let's you and I march for the camp, and you can tell me about how you came to be here at all rather than face down in the mud on the other side of the river. And, for that matter, how you managed to scatter barbarian dead around quite so liberally, given your men's lack of any battle experience . . . '

* * *

Martos led his warriors away from the ford without any of the defenders seeming to notice, climbing the steep hill to the south of the defences in long rangy strides that put them on the flat summit within two minutes. With their leader setting the pace the Votadini headed south along the crest's rolling surface, Martos staring intently down into the mist for a sight of the place he was looking for. After a few minutes he saw the Hamians marching tiredly north along the river's bank, followed closely by the survivors of the Tungrian century.

'Can't be too far now . . . '

He led his men cautiously down the valley's steep slope, their swords drawn and ready, his eyes scanning the ground.

'There!'

A man to his right had spotted the scene of the battle to hold the riverbank, marked by both the burning trees' billowing smoke and the corpses scattered across the river's narrow plain by the score. Martos waved his men forward and down the hill.

'Make it quick. The longer we're here, the more chance of our being surprised . . . '

* * *

Julius took his four centuries south at a gentle jog, balancing the need to make haste with that of his men being ready to fight when they met the inevitable opposition. The other three centurions ran alongside him, their faces grim as they listened to his instructions.

'It has to be another warband. That's the reason those lads back at the ford haven't attacked again, they're waiting for this lot to turn our right flank. They'll be building up their strength ready to attack the riverbank, hoping to sweep away any blocking force and fall on the defenders at the ford without warning. When we find them, we form a three-century line and then advance to make contact, with the Bear's lads held back in reserve. We kill every blue-nose we can find, then we let the axemen loose on whatever they're using as a bridge while the rest of us use our shields and spears to protect them as best we can. Right, it's time to slow down and listen.'

He signalled the advance to slow to walking

pace, and ordered a quiet deployment into battle line, the muffled jingling of the soldiers' equipment the only clue to their presence as they drew their swords and hefted their shields, ready to fight. They could hear the enemy now, a distant murmur of voices in the mist as they advanced cautiously down the riverbank. Julius signalled to his brother officers, pointing to his eyes and calling softly to them.

'They're closer than they sound in this fucking mist. Keep your eyes open.'

With a gentle gust of wind the mist shifted, momentarily opening a window on the Venicones gathered by the river's bank.

'*Fuck me sideways . . .* '

The veteran Scarface, in his usual place at the centre of the 9th Century's line, stared aghast at the scene revealed as the mist rolled aside for a moment. Hundreds of Venico warriors were milling about on the riverbank less than fifty paces in front of them, clearly waiting for their leaders to send them along the river in force. Behind them a continual stream of men were crossing the trunks of three trees that had been felled and lashed together to span the river's churning course. The Red now foamed and gurgled around rocks that protruded from the water, as the river approached the first in a series of falls that dropped it abruptly into a stone-walled canyon that would prevent any further progress down either of the river's banks.

Behind the Roman line Julius took one look at the scene laid out before them and stepped up behind his men, taking a deep breath and bellowing his orders.

'Spears ready! Advance!'

The Venicone warriors, alerted to the presence of their enemy by his voice, came bounding forward to the attack, their voices raised in a clamour of screamed abuse and swords brandished over their heads.

'*Front rank, throw . . .* '

The front rankers ran swiftly forward and launched their spears across the twenty-five-yard gap between their line and the oncoming warriors, the heavy-bladed missiles slamming into the barbarian charge and dropping dozens of the Venicones to the steaming turf screaming in agony.

'*Rear rank, throw . . .* '

The front rank had followed their training and gone down on one knee once their spears were in the air, ignoring the oncoming warriors to allow their fellows an unrestricted throw. The second volley of spears was thrown lower than the first, their trajectories flatter as their targets raced closer, and the missiles again took a vicious toll of the attackers, who were for the most part unarmoured. All along the front of the mass of charging warriors men fell under the thumping impact of the spears, the flying blades piercing their limbs and bodies and dropping them helplessly to the ground, impeding their fellows, who trampled over the fallen in their urgency to get at the Romans.

'*Line!*'

The Tungrian front rank drew their swords with a massed scrape of iron on scabbard fittings, slamming their shields into an unbroken wall that stretched from the riverbank to almost a third of the way up the valley's side. With a mighty roar the tribesmen recovered the momentum stolen from them by the volleys of spears and dashed themselves against the Roman shields, swords flashing as they rose and fell in vicious arcs. Unlike the Selgovae tribesmen that the cohort had fought to a standstill at the battle of Lost Eagle the Venicones were incandescent in their battle fury, disdaining any pretence of self-preservation as they hacked and chopped at the Tungrians' shields and the helmeted heads that peered over them, taking any opportunity to attack the men behind them even if it opened them up to devastating counter-attack from the soldiers' short thrusting swords.

Julius stalked down the rear of his command's line to find Rufius marshalling his century's defences, feeding men into the line as the soldiers to their front suffered under the barbarian swords. His brother officer nodded grimly, inclining his head to the warriors railing at the shields, almost close enough to reach out and touch, and shouted over the clamour of their assault.

'This is more like the old days. If the lads that faced us at Lost Eagle had been this fired up I doubt we would have survived long enough for the legions to show up.'

Julius nodded grimly, one hand gripping his sword's hilt tightly.

'And they've still got men crossing the river behind them. Unless we can chop that bridge off they'll just wear us down with numbers.'

A soldier to their left went down under a barbarian axe-blow that cleaved through the curved iron plate of his helmet, staggering blank eyed back from the shield wall before pitching headlong to the bloody grass with the weapon still embedded in his head. Rufius's chosen man thrust a rear ranker into the breach, the soldier stepping forward to put his sword into the disarmed axeman's throat as the man leapt at him with only his teeth and nails for weapons. Rufius raised an eyebrow, ducking momentarily as a spear flashed past the two men, clearly aimed at the enticing target of their helmet crests.

'Fuck me, they're keen. Perhaps we should send the Bear's boys round them to attack the bridge?'

'Perhaps not, little brother.'

They turned to find Titus standing behind them, surveying the Venicones' strength beyond their shields with a face equally as grim as their own.

'There must be five hundred of them. We wouldn't even get to the bridge before they cut us down like dogs. What this little skirmish is crying out for is a flank attack to get them fighting on two sides . . . then I'd have some chance of succeeding. Without something to distract them we'll only hold them off until they get enough men across that bridge to overwhelm us . . . '

Julius started, looking over Rufius's shoulder.

'*Fuck!*'

He started running up the Tungrian line, his sword out of its scabbard, and Rufius and Titus turned to look at what had caught his eye. In the shield wall to their right, where the valley floor met the steep hillside that rose above it, the crested helmet of a centurion rose proudly above the helmets of the men to either side. Barbarian swords were rising and falling in flashing arcs around the embattled officer, clearly drawn to their chance of taking a Roman officer's head like wasps to honey.

'*Dubnus!*'

Even as Rufius realised his friend's predicament the centurion staggered back out of the line, and a mighty roar went up from the men facing the 9th Century, pressing forward with the scent of victory in their nostrils.

* * *

Antenoch and Lupus's afternoon had been relatively non-eventful. The pair had been kept busy taking rations to the centuries manning the riverbank. With each brief visit to their comrades both had taken a moment to stare out between the waiting soldiers at their enemy, standing with apparent patience on the opposite bank. Antenoch pulled the child away from the Tungrian line, thinned out by the removal of the four centuries the first spear had taken south down the riverbank to the degree that the boy no longer had to duck to stare between the soldiers' legs to see the Venicone warriors lurking on the far bank.

'There's more of them over there than we can see in this bloody mist. That lot are waiting there because their leaders know they keep us here to face them down just by being there. The question is, where are the rest of them?'

Prefect Scaurus was asking the same question of himself, two or three times on the verge of sending another two centuries down after the first four. Each time he weakened, however, one look at his colleague's face was enough to convince him not to do so. Prefect Furius was staring pale faced and trembling down at the massed warriors on the far bank, his eyes wide with the same fear that Scaurus had seen on his face ten years before. He watched Antenoch and the boy toil past his perch on the hillside once more and smiled wanly, wondering whether a position with such simple responsibilities would be better than the crushing burden of command bearing down on him.

Movement in the mist to the south caught his eye, a century or so of weary men marching over the brow of the steep escarpment from the south. His first reaction, as he recognised the centurion leading the soldiers behind him out of the murk alongside First Spear Frontinius, was a wolfish smile of triumph, but the emotion faded quickly as he realised the sheer number of men missing from the ranks marching exhaustedly behind his officers, even with what appeared to be another century bringing up the rear. The Hamians staggered to a halt, clearly at the end of their tether, most of them bearing the marks of men that had been in a desperate fight, their shields scored and notched and their armour black with the drying blood of their enemies. Many of them were supporting walking wounded. As he watched his men's obvious distress with pity and pride, Scaurus's attention was drawn away from what was happening in front of him for a terrible, fateful moment.

Antenoch saw them first, half a dozen ragged warriors loping down the hill in front of them towards the unguarded supply carts in the Tungrian rear, their swords gleaming dully in the mist. He pushed the child under the cart from which they were unloading the rations, snatching up his shield and unsheathing his own blade as he turned to face the barbarians bounding down the slope to attack, shouting a warning to the soldiers two hundred paces away on the far side of what remained of the previous night's camp. His cry sounded weak and muffled in the mist's dampness, and the Venicone warrior leading the pack grinned in anticipation, swinging his sword in a vicious hacking blow at the lone soldier.

Antenoch parried the strike upwards with his gladius, stepping in fast to drive his helmet's brow guard into the other man's face so hard that he felt bone shatter under the blow's force. Reversing his grip on the sword's hilt he ducked under the next man's spear-thrust, burying the gladius's length in his side and snatching away the spear, leaving the blade sheathed in the crippled barbarian's liver. The remaining warriors spread out around him, wary of the spear's long reach but quickly surrounding him with blades and forcing him to twist and turn, continually stabbing with the weapon's wide blade in a doomed attempt to hold them off. One of the warriors slid silently around to his rear, stepping close to the cart and landing a slashing blow across the back of the Roman's thigh, dropping him on to one knee with his hamstring severed. The warrior's howl of victory became a scream of pain as Lupus scuttled out from under the cart and dragged the razor-sharp blade of his knife across the back of the barbarian's ankle. The tendon parted with an audible thump, and the Venicone staggered away on his good leg and fell to his knees, waving his sword at the child and screaming with fury. Antenoch turned to the boy, grimacing with pain, and muttered a single word between gritted teeth.

'*Run!*'

As Lupus watched, his eyes wide with the shock of combat, another warrior stepped in and butchered the stricken soldier, grabbing his helmet's broad neck protector and jerking it up to expose the back of his neck. Slamming his sword through the space between Antenoch's mail coat and his helmeted head, the tribesman speared the sword's blade through his throat. A fine drizzle of the dying man's blood flicked across the boy's face as he stared without comprehension at the horror inches from his face. Antenoch's mouth gaped open, but no sound issued other than his croaking death rattle. His eyes rolled upwards as he lost consciousness, and his body sagged twitching to the ground. Lupus, still frozen to the spot, looked up into the face of his protector's killer as the warrior ripped his sword free from Antenoch's neck, then drew back his arm to hack the child down, swinging the blade out in a wide arc that held Lupus mesmerised as the Venicone screamed his rage into the boy's face.

In a sudden blur of motion and with a crunching impact the barbarian was gone, punched away by the impact of a shield smashed into his body by a figure sprinting out of the mist. The warrior went down with his face wrecked, battered out of shape by the impact of the shield's heavy bronze boss, and with blood pouring from his shattered nose. He groaned once, put a hand to his ruined cheekbone and collapsed to the grass only partially conscious. Lupus stared up from his crouch between the cart's traces, watching numbly as Marcus tossed the shield aside, flashed out his gladius alongside the longer-bladed spatha and turned his ire on the man the child had wounded. Swinging the cavalry sword at the hobbling warrior's throat in a precise arc, he dropped the wounded man to the turf with blood sheeting from his opened neck, then turned back to the remaining barbarians with a tight-lipped snarl that hardened to barely restrained rage as he lined up the blades' points. He drew in a long breath and allowed it to escape in a slow exhalation as he paced slowly forward, eying the three remaining barbarians with cold calculation as they dithered between fight and flight, his eyes meeting the child's empty stare and hardening as they flicked back to the Venicones. For all their numerical advantage the warriors quailed at the sight of a helmetless soldier daubed with mud and blood, his eyes flint hard above a mouth slitted with contempt. One of them groped on the floor in front of him, unable to take his eyes from the Roman's approach as he picked up the spear that Antenoch had dropped.

The attack, delivered after several long seconds of silence, was all the more shocking for the speed with which Marcus took his iron to the barbarians, too fast for the stunned child to follow from his hiding place. Turning aside the spearman's frantic defence and punching his gladius through the man's ribs, he deflected a stabbing sword from his left with an almost absent-minded parry with the spatha, slanting the long sword to allow the man's attack to slide along its polished surface and extend the attack farther than the barbarian had intended, then kicked his legs out from under him and pitched him face first to the ground. Leaving the short sword in the spearman's chest, he feinted momentarily at the last man standing to put him on the back foot, then finished the fallen barbarian with brutal speed, hacking the spatha deep into his spine before turning away to tackle the last remaining warrior. Ripping his gladius free as he passed the dying spearman, he brutally kicked him face first into the mud. The last man turned to run, but managed less than five paces before the enraged officer ran him down, spearing the long sword through his left thigh and dropping him howling to the ground. He waited for the Venicone warrior to roll on to his back before finishing the fight, batting aside the man's sword with something close to contempt before pushing his spatha into his chest in a slow, measured thrust, watching the barbarian contort in agony as the iron's cold bite pushed through his organs. The stink of faeces hung in the air as the dying warrior's bowels voided themselves.

'A hard death.'

Marcus turned to find Scaurus and Arminius standing behind him, their swords unsheathed. Both men were breathing hard from their run from the opposite hill. Marcus twisted the sword and pulled it from the dying man's body, inspecting the point for any damage, then casually ran the blade through the throat of the concussed warrior he had smashed aside with his shield.

'Not hard enough. They killed my clerk.'

The prefect nodded simple agreement, turning away to look for Lupus and finding him staring at the hill above them.

'At least you managed to save the child, that's some . . .'

He turned to look at whatever was holding the child's attention, seeing another group of warriors staring down at them from the hill's crest, nine or ten strong. Marcus and Arminius followed his glance, their faces hardening as the barbarians started down the slope towards them.

'If you'll allow me, Prefect, this is a job for your man here and me . . .'

Marcus fell silent as the prefect bent to pick up one of the dead Venicone warriors' swords, seeing an amused smile touch Arminius's face.

Scaurus drew his gladius, taking up a two-handed fighting stance without ever taking his eyes off the oncoming warriors.

'Thank you, Centurion, but I'll take my chances alongside the pair of you if it's all the same to you.'

The first warriors stormed in to attack the trio before Marcus had any chance to reply, assaulting the Romans in a furious whirl of swords and axes. In a second Marcus was fighting for his life, ducking under a wild sword-blow and hacking his gladius deep into his attacker's thigh before shouldering the man into the path of another warrior. Sensing movement behind him, he swayed his upper body back out of the path of a spear-thrust, watching the wickedly sharp iron blade slide past within inches of his face. He flicked the spatha's blade down into the muddy ground, relinquishing the sword's hilt and grabbing the spear's shaft with his right hand, then leaned in to thrust his gladius up under the spearman's jaw, leaving the sword embedded in the dying man's throat. Lifting the spear from the warrior's numb fingers he pivoted back to the wounded barbarian and the man into whose path he had pushed him, reversing the weapon with a casual flourish and stepping in to plant the butt spike in the wounded barbarian's throat in a spectacular shower of blood as the spike tore into the man's neck. Shifting on to his back foot, he flipped the spear lengthwise again to present its razor-sharp blade before stamping his right foot forward again, thrusting the iron head deep into the other barbarian's guts and ripping it free with a savage twist that contorted the warrior's face with pain, the contents of his bowels gushing down his legs as his eyes rolled up. He watched the man's face with savage intent, lost to blood rage as the barbarian slumped to the floor, ramming the spear's blade between his ribs and through his heart. Arminius's guttural shout snapped him back into the fight.

'Behind you!'

He pivoted, ripping the spear free of the fallen warrior's body to find a pair of warriors within a half-dozen paces and charging in fast. Without time either to pull the weapon back for the throw or turn fully enough to use the blade, he dived forward beneath their raised swords, tripping his attackers with the spear's shaft and rolling out from beneath their tumbling bodies to where his spatha waited, its point buried in the mud. Dropping the spear and snatching at the sword's hilt, he sprinted back into the fight, hacking at the closer of the two, the sword's razor-sharp blade opening the man's head up like ripe fruit, then kicked the sword loose from the lolling corpse to parry an attack from his companion. Too slow. The man's booted foot hooked his leg and pitched him to the ground with a thump, driving the breath from his body and breaking his hold on the spatha's hilt. The sword fell uselessly to the ground beside him and the barbarian smiled at him in triumph, his sword's point suddenly at Marcus's throat with a cold bite that froze his attempts to regain his feet. Groping unnoticed at his belt for his dagger he found instead the tribulus given to him on a cold spring hillside far to the south and months before by Rufius and tugged the vicious little device free, forming a fist around its iron spikes.

The Venico standing astride him laughed down at him, lifting his shoulders and taking a firm grip on his sword's hilt in readiness to ram the blade home into the Roman's windpipe. Marcus was a split second faster, slamming his fist up into the man's unprotected groin and spearing the iron barb that protruded from between his fingers between his balls and deep into the root of his penis. The barbarian threw his head back and screamed in agony, his sword dangling forgotten as he staggered away, and Marcus rolled to one side, scooping up the spatha and surging to his feet to behead the man with a single blow. He looked to his comrades, fearful of what he might find.

* * *

A mile down the river, the fight was slowly but certainly turning against the Tungrian detachment sent to cover the defence's southern flank. Julius watched with growing consternation as the number of Venico warriors ranged against the three centuries in his defensive line strengthened by the minute, a stream of tattooed barbarians crossing the river behind them to add two men to their strength for every one killed by the Tungrians. His men were tiring now, their initial battle fury exhausted, and while he knew they would fight on for a good deal longer he could tell that they were no longer battling as hard as before. While the Tungrians were increasingly huddled behind their shields, striking out with their short swords when the opportunity presented itself, the Venicones, bolstered by the flow of fresh warriors from the mass waiting on the other side of the river, were gradually gaining the upper hand, growing in confidence as their strength increased.

He looked to the rear, peering past the stolid lines of the 10th Century's axemen waiting for their turn to join the fight in the mist, knowing that the rest of the cohort probably had problems enough that reinforcement was unlikely.

'Another five minutes of this and we'll have to start putting the Bear's lads into the fight.'

Julius nodded at Rufius's muttered statement.

'How's the boy?'

The older man glanced down at Dubnus's prone form, his wound temporarily staunched by the bandage stuffed through the hole in his armour by a bandage carrier who had shaken his head unhappily and moved on to the next casualty with the hardbitten detachment of a man who had seen death and mutilation too many times before to be affected by anything as prosaic as a spear wound.

'Still with us. I'd say he'll pull through, if only we can get him out of here . . .'

Julius snorted, pushing another of his century's rear rank forward as a front ranker went down with an axe buried deeply in his head, the heavy blade cleft clean through his helmet's bracing bars and deep into his skull.

The rear rankers to either side grabbed him by the shoulders of his mail coat and threw him backwards past the officers and out from under the soldiers' feet to lie wide eyed and spasming intermittently on the wet ground. The bandage carrier gave his twitching body a cursory glance before turning back to the task of bandaging a wounded man's arm, opened up from wrist to elbow by a Venicone sword.

'Not much chance of that. We stand here and most likely we'll die like rats in a barrel. Bear, get your boys ready to . . . '

His head jerked up as he caught movement on the hill above them out of the corner of his eye.

'*What the fuck . . . ?*'

Men were mustering on the slope to the barbarian left, perfectly positioned for an attack down into their unprotected rear. Rufius stared up the hill alongside him, straining tired eyes to make out the detail masked by the curtains of mist drifting across the battlefield.

'It's a century of our lads, although they look bloody odd to me. Scruffy bastards from the look of it . . . '

Julius laughed grimly, tucking his vine stick into his belt and drawing his gladius as the men on the hill above gave a guttural war cry and poured down the hill in an undisciplined charge that narrowed Rufius's eyes with bafflement.

'Those boys aren't ours, Grandfather, you need a new set of peepers. That's Martos and what's left of his warband, wearing our kit and getting stuck into the Venicones. I might not like the man, but I'll be buggered if I'll let this chance go begging. Bear, get ready to attack to the bridge!'

He elbowed the trumpeter in the ribs.

'Blow the advance, boy! *Burst your fucking lungs!*'

The trumpet's call sang out over the riverbank, the notes stiffening backs previously bent to huddle into the cover of their shields as standard-bearers bellowed encouragement to their comrades. Julius stepped up to the line, motioning with both arms to the three centuries' chosen men to put their poles to the soldier's backs and start pushing. He took a deep breath and roared his command, the bellowed words cutting across the sounds of clashing metal.

'*Tungrians, either we deal with these barbarian arse-fuckers now or we die before our time. Advance!*'

As the newcomers burst on to the Venicones' left flank in a flurry of hacking swords, the Tungrians took their iron to the distracted tribesmen with renewed vigour, spending the last of their strength recklessly as they saw their one chance to snatch victory from the certainty of defeat. As they stepped up to the Venicones with new purpose, hammering at the warriors with their shields before stabbing their swords in drilled unison, the 10th Century took their chance, trotting around the end of the Tungrian line and past the mass of enraged Votadini assaulting the enemy flank before breaking into two halves. Five tent parties assaulted the barbarian rear, while the remainder, led by Titus, charged into the Venicones still coming across the improvised bridge. Their already bloodied axes rose and fell in pitiless arcs, each blow chopping a Venico warrior to the ground in bloodied ruin. Attacking unprepared and unarmoured warriors from the rear, the forty men at the Venicones' rear killed three times their strength in less than a minute, before the barbarians even had time to turn and fight. The warband, beset from the rear by blood-painted giants wielding their weapons with terrible ferocity, promptly lost all reason and threw themselves at the Tungrian line in a desperate attempt to escape, their abandon opening them up to vengeful soldiers who only seconds before had been suffering under their swords. With a sudden collective shudder of men at the end of their tether, the warband broke into a melee of fleeing warriors, pursued across the battlefield by soldiers and Votadini warriors whose blood was well and truly up, and whose only desire was to complete the slaughter of their mutual enemy.

Julius fought his way through the chaos to Martos, nodding in respect at the panting chieftain.

'Well fought, Votadini. Can you finish them?'

The other man nodded.

'We'll hunt them down to the last man. I have a score to settle with these bastards.'

Julius nodded, turning back to his men.

'*To the bridge!*'

* * *

'So Martos broke the deadlock? In that case he's been instrumental in more than one last-minute rescue. I thought we were dead men when the barbarians came out of the mist to our front with their swords ready, back there on the other side of the river. My lads were terrified, of course, so it was a good thing that it was him and his men and not the real thing, or we'd all have been dead inside a minute.'

Marcus rubbed at his still-wet hair with one bloody hand, his eyes blank as he remembered the frantic retreat from the Venicone warband.

'He saved us, of course. Led us up the hill to our left, took us out of sight of the warband when they came thundering past a few minutes later. After that we just walked south until we came to the outcrop and climbed down it to reach the far bank of the Red. You know the rest, and you've seen the mess that the Venicones made of the Eighth, but I'll wager when we count the corpses we'll have killed five men for every one we lost. They've earned their right to be called Tungrians, I'd say. What happened after the Votadini came down the hill in our armour then?'

Julius grinned, still elated with their victory.

'You should have seen it, man, the Bear's lads just ran wild. They hacked their way to the bridge those Venico bastards had thrown across the river and left a trail of bodies with their heads stove in and arms and legs lopped off. The barbarians tried to put them off, of course, chucked bucket-loads of arrows and spears at us from the other side of the Red, but we put a double line of shields on the riverbank and the Tenth took turns chopping at the trees behind them. Once the tops were off it was easy enough to push the trunks into the river, and that was that, pretty much. If only they hadn't managed to put a spear into Dubnus I'd be counting this as a right result. As it is . . . '

Julius's face darkened. Marcus shook his head sadly.

'He shouldn't have been in the front rank. He kicked my backside hard enough when I did it . . . '

Both men were silent for a moment, staring out across the river at the thousands of Venicone warriors still waiting in silence. The four centuries that Julius had led down the riverbank to deny them their last chance of crossing the river were now back in place at the ford, the two cohorts' massed spears sufficient to deter any further attempt to force the crossing. The river itself was running slightly lower than had been the case during their first abortive attempt, but still had too much power for the warband's leaders to seriously consider throwing their men across the river to die on the Roman defences.

'I heard about Antenoch. He died defending the child?'

Marcus shrugged tiredly.

'He died defending the supplies. Lupus was an incidental. Our prefect was a bit of a revelation, though . . . '

Julius raised an eyebrow.

'Oh yes?'

'Yes. I fought off the first group to come over

the hill, but then another group followed them in and took the three of us on, me, Arminius and the prefect. I suggested that he stand back and let the German and me do the fighting, but he just laughed at me and stood his ground.'

'And . . . ?'

'And put down three of them without much difficulty, from what I gather. I was too busy while it was happening, but I had a quick word with Arminius after the fight was done, while Scaurus was busy making sure that they were all dead. All this time we've been assuming that the bodyguard's the fighter, but it turns out he's been taking lessons from the prefect since the day he was taken prisoner.'

Tiberius Rufius walked up with a weary demeanour, squatting down on his haunches opposite the other two, who both stared at him with open curiosity. He shrugged.

'He'll live, just as long as the gods keep smiling on him. The prefect's got half a dozen tents up for the wounded and he's warm enough, plus his wound's stopped bleeding for the time being. Got any water left?'

Marcus passed over his water skin, waiting until his friend had drunk his fill before speaking again.

'We need to get him back to Noisy Valley. That wound needs to be cleaned out before it closes up . . . '

'In which case, that's probably good news.'

Julius pointed up the road away from the ford. Half a mile distant, where the track met the skyline, the distant silhouettes of Roman soldiers were appearing against the bright evening sky. He stood up, looking back over his shoulder at the Venicones still waiting on the other side of the slowly subsiding river.

'It's their turn to run now. If that's one full legion, never mind two, they'll not want to be anywhere close to hand when that lot cross to the far side. Come on, let's go and watch them leg it. And remember to put on a brave face for the troops; they need better from us than the despondency we're feeling to show in our faces. We faced ten times our strength of the nastiest bastards in this whole shitty country and lived. Again. There are few enough men that have done that once, never mind twice in one year.'

11

The Tungrian cohorts marched into Noisy Valley behind the Petriana cavalry wing late the next day, having slogged back down the north road that afternoon. The surviving wounded had been carried on the carts that usually mounted the cohorts' tents and cooking equipment, the dead left for burial by the soldiers of the 6th and 20th Legions. Scaurus had received his orders from the governor in the quiet of the man's command tent the previous night, once the Legions had set up camp for the night beside the now quiescent Red River.

'You've done a good job here, Prefect Scaurus, saved us from being ambushed by those ugly tattooed buggers. How many men did you lose?'

Scaurus made a show of consulting his tablet, although in truth the numbers, and their significance, were already burned into his brain.

'Seventy-three men dead and a hundred and twenty-one wounded, seventy-six of them walking. The medics expect another dozen of the wounded to die before sunrise.'

The governor waited for a long moment.

'And the Second Cohort . . . ?'

'Thirteen dead and twenty-five wounded, sir. Only one of their centuries actually saw any real combat.'

The tone of the governor's reply made clear the frustration that was taking hold of his superior officer.

'I know. I also know that a makeshift century composed mainly of Arab archers took more than double that number of casualties in the same action and still managed to frustrate an attempt by the Venicones to get over the river. I had Legatus Equitius make discreet enquiries of your first spear, and you'll be aware of the mutual esteem in which your centurions and their former commander hold each other. Not to mention the off-the-record comments I've had from Tribune Licinius after his debriefing of his message riders. It seems you were forced to take control of his cohort for fear that he would panic and scare his men into running?'

'Governor, I must . . . '

'No. I think not, Rutilius Scaurus. I knew you would try to protect that fool Furius, just as you did ten years ago when he panicked in battle against the Quadi, although for the life of me the reason for your doing so still eludes me.'

Scaurus squared his shoulders.

'I will not condemn a fellow officer, sir, no matter how great the provocation.'

The governor snorted his amusement.

'Perhaps you won't, but your fellow officer seems to be carved from less noble material. He was in here not fifteen minutes ago protesting at your behaviour today in the most graphic terms. Apparently I would be well advised to have you relieved of command and sent back to Rome. It would also seem that his father wields great power in Rome . . . although I'd say he's mistaking affluence for influence.'

He sniffed dismissively, taking a seat while

Scaurus maintained his stiff posture. His next comment was made offhandedly, in an almost dismissive tone, but if the comment was made lightly enough, the words themselves rooted the younger man to the spot.

'He was also spouting some nonsense about your cohort playing host to a fugitive from imperial justice . . . He showed me a piece of jewellery, a gold cloak pin with an inscription of some kind. 'Irrefutable proof,' he said, but by then my patience with the man was exhausted so I threw him out. It is nonsense, I presume?'

The prefect raised an eyebrow with an apparent lack of concern that he was a long way from feeling.

'Yes, Governor, Prefect Furius has taken it into his head that one of my officers is this man Valerius Aquila that went missing a few months ago.'

'Whereas . . . ?'

'Whereas, Governor, as both Legatus Equitius and Tribune Licinius will stand witness, my man's simply a patriotic son of Rome doing his duty for the empire, nothing more and nothing less. It seems that every young officer with dark hair and brown eyes on the frontier should now be considered as suspicious.'

Ulpius Marcellus gave him a hard stare, then nodded his agreement.

'If Licinius will back the man that's good enough for me, he's got no axe to grind. And nothing that fool Furius says can be treated with any sort of respect. He would keep insisting that I dismiss you from the service . . . '

Scaurus shrugged, keeping his face expressionless.

'In this, as in every other matter, sir, I am your faithful servant. If you deem it fit to send me away from here I will accept your judgement.'

The governor snorted again, slapping a hand down on the table in front of him.

'Not likely, young man! Your cohort has surprised and then held off two Venico warbands, only for that self-serving fool to tell me that I ought to cashier you? No, Rutilius Scaurus, you are to take your wounded south to Noisy Valley using the legions' supply wagons, get your men into the hospital, re-equip with whatever you need from the legion stores and then pick up a full load of food and get yourselves back here before dark in two days' time, no more. I'll use the legions' cavalry and the auxiliary horse to keep the barbarians' necks tucked in, and we'll attack their stronghold once we're properly positioned. I want your men back in the line before that happens, they're too experienced to sit out such a fight and I've got a particular part of the battle plan in mind for them.'

Scaurus saluted and turned away, his mind already racing around the challenge of getting his wounded across the difficult early stages of the twenty-mile march to Noisy Valley.

'One more thing, Rutilius Scaurus.'

The prefect turned back from the tent's door to find the governor on his feet and holding out a sealed tablet.

'I'm sending Licinius and the Petriana with

you. They can make sure you make it back down the north road without being harassed, and provide a show of force to keep the Brigantes quiet. When you get to Noisy Valley hand this tablet to Licinius. He'll know what to do.'

* * *

With the Tungrians settled into the Noisy Valley barracks previously occupied by the 6th Legion, Scaurus sent his officers to organise the loading of the supply carts, and his bandage carriers to the hospital to offer any help that might be required by the hard-pressed medical staff. With no more commands to issue he sought out Tribune Licinius, finding him in the officers' mess with a beaker of wine in front of him. The grizzled senior officer stood and shook the younger man's hand, calling for more wine.

'Well, Cohort Prefect Scaurus, I was hoping to get a moment or two with you. You Tungrian buggers don't seem to be able to stay out of trouble, but then y'don't seem to have much of a problem fighting your way out of it either, eh? I salute you!'

He lifted his beaker, taking a slug of the wine, and watched Scaurus as he sipped his own drink.

'Something wrong, eh, young 'un?'

Scaurus placed the governor's tablet, still sealed, gently on the table in front of him, the writing block's polished case making a soft click as it made contact with the scarred wooden surface.

'There may well be, Tribune. This is a message from . . . '

'. . . the governor. I can recognise his seal, y'know.' He split the wax seal with a thumbnail, reading the contents of the tablet with an expressionless face. 'That old bastard doesn't muck about when he wants dirty work doing. You have no idea what's in this message?'

Scaurus shrugged.

'I have a good enough idea who it concerns, but no idea as to the precise contents.'

Licinius leaned across the table, putting out his hand.

'Well, it seems that congratulations are in order, young man. You're provisionally promoted to cohort *tribune*, with command of the combined First and Second Tungrian cohorts. I can't make any promises on Ulpius Marcellus's behalf, of course, but we both know that the rank is rarely rescinded once granted. Well done, young man.'

Scaurus stared back at him disbelievingly.

'But . . . '

'No, there's no mention of any 'buts' in this message. The governor stresses that you are directed to assume command of the Second Cohort *immediately*.'

'And Furius?'

Licinius smiled evenly, reaching for his helmet.

'Former Prefect Furius is to be relieved of his command and shipped out to Rome as quickly as the act can be made to happen. Sounds like the governor has about the same opinion of your colleague that I do, given the dismal tactical skill and military acumen he's displayed to date, not to mention his apparent lack of anything remotely resembling a set of balls. We're better off without him, and you'll have a nice big double-strength cohort to play with.' He got to his feet, heading for the door, but turned back after a couple of strides. 'Oh yes, and why not give what's left of your archers to the Hamian cohort while you're here, there's a good lad? That energetic young centurion of yours has managed to get half of them killed in less than a month, so I think the rest of them have earned some time off for good behaviour, don't you?'

* * *

In the base hospital a disciplined chaos ruled, half a dozen of Felicia's assistants working to put the surviving Tungrian wounded on to the doctor's table in something like the order of their medical priority. Marcus and Rufius found Dubnus dozing uneasily through the racket, his face pale from the blood he'd lost the previous day.

'He looks dreadful. Why haven't they dealt with him yet?'

Rufius waved an arm at the room in response to his friend's question.

'Look around you. Every man that goes on to the table before him has a worse wound.'

As they watched a soldier was carried from the surgery on a stretcher, his right leg swathed in bandages down to the knee, below which the remainder of the limb was missing.

'See, that poor bastard's lost his leg. Dubnus has it comparatively easy by comparison.'

'Easy . . . you come and lie here for a few minutes and then tell me this is easy . . . '

They turned back to find Dubnus lying with his eyes barely open. He closed them again after a moment, the effort clearly tiring him.

'I feel like I've been beaten with hammers.'

Rufius lifted a bottle of water to his lips.

'Drink some of this. You'll be in surgery soon enough. Get that wound cleaned out and stitched, and soon enough you'll be scaring the shit out of the recruits like a new man. Can you remember what happened?'

The young centurion snorted, then winced at the pain that the action caused.

'Of course I bloody can. I got a spear in the guts, not through my head. Some big bastard with an axe set about the front rank, killed three men in the time it takes to tell it, and I was stupid enough to jump in to deal with him . . . '

He paused, grasping the water bottle and taking another sip.

'He swung at me and buried his axe in my shield . . . actually put the blade's edge right through my board, and while he was trying to pull it free I gutted the fucker.'

'Keeping your attention on the men to either side, of course . . . ?'

Dubnus sighed.

'As a matter of fact, you superior old bastard, yes, I was. What I wasn't looking out for was a spear-thrust from behind their front rankers. The bastard must have taken a running jump at me; the blade ripped straight through my armour and skewered me like a piece of liver. I went down like a sack of shit with the whole warband baying for my head, but the rear rank managed to pull me out of the fight while good old Cyclops closed the gap and kept them off me. Remind me to buy that bad-tempered sod a beer next time I see him . . . '

Rufius nodded sagely.

'I'd say you owe him a good deal more than that. Let's have a look at your wound, then.'

He lifted the sheet to reveal Dubnus's stomach. The wound was a four-inch-long gash, its edges a livid purple and joined by a crust of dried blood.

'Not too bad. Of course, the first thing that our friend's wife-to-be is going to have to do to you is open that up again and make sure it's clean. I wonder if she'll let us watch?'

* * *

Licinius found Furius in his temporary quarters with a terracotta flask of wine. The younger man rose and greeted him, lifting the wine in salute.

'Tribune Licinius, welcome. Join me in a beaker or two of wine, to celebrate our escape from certain death yesterday . . . '

His smile faded as he realised that the senior officer hadn't moved from his place in the barrack's entrance, his stance formal and a writing tablet held open in one hand.

'Cohort Prefect Gracilus Furius, I am hereby ordered by Governor Ulpius Marcellus to direct that you relinquish your command with immediate effect. I suggest that you accompany me to the commander's residence. You can stay the night there, and avoid all the awkwardness that goes with sudden changes of command . . .'

The wine flask dropped from Furius's hand and cracked on the wooden floor, his fingers suddenly numb with the shock. The wine trickled out across the floorboards unnoticed by either man.

'There must be some . . . '

'There's no mistake . . . ' Licinius's tone was gentle; he knew the enormity of the blow being dealt to the other man. 'I can assure you that the governor is very specific in his instructions.'

'But this simply cannot be. If anyone should be relieved of command it's that jumped-up puppy Scaurus, not me. He . . . '

The grim look on Licinius's face as he advanced across the room silenced him.

'Citizen Furius, you were, to be brutally honest, *quite* the worst commanding officer I've met in several years of service in this province. You are a coward, which I'm told you've proved on more than one occasion, but worse than that you lack any real aptitude for the command of soldiers in the field. If you leave with me now, quietly and without making a drama out of your departure, you can at least go home with some dignity. The governor will send you home with the next set of dispatches to the emperor, and you can tell your friends that you took part in a battle with a fearsome tribe from the far north. Tell them it was a great victory and that you were sent home to report on it as a mark of favour. If you kick up a fuss, however, the story will get home long before you do. *You* don't want that to happen, and neither will your *father*. Keep the family name proud, eh? Don't embarrass the old man any more than you probably already have. Come on, I'll have your gear sorted out and brought over later.'

Furius stared at the senior officer for a moment, the fight going out of him as he sensed the deep anger underlying the older man's gentle tones in the hard lines of his face.

'I'll come with you. It wouldn't do to make a scene . . . '

They walked from the tent and into the cool evening air, the sentry snapping to attention and saluting. Licinius nodded to the man, but Furius was lost in a world of his own, his downcast face a study in misery. The sentry waited until the two men were out of sight then whistled to his mate, walking a patrol beat along the line of barracks.

'Crucifix Boy just left with that old bugger from the cavalry, and he wasn't looking happy. Best tip the wink to the first spear . . . '

As he crossed the fort a pace behind Licinius, a thought occurred to Furius, a sudden shocking idea that wormed its way into his mind and sat festering for all of ten seconds before he blurted it out, his tone both aggressive and fearful.

'It occurs to me, Tribune Licinius, that there are only two options for my immediate replacement. Either you'll put a man of your own choosing into my place, or else . . . ' He looked at the man walking slightly ahead of him, finding his face imperturbable. ' . . . or else my former colleague Scaurus will command both his own cohort and mine. Which is it, Tribune?'

Licinius stopped walking and turned to face him, his features skull-like in the fort's deep shadows. His voice was harsher than before, as if he were holding on to some last vestige of patience.

'Leave it *alone*, Furius. Let go of this failed attempt to regain a life to which you're not suited, and turn back to that which you can manage.'

Furius put a hand to his head, staring up at the stars in genuine amazement.

'So I am removed from my command and replaced by him. By him! Zeus, Jupiter and Mars, but I'll see someone damned for this indignity. My father will . . . '

He quailed back against a barrack's wooden wall as Licinius took a handful of his tunic and twisted it harshly.

'Your father? You think the influence of a moderately successful merchant will be enough to protect you while you spread your poison round Rome. You bloody *fool*, do you have any idea who Cohort *Tribune* Scaurus's sponsor is?'

He waited for a moment until Furius shook his head.

'I had assumed from his slow progression . . . '

' . . . that he was without patronage? Well then, how does this name suit you?'

He leant in close to the wide-eyed Furius and whispered a single word in his ear.

'No.'

'Oh yes, you heard me correctly. I heard your

father had to pay a small fortune to get you back into legion service, to find a legatus willing to overlook your reputation from the last time you were allowed into uniform. And even then you lasted only a matter of months before you gave him the excuse he was waiting for to ship you on to another province, once he realised just what a liability you were. All those years that you sat on your arse at home, whoring, drinking and waiting for Daddy to buy you another chance, your colleague Scaurus concentrated on building up his military skills the hard way. His backer could snap your family's power with a crook of his little finger, but Scaurus was never willing to take advantage of that influence, quite the opposite, as it happens. He loved the joy of commanding men in battle far too much to consider promotion away from the sharp end of the spear, and so for years he was content to be a legion tribune. He might have frustrated his sponsor in the process, but the man recognised his quality and never stopped backing him, and I'll warn you just this once, you'll spread evil gossip about the man at your peril. Just a few quiet words in the right ear and you'll find yourself robbed, buggered and murdered in some Roman back alley. I advise you to accept your lot and get on with the rest of your life.'

Furius nodded slowly, his eyes fixed on the older man's. Licinius relaxed, judging that his words had beaten the last resistance from the man.

'Come on, then, let's get you into the residence and away from prying eyes.'

* * *

In the hospital, Felicia's assessment of Dubnus's condition was delivered to his friends in a quiet, tired voice as she leant across the big centurion to look closely at his wound, taking a slow long breath in through her nose with her face close to the blood-crusted gash.

'A spear, yes? Good, the wound won't be too deep, then. It looks like his mail did its job and took most of the force of the blow. And there's no smell of infection, that's a good sign. Now we can do this one of two ways, Centurion. I can dose you with something to make you sleepy, or we can just get it over with now. It will hurt either way, but with the tincture the unpleasantness will seem to have happened in a dream, whereas you'll know every second of the pain without it.'

Dubnus closed his eyes with exhaustion, shaking his head slowly.

'I already feel like a dead man, lady, so let's get this done and over with.'

The doctor nodded to her assistants.

'Strap his legs down well. I'll need the small-wound forceps, vinegar, clean linen swabs and a small drain tube. Oh yes, and the honeycomb. And you two gentlemen . . . ' She smiled wanly at the waiting centurions. ' . . . can help me by putting down those helmets and sticks and coming over here to hold his arms. Once we get the wound open he's going to be in more pain than when the blade went in.'

By the time Julius arrived an hour later

Dubnus was sleeping exhaustedly in his bed, his stomach heavily bandaged and a tiny bronze tube protruding from the wrappings.

'He'll live, I presume?'

Rufius nodded tiredly.

'He will, if our colleague's woman has anything to do with it. I've not seen a wound cleaned out with such care for many a year, nor a man take such torture without even a grunt.'

Julius nodded, knowing from grim experience what his comrade had been through.

'I did a bloody sight more than grunt when they cleaned mine out. It's packed with the honeycomb, I presume?'

Rufius nodded, raising his hands.

'Crushed it myself . . . '

'So he should be fine. That's a relief . . . '

Marcus and Rufius exchanged glances.

'What?'

'It's probably nothing . . . '

'But . . . ? Come on, Centurion Corvus, I'm a big boy, I can take bad news.'

Marcus frowned.

'Fel . . . the doctor told us that there's some damage to his liver, just a nick, but there's no way of telling what might have been on the blade that creased him. We'll just have to wait and see.'

Julius took a deep breath, shaking his head slowly.

'And so it goes . . . Very well, gentlemen, orders from the first spear. We're to get a beaker of wine down our necks, get to bed and be ready to march again at dawn. We go north again at first light, and he wants us as fresh as possible, not bleary from a night spent watching a wounded man sleep off his surgery. Two Knives, take a moment to say hello to your woman properly and then join us in the officers' mess for a quick one. You'll sleep better with a beaker of half-decent wine under your ribs.'

Marcus nodded agreement, tapping fists with both men and making his way cautiously to the surgery door. Felicia, bent over another patient, sniffing for decay, caught his eye as he put his head around the door frame and smiled, standing up from the patient and nodding.

'Clean enough, if my nose isn't getting tired from all this practice. Let's make this the last one tonight, there's nothing out there that won't wait until I've had a few hours' sleep. Get him ready for cleaning out, please.'

She walked to the door, and pushed Marcus into the ward, wrapping her arms around him, muttering tiredly into his chest.

'How long have you got in camp?'

He snorted into her hair, laughing despite himself.

'About six hours. We're going back north at dawn.'

She pushed herself away from him, holding him out at arms' length and looking critically at his black-ringed eyes.

'You were in action yesterday. From the look of it you were right in the middle of it, as usual . . . '

His eyes were suddenly misty, the gentle challenge breaking down defences that he'd thought secure against the emotions surging around them.

'We fought off a warband from the far north. My archers fought better than I could ever have imagined . . . but I lost so many of them. And Antenoch . . . '

A tear escaped from his right eye, rolling down his cheek and falling on to his armoured chest. Felicia pulled his head on to her shoulder, holding him close again and biting her lip to suppress her own tears.

'My love. My poor, poor love. They were soldiers . . . '

Marcus pulled away a little and tried to speak, but she put a finger to his lips, shaking her head.

'No! No guilt. They may not have been fighting men to match your Tungrians, but they were still soldiers. They knew what they were volunteering for. And as for your clerk . . . '

'He died saving the boy's life. I was too late to do anything other than butcher the men that killed him. Perhaps that's all I'm good for . . . '

'Rubbish!' Her voice hardened, and she took a grip of his mail shirt's collar and dragged him close again, whispering vehemently in his face. 'You're a fine officer and a good man, and I love you. So pull yourself together, go and get some sleep and come back to me in one piece when this is all over. I want a live husband, not a dead hero, so keep your wits about you!'

He smiled wanly and kissed her gently, squeezing her to him for a moment. Disengaging and moving towards the surgery door, she turned back, a wry smile on her face.

'And if you want a way to remember your clerk that doesn't involve yesterday, just remember all the times he drove you to the point of tearing your hair out.'

He smiled back at her, his mood lifted by the thought of better days.

'I threw a copy of *Commentaries on the Gallic War* at his head in the hospital at Cauldron Fort.'

'I know, he told me. I think he was rather proud of the achievement . . . Now, away with you. I've got a patient to deal with, and my records to scribble out before I forget what to write.'

Marcus gathered up his helmet and followed her to the door, his mind already fixed on the thought of a few hours' sleep and the next day's march.

* * *

Furius drained the last of the wine that had been left for him and lifted the flask, shaking it to ensure that no drop remained within.

'Empty. Bastards couldn't even leave me enough wine to put me to sleep.'

Rising from the chair in which he'd been sitting since Licinius had left him in the residence's comfortable main bedroom, with the command to get some sleep, the disgruntled ex-officer shambled off into the house in search of more wine. Finding nothing to drink in any of the rooms, he pulled his boots back on and went to the front door, opening it cautiously to peer into the fort's empty street. A pair of the Petriana's cavalrymen turned to face him, their faces stony with dispassionate disapproval and their spears crossed to bar him from exiting the residence. Closing the door, he retreated to the kitchen, searching until he found a suitably heavy bladed cooking knife. Back in the bedroom, at the building's rear, he got to work on the locked wooden catch that secured the window's shutter, prying it away from the frame until the wood splintered and broke, allowing the shutter to open.

Blowing out the lamp that was the room's only illumination, he eased the shutter open a crack and looked cautiously through the thin slit. The street between the residence and the fort's defensive wall was quiet, and he was about to open the shutter properly and climb through it when a helmeted soldier appeared in his restricted field of view, having passed by the window without noticing that it was ajar. He waited until the guard had turned the corner and then eased himself noiselessly to the ground and pushed the shutter closed again, hurrying to the corner of the residence around which the guard had disappeared. Peeping round the brickwork in trepidation, fearing that the man might have reversed his steps and be advancing towards him, he saw to his relief that the sentry was just turning the next corner, clearly walking a simple path around the residence. He had a couple of minutes before the soldier could cover the other two sides of the building and come up behind him. Taking a moment to calm his breathing, he took the only course of action open to him, walking boldly across the road and into the cover of the barrack block facing the residence, waiting for the sounds of pursuit. None came. If the guards watching the building's front door for Licinius had spotted him, they had failed to connect the apparently confident figure crossing the street with the man held captive within.

He moved quickly now, sticking to the shadows and heading for the barrack block in which his temporary quarters were located. The patrolling Tungrian guard coughed in the cold evening air, standing in his position at the far end of the block. There was no sign of the man who would normally be posted in front of the prefect's rooms.

'No need, given my new status . . .'

Finding what he believed to be the right door, he opened it and stepped inside with light feet, not sure whether there would be a guard placed inside, but the room was empty. His sword and dagger were lying on the bed alongside his other effects, and he picked them up, strapping the belt and baldric over his tunic. Stepping over to the window, he cautiously peered through the shutters at the hospital opposite. A group of four orderlies came out of the building, the sleeves of their tunics spattered black where their aprons had failed to provide protection from the blood of the wounded men they had been treating throughout the evening. They headed off towards the main gates, and the fort's vicus.

'Off to the beer shop, are we, gentlemen? Who does that leave minding the patients while you're wetting your whistles? I wonder.'

He searched down the building's row of windows until he found what he'd been hoping for.

'Oh yes, that would make a *very* acceptable reward for refusing to go quietly.'

* * *

In the officers' mess, crowded with the presence of the centurions of both infantry cohorts and the Petriana's decurions, First Spear Frontinius was enjoying a rare moment of leisure with his men. The Votadini prince Martos stood among them self-consciously with his drinking horn held in one hand. He had sought to avoid the invitation at first, but Frontinius had refused to take no for an answer.

'You pulled our backsides out of the fire yesterday, and as far as we're concerned you're a brother now, no matter what happened before or might happen in the future. Besides, if you refuse I'm pretty sure that the Bear will just come down here and carry you over to the mess, so why not make it easy on yourself?'

Frontinius lifted his beaker, and the cohort's centurions gathered more tightly around their leader to hear his toast. His voice rung around the room in the sudden hush, as all three groups of officers strained to hear the words.

'Brothers, we drink to the Venicones. May they long remember the day that two cohorts of Tungrians repelled ten thousand of the bastards . . . ' He lowered his voice theatrically, knowing that he had the whole room's attention. ' . . . with a little help from Jupiter, sender of rain . . . ' He raised his voice to shout out the last few words of the toast. ' . . . and an honourable mention for the Red River!'

A cheer rang out, every man in the room lifting his drink in salute. Frontinius turned to Julius with a raised eyebrow.

'Dubnus?'

'Should be fine, if a small nick to his liver heals clean.' He raised his beaker to Martos, speaking in quiet tones that would be heard only by the tight knot of men standing around him. 'To you, Martos, and your warriors. Without you our brother Dubnus would be dead now, and likely most of the rest of us too.'

The Briton nodded acknowledgement of the honour as the officers raised their cups, taking a draught of beer from the drinking horn.

'You may yet have to return the favour, Centurion, but I thank you for your kind words. Here's my toast, if I may . . . ?' Frontinius nodded, motioning him to continue. 'I'll drink to your archers. Untrained and unready for the fight they may have been, but they stood taller than all the rest of us so-called 'warriors' by their deeds yesterday. They were the real champions of the fight.'

He lifted the drinking horn and the Tungrian officers nodded soberly, starkly aware that half of Marcus's century had been killed or badly wounded in the battle on the banks of the Red. The first spear drained his beaker and set it down on the nearest table.

'Well said. And now, my brothers, I'll bid you goodnight. Drink up and get yourselves into your racks for a few hours. Tomorrow's march will be just as savage as today's was, and I'll have you bright eyed and ready for anything if it's all the same to you.'

He made his way out of the mess, walking past the 2nd Cohort's barracks as he headed towards the main gate and his own cohort's quarters, returning the guards' respectful salutes as he mused on their marching route for the following day.

Furius watched him from inside the hospital's lobby until he was out of sight, waiting another moment in case he turned around for any reason. When he was satisfied that there was no risk of the veteran officer discovering him, he turned to the hospital's main corridor, walking quietly down the passageway off which the wards opened, his boots making quiet creaking noises with each step. Each room was packed with wounded men, all oblivious to his presence as a combination of the brutal shock of their treatment and the drugs prescribed for them by the doctor had rendered them senseless. At the end of the corridor he stopped and listened, hearing his quarry's quiet voice as the doctor talked herself through the notes she was making on each of the surgical cases she had dealt with that evening. He opened the door and walked into her cramped office, enjoying the warmth of the fire burning in a small hearth on the far wall. The woman started at his unexpected presence, relaxing as she realised who the newcomer was.

That, he mused with an inward smile, would change soon enough.

'Good evening, Prefect Furius. You've come to see your wounded, I suppose. They're . . . '

Furius rode over her tired voice, his tone harsh enough to make Felicia lean back in her chair.

'No, Doctor, the person I've come to see is you. And you're a little out of date with your greeting; I am no longer Prefect Furius, but just plain Furius now. Furius the *failure*, the *coward*. Furius the *dismissed* is what I am now, but strangely enough my new-found status has finally liberated me from expectations of how a senior officer should behave.' He closed the door behind him, smiling hungrily down at the seated woman. 'You won't be aware of it, but my sexual tastes have troubled me for most of my adult life. You see, my dear, I enjoy women the most when they struggle . . . ' Felicia stared up at him in dawning horror, then around the office for some way to defend herself. 'The problem is that some of the women I've favoured with my manhood have struggled so hard that I've been accused of rape.' He sighed, shaking his head sadly. 'My father paid off the families the first couple of times, but I soon took to strangling the women whose bodies I enjoyed in order to ensure their silence. That's how I ended up being moved on from First *Minervia*, a pretty young thing that I took a fancy to but who was just a little bit too well connected for the matter to be brushed under the mat. Nobody could prove anything, but there was enough suspicion for the legatus to send me away. In my own best interests, of course, or so he told me. The lady's brothers had sworn their revenge on an altar to Nemesis, apparently.' He raised an arm and declaimed: '"Nemesis, winged balancer of life, dark-faced goddess, daughter of Justice."'

He smiled, and Felicia recoiled again at the blank look in his eyes. 'Of course, the legatus couldn't tell my new superiors why he was moving me on, or they would have refused to accept my onward posting, and so here I was with no one any the wiser as to my very particular needs. Nemesis, daughter of justice? Hah! There is no justice.' He squatted down, bringing his face close to hers. 'If there were I would not be locked up safely in the prefect's residence waiting for a quiet and ignominious departure tomorrow morning, or so everyone else but you and me believes. Which, of course, gives me licence to do whatever I please with you, my dear, and without fear of discovery as long as I cover my tracks well . . . I presume you'll be well aware of what I like to do to my partners, given that you examined one of my victims once I was done with her?'

The horrified doctor nodded slowly, unable to take her eyes from the face in front of her. Furius smiled slowly, then reached out with sudden speed and gripped the collar of her tunic with both hands, rending the garment apart with his immense strength. He put a hand around her throat and forced her to her feet, pushing her up against the wall while using the other hand to tear away the ruined tunic, revealing her body to him.

'Oh yes, *exactly* what I need. You, my dear, are going to be squealing like a stuck pig in a minute or two.'

He pulled down the linen band restraining her breasts, allowing them to bob loose, and gripped a nipple with a fierce tweak. The abused flesh stiffened in protest, as an amused grin played across his face.

'See, your body is already betraying you . . . you bitches always enjoy what I've got to offer, even if you pretend to resist!'

The door opened behind him with a groan of hinges. Cornelius Felix walked gingerly through the doorway, his right arm tightly bound in a sling.

'Doctor, I . . . good grief, what in Hades are . . . '

Furius pivoted swiftly, driving a bunched fist into his face and catapulting him across the corridor and off the far wall. The wounded cavalry officer slumped to the floor, already unconscious. Furius turned back to find the naked woman clawing frantically at the room's shutter. Pulling her away from the window and pushing her to the floor with a triumphant laugh, he delivered a stinging backhanded slap to her face.

'No you don't. Let's have those undergarments off, shall we. Open wide!'

* * *

In the officers' mess Marcus drained his beaker, putting it down on the table and picking up his helmet, looking around for a moment.

'Damn.'

Rufius raised an eyebrow.

'My vine stick. I must have left it in the hospital.'

His friend drank his wine and picked up his own helmet.

'It's only round the corner, I'll come with you. It'll give us a chance to see how Dubnus is doing. You coming, Martos?'

The Briton nodded, tipping back the contents of his drinking horn and shoving it into his belt. Julius picked up his helmet, shooting Marcus a wry smile.

'I'll come too. Someone's got to make sure you come back to your barrack nice and promptly, or we'll have a repeat of what happened the last time you were left alone with her. Can't have you turning up on parade in the morning looking like you've been pulled through a hedge, can we?'

The four men made their way to the door, stepping out into the cold night air under a blaze of stars and strolling down the street towards the hospital. The light of a lamp flickered through the shutters of the doctor's office window, making Marcus shake his head.

'She's still at it. So much for 'you go and get some slee . . . ''

'Quiet!'

They turned and looked at Martos, his head cocked the better to listen. In the silence they all heard the sound, a woman's cry of distress. Rufius made the connection first, dashing off along the street with the other men in close pursuit. He took the steps into the hospital's lobby two at a time and lunged into the corridor, his pace hastened further by the slumped body at its far end. Drawing his sword, he sprinted down the length of the building, kicking the office door open to find the helpless Felicia pinned to the floor with Furius on top of her, her legs forced open by his muscular thighs, one hand stifling her screams and the other between their bodies, his buttocks moving slightly as he readied himself to thrust into her. The doctor saw Rufius over her attacker's shoulder, her eyes bulging as he stepped into the office and stooped to put his blade's point against her rapist's anus. Furius froze into immobility with the weapon's first touch, looking over his shoulder in amazement at the furious centurion.

'Get off her now, or I'll put my iron so far up you it'll stop your heart without ever disturbing your ribs, you piece of shit.'

The other officers appeared in the door behind him, Julius sizing up the situation in an instant.

'Keep him there. Lady, bring yourself out from under him, nice and easy.'

Felicia struggled out from beneath Furius's weight, spitting into his face with shocked anger. Julius tapped Marcus on the shoulder hard, seeing his friend's ash-white face and knowing that the man was seconds from taking a blade to the prostrate former officer.

'Get your woman out of here, Centurion, and give her some decency. We'll deal with this bastard once she's safely out of the way.'

He stepped into the office and put an iron-nailed boot on to Furius's neck, crushing the man's face into the hard stone floor.

'Tie his hands behind his back with your belt.' He waited while the older man secured their prisoner's wrists. 'Good. Now sheathe your blade, Rufius; this one won't struggle, not now he's dealing with fighting men and not trying to violate a defenceless woman. And besides, I'm rather looking forward to seeing his face when we scourge his back off and then nail him up tomorrow morning. That *is* your preferred method of punishment, I believe . . . ?'

Furius lay helpless under the centurion's booted foot, but his snarled response was anything but.

'You won't dare bring me to justice, Centurion, I know things that you can't afford to have made public!'

The boot pinning him to the floor pushed down harder, Julius turning to his brother centurion.

'Go on; get whoever that is lying outside sorted out.'

Rufius sheathed his sword, leaving the room and allowing Martos through the door to get his first glimpse of the prostrate Furius. Julius bent and took a handful of Furius's hair, pulling his head off the floor despite the foot pinning his neck.

'Go on, then, let's hear these things we don't want to be known.'

Furius spat his frustration into the words, half

choked by the position the angry centurion had forced him into.

'Your centurion . . . the boy with the . . . unconvincing name . . . I know he's a fugitive . . . and that you're all . . . hiding him.' He paused, swallowing painfully. 'You put me on display . . . and I'll shout that so long and loud . . . the gods will hear it.'

Julius laughed, wrenching the helpless man's head to one side so that he could see the centurion standing over him.

'Very good, *ex-Prefect*. You've just earned yourself a private death.' He pulled a dagger from his belt, putting the blade close to Furius's face. 'I might blind you first, and then we'll truss you up and take you out into the woods. I fancy staking you out and leaving you for the animals to find you . . . '

Disquietingly, the former officer laughed back at him in spite of his discomfort.

'That would be . . . brave of you . . . No, I mean it!'

Julius had pulled his head back farther, threatening to finish the job of choking him to death, and he exchanged an uneasy glance with Martos.

'Brave, eh?'

'Yes . . . anything that brings . . . the corn officers . . . will bring your lies . . . crashing down . . . expose the fugitive . . . crush you all.'

Martos tapped Julius on the shoulder.

'I think that what's needed here is for this man to die an unremarkable death. Something to arouse no suspicion, perhaps?'

Julius nodded, raising an eyebrow.

'And you know how to make this happen?'

The Briton nodded, pulling the drinking horn from his belt and pointing to their captive's bare backside. Julius frowned uncomprehendingly.

'We're going to bugger him to death with a drinking horn?'

Martos shook his head, raising a hand to forestall any more questions.

'I'll be back in a moment.' He leaned in closer, bending to slap Furius's ear hard enough to provoke a howl of rage that covered his brief whisper to the centurion. 'Make him believe he's won. He mustn't struggle for the next few minutes; we want no marks on his body. Just do one thing for me while I'm gone . . .'

Having explained what he wanted, he left the office and went to the surgery, looking around for the tool he wanted. Finding a suitably robust bone saw he worked swiftly, cutting off the last inch of the horn's tip to reveal a hole as wide as his middle finger.

'Perfect.'

He pocketed the horn's tip, and then went in search of the other centurions. He found them both in the main ward, watching as the doctor, dressed in a spare tunic and apparently recovered from her ordeal, fussed over the young man they had found unconscious in the corridor.

'He seems to have nothing worse than a slight concussion. Poor man, I thought that animal had managed to do what the barbarian archers had failed to achieve.'

She looked up as Martos approached the

small group. He nodded to her, speaking to the two centurions.

'Brothers, I need your help with our prisoner.'

Rufius and Marcus followed the Briton to the office door, where he stopped them and spoke quickly, showing them the horn and explaining what he proposed. All three men crowded into the office, almost filling the small room with their bulk. Julius gave them an exasperated stare, while Furius, hearing the rapping of boot nails on the stone floor, renewed his harangue of his captors.

'Just surrender to the inevitable, you fools! Release me now and I may choose to overlook this stupidity. Hold me here any longer and I'll insist on fucking the doctor's lovely tight arse as part of the deal!'

Julius stared down at the prone figure, clearly at the end of his patience with the man's imprecations.

'Whatever it is you have in mind, Martos, could we just get on with it?'

Martos nodded, showing him the truncated horn with raised eyebrows. After a second the realisation dawned on the centurion, and a slow smile spread across his face.

'Very well, Prefect Furius, I suppose you're right. You two, unbind his wrists.'

Marcus and Rufius unfastened the belt tying Furius's arms, but rather than allowing him up as he expected, they each pinned an arm to the floor, spreadeagling him across the stone while Julius deftly wrapped a powerful arm around his legs, preventing him from kicking out. With his neck no longer under Julius's boot the disgraced officer craned his head round in amazement.

'What?! Free me now, or you'll leave me no option but to . . . '

He went quiet as Martos squatted down by his head, showing him the ruined drinking horn.

'This was my father's, and his father's before him. I don't appreciate having to destroy it for the sake of a piece of shit like you, but I have. A man that will attack a woman like that, one of his own people, does not deserve either to live or to leave this life quietly. And so . . . '

He picked up Felicia's undergarment from the floor where the disgraced officer had discarded it in his haste to violate the helpless woman. Wadding the linen into a ball he slapped the man's ear again, then deftly pushed the gag into his mouth as he opened it to bellow another protest.

'Make the most of that, it's the last contact with a woman you'll have in this life.'

He joined Julius, taking a strong grip of one of Furius's legs. The two men nodded to each other, pulling the man's legs apart and revealing the Roman's genitals and his puckered anus. Moving quickly, the Briton pushed the tapered end of the horn into Furius's rectum, ignoring the muffled protests the helpless captive was now making.

'Hold this.'

Passing the leg he was gripping to Julius, who flexed his powerful shoulders to hold the limbs in place despite Furius's increasingly desperate struggles, he picked up the remnants of the doctor's torn tunic and wrapped it round his hand before reaching for the poker, whose blade Julius had plunged deep into the fire's coals moments before. Regarding the red-hot metal critically, he pushed it deep into the fire again, stirring up the coals for maximum heat.

'Well, Roman, it seems we have a moment or two to kill, so I'll tell you a story.'

Furius goggled at him, his eyes bulging in disbelief.

'You will probably have heard it before, it's as old as the hills themselves, but that's no reason not to spend a moment telling it again. There was once, my grandmother told me when I was very young, a snake whose delight was to bite and kill other creatures, even those — or perhaps especially those — it could not eat. The other beasts of the forest hated and feared the snake in equal measure, since it killed simply to enjoy the sensation. One day, at the height of summer, there was a fire in the forest, and the flames leapt from tree to tree faster than the snake could slither. The snake was afraid of being burned to death, but just when all seemed lost he saw a fox, an intelligent and wily animal, running towards him, for foxes, as I am sure you know, can run fast enough to outpace a forest fire, and for many miles too.

'So, he called to the fox and begged it to carry him away to safety. The fox, of course, was unimpressed with the request. He knew of this particular snake's reputation, and he feared that to carry the snake on his back would be his death sentence, but the snake had one powerful argument that he knew would sway the fox. 'If I bite you,' he reasoned, 'I will burn to death when I fall from your back. Why would I do such a stupid thing?' And so the fox agreed to carry the snake to a safe distance from the fire in return for the reptile's future favour.

'Of course, halfway across the forest, where the trees were at their thickest and the fire threatened to overtake them, the snake suddenly sank his fangs into the fox's neck and delivered a dose of poison that was sure to kill him in seconds. As the fox was struggling in his death agonies, with his sight going dim and his ancestors calling him to join them, and as the fire started to rage around them, he raised himself up with one last mighty effort, and asked the terrified snake the obvious question: 'Why have you killed me, when it means your own death?' And the snake, sliding off his back and into the flames that would burn him to death, hissed the answer with fear and shame, but with the certainty of truth. And do you know what he said?'

The Briton gave the gagged Roman a moment to respond. Furius stared at him mutely, his eyes filled with hate.

'No? What he said was simply this: 'I can't help it. It is in my nature.''

'By now, of course, you will have guessed why I have taken this time to tell you this story, apart from the fact the poker needed a little more time to be hot enough for my purposes. You, although I have not known you for very long, clearly have the same lust for death and suffering as the snake in my story. You are a man who is dangerous to all around you, and you will remain so for as long as you live. Some people would be filled with curiosity as to what can lead a man to become so debased, but I am of a more practical mind. I simply want to put you out of this misery you call a life without your evil leading to any more death. And now, it seems that the means of delivering you to Hades without springing these traps of which you speak is ready.'

He hefted the white-hot poker in front of the Roman's face, watching a bead of sweat trickle down the man's forehead, then moved to where the horn protruded from between his legs.

'Brace yourselves, he's going to struggle with the strength of a bear once this starts.'

He slid the poker into the horn's conical opening, the smell of burning filling the air as the hot metal seared its interior, then pushed the metal forcefully through its tip and into the prostrate man's body. Without the gag Furius's anguished screams would have woken the entire camp, and his body thrashed across the floor despite the four men fighting to hold him down as the hot metal blade tore through his internal organs. With one last massive shudder the dying man sagged lifelessly to the stone floor, his eyes suddenly glassy and empty of life. Martos withdrew the poker, filling the room with the stench of burning offal, then pushed it back into the fire to burn off the residue of Furius's organs clinging to its surface, and tossed the ruined drinking horn on to the coals. Julius stared down at the body, shaking his head in wonder.

'The perfect murder. No signs on the victim's body, and no trace of the means of death. Get him dressed, brothers.'

* * *

Tribune Licinius, summoned from the bed into which he had just gratefully slumped, took one look at Furius's corpse laid out on the operating table in his boots and tunic and called for the doctor.

'What can you tell me about this, my dear? I'll have to explain this to more than one very senior officer and I'd like to get my story straight before the questions begin.'

If he noticed the tense air in the room he chose to ignore it, waiting for Felicia to make her reply.

'He had come to see his men. He was talking to me in my office when he collapsed without any warning, clutching his chest and shouting with the pain, then passed out. I couldn't find a pulse, so I called for the officers here to help me.'

'And all of you saw this?'

Julius answered for the three of them.

'Not really, Tribune. We were having a quiet look at our brother officer when we heard the prefect here hit the floor, and then the doctor called for help. He was as limp as a rag when we picked him up to put him on the table.'

'You knew that he'd been relieved of command?'

'Yes, sir, our first spear told us about it. We just thought the prefect might have seen the error of his ways and come to visit his wounded . . . '

'Hmmm. And not a mark on him, eh, Doctor?'

Felicia looked him square in the eye.

'Not that I could find, Tribune Licinius, not a cut, nor a bruise of any significance. You're welcome to have a look yourself, if you like?'

Licinius's eyes narrowed, and he sniffed the room's air ostentatiously, raising an eyebrow at windows opened wide despite the night air's chill.

'No need, Doctor; you're the expert here. But that's a nasty bruise you've got coming up round your left eye.'

Felicia stared straight back at him, her eyes suddenly glassy with barely restrained tears and her answer delivered in a quavering voice.

'A patient managed to get his arm free during surgery, Prefect. It happens sometimes, and he managed to catch me a nasty blow on the face before he could be restrained. I'll live.'

The tribune's face softened.

'I'm sorry, my dear, if I'd known there was a risk of any such thing happening I would have made sure he was restrained more effectively. And you, gentlemen . . . '

The centurions waited stiffly, pondering their fate while the senior officer paced around the table to stand close to them, speaking in a low voice that was intended for their ears alone.

'I have no idea how you managed to achieve this, but given what I am guessing has happened here, I'm mightily relieved that this is such an obvious case of death by *natural* causes.' He cocked an eyebrow at Frontinius and Scaurus, waiting silently to one side. 'And now, gentlemen, since we're kept from our beds by this unfortunate occurrence, we might as well go and get a cup of wine. I'll drink to your promotion and to this fool's timely demise in equal measure.'

⋆ ⋆ ⋆

The two cohorts paraded at dawn that morning, fifteen hundred infantrymen cursing the thought of another long day's hard marching. Morban nudged Qadir in the ribs, tipping his head towards the Petriana wing as they clattered past the parade ground, heading for the road north and their main task for the day, hunting for any barbarian ambush.

'They won't be sweating all bloody day like we will, they'll be sat nice and comfy on their bloody horses giving the bushes an occasional poke with their spears.'

The Hamian shrugged, muttering his response so quietly that only Morban could hear it.

'If you can't take a joke, Standard-bearer, you should not have joined the army in the first place.'

Morban gave him a dirty look.

'All you need to do is learn to swear and you'll be nicely positioned for a vine stick when the next one dies . . . '

He withered under Marcus's stare as the young centurion turned and glared at him. Qadir looked down his nose at him, shaking his head almost imperceptibly

'*Not* so clever. Not with his friend still in the camp hospital.'

Morban nodded glumly, watching as Scaurus strode out on to the parade ground with Frontinius and Neuto flanking him to either side.

'Tungrians, hear me! By the command of Ulpius Marcellus, governor of this province, I have been appointed to the command of both the First and Second Tungrian cohorts, with the rank of cohort tribune . . . ' The parade ground was suddenly deathly quiet, as the much-anticipated news became reality. Scaurus continued, walking slowly across the gravel with both hands on his hips. 'For the time being nothing changes. Your officers before this announcement are still your officers now. I will, however, be reviewing the strengths and weaknesses of both cohorts, and making selective changes where I and my first spears feel they are required.'

The new tribune stopped speaking and stared across the ranks of his command, allowing time for the last sentence to sink in before speaking again.

'We march north now to rejoin the legions, and I expect that once again we'll have a front-row seat when the time comes to finish this war by finding and destroying the enemy. With that in mind, and given the price paid in blood by the First Cohort's Eighth Century, I have decided to release the remainder of that century to serve with the First Hamian cohort, who are currently manning this fort. Centurion Corvus will command the Ninth Century while their officer is recovering from his wound, and the First Cohort will carry the Eighth as an empty century until sufficient reinforcements are received to reconstitute it. So, I call upon our Hamian brothers to come forward and accept your acclamation before we march north . . . '

Marcus walked from his place in front of the 8th to one end of their short line, beckoning Morban and the trumpeter to join him behind the archers. Extending an arm to Qadir, he shook his chosen man's hand before pointing to the waiting tribune.

'Just march them over to Tribune Scaurus. He'll probably want to shake your hand, and then I'd imagine he'll appoint you centurion before the Hamian prefect gets his hands on your men. I'd say you've earned it.'

The chosen man stared at him in amazement. 'Centurion?'

Marcus nodded, a smile creasing his face.

'Yes. If Scaurus appoints you now, then rather than your reverting to temporary status you'll get to keep the position. No matter how many other good candidates the Hamian prefect might have queued up for the job. Once your wounded have recovered you'll have a good-sized century to chase around the hills.'

Qadir's mouth opened and closed soundlessly. 'I do not . . . '

'Know what to say? The words 'thank you, Tribune' will make a good start. And he's still waiting for you, so I suggest you get your men out there and take what you've earned.'

The Hamian nodded, ordering his men to

march forward to the spot where the tribune was waiting. Marcus watched as he stepped through their line and snapped off a smart salute to Scaurus, then took the offered hand and shook it, all the while apparently speaking to the tribune rather than allowing him a chance to say the words he had prepared for the occasion.

'So, back to the Ninth again. It'll be good to be in front of the lads with a statue again.'

Marcus raised an eyebrow in apparent surprise.

'Who said you'd be the Ninth's standard-bearer?'

'But you . . . '

'They haven't got a centurion, but they're not missing a standard-bearer . . . ' The centurion waited for a moment until the trumpeter smirked at Morban's back before adding, ' . . . or a trumpeter.' He turned back to the 8th, noting that Scaurus was now speaking, the expression on his face earnest and yet not entirely displeased. 'What in Hades is keeping them?'

Morban sniffed loudly, wounded pride dripping from his words.

'Qadir's probably turning down the chance to sit out the war here in peace and comfort and asking to be assigned to the Ninth with *you*, Centurion.'

Marcus glanced round at him with an incredulous look before returning his gaze to the scene playing out in front of the cohort.

'*Nobody*, Standard-bearer, is that stupid.'

The older man's face stayed perfectly straight,

and he nudged the trumpeter with his foot, unseen by Marcus.

'A small wager, Centurion? Say . . . ten denarii at five to one?'

Marcus answered without even turning round. 'Done.'

The discussion seemed to have finished, but before Marcus had a chance to comment the newly appointed tribune beckoned to him with a raised hand.

'Centurion Corvus, join us, please.'

He walked across the parade ground with a sinking feeling, snapping off a crisp salute and waiting for the tribune to speak. Scaurus's face was a picture of irritated bemusement.

'It seems that your former chosen man doesn't want to accept the position of centurion I've offered him. He seems to prefer serving with you in the Ninth Century, even if that means accepting a lower rank. Several of his men are of the same opinion, it seems. Perhaps you can talk some sense into him, while the position's still on the table?'

Qadir turned to face him, his face set obdurately.

'Qadir, as a centurion you'll have . . . '

' . . . everything I could possibly desire, my friend, except the knowledge that I am part of the best infantry cohort in the province. A month ago I would have accepted the tribune's offer with joy for my men's future safety. Today I cannot accept that safety while I know that you and my other brothers will face such risk again, not while there is a fight waiting for us over the horizon. I'm sorry to throw this offer back in your faces, but I cannot accept it and remain my own man. And I am not the only one who feels this way.'

The tribune spoke up, his voice no longer employing tones of persuasion but now harsh with his authority.

'Very well. It seems the Eighth-Century do not all wish to join the Hamian cohort. Those men that wish to leave us, and serve with their own people, step forward three paces.'

Of the seventy-odd men remaining in the 8th, roughly two-thirds stepped forward, some with sad glances back at Qadir and their remaining comrades.

'Those men that wish to remain with the First Tungrian cohort, step back three paces.'

Marcus watched the remaining men as they made the three fateful steps, noting that for the most part they were the men who had made tolerable swordsmen and had coped best under the burden of their weapons and armour. He turned to Scaurus, raising a hand.

'If I might speak with these men for a moment, Tribune?'

Scaurus nodded, and the young centurion walked out in front of the soldiers who had stepped back to rejoin the Tungrians, clearing his throat and addressing his comments not just to the Hamians before him but to the entire cohort, his voice raised to a parade-ground-spanning bark.

'Hamians, you wish to remain with the Tungrians with whom you have made your home this last few weeks! You have proved your bravery in the battle at the Red River, where you saved every man here from near-certain ruin and death! But now you seek admission to a brotherhood of arms that can make no further allowances for you! When we march at the forced march you will either cope with that pace or you will fall out of the line of march and take your chances! You will be expected to carry two spears, and to sling them into a man-sized target at twenty paces! Any weaknesses or failings will no longer be tolerated as understandable, given your previous training; they will be run, and practised, and if need be *beaten* out of you! You will become *Tungrians*, with everything that implies! Can you accept those terms to your remaining with us?!'

The men in front of him answered in ones and twos, their abashed faces staring at the ground.

'Not good enough, not if you want to be Tungrians! Can you accept those terms? If you can, the only answer is '*Yes, Centurion!*' '

The response wasn't perfect, delivered as a rolling chorus rather than as one crisp response, but it was good enough.

'*Yes, Centurion!*'

'Very well, under those terms I am happy to recommend to the tribune that we retain you on the cohort's strength and give you a chance to meet our standards. One more thing, though . . . your bows . . . '

Inwardly amused, he kept his expression utterly neutral as their faces lengthened, only Qadir gazing at him quizzically as if he already knew what was coming.

'You'd best keep them, and make sure you have a good supply of arrows. You might be needing them.'

With the Hamians back in their place the prefect dismissed the cohorts to their preparations for the march, the centurions and their chosen men busying themselves checking that their men had all their kit and were ready for the imminent command to move. In the middle of the bustle of getting the 9th Century, now back to full strength with the addition of the Hamians, ready for the day's marching, Marcus felt a tap on his shoulder. He turned to find First Spear Neuto standing behind him at a respectful distance, and saluted smartly.

'Can I help you, First Spear?'

The older man held out a small cloth-wrapped package to him.

'I found this in Prefect Furius's kit last night, while I was sorting out his personal effects to send to his family once all this is done with. I thought you ought to have it, given what's inside it.'

Marcus lifted the cloth covering, and the gold cloak pin underneath it winked at him in the morning sunlight.

'Ah. I wondered where that had got to. Thank you, sir.'

Neuto inclined his head gravely.

'It was accompanied by a scroll detailing some rather colourful allegations against you and your brother officers. I took the liberty of putting it into the night guard's brazier.' He looked around himself for a moment before speaking again. 'The men that fought with you down at the riverbank told me you gave Centurion Appius his dignity in death, and that you helped them to face the blue-noses when all seemed lost. All things considered I'd say your place is here, not being carted off to Rome to make some bastard in a purple toga feel better about himself.' He nodded and turned to go, then turned back with a final thought. 'One thing, though. You might find it a good idea to scratch off that inscription . . . '

Marcus saluted, returning the first spear's level gaze.

'Yes, First Spear. I might.'

We do hope that you have enjoyed reading this large print book.

Did you know that all of our titles are available for purchase?

We publish a wide range of high quality large print books including:

Romances, Mysteries, Classics
General Fiction
Non Fiction and Westerns

Special interest titles available in large print are:

The Little Oxford Dictionary
Music Book
Song Book
Hymn Book
Service Book

Also available from us courtesy of Oxford University Press:

Young Readers' Dictionary
(large print edition)
Young Readers' Thesaurus
(large print edition)

For further information or a free brochure, please contact us at:

Other titles published by The House of Ulverscroft:

WOUNDS OF HONOUR

Anthony Riches

Marcus Valerius Aquila has scarcely landed in Britannia when he has to run for his life — condemned to dishonourable death by power-crazed Emperor Commodus. Desperate, the Praetorian Guard officer agrees to take a new name, serve in an obscure regiment on Hadrian's Wall and lie low until he can hope for justice. Then a rebel army sweeps down from the wastes north of the Wall, and Marcus has to prove he's hard enough to lead a century in the front line of a brutal war with a merciless enemy.

THE TENTH CHAMBER

Glenn Cooper

Abbey of Ruac, rural France: A medieval script is discovered, and sent to Paris for restoration. There, literary historian Hugo Pineau finds therein a description of a painted cave with the secrets it contains — and a map showing its position close to the abbey. Hugo, aided by archaeologist Luc Simard, goes exploring. They discover a vast network of prehistoric caves deep within the cliffs. At the core of the labyrinth lies the most astonishing chamber of all — as the manuscript chronicled. They set up camp with a team of experts to bring their find to the world. But they are drawn into a dangerous game as one 'accidental' death leads to another. Someone will stop at nothing to protect the enigma of the tenth chamber . . .